# THE
# TUTOR'S DAUGHTER

## Books by Julie Klassen

### From Bethany House Publishers

# THE TUTOR'S DAUGHTER

# JULIE KLASSEN

BETHANYHOUSE

*a division of Baker Publishing Group*
Minneapolis, Minnesota

Published by Bethany House Publishers
11400 Hampshire Avenue South
Bloomington, Minnesota 55438
www.bethanyhouse.com

Bethany House Publishers is a division of
Baker Publishing Group, Grand Rapids, Michigan

Printed in the United States of America

Library of Congress Cataloging-in-Publication Data
Klassen, Julie.
     The tutor's daughter / Julie Klassen
        p.   cm.
     ISBN 978-0-7642-1069-3 (pbk.)
     1. Regency fiction. 2. Love stories. 3. Christian fiction. I. Title.
PS3611.L37T88 2012
813'.6—dc23                                                       2012034244

Scripture quotations are from the King James Version of the Bible.

This is a work of historical reconstruction; the appearances of certain historical figures are therefore inevitable. All other characters, however, are products of the author's imagination, and any resemblance to actual persons, living or dead, is coincidental.

Cover design by Jennifer Parker

Cover photography by Mike Habermann Photography, LLC

Author represented by Books and Such Literary Agency

12   13   14   15   16   17   18          7   6   5   4   3   2   1

With love to my uncles,

Al, Ed,
Hank & John

And in loving memory of
Uncle Bill

*YOUNG GENTLEMEN*
*are boarded and instructed in English,*
*Writing, and Arithmetic, at Eighteen Guineas*
*per Annum. They are likewise carefully*
*instructed in the CLASSICS. Drawing,*
*Geography, and the use of the Globes,*
*taught separately on moderate Terms.*

—*Hampshire Chronicle* advertisement, 1797

*E. England begs leave to acquaint his*
*friends and the public that he receives a*
*limited number of pupils under his care,*
*who are boarded at the rate of fourteen*
*guineas, and carefully instructed in English*
*Grammar, Penmanship and a regular course*
*of Mathematics, together with History,*
*Geography, the use of Globes, and the*
*method of Drawing in Perspective.*

—*Stamford Mercury* advertisement, 1808

# Prologue

LONGSTAPLE, DEVONSHIRE
1812

*S*omething *is amiss,* Emma thought, immediately upon entering her tidy bedchamber. *What is it . . . ?*

She scanned the neatly made bed, orderly side table, and dressing chest. . . . *There.* She stepped forward, heart squeezing.

In the special teacup she kept as decoration nestled a clutch of tiny pink roses. The flowers had likely been picked from her aunt's garden next door, but they had been picked for her, and they had been picked by him, and that was all that mattered.

She knew instantly who had left them—Phillip Weston. Her favorite from among her father's many pupils. And likely the only one who knew it was her birthday—her sixteenth. How much kinder Phillip was than his older brother, Henry, who had boarded with them a few years before.

Emma carefully lifted the cup, bringing the flowers to her nose and breathing in the fragrance of apple-sweet roses and fresh greenery. *Mmm . . .* She held the cup away, admiring how the flowers' pink petals and green leaves brought out the colorful painting on its side.

She found herself thinking back to the day her mother had given her this teacup three years before. The very day Henry Weston had nearly broken it. . . .

Emma untied the ribbon, peeled back the tissue paper—careful not to rip it—and opened the box. Looking inside, pleasure filled her. She had been right about its contents. For she had noticed the prized teacup missing from its place in the china cupboard.

"It was your grandmother's," her mother said. "She purchased it on her wedding trip. All the way to Italy. Can you imagine?"

"Yes," Emma breathed, admiring anew the gold-rimmed cup with its detailed painting of a Venetian gondola and bridge. "It's beautiful. I've always admired it."

A rare dimple appeared in her mother's pale cheek. "I know you have."

Emma smiled. "Thank you, Mamma."

"Happy birthday, my dear."

Emma returned the cup and saucer gingerly into the box, planning to carry it up to her bedchamber. She stepped out of the sitting room and—*wham*—a wooden ball slammed into the wall opposite, nearly knocking the box from her hands. She looked up, infuriated to see one of her father's pupils smirking at her.

"Henry Weston!" Emma clutched the box to her young bosom, shielding it with her arms. "Do be careful."

His green eyes slid from her face to her arms, and he stepped closer. "What is in the box?"

"A gift."

"Ah, that's right. It is your birthday. How old are you now—ten?"

She lifted her chin. "I am thirteen, as you very well know."

He reached over, pulled back the paper, and peered into the box. His eyes glinted, and then he chuckled, the chuckle soon growing into a laugh.

She glared at the smug sixteen-year-old. "I don't see what is so funny."

"It is the perfect gift for you, Emma Smallwood. A single teacup. A single solitary teacup. Have I not often said you will end a spinster?"

"I will not," she insisted.

"Sitting about and reading all day as you do, your head will continue to grow but your limbs will shrivel, and who would want to marry *that*?"

"Someone far better than you."

He snorted. "If someone marries you, Emma Smallwood, I shall . . . I shall perform the dance of the swords at your wedding breakfast." He grinned. "Naked."

She scoffed in disgust. "Who would want to see *that*? Besides, who says I would invite you to my wedding?"

He tweaked her chin in a patronizing fashion. "Bluestocking."

She scowled. "Jackanapes!"

"Emma Smallwood . . ." Her mother appeared in the doorway, eyes flashing. "What word did I hear coming from your mouth? I give you a beautiful gift and you repay me with an ugly word?"

"Sorry, Mamma."

"Hello, Mr. Weston." Her mother slanted Henry a dismissive look. "Do excuse us."

"Mrs. Smallwood." He bowed and then turned toward the stairs.

"Emma," her mother hissed. "Young ladies do not speak to gentlemen in such a manner."

"He's no gentleman," Emma said, hoping Henry would hear. "He certainly does not act like one."

Her mother's lips tightened. "Be that as it may, it isn't proper. I want you to go to your room and read the chapter on polite manners in the book I gave you."

Emma protested, "*Mamma* . . ."

Her mother held up her hand. "Not another word. I know I say you read too many books, but I would rather you read one on the feminine graces than those horrid scholarly tomes of your father's."

"Yes, Mamma." Emma sighed and carried her cup upstairs.

Unhappy memory fading, Emma smiled at the sweet bouquet left for her by Henry's younger brother, Phillip. She wondered what

Henry Weston would say if he could see her now and knew who had given her flowers.

When Henry Weston left the Smallwood Academy, Emma had been relieved, but she would be sad to see Phillip depart. It was difficult to believe two brothers could be so very different.

*Before, however, Lucy had been an hour
in the house she had contrived a place for
everything and put everything in its place.*

—*The Naughty Girl Won*, circa 1800

# Chapter 1

FIVE YEARS LATER
APRIL 1817

Twenty-one-year-old Emma Smallwood carefully dusted the collection of favorite books atop her dressing chest. It was the one bit of housekeeping she insisted on doing herself, despite Mrs. Malloy's protestations. She then carefully wiped her cherished teacup against any dust particle daring to lodge there. The cup and saucer were a gift from her mother—fine porcelain rimmed with real gold.

Emma set the cup and saucer back atop the leather-bound volume of Sterne's *A Sentimental Journey Through France and Italy.* She angled the cup to best display the image on its side—a lovely painting of a graceful gondola in Venice.

Emma had never sipped from the gold-rimmed cup. But she did like to look at it. To remember her mother, gone these two years. To remember a young man who had once left roses inside it. And to imagine visiting Italy someday herself.

Morning ritual finished, Emma stowed her cleaning supplies and checked the chatelaine watch hooked to her bodice. She closed the cover with a satisfying *snap*. Precisely as she'd thought. Time to go down and send off their last remaining pupil.

Reaching the bottom of the stairs, she saw Edward Sims standing in the hall, fidgeting with his valise. He wore a smart frock coat and top hat, and looked the picture of a young man ready to take on the world.

"All set, Mr. Sims?"

He turned. "Yes, Miss Smallwood."

Though she was only four years his senior, Emma felt a fondness bordering on the maternal when she looked at the young man who had lived with them for most of the last three years. She glanced around the empty hall. "Has my father bid you farewell?"

Mr. Sims shifted and shook his head. "I have not seen him this morning."

Emma forced a smile. "What a pity. He shall be so sorry to have missed you. I know he wanted to be here to see you off."

Her father ought to have been there. But no doubt he had gone to the churchyard to visit her grave. Again.

Mr. Sims gave an awkward smile. "Tell him good-bye for me, and thank him for everything."

"I shall."

"And I thank you especially, Miss Smallwood. I learned a great deal from you."

"You are very welcome, Mr. Sims. I wish you every success at university."

From the front window, she watched the young man walk past the *Smallwood Academy* sign, and down the cobbled lane, feeling the wistful letdown she often felt when a pupil left them. This time all the more, since there were no new students to replace him.

The house seemed suddenly quiet and empty. She wished Mr. Sims had a younger brother. *Six* younger brothers. She sighed. Perhaps even amiable Mr. Sims would hesitate to recommend Mr. Smallwood as tutor, considering how little her father had actually been involved in his education. But how would they pay their cook-housekeeper and maid, not to mention the languishing pile of bills, without more pupils?

Emma walked to the desk in the family sitting room, pulled out the bound notebook she kept there, and flipped past previous lists:

*Books read this year.*

*Books to read next.*

*Improvements needed to boys' chambers.*

*Economizing measures.*

*Places to visit someday.*

*New texts and primers to order for next term: None.*

*Diversions to improve Papa's moods/Improvement noted: None.*

*Pupils by year.*

Her pupil lists, which had grown shorter with each passing year, included notes on each young man's character and his plans for the future.

She turned to the list from three years before, running her finger over the few names, lingering on one in particular.

*Phillip Weston. Kind and amiable. Second son. Plans to follow his brother to Oxford and read the law.*

The brief note hardly did him justice. Phillip Weston had been her only true friend among her father's pupils over the years.

Seeing his name caused her to turn to another page. Another list.

*Prospective pupils for the future: Rowan and Julian Weston?*

Emma thought again of the letter she had sent a fortnight before. She knew perfectly well Henry and Phillip Weston had two younger half brothers. Phillip had mentioned them often enough. Julian and Rowan were at least fifteen by now—older than Phillip when he'd been sent to the academy.

But they had not come.

She had broached the subject with her father several times in the past, suggesting he write to the boys' father. But he had hemmed, hawed, and sighed, saying he was sure, if Sir Giles meant to send his younger sons to them, he would have done so already. No, more likely, Sir Giles and his second wife had eschewed their humble establishment in favor of prestigious Winchester, Harrow, or Eton.

"Well, it would not hurt to ask," Emma had urged.

But her father had grimaced and said maybe another day.

Therefore Emma, who had been acting with increasing frequency as her father's secretary, had taken up quill and ink and written to Sir Giles in her father's stead, to ask if he might consider sending his younger sons, as he had his older two.

She still could hardly believe she had done so. What had come over her? In hindsight, she knew very well. She had read an account of the daring travels of the Russian princess Catherine Dashkov. Reading about the princess's exploits had inspired Emma's rare act of bravery—or foolishness—whichever the letter had been. In the end, her letter apparently made no difference. Her assertiveness had been in vain, for there had been no reply. She hoped if Sir Giles had been offended at their presumption that word of it had not reached Phillip, who was, she believed, still away at university.

Turning a page in her notebook, Emma tapped a quill in ink and began a new list.

*Measures to acquire new pupils.*

Someone knocked on the doorjamb, and Emma looked up. There stood Aunt Jane, who had let herself in through the side door as usual.

"Mr. Sims departed on schedule?" Jane asked with one of her frequent smiles, punctuated by slightly crooked eyeteeth.

"Yes. You only just missed him." Emma set her quill back in its holder.

Her aunt laid her bonnet on the sideboard and smoothed back her hair. Amidst the brown, Emma glimpsed a few silver hairs that had escaped her ruthless plucking.

Jane, her father's sister, younger by six years, had never married. She lived in the house next door, which had been their parents' home. There she ran a sister school to the Smallwood Academy—a boarding school for young ladies.

Jane peeled off her gloves. "Dare I ask where your father is?"

Emma shook her head. "He's been gone since breakfast."

Aunt Jane pulled in her lips in a regretful expression, her shaking head mirroring Emma's.

Mrs. Malloy, the Smallwoods' cook-housekeeper, brought in the tea tray and seemed not in the least surprised to see Jane Smallwood there. In fact, three cups already sat upon the tray.

"You will join me, I hope?" Emma asked politely, knowing full well her aunt had planned to do so all along.

"Thank you, my dear."

As if drawn by the warm trail of steam from the kettle or the smell of Mrs. Malloy's shortbread, the front door opened and Emma's father shuffled in, head bowed, thin mouth downturned, looking older than his forty-eight years.

Mrs. Malloy bustled over to take his hat and muffler, scolding, "Mr. Smallwood . . . yer shoes are a right mess! And wet trouser 'ems in the bargain. Did ya swim 'ome?"

"Do forgive me, Mrs. Malloy," he said dryly. Irony glinted in his round, blue eyes. "I did not step in that puddle to spite you." He wiped his shoes and looked across at his daughter and sister. "Am I in time for tea?"

"Yes," Emma replied. "Though you have missed Mr. Sims."

Her father blinked, clearly surprised and chagrined. "Left already? Good heavens. I wanted to be here. I do hope you passed along my gratitude and farewells."

"Of course I did."

Her father sat down, rubbing his hands together. "Chilly day. Damp too."

"You ought not to have stayed outdoors so long, John," Jane said. "You'll catch your death."

"I should be so lucky," he murmured.

Aunt and niece shared a look of concern.

Emma poured tea into their plain everyday cups, and conversation dwindled while they partook of the simple repast of hot tea, bread, cheese, and shortbread. Her father ate a little of everything, she noticed, though his appetite was not what it once was.

Emma nibbled bread and cheese but resisted the shortbread, though it was her favorite. Her slim figure was one of the few things her mother had praised. Emma allowed herself sweets only at Christmas and her birthday.

She sipped her tea, then set down her cup. "Well, Papa," she began, "I have started a list."

"Another? What is it this time?"

She felt a flicker of annoyance at his condescending tone but replied evenly, "A list of things we might try to acquire new pupils."

"Ah." He waved a dismissive hand as though the topic were trivial.

Her aunt said more encouragingly, "And what have you thought of so far?"

Emma looked at her gratefully. "A new advertisement in the paper. Perhaps expanding to other newspapers as well, though that would be expensive. A larger sign might help. Our old one is showing signs of wear, I fear. And hardly visible unless one is looking for it."

Aunt Jane nodded. "Yes, a smart, well-maintained sign is very important, I feel."

"Ours is fine," John Smallwood muttered into his tea. "It is not as though parents go wandering through the streets in search of a tutor."

Emma weighed her best course, then said, "You are exactly right, Papa. It is not passersby we need to attract, but rather well-to-do families farther afield."

His eyes dulled, and his mouth slackened. "I just don't have the energy for all of that, Emma. I am not a young man anymore."

"Oh come, John," his sister said. "You have many good years ahead of you."

He sighed. "What a depressing thought."

With a glance at her niece, Jane said, "You have Emma to think of, John, if not yourself."

He shrugged, unconvinced. "Emma is more than capable of taking care of herself. As are you."

At that, Emma and her aunt shared another long look.

If Emma didn't think of some way to help her father soon, they would be in serious trouble, both financially and otherwise. They might very well lose their home and school—his only livelihood . . . and hers.

Emma spent the next two days combing her memory and the newspapers for names of families with sons who were not already enrolled elsewhere, as far as she knew. She was hunched over the desk when Mrs. Malloy entered the sitting room with the day's post. "'Ere you go, love."

Needing to stretch, Emma rose and looked idly through the stack, dreading to find more bills or final notices. Her hand hesitated on one of the letters addressed to her father. The return direction: *Ebbington Manor, Ebford, Cornwall.*

Ebbington Manor was the primary estate of Sir Giles Weston and his family. Excitement and fear twisted through her stomach and along her spine. She had all but given up hope of a reply.

Because her father left it to her to open his correspondence— especially the increasingly depressing bills—she felt only minor qualms about lifting the seal and unfolding this letter as she had so many others.

She glanced toward the door with a twinge of self-consciousness, then read the lines written in what appeared to be a somewhat hurried hand:

*My dear Mr. Smallwood,*

*Thank you for your letter and your kind interest in my younger sons. You are correct that they have reached—nay, surpassed— the age when my two older boys left us to spend a few years with you there in Longstaple. However, Lady Weston feels that our youngest are too delicate to live apart from their mamma. While*

*I personally think the experience would be as good for them as it was for Henry and Phillip, and would no doubt strengthen their developing characters in the bargain, I feel I must defer to my wife's wishes in this matter.*

*I don't suppose you would consider coming to Ebbington Manor and teaching the boys here at, say, twice the boarding rate? If you could but spend one year here preparing them for university, how ideal that would be for us. Of course I realize that is a great deal to ask, especially considering the loss of your wife, which I was very sorry to hear of. But if you ever desire a change of scenery, do not hesitate to let me know. You would be most welcome. Your daughter as well.*

> *Yours most sincerely,*
> *Sir Giles Weston, Bart*

Good heavens, what a thought. That her father would give up his established academy to tutor two pupils. What personal service that would be! Many young gentlemen, fresh from university but without fortune, served as tutors in grand houses. But to presume that Mr. John Smallwood would leave his home and academy to do the same . . . ? Emma felt offended on her father's behalf. Had word gotten around that the Smallwoods were in dire straits? Emma huffed and tossed the letter back onto the pile.

She stood there, stewing. But after vexation passed, she read the letter again. In reality, Sir Giles's tone was perfectly polite, nearly apologetic to even suggest such an idea. He merely wanted to see his sons well educated—all while kowtowing to his wife's irrational coddling.

The first Lady Weston, Phillip and Henry's mother, had died when the boys were quite young. And Emma knew from comments Phillip had made that his stepmother, the second Lady Weston, was somewhat difficult—and that she favored her sons by birth far above her sons by marriage. Emma recalled feeling sorry for Phillip when he'd described his tenuous relationship with the woman.

Emma did not recall Henry speaking of his stepmother one way or the other, though she and Henry had not been friends and therefore had not spoken of such personal matters.

Emma thought of Ebbington Manor, a place she had never seen but had often imagined, high on a cliff on the windswept Cornwall coast. Of course she would enjoy seeing Phillip Weston again. But she reminded herself that he was away at Oxford, likely in his third year at Balliol. Not sitting at home waiting for her to visit.

Should she show the letter to her father? She doubted he would even consider the notion, not when he spent hours each day visiting his wife's grave. And if he did agree, what would she do—pack up her father and send him off to Cornwall for a year while she remained behind with Aunt Jane?

On one hand, that scenario appealed to her. How many times had her aunt suggested Emma teach with her someday, eventually becoming Jane's partner in the girls' school, if and when she felt comfortable leaving her father on his own?

But her father still needed her. Emma had been helping him for years—first during her mother's long illness and then even more so after she'd passed on and her father's depression of spirits began. Emma wasn't certain he was capable of managing on his own. Although, at Ebbington Manor, he would be responsible for only the boys' education, and not the administration of an entire academy—juggling day scholars, tuition notices, as well as special sessions with the dancing master, drawing instructor, and French tutor. Yes, it might help her father if his focus were narrowed. Yet Emma couldn't be certain, and she couldn't abide the thought of sending him away on his own. What if he should fail? Embarrass himself and suffer the mortification of being dismissed? That would be too much for him to bear in his current state.

*You're fretting over nothing, Emma,* she chided herself. *He won't want to go.*

But when she broached the subject after dinner, her father stunned her by straightening and becoming alert, looking at her with more animation than she'd seen in years.

"Did Sir Giles really invite us to come and live there?" he asked.

"Yes, but . . ."

"Interesting notion . . ." His eyes brightened as he looked toward the ceiling in thought.

"Father, I assure you I did not hint at any such arrangement, only asked if he might consider sending his younger sons to us here."

Her father nodded, but he seemed not at all vexed about the invitation, nor her presumption in writing.

He asked to see the letter, and she produced it.

He read it, lowered his spectacles, and said, "In all honesty, my dear, I long for a change. Being here in this house, day after day, night after night. The place where my dear one suffered so long . . . Constantly surrounded by things that remind me—not of the happy years, as I should like, but of the last years. The painful years. Why do you think I leave so often?"

"I . . . thought it was to visit her in the churchyard," Emma said quietly.

He shrugged. "I go there now and again, to make certain the plot is kept up. To pull weeds or lay a few flowers. But not to visit her. She is not there, Emma. She is somewhere far better than a dreary Longstaple churchyard."

Tears brightened his eyes, and Emma blinked back her own tears. At the moment she was too worried about the future to mourn the past.

"But . . . Ebford is . . . such a long way," she stammered. "In the very north of Cornwall."

"Not so very far. And it would only be for a year." He sat back, musing, "I remember Phillip describing Ebbington Manor. Rambling old house, high on a cliff near the sea. Beautiful paths along the coast. . . ."

"But you would not be there to walk along the coast," Emma reminded him. "You would be there to teach."

"Yes, I know. But certainly we would have some time to enjoy the out-of-doors." He hesitated for the first time. "Though I should not presume you would wish to go with me, my dear. I realize you are not a little girl any longer."

Emma rose and stepped to the window, thoughts whirling. Could she really do it—uproot herself and leave all she knew to live in Cornwall for a year? Emma felt her sense of control slipping away and her panic rising. "I . . . I need to think."

"Of course you do, my dear. This is all very sudden. Quite a shock, though a pleasant one, at least for me. But you consider what is best. I shall abide by your decision."

Such responsibility! Should she, could she, accept and thereby place herself under the same roof as Henry and Phillip Weston? At least she assumed Phillip would be there during school vacations. She wasn't sure where his older brother was nowadays.

In her mind's eye, she saw Henry Weston, wavy dark hair wild about his sharp-featured face. His eerie green eyes narrowing in menace as he commanded her to stay out of his room or pulled some nasty trick on her.

She shivered.

Fire irons clanged belowstairs, and Emma started. *How foolish,* she thought, despising irrational emotion.

She rose with determination. She knew what to do. She would go and speak with levelheaded Aunt Jane. Aunt Jane who would hate to see them go. Aunt Jane who so often spoke of a fond "someday" when she and Emma might teach together in her school. Cautious Aunt Jane who had avoided the attentions of men all her days. Yes, Aunt Jane would help her decide.

❦

Sitting in her aunt's snug parlor that evening, Emma handed her the letter and sat back while Jane read it. While she waited, Emma looked from the plain, chipped teacup in her hand to the fine rose-and-white tea set—cups, saucers, small plates—displayed in the corner cabinet. How often she had admired the set. She remembered asking Aunt Jane why she never used it—instead using the same old mismatched cups and saucers for years.

"Those are too good for everyday use," she'd said. "I'm saving them."

"Saving them for what?" young Emma had asked. "Your wedding?"

"My wedding? Heavens no." Jane had winked and tweaked Emma's nose. "Maybe yours." Then her eyes had grown thoughtful and distant. "I . . . don't know really. Someday I'll use it. But not today."

Now, again eyeing the lovely tea set sitting on the shelf, Emma's heart twisted. The sight saddened her, though she knew it should not. She thought of her own special teacup from her mother. Emma polished and admired it but never used it either, so who was she to question Aunt Jane?

Emma returned her gaze to Jane Smallwood's angular face with pointed nose and chin. Her eyes were large and soft green, like Emma's. It was a face Emma loved, had always loved. With each passing year, the lines around her aunt's eyes and across her forehead became more pronounced. Even so, Emma thought it a beautiful face, though she imagined not everyone shared her opinion.

Jane's brow furrowed as she neared the end of the letter. She said quietly, "He mentions his sons, Henry and Phillip. . . . I remember them both."

Yes, her aunt had met them both on many occasions—when slipping over for tea as she did, or walking to church together and sharing a meal afterward, as she so often had over the years.

She looked at Emma from beneath her lashes. "I believe you were rather fond of one of them."

Emma felt her cheeks grow warm. "Phillip and I were friends—that is all. But that was years ago."

Aunt Jane pursed her thin lips. "What has your father said?"

"Oddly enough, he seems keen on the idea. Though he says he'll leave the decision to me. But I have no desire to pack up and move. And what would become of our house? And all of our books?"

"A tenant might easily be found," Jane said. "And I can look after the place for you in your absence."

Emma stared in disbelief. This wasn't the reaction she had expected. Hoped for. "But I don't *want* to go." Her voice rose plaintively, very unlike her normally reserved tone.

Jane said, "I know you have read about Cornwall. Here is your opportunity to see it for yourself."

"You want us to leave?"

"Emma . . ." Jane's forehead crinkled once more, her eyes large and expressive. "This isn't about what *I* want."

"But . . . " Emma pulled a face. "You have never felt it necessary to leave here, to go gallivanting off on some ill-conceived venture. To put yourself in the path of gentlemen."

Jane looked off into the distance. "Perhaps I should have."

Emma sat speechless. She wondered if her aunt was thinking of Mr. Farley, an admirer she once turned down to continue teaching. Emma had never met Mr. Farley, but her aunt had described their meeting, and allowed her to read his letter.

Jane Smallwood reached over and laid a hand on hers. "Don't misunderstand me, Emma. I am content with my lot. I derive great satisfaction from teaching. But that does not mean I don't sometimes wonder what I have missed. What my life might have been like, had I said yes to a little adventure of my own."

*Edward Ferrars was privately tutored*
*in the home of the Reverend Mr. Pratt*
*at Longstaple, near Plymouth. . . .*

—Deirdre Le Faye, *Jane Austen:*
*The World of Her Novels*

# Chapter 2

On her father's behalf, Emma wrote to Sir Giles, accepting his invitation to tutor his younger sons for a year at Ebbington Manor at the salary he'd offered.

Emma still felt nervous about the prospect, worrying how Phillip and Henry Weston might react to learning they—*she*—would be coming to their home. She fervently hoped neither of them thought it forward of her or suspected any motive beyond what it was—a good opportunity for her father.

At least, she hoped it would be good for him. She almost prayed it would be so. But, in truth, Emma rarely prayed these days. It seemed clear to her that God had ceased to answer her prayers, so she had ceased asking. She had learned over the years, especially since her mother's death, to rely on no one but herself. If something needed doing, it would likely be left to her. Had not her recent act—sending an inquiry to Sir Giles—proved that truth once again?

So, as much as she dreaded it, to restore their finances and hopefully her father's spirits, she would leave her safe, ordered life to help her father teach two pupils in Cornwall. In the home of Phillip and Henry Weston.

Even thinking those words caused Emma's palms to perspire.

As Aunt Jane had predicted, tenants were easily found for the house. Jane had recalled that the vicar was looking for nearby lodgings for his married sister while her husband was away at sea. She might have stayed with him, but the small vicarage had only one spare room, and the clergyman's sister had many children.

Emma's father spoke with the Reverend Mr. Lewis, and arrangements were quickly made. More quickly than Emma had wished. She knew the vicar, yes. But not his sister or her children. What if they did not take care of the furniture and things she and her father were leaving behind? Inwardly, Emma checked herself. The truth was, she cared little how the furnishings fared in their absence. What she did care about were her mother's teacup and their books. She wondered how many volumes they would be able to take along.

On the same day her father agreed to the terms of the lease, they received a brief reply from Sir Giles, saying he was surprised but pleased the Smallwoods were willing to accept his offer, and that they were welcome to come at their convenience.

The next morning, Emma and her father went to see the booking clerk at the local coaching inn and, with his timetables and advice, planned their best route for the journey. Emma wrote back again to apprise Sir Giles of their expected arrival date and time.

Then they began packing in earnest.

Considering the cost to transport luggage, Emma realized that she and her father could reasonably take only one modest-sized trunk apiece. They would not be able to take all their books. Not by far. She would need to select only her very favorites. With a heavy heart, Emma began the difficult process of sorting and choosing.

She packed up one crate of books she would not take with her, but that she could not bear to leave lying about the house for sticky fingers to find. These she delivered to Aunt Jane's and asked if she would store them for her.

Jane fingered through the volumes in the crate. *Robinson Crusoe,*

*The History of Peter the Great, Gulliver's Travels, The Juvenile Anec-dotes,* and more.

"So many children's books, Emma," Jane observed. "I doubt you will ever read these again. Why not give them to the church or the parish poor?"

Emma's stomach twisted. "But I love these old books. I could never give them up. Never."

Jane held up an old volume of *Aesop's Fables.* "You must know these by heart by now."

With an apologetic shake of her head, Emma gently took the book from her aunt and slid it back into the crate. "Just promise me you will keep them safe."

That afternoon, her father paused at the open door of Emma's bedchamber. He looked from her, to the open trunk, to the gowns spread on the bed.

"How goes the packing, my dear?"

"I am finding it very difficult to fit everything I want into one trunk." Biting her lip, she extracted a bandbox and filled the resulting space with another stack of books. One hat and one bonnet would have to suffice. Then she eyed the two evening gowns.

Watching her, her father said, "Remember it shall not be forever, my dear. Your books will be here waiting for you when we return."

Emma set aside one evening gown. How many would she really need? It was unlikely they would be asked to join in any formal dinners or parties. They would likely be viewed, after all, as little higher than servants.

Yes, her books would be far more comfort on a cold Cornwall eve than a gown of cool, crisp silk or gauzy muslin.

Other necessities? Her teacup, of course. A small chess set, to help her and her father pass the long evenings. One pair of indoor shoes and a pair of half boots for the coastal walks her father seemed determined to pursue. A warm pelisse, cape, shawl, and gloves, of course. Emma stood there, trying to decide between the Ann Radcliffe novel she held in one hand and the jewelry box she held in the other. Really it might be safer to leave most of her jewelry, modest collection though it was, with Aunt Jane as well.

Finally, she wavered over a small bottle of *eau de cologne*. Phillip Weston had given it to her the day he left the Smallwood Academy. He had given it to her without fanfare, with only a self-conscious shrug and a mumbled, "Thought you might like to have it."

It seemed almost ungrateful not to take it with her now. Making up her mind, Emma crammed it into her already-stuffed reticule and pulled the drawstrings tight.

On the first Monday in May, Emma and her father visited Rachel Smallwood's grave in the churchyard, stopped to say good-bye to the vicar, and then went next door to bid Aunt Jane farewell. Standing there on the path between their houses, Emma received her aunt's kiss and bestowed a brave smile in return. While her father embraced his sister, Emma turned with a determined sniff and followed the boy and cart transporting their trunks to the coaching inn.

They traveled by stage from Longstaple, Devonshire, to Ebford, Cornwall, stopping every ten to fifteen miles to pay tolls or change horses at one inn or another. Other passengers came and went at various stops along the way—some squeezing beside them inside the coach, others sitting on its roof. At least Emma and her father had inside seats for the daylong journey.

From time to time, she felt her father studying her. When their eyes finally met, he raised his brows in unspoken query, *Are you all right?* Emma forced a reassuring smile. She did not share his enthusiasm, but she reminded herself—even remonstrated herself—that this had all been her doing. It was too late for second-guessing now.

As the coach jostled onward, Emma tried to keep images and memories of Henry Weston at bay, but they returned to worry her. She tried to read, but doing so in the rocking carriage made her queasy. She clutched her volume of *The Female Travellers* to her chest and told herself to think of Phillip Weston instead. She and Phillip practicing the minuet in the schoolroom or looking up at the stars together at night. Gentle Phillip comforting her when her mother had fallen ill. . . . But thoughts of his foul-tempered brother prevailed and pestered her throughout the bone-jarring journey.

When Henry Weston had first come to Longstaple, he had been sullen and resentful, keeping to his room, snapping at her whenever she dared speak to him, and forbidding her to touch his belongings. She had quickly learned to avoid him.

The next term, Henry had arrived early, before the other pupils. He seemed less angry and more resigned to being there. When he had quickly become bored with no other boys about, he had even asked *her* to join him in one game then another—football, cricket, shooting, fencing. . . . But, not being athletically inclined, Emma had refused each boisterous activity in its turn.

"Cards?" he'd asked rather desperately.

"I detest cards," Emma had said.

"Riding?"

"I haven't a horse, as you very well know by now."

Frustrated, he'd scoffed, "Is there nothing you are good for?"

How she had wanted to return the insult with one of her own, but she bit back the angry retort burning on her lips. Very calmly, she'd said they might play a game of chess, if he liked.

Henry had reluctantly agreed. She quickly realized they were rather evenly matched and wisely allowed him to win. After that, chess was the only game he'd asked her to play.

When the other boys arrived, however, Henry began acting surly again, and critical in the bargain. When he came upon her reading— a frequent occurrence—he would pronounce some ominous prediction like, "Boys don't like bookish bluestockings, you know. You shall end an old maid. See if you don't."

And then the pranks had started. . . .

No, Emma did not look forward to seeing Henry Weston again. If only Phillip might be there instead. She sighed, consoling herself with the fact that it was very unlikely self-important Henry Weston would seek out the company of a humble tutor's daughter he'd once despised.

They arrived in the village of Ebford that evening, and there was no one to meet them. The guard and groom set down their trunks outside the inn, while the hostlers led the weary horses to the back of the establishment to be stabled. Apparently Ebford was the end of the line, at least for the night.

Emma and her father stepped tentatively inside the inn. The dim, low-beamed room was filled with roughly dressed men, pipe and peat smoke, and the odors of ale and fish.

"Wait here," he whispered, and Emma stood beside the door while her father approached the publican.

Around the room, men cast suspicious looks at him. Emma looked nervously about but saw no sign of Sir Giles or anyone dressed well enough to work for him.

Her father asked the publican if anyone from Ebbington Manor had been in that evening.

The gap-toothed man shook his bald head and said, "No. Now, do 'ee want a pint or don't 'ee?"

"No, my good man, I am simply inquiring."

The man stared at John Smallwood a moment longer, then went back to wiping the tankard in his hand.

Giving up, her father turned and led her back outside.

Emma looked up one side of the cobbled lane and down the other. The small village curved in a crescent around the harbor. On either side of the inlet, cliffs rose.

Her father asked, "You wrote and told Sir Giles when to expect us, did you not?"

"Yes. Perhaps he forgot. Or something more important came up."

He shook his head in frustration. "Sir Giles is too considerate to knowingly neglect us. More likely the letter was misdirected, or the coachman he sent for us has been delayed."

Emma hoped her father was right.

After waiting another quarter hour, they gave up and hired a youth with a donkey cart to transport them and their trunks to Ebbington Manor.

"Goin' to the big 'ouse are thee?" the young man asked, his accent deliciously different.

"Yes," Emma replied. "Do you know where it is?"

"'Course I do. Ever'soul in the parish knaws Ebb-ton." He pointed to the cliff top on the other side of the harbor. There, a red-gold manor house loomed in the twilight.

The brawny youth helped her into the cart. Her father clambered up beside her, and the young man urged his donkey into motion. They left the village, crossed a river bridge, and began slogging up a steep road, ascending the cliff. The wind increased as they climbed, and the temperature dropped. Emma pulled her pelisse more tightly around herself. The path turned at a sharp switchback and continued to climb.

Below, the village and moored boats in the harbor appeared smaller and smaller. The donkey strained and the young man urged until finally they crested the rise and the path leveled out onto a grassy headland.

Again the sprawling stone manor came into view, its rooflines of varying heights, crowned by fortress-like chimney stacks built, no doubt, to withstand the ravages of the westerly gales.

The path before the manor widened into a drive that forked into two.

"The front er the back of the 'ouse?" their driver asked.

"Oh . . ." Emma hesitated, recalling her earlier supposition that their status at Ebbington Manor would be little higher than servants. But how much higher?

"The front, of course," her father replied, chin lifted high. "I am an old friend of Sir Giles and the Weston family."

The young man shrugged, unimpressed, but directed the donkey toward the front of the house.

Emma winced at the picture they must have made. Presuming to come to the front door, not in a fine carriage but in a donkey cart. She wondered what snide comment Henry Weston might have to say about that.

"Perhaps we ought to have gone to the back, Papa," she whispered. "With our trunks and all."

"Nonsense."

Closer now, Emma could see more detail of the house. The stone exterior shone a mellow, pinkish gray by twilight, with newer Georgian sash windows in one section, and older mullioned windows in another. The front door was massive and medieval—dark oak with black iron scrollwork and fittings.

No servant hurried out to meet them, so while the young man helped her down, her father alighted, strode up to the door, and gave three raps with his walking stick.

A minute later, the door was opened a few inches by a manservant in his late fifties.

"Yes?" he asked, squinting from her father to the donkey cart and trunks behind him.

"I am Mr. Smallwood, and this is my daughter, Miss Smallwood."

The servant blinked. "Are you expected?"

"Yes. I am here to tutor the younger Weston sons."

Face puckered, the man regarded her father, chewing his lip in worry.

"Who is it, Davies?" a woman asked from behind the door, her voice polished and genteel.

The servant turned his head to reply. "Says his name is Smallwood, my lady. Says he's the new tutor."

"Tutor? What tutor?"

At the incredulity in the woman's tone, Emma's stomach churned. She opened her reticule to extract Sir Giles's letter as proof of their invitation. She had not thought she would need it.

The manservant backed from the door, and his face was soon replaced by that of a handsome gentlewoman in evening dress, though Emma noticed her hair was somewhat disheveled and she held the door partially closed.

She said, "Mr. Smallwood, is it?"

Her father removed his hat and bowed. "John Smallwood. And you are Lady Weston, I presume. We have not met in person, but

I have had the pleasure of hosting your sons Henry and Phillip at my academy in Longstaple."

"My stepsons. Yes. I recall hearing your name." Her countenance rippled with several emotions, there and gone too quickly for Emma to catalog. Then the woman forced an apologetic smile. "I am sorry. We were not expecting you."

Emma felt her cheeks heat. She could not distinguish her father's countenance in the dim light but did hear his tone grow mildly defensive. "Were you not? But Sir Giles requested that my daughter and I tutor your younger sons here in the comfort of your own home."

One arched brow rose. "Did he indeed?"

"Yes. We wrote back to accept more than a fortnight ago."

Emma added, "And sent word of our travel plans."

Lady Weston flicked a look at her but addressed her father. "He must have forgotten to mention it." She glanced over her shoulder, then said, "Unfortunately, you have come upon us at an inopportune time." She glanced to the waiting trunks. "But I cannot in good conscience, I suppose, ask you to return another time, considering the hour. . . ."

Her father stiffened. "We are very sorry to inconvenience you, my lady. Perhaps this young man will not mind taking us back down to the village. . . ."

Another voice rose from behind the door. A low male voice. "What? Who? . . . Good heavens. I quite forgot that was tonight. . . . I know, but it cannot be helped."

The door opened farther, and there stood fifty-something Sir Giles in evening attire, though his cravat was missing, exposing the loose skin of his aging neck as it draped into his shirt collar.

"Mr. Smallwood. Please forgive the rude reception. My fault entirely. I am afraid communication is not one of my strong points, as dear Lady Weston is forever reminding me, and with good cause, I fear." He ducked his head apologetically and looked up from beneath bushy eyebrows. "Please do come in."

Her father turned to her. "You remember my daughter, Emma?"

The baronet's eyes widened. "This is little Emma? Why, last I saw her she was no bigger than this." He stretched forth a hand, chest high.

"Yes, well, children do grow up. As no doubt Henry and Phillip have as well."

Behind them their driver cleared his throat, and her father turned, digging into his purse. But Sir Giles pulled a crown from his pocket and said, "Allow me." He tossed the silver coin to the driver. "Thank you, Tommy. Good night."

The youth caught it handily. "Thank *'ee,* sir."

Her father bent to pick up his smaller valise, but Sir Giles stayed him.

"No, no. Leave them. Our steward shall have them delivered up to your . . . uh, rooms . . . directly. Well, not directly, but do come in." He held the door open.

Her father gestured for Emma to precede him.

Emma entered the vast two-story hall, trying not to gape. The hall was clearly quite ancient, unlike the modern windows of the side wings she had seen from outside. The hall's darkly paneled walls were hung with crossed swords and shields.

Sir Giles led the way over the flagstone floor to an open door across the hall. "Do come into the drawing room here." He turned to his wife. "My dear, would you mind terribly calling for tea and something to eat? I am certain Mr. and Miss Smallwood must be hungry after their long journey."

Lady Weston's smile was brittle. "Very well, my dear." She turned back. "Any preference as to which rooms I have made up?"

Sir Giles appeared embarrassed, no doubt wishing he might have spared his guests the realization that no rooms had yet been prepared for them. He escorted the Smallwoods into the drawing room, gave them another apologetic look, and asked them to excuse him for just a moment.

Even though Sir Giles closed the doors behind him, Emma heard a few words of the tense conversation beyond.

" . . . north wing."

"No way to foresee . . ."

" . . . nothing about a young woman . . ."

"For now."

A moment later, Sir Giles stepped back into the room. Emma pretended to study a framed map of Cornwall on the wall.

Sir Giles smiled and rubbed his hands together. "Tea and refreshments shall be arriving soon. Might I offer either of you a glass of something while we wait?"

"I wouldn't say no to a cheerful glass," her father said.

Emma added, "I shall wait for tea, thank you."

Sir Giles unstopped a crystal decanter and poured two glasses of brandy. "I imagine it has been quite a taxing day for you. First the journey, then a slapdash reception. I do hope to make it up to you."

John Smallwood said, "Think nothing of it. We only hope we did not presume in coming."

"Not at all. Not at all. I am only surprised and delighted you would come."

"But . . . did you not receive our letters in reply?"

"Oh . . . uh . . . yes. But, well, they reached me at a busy time, and I'm afraid I was not able to give them my full attention. But all shall be taken care of now that you're here."

Sir Giles carried a glass to her father, then said, "You will be glad to know we have not neglected the boys' education entirely. The local vicar has been tutoring them in Latin and Greek, so they are not *complete* savages." He chuckled awkwardly.

Her father smiled. "I am glad to hear it."

Sir Giles carried his own glass to an armchair, where he settled himself comfortably against the cushions. "You mentioned Henry and Phillip."

"How are they?" her father asked. "Will we be seeing them while we are here?"

"Yes. Phillip is away in Oxford, but he will return home at term end. Henry has just left for a few days on . . . em, family business, but he shall be returning soon."

Her father beamed. "Excellent."

Emma forced a smile, even as her stomach knotted at the thought.

*Such a trip as we had into Cornwall. . . . If*
*you could have followed us into the earthy old*
*churches . . . and into the strange caverns on*
*the gloomy seashore, and down into the depths*
*of mines, and up to the tops of giddy heights,*
*where the unspeakably green water was roaring.*

—Charles Dickens

# Chapter 3

E mma and her father were left alone to eat a light supper. Then
the housekeeper appeared to lead them to their rooms, candle
lamp in hand to light the way.

"You are to have rooms in the south wing," Mrs. Prowse said as
they crossed the hall to a simple Georgian staircase, another addition to the far older main hall.

When they reached the half landing, her father paused, looking up. Emma followed his gaze as he surveyed the soaring ceiling
striped by ancient roof timbers, massive and black as pitch.

He asked the housekeeper, "How old is the manor?"

Mrs. Prowse turned and swept her arm in a wide arc. "The hall
itself dates back three hundred years. Originally it was all there
was to the house, save for side wings for kitchens and stables. But
over the centuries additional wings and floors have been built on."

*Ah,* Emma thought. That explained the uneasy marriage of
Medieval, Tudor, and Georgian architecture she had noticed, both
in the exterior and now interior as well.

The middle-aged housekeeper led them up two flights of creaking stairs, pausing to light the candle lamps at each landing. "The north wing lies in that direction," she said, with a jerk of her chin. "You are not to venture there." She turned in the opposite direction and guided them down a long corridor, its floor slanting after years of warping and shifting.

She halted before a door midway along its length. "You are to have this room, Mr. Smallwood. And Miss Smallwood shall be around the corner at the end of the next passage."

Her father frowned. "May we not be closer?"

Knowing how much trouble the housekeeper and her maids had likely already been put to, Emma hurried to say, "It's all right, Papa. We shall find each other easily enough."

Mrs. Prowse nodded her approval, then continued officiously, "You haven't your own man, I take it, Mr. Smallwood?"

"No, I'm afraid not. But I shan't require much help."

"Our footman, Jory, will valet for you. And you, miss. Traveling without a maid, I understand?"

"That's right." At home, Mrs. Malloy or their maid, Nancy, had helped her dress. And Emma had taken care of her own hair.

"Then I shall send up the second housemaid to assist you."

Emma felt a twinge of unease, as she always did when acknowledging she needed anyone's help. But she did. Stays laced up the back, as did most of her frocks. "Thank you," she murmured.

Mrs. Prowse started to turn away but then lifted a finger. "Oh, and before I forget. You are both to take your meals in the steward's office from this point forward. Mr. Davies shall be expecting you."

"I see. Thank you." Emma realized she had been correct to foresee their status at Ebbington Manor as little higher than the servants. But she felt no pleasure at being right.

Emma bid her father good night and followed the housekeeper around the corner and down a narrower passage. Glancing up, Emma noticed old portraits high on the walls, their many pairs of eyes glaring down at her in the flickering candlelight. A shiver crept up her neck, and Emma suddenly shared her father's wish that their rooms were closer together.

When Mrs. Prowse opened a door near the end of the passage, Emma stepped inside the room and was pleased to see a candle glowing on the bedside table and a modest fire burning in the hearth.

"Do let me know if you need anything," the woman said, a hint of kindness in her voice.

"Thank you," Emma said once more, feeling like a parrot who knew only one phrase by rote. She added a smile to warm her words.

Assuring Emma the maid would be up soon to attend her, the housekeeper took her leave, closing the door behind her.

Emma stepped farther inside and surveyed the room. Her trunk sat near the wardrobe, but she hadn't the energy to begin unpacking. She'd had the foresight to pack a nightdress, comb, and tooth powder in her hand luggage and would make do with those for the night.

She had only just set these things out on the washstand when a quiet knock sounded. Emma turned. "Yes?"

The door creaked open and a girl's head appeared. "May I come in?"

Emma was surprised the maid would bother to ask. "Of course."

The young woman grinned impishly, bouncy dark ringlets framing her charming, freckled face. She wore no apron, and her ivory gown seemed too fine for her station.

Emma said bluntly, "You don't look like a housemaid."

The girl curtsied. "I thank you, miss. For I am not a housemaid."

Emma's face heated. "Forgive me. It is only that the housekeeper said she would send up the housemaid directly."

"Did she? Good. I was afraid the old thing wouldn't think to do so and you'd be left to fend for yourself. So I thought I would pop up and see if you needed any help. I haven't a lady's maid either. The housemaid attends me as well."

"I see." Emma waited for the young woman to introduce herself, but she merely stood there, smiling sweetly. A pretty girl, Emma thought. Probably seventeen or so. Several years younger than herself.

Emma took the matter in hand, saying, "Allow me to introduce myself. I am Miss Emma Smallwood." She raised her brows expectantly.

"Oh!" the girl exclaimed. "Do forgive me. How silly I am. I am Lizzie. Lizzie Henshaw."

Emma waited for her to explain her connection to the family. When she said nothing, Emma prodded, "And you are . . . ?"

The girl gaped. "You've never heard of me?" She huffed. "Those boys. I shouldn't wonder. I am Lady Weston's ward. I thought you'd know. I've lived here for more than three years now. Phillip never mentioned me?"

"Not that I recall."

Seeing the girl's crestfallen expression, Emma hastened to add, "I have not seen Phillip for nearly three years, so he very well may have mentioned you and I simply forgot."

Lizzie shrugged in easy acceptance. "That's all right. If he did mention me, it was probably full of teasing and jokes. Always likes to tease me. But that's how young men are, I suppose."

Lizzie cocked her head to one side, dark eyes glinting. "That reminds me. Have you met the twins yet?"

"No."

"Your father will have his hands full with those two, if I don't miss my guess."

"Oh? How so?"

"They're not accustomed to sitting in the schoolroom all day. At least not since their governess ran off with the drawing master. And that was years ago now."

"I thought Sir Giles mentioned a Latin and Greek tutor?"

"Mr. McShane?" The girl nodded. "The vicar comes a few hours each week. And handsome he is too. Though a bit . . . well fed."

"But is he a good teacher?"

Lizzie wrinkled a freckled nose. "I wouldn't have any idea about that, would I? I walk by the library now and again to take an eyeful, I confess. But most of what he says is so much gibberish to me."

*How sad,* Emma thought. Though she knew things like Latin

were "so much gibberish" to most females. And that men—and the majority of women —preferred it that way.

Lizzie continued. "But otherwise, the boys have been allowed to run wild for the most part. Worse than their elder brothers, they are." She shrugged. "But as I said, that's how boys are."

"Well. I suppose we shall meet them tomorrow."

Another knock sounded, and a diminutive housemaid entered in mobcap and apron. She dropped a curtsy, then hesitated at seeing Lizzie in the room.

"Were you looking for me, Morva?" Lizzie asked.

"Ess, miss. I be in yer room, waitin' for thee. Her ladyship told me to see to thee first."

"Well, never mind that," Lizzie said. "Attend Miss Smallwood first. I am in no hurry, whereas she must be exhausted."

The young housemaid bit her lip.

"Go on." Lizzie gestured toward Emma. "And if Lady W. fusses, just tell her I commanded you most imperiously."

The maid's brow puckered. "Most what?"

Lizzie paraphrased, "Blame me." She opened the door, then turned back to wink at Emma. "I shall see you in the morning, I trust?"

"Yes. I should think so."

"I hope we see a great deal of each other." Lizzie smiled. "I for one am very glad you're here."

Emma smiled stiffly, the girl's innocent words jabbing her throat—I *for one* am glad you're here.

Within minutes the housemaid had helped Emma undress and left to assist Lizzie. Though tired, Emma decided to write in her journal, as she usually did before blowing out her bedside candle at night. She thought it might settle her. She sat in bed, smoothed the bedclothes over her legs, and situated her small, portable writing desk on her lap. Uncorking the inkpot, she dipped her quill and wrote.

*How very disconcerting to arrive at Ebbington Manor after care-*
*ful planning only to find ourselves unexpected and, apparently,*

*unwanted guests. Had we not already let our house, I would have been tempted to turn right around and return home. But it is no longer our home, at least not for the next twelvemonth.*

*Hopefully, Lady Weston will come around to our being here. If only the younger Westons might take a liking to Papa as Phillip and even Henry Weston did as boys. I do hope Papa will rise to the occasion after his months of gloomy apathy. For if the Weston sons speak highly of their new teacher, that, I think, would go a long way in warming Lady Weston to the idea of an in-residence tutor. Not to mention the tutor's daughter. Tomorrow will be an important day. I must do what I can to help Papa make a good first impression.*

*Our cool reception has been salved somewhat by two unexpected consolations. One, Henry Weston is not present at the moment. And two, an unexpected young woman is. Her name is Miss Lizzie Henshaw. Lady Weston's ward, she said. I suppose she is the daughter of some relation of Lady Weston's, likely orphaned to have come to live here, apparently permanently. I don't believe Phillip mentioned her arrival. I wonder why.*

*At all events, Lizzie seems the most pleasant of the lot, or at least the only one truly glad to see us. She is several years younger than I. Still, I hope we might be friends. I would enjoy having a female friend, I think. It is not my habit to make quick judgments of anyone's character. But early indications seem quite—*

A strange howl reverberated through the door and up Emma's spine. She froze, quill in hand, heart pounding. There it came again, a high-pitched wail like an ailing child, or a frightened woman, or . . . a ghost. She told herself not to be silly. There was undoubtedly a simple, earthly explanation for the unearthly sound.

Emma squeezed her eyes shut, listening. She heard no answering cry of alarm, but distant footsteps padded rapidly down the corridor. A servant, she guessed. But why would he . . . or she . . . be running unless something was wrong?

Emma reminded herself that she was no longer in their modest household with only Mrs. Malloy and Nancy to look after them. Here at Ebbington Manor, there would be a whole army of servants busy about the place at all hours, lighting fires, bringing water, and who knew what all. It didn't necessarily mean that anything was amiss.

Did it ... ?

*Plop.* A drip of ink landed on her journal page, barely missing her white nightdress. It was enough to shake Emma from her fear-induced stupor. She quickly blotted the ink and stowed her writing things neatly away. Then she forced herself to blow out her candle and close her eyes.

But it was quite some time before she calmed down enough to fall asleep.

In the morning, Emma rose and washed with cold water left in the pitcher from the previous night. She then dressed herself as best she could, checking her watch and hoping the housemaid would arrive so she could finish dressing and get an early start on the day.

Morva finally bustled in, muttering apologies. "Sorry, miss. Not used to having two ladies to attend, along with my other duties."

Morva helped fasten her long stays and the back of her pin-tucked lavender frock. "There 'ee be. Anything else?"

"Fresh water might be nice, when you have a chance."

"Oh. Right. And I shall see to the slops. But just now I'm off to ..." Emma didn't hear the rest of the small woman's sentence, for she was already out the door.

Emma looked at herself in the mirror above the washstand. Her green eyes appeared large in her long oval face. Her cheeks pale. She had pinned her hair in a coil at the back of her head, but tawny dark blond fringe fell in wisps over her forehead, and a strand curled over each ear. She reached up to pinch her cheeks, then stopped herself. She should appear well-groomed and competent to make a good impression on their pupils. But beyond that, there was no need to try to look pretty.

Inwardly, she scolded herself for her tense countenance and rapid pulse. She reminded herself that neither Phillip nor Henry Weston were there to see her that morning. Not that she harbored any romantic notions about either man. . . . Still, one did wish to appear improved with age.

Her father was not in his room when Emma passed, so she went down alone. When Emma descended the stairs, there stood Lizzie Henshaw waiting for her, arms spread wide.

"Look at me, up early. It is not my custom, I assure you. Threw Morva into a spin this morning—my ringing for her so early and then having to attend you as well. It's good for her, I say. Cheeky thing."

Lizzie winked and propped a fist on her hip. "Why am I up with the birds this morning, you ask? Because I guessed you didn't even know where to take your breakfast. Am I right?"

"The housekeeper mentioned the steward's office, I believe."

"And do you know where that is?"

Emma shook her head. "No idea."

"That's what I thought." Lizzie cheerfully took her arm and led Emma across the hall. "This way."

"But my father—"

"Has already eaten, gone for a walk, and is no doubt pottering about in the schoolroom by now. Early riser, your papa."

"Yes," Emma agreed, disconcerted to find herself getting such a late start on their first day. She had not slept well.

"Lizzie, did you hear anything last night?"

"Like what?"

"A strange wailing?"

Lizzie shook her head. "Probably the wind. It makes strange sounds sometimes. Julian says it's a ghost, but Lady Weston assures me it's only the wind."

She added, "I don't know why Lady W. insisted on putting you in that drafty room, so far from the rest of the family. . . ." She halted midstride, jerking Emma to a stop beside her. "That's not true. I do know why. She's unhappy to find Mr. Smallwood's daughter so grown. Doesn't want any unattached females near her precious sons, I imagine. She said to me last night, 'At least Miss Smallwood is plain.'" Lizzie looked at Emma closely and shook her head. "But I don't think you're plain. I think you're quite lovely, actually. In a quiet sort of way."

"Th-thank you," Emma murmured, taken aback by the young woman's forthright speech and uncomfortable revelations. Lady Weston was an unkind woman, Emma thought, before reminding herself not to judge anyone too quickly.

"I had hoped you would be dining with us," Lizzie said. "But Lady W. is a stickler about station. Pity. Meals are an absolute bore, especially with both Phillip and Henry away." She sighed. "Ah, well. Mr. Davies is a decent chap, though a bit long in the tooth and grey in the side-whiskers for you. But perhaps Mr. McShane might suit you."

Emma frowned. "Miss Henshaw, I—"

"*Lizzie*, please," the girl insisted.

"Very well. Lizzie." Emma did not offer the use of her own Christian name. Not yet. "I hope you aren't under the misapprehension that I have come here looking for romance."

Again Lizzie halted. "Have you not? Well, Lady W. shall be relieved to hear it."

"Why would she think that is why I've come?" Emma asked, incredulous.

Lizzie studied Emma shrewdly. "Then, why are you here?"

"To help my father. As I have done for years. We . . . that is, my father teaches a great many subjects, and I assist him. Besides . . . my mother is no longer living. I should not want to be apart from him."

Lizzie took this in. "I see."

Emma noticed the girl did not offer any empathetic information about the fate of her own parents, but did not feel she ought to pry. Instead she asked, "Is there a particular reason our arrival came at a bad time?"

Lizzie shrugged. "I don't know. Everyone was in a frenzy yesterday. I was sent to my room to stay out from underfoot. Something about Henry."

"Sir Giles mentioned he left on some sort of family business."

"Did he? I wouldn't know about that. No one tells me anything. They think I can't keep a secret." She leaned nearer and winked. "And between you and me . . . they're mostly right."

Emma made a mental note to remember that.

Lizzie tugged on Emma's arm once more and led her down a side passage. "Mr. Davies has his office back here by the tradesmen's entrance." The girl paused at an open doorway. "Here we are." She gave Emma a wry glance. "Now, don't get used to a personal escort. I plan to return to my lazy lay-abed ways tomorrow." She smirked, and Emma could not help grinning in reply.

Lizzie left her, and Emma entered the room alone. Inside, she observed a modest table set with everyday linen and cutlery, and a sideboard bearing a spigot urn, teapot, and trays of assorted breads, cold meats, boiled eggs, and baked goods. A scattering of crumbs and used teacups on the tablecloth told her at least two people had eaten there before her. She helped herself to a cup of tepid tea and a cold egg and sat down to a solitary meal.

Half an hour later, Emma made her way up three flights of stairs to the schoolroom. There she found her father sitting at the desk, paging through a book. Two youths slumped at a table facing him. The room was long and narrow, its ceiling pitched steeply along one wall, with dormer windows overlooking the roof and a patch of coastline beyond.

Her father glanced up when she entered. "Ah, Emma. There you are." He gestured her forward.

Emma crossed the room and stood beside his desk. How many times had she endured these awkward introductions back in Longstaple whenever new pupils arrived? Somehow she felt even more self-conscious in the Weston schoolroom than she ever had in their own.

"Boys, this is Miss Smallwood, my daughter, who will be assisting me from time to time." He lifted a hand to each fifteen-year-old as he made the introductions. "Emma, may I present Julian and Rowan Weston."

"I'm Rowan. He's Julian," one of them corrected.

"Oh. Forgive me."

Emma looked at the boys. Young men, really. They were not identical, she instantly saw, but she could understand how her father might confuse them. Both had dark hair, worn short. Both had blue eyes. But Julian had a rounder face and a smattering of freckles across the bridge of his nose, which made him look younger. His eyes were a pale icy blue.

Rowan's face was longer and more angular, his complexion slightly darker and clear of freckles. His eyes were a deeper blue than Julian's, his nose wider and his upper lip more pronounced.

Both were handsome, but Julian appeared to be perched on the cusp of manhood, whereas Rowan had already arrived—he could have easily passed for seventeen. At all events, both looked older than she had imagined them.

"I am afraid we have yet to begin," her father said. "When I arrived up here this morning, I was surprised to find the room in disuse and the trunk still packed."

Her father had filled his trunk with the maps, schoolbooks, and other texts he'd used in his academy for years.

He continued, "I had to call for the housekeeper and ask for it to be dusted and swept. I am still not organized."

"I shall put the room to rights," Emma said. "You go on with your lesson."

Her father nodded. "Thank you, my dear. Apparently, the vicar has been teaching the boys in their father's library."

"Mr. McShane said the schoolroom is for children," the larger Rowan said, his pronounced upper lip curled. "And we are nearly sixteen."

Mr. Smallwood gave him a patronizing smile. "I suppose that is true—you are young men now. And perhaps this is a fortuitous arrangement. For I might have my own domain and Mr. McShane his." He looked at Emma and explained, "I spoke with Sir Giles this morning, and we have decided the vicar shall continue teaching Latin and Greek for now—finish out the week at least. That will allow us a bit more time to settle in here at Ebbington."

Emma nodded her understanding, and her father returned his attention to the book he'd been paging through.

"Emma, I am trying to find that passage about the importance of the classics in education. Do you recall where it is?"

"Chapter two, I believe. About midway through."

After flipping a few more pages, his eyes lit. "Ah yes. Here it is. Boys, please turn to page fifteen in your texts."

The boys opened their books—Julian eagerly, Rowan lethargically.

Her father looked at Julian. "If you will read the first paragraph, Rowan?"

"Julian," the smaller youth gritted out, his tone not matching his sweet, boyish face.

"Right. I beg your pardon."

*Oh dear,* Emma thought. *Not a good start.* She would have to help her father learn to differentiate the boys and remember which was which.

And perhaps insist he wear his spectacles.

Leaving the males to their first lesson, Emma moved to the trunk in the corner and began to quietly and she hoped unobtrusively unpack her father's books and supplies. She decided to organize a separate shelf of their own books, to make it easier to extract their volumes when it was time to leave.

She barely noticed when her father released the boys for a respite. And when he announced he was going to take a turn about the grounds to stretch his limbs, she mumbled something and went on sorting. There were many good books on the schoolroom shelves. Books that had likely sat there for years, unread. There was no logic to their order, but Emma began to remedy that. She decided to create an index by subject and author to aid in future reference. She loved to catalog, organize, and make order of chaos.

Those books she was unfamiliar with, she flipped through, reading enough to catalog its subject. Many she found fascinating. What a shame no one read them. If such treasures had been left here in the schoolroom, what must Sir Giles's library hold? She wondered if he would invite her to peruse it while she was there.

Although, if he was anything like his son Henry, perhaps not.

When Phillip had come to Longstaple, he had happily shared the few books he had brought with him. His older brother, on the other hand, had not. That was what she remembered most about Henry Weston's arrival all those years ago. . . .

She had been a girl of eleven when he'd first arrived—fourteen, sullen, and resentful. She had only asked if he might like some help putting away his things, her eyes drawn to the stack of books in his trunk. But he had slammed the lid closed.

"I'll thank you to leave my things alone. There are no dolls here."

She pointed to two cases of tin soldiers lying on his bed. "Then what are those?"

His green eyes narrowed, hardened. "Miniature military figures. And if I hear them referred to by any other name, or if I find you have so much as touched them, I shall make you very sorry."

She gasped, then snapped, "I can certainly see why your family sent you away."

Emma could hardly believe those words had come from her mouth. Never had she said anything so meanspirited in her life. And certainly not to a new pupil. What had come over her? His cold, superior attitude and rudeness were vexing, yes. But no excuse. She had always controlled her tongue, regardless of provocation.

For a second, the flinty layer of glass fell from his eyes, and she glimpsed an unexpected vulnerability. But a moment later, his eyes hardened once more, and his mouth cinched tight. He shut the door in her face—leaving her out in the passage alone.

A girl's voice interrupted Emma's reminiscing. "Are you never going to come away?"

Emma turned to see Lizzie standing in the schoolroom doorway, dimples in her cheeks.

"How dedicated you are," Lizzie continued. "Still working away after all the males have gone. I gather your father decided to start with only half a day today."

Emma looked around and frowned. "What time is it?"

"After four. You've missed tea and will be late for dinner if you don't go and change now."

Emma rose from knees she'd just realized were stiff and aching. "Change?"

"Yes, we dress for dinner here, even in *uncivilized* Cornwall," Lizzie teased. "And so shall you. For you've dust on your hems and on your cheek."

Self-conscious, Emma's hand went to her face.

Lizzie withdrew a handkerchief from her sleeve and handed it to her, pointing to the mirror spot on her own cheek as guide.

Emma wiped the spot. "Gone?"

"Better." Lizzie tugged her hand. "Come on, I shall help you change your frock. Who knows where Morva is this time of day."

"But don't you need to change as well?"

"Oh, I have plenty of time," Lizzie explained. "The family eats a bit later."

"Ah." Was Lizzie family, then?

On their way down to Emma's room, Emma heard Lady Weston greeting her sons on the landing below.

Lizzie grasped her arm and put a finger to her lips. "Shh . . ."

"So how went your first day with the new tutor?" Lady Weston asked.

"A dead bore, Mamma," Rowan replied in his low voice.

"Oh, it wasn't so bad," boyish Julian amended. "And Miss Small-wood seems amiable."

Rowan added, "More so than her crusty old father, at any rate."

Sir Giles spoke up. "Rowan, mind your tongue. Mr. Smallwood is a well-reputed and learned gentleman. He deserves your respect."

"What has that to say to anything?" Lady Weston objected. "Really, my dear. You mustn't chastise Rowan for merely stating his opinion."

Emma was glad her father wasn't standing there with her, over-hearing their words. Increasingly uncomfortable to be eavesdropping, Emma gestured for Lizzie to come away. Giving in, Lizzie followed her quietly down the corridor.

When they'd turned the corner, Lizzie whispered, "Don't take it to heart. I told you the twins weren't accustomed to sitting in the schoolroom—except for the few hours Mr. McShane is here, making them recite Latin verbs or some such."

"But they have never been to school?"

"Oh yes. They did go away to school once. 'A good old-fashioned West Country school,' Lady Weston called it."

Emma was astonished. No one had mentioned a school. "Oh? Which one?"

Lizzie puckered up her face. "I don't know. Anyway, they didn't like it. I gather the schoolmaster was a hard man. And the other students a mean lot. So Lady W. fetched them home."

Emma recalled something Sir Giles had said in his letter about Lady Weston feeling their youngest sons were too delicate to live apart from their mamma. She wondered why they had sent the boys to some unknown school, when surely Phillip must have spoken highly of his years at the Smallwood Academy. She didn't think even Henry Weston would disparage her father, regardless of his opinion of her.

Inside Emma's room, Lizzie flung open the wardrobe and flipped through the few gowns hanging there, as eagerly as Emma might flip through a book. "Surely these are not all you brought?"

"Yes, actually."

Lizzie tsked. "Are tutors really so poor?" She asked it matter-of-factly, without apparent criticism.

"I have a few more at home," Emma said. "But I could only bring one trunk."

Lizzie looked at all the books—piled on the floor and stacked on the side table, where Morva had displaced them to unearth the clothing—and said with a wry grin, "And you must have your books."

"Exactly."

Lizzie idly picked up the top book on the stack. "I have never cared much for reading."

Emma jested, "And here I'd hoped we were going to be friends."

Lizzie looked up at her sharply.

Emma hurried to say, "I was only joking. I realize most women are not as keen on books as I am."

"A real bluestocking," Lizzie said. "That's how Henry described you once when he and Phillip were speaking of your academy."

Emma lifted her mouth in a humorless smile. "Yes, that sounds like something he would say."

Lizzie picked up another volume from the bedside table, and Emma's heart lurched.

"Oh, that's only my journal," she said, hurrying over. "You don't want that." Emma held out her palm, barely resisting the urge to snatch the journal from the girl's hand.

Was it her imagination, or did Lizzie hesitate? But a moment later, Lizzie handed it over with her usual dimpled grin.

"Ooh la la! A real gothic romance, I don't doubt. What secrets and scandals it must contain." She wagged her eyebrows comically. "Now *that's* a book that might very well hold my attention."

Cradling her journal, Emma made a mental note to add *nosy* to her list of Lizzie Henshaw's qualities.

Lizzie helped her change into her favorite gown of ivory muslin with pink flowers embroidered at bodice and hem. Then Emma slipped her arms into an open robe of dusty rose, which buttoned under her bosom and was trimmed with lace at the neckline and cuffs. Lizzie commented that she thought the old-fashioned over-dress quite charming and had not seen one in an age. Emma forced a smile and thanked her, and then the two walked downstairs together.

Conversationally, Emma asked, "Phillip was home for Easter, I trust?"

"Yes. For nearly a fortnight before he had to return for the next term."

"And how did he seem to you?"

"Homesick."

Emma gave the girl a sidelong glance. "He is not enjoying university?"

"Who could enjoy school? No offense, Miss Smallwood."

They arrived at the steward's office, sparing Emma the need to reply. Her father stood just inside, waiting as Mr. Davies poured two glasses of something.

"This is my father, Mr. Smallwood," Emma began. "May I present Miss Lizzie Henshaw."

"How do you do, Miss Henshaw."

At her father's inquisitive look, Emma added, "Miss Henshaw is Lady Weston's ward."

"Ah. I see. Well, a pleasure to make your acquaintance."

The steward turned and made a sharp bow. "Good evening, Miss Smallwood. Liz—Miss Henshaw."

"Mr. Davies," Emma greeted the man, whom she had met briefly when they arrived. He wore the clothes of a gentleman, in bleak black. His slicked-down hair was still dark, though his side-whiskers bristled silver. His face sagged in a weary, hound-dog fashion, and his voice carried an accent strange to her ear. Faded Scots, perhaps?

Her father accepted a glass of sherry. "I was about to ask Mr. Davies when we might be seeing Henry." He addressed Lizzie, "But perhaps you know?"

Lizzie reared her head back. "I don't know. I've no idea where he's even gone. Do you know, Davies?"

The steward's face wrinkled into a grimace. "I . . . That is . . ." He cleared his throat. "I don't know when Master Henry shall be returning; don't think anyone knows exactly."

Lizzie shot Emma an exasperated look. "Told you no one trusts me." She narrowed her eyes at the steward. "Apparently, not even our Mr. Davies here. Well." She drew herself up. "I shall leave you to your dinner. Don't talk about me now." She fluttered a wave, grinned at Emma, then whirled from the room.

After she had gone, Emma sat at the small table while a servant—by appearance even younger than Julian—served their meal. As they ate, Mr. Davies told them a little about himself. He had been with Lady Weston's family as their butler when she was a girl. Upon her marriage to Sir Giles, Davies had come with Violet Heale-Weston to Ebbington Manor as steward—overseeing the estate accounts, tenants, and servants. He had been married, but his wife had died several years ago.

Emma's father mentioned the loss of his own wife, and the two widowers spoke in quiet empathy for some time, allowing Emma—weary from all the upheaval of recent weeks—the luxury of lapsing into silence.

She excused herself as soon as etiquette allowed, retreated to her room, and rang for Morva to help her undress. After the maid left her, Emma sank gratefully into bed with her journal but fell asleep before writing a single word.

*Clever girls were looked at with suspicion.*
*They earned the title "bluestockings,"*
*and it was not a term of admiration.*

—Sharon Laudermilk and Teresa L. Hamlin,
*The Regency Companion*

# Chapter 4

The next morning, Emma again found her father's room empty and went downstairs alone. When she neared the steward's office, she heard low male voices and assumed Mr. Davies and her father were breakfasting together. But when she entered, she found Mr. Davies seated at his desk, in conversation with a man she had not seen before—a man still wearing his outdoor coat and cap.

*Not very polite of him,* Emma thought.

From beneath the man's tweed cap, red hair in need of a comb hung over his collar. Some tradesman or estate worker Emma guessed, though his well-made suit of clothes seemed incongruous with his flat cap and unkempt hair.

The man looked at her, his gaze running from her head to bosom and back again. Emma was grateful to have a modest fichu tucked into her neckline—not that she had much to cover up.

Mr. Davies rose from behind his desk. "Good morning, miss."

"Good morning."

She waited, but Davies did not introduce the man.

She faltered, "Should I . . . come back another time? I am really not very hungry."

"No, miss." Davies looked at the man pointedly. "This fellow was just leaving."

"Pray, don't leave on my account." The man smiled archly. "Miss, thee say?"

Again Mr. Davies offered no introduction, so Emma made do with an awkward nod.

The man's smile stretched across his thin face. "I'd heard new folks come to Ebb-ton. But not that one be so well favored."

Cheeks burning, Emma turned away. Aware of his gaze following her, she stepped to the sideboard and self-consciously selected a small breakfast. How would she eat half of it if the man kept watching her?

But she had no sooner set her plate on the table than the man rose.

"Until the first, then, Davies. I shan't wait a day longer."

Davies sighed heavily. "I shall do what I can."

With a grin in her direction, the red-haired man tugged his cap brim and took his leave.

Davies remained only long enough to ask her if she had everything she needed before excusing himself as well.

Emma ate her breakfast alone.

When she exited the steward's office a short time later, she was surprised to find her father buttoning his greatcoat and taking up his walking stick from the stand near the back door. She hoped he was not neglecting his duties already.

"Good morning, Papa."

"Ah, Emma. Good morning."

"Where are you off to?" She steeled herself to be called upon to teach the morning lesson in his stead. She hated to think what Lady Weston would say when she heard.

"I'm off for a morning stroll. Rowan and Julian are in the library with the vicar."

"Do you mind?" she asked gently.

"Not at all," he said. "I imagine the vicar's Latin and certainly his Greek are superior to mine."

Emma was surprised her father would acknowledge that.

"At all events," he continued, "I plan to use my free time to become more acquainted with the countryside. Would you like to accompany me?"

"No thank you, Papa."

"You don't know what you're missing, my dear. The property stretches out to sheer cliffs which drop straight down to the Atlantic—crashing waves, bracing ocean breezes. Nothing like it in Longstaple, I can tell you. There's something refreshing about it, Emma. You simply must see it for yourself."

Already her father's cheeks were bright—either from his walk the day before or in anticipation of that morning's pleasure. Whatever the case, he looked more alert and alive than she'd seen him in months.

"I shall," she assured him. "But not today. I made good progress in organizing the schoolroom yesterday, and I shall take advantage of its not being in use this morning to continue." Guilt niggled her. Had she not come here to help her father? She would have to make a point to spend more time with him in future.

Bidding him be careful near the cliffs, Emma watched her father leave. Then she turned and walked up the passage and across the hall. Seeing no one about, she gingerly approached the library door, partially ajar.

She peeked inside. There at the library table sat Rowan and Julian, hunched over paper and quills, translating something, she imagined. Pacing before them was a slightly portly man with auburn hair that almost, but not quite, covered his somewhat prominent ears. He was dressed in a black coat and trousers with a cleric's white, tabbed collar.

He stopped pacing, crossed his arms, and regarded his pupils. In that position, she got a better look at his face. His nose was well proportioned, his mouth wide, its upper lip a well-defined archer's bow. A pleasing face, Emma thought, though perhaps not quite as handsome as Lizzie had led her to believe.

Apparently bored or eager for the boys to finish, he wadded up a scrap of paper and tossed it at Rowan.

Emma frowned at this, as did Rowan, who glanced up in surprise.

Mr. McShane said, "Just wanted to make sure you were awake, Rowan."

"I am. But this is dashed difficult."

"Of course it is," he said, tone wry. "Most worthwhile things are."

Rowan's face puckered, but he begrudgingly bent back over his work.

"And you, Julian?" the vicar asked, pausing beside his second pupil.

Julian had not reacted during the exchange with his brother, nor even glanced up.

Still eliciting no response, Mr. McShane poked him in the arm with his index finger. It was a playful gesture, not hard or cruel, but Julian's head snapped up, his eyes sparking with fury. Gone was the charming boy Emma had seen upon first meeting. In his place sat a furious young man ready to strike.

"Poke me again and you shall draw back a stump."

Emma stifled a gasp—and the urge to stalk inside and take the situation in hand.

In a flash Rowan leapt to his feet and placed himself between his brother and the stunned vicar. Rowan was nearly as tall as the clergyman. He stood, tense and alert, poised to . . . what? Defend his brother, or threaten his provoker?

He said quietly, "I would advise you not to do that again, Mr. McShane."

The vicar's hand went to his chest in a regretful gesture. He said earnestly, "*Mea maxima culpa.* I beg your pardon. I had no intention of harming or offending either of you. I apologize."

Rowan remained where he was a moment longer, then turned, and both men faced Julian. For a moment Julian's hard glare didn't waver. Emma tensed, fearing a fight was about to break out.

But then Julian leaned back against his chair, slowly grinning as though it had all been a joke. "*Te absolvo,*" he said. "This time."

Emma quietly turned away and started up the many stairs toward the schoolroom. One part of her was oddly relieved that the vicar had some difficulty with the boys, as her father had. But another part of her was unsettled by such a lack of respect demonstrated to a teacher, and a clergyman in the bargain.

Reaching the schoolroom, she returned her attention to the review and cataloging of the books on the schoolroom shelves. One dusty volume promised a history of the village of Ebford. Kneeling before the bookcase, she skimmed through the volume, noting a list of prominent families who'd settled the parish—the Heales, Trewins, Teagues, and Morgans. *Heale*... Was that not the name Mr. Davies had mentioned—Lady Weston's maiden name? She thought so, but could not recall with certainty.

That afternoon Lizzie offered to give Emma a thorough tour of Ebbington Manor, showing her not only a general sweep of the public rooms as Mrs. Prowse had done, but promising to include more interesting areas of the house as well. Emma was surprised Mrs. Prowse had not offered such a tour herself. But as she thought about it, Emma realized she had barely laid eyes on the housekeeper since she'd shown them to their rooms the night they arrived.

Lizzie led her first through the ground level, pointing out rooms opening onto the hall. "You've seen most of this already. The drawing room, dining room, breakfast room, library. Have you seen the music room yet?"

"No."

Lizzie opened the door and gestured across the room. Emma peered inside, noting the tapestries and portraits on the walls, a pianoforte front and center, and a harp off to one side.

"Who plays?" she asked.

"The harp? Nobody, I don't think."

"And the pianoforte?"

"Julian and Rowan have both had lessons. But Julian is supposedly the better player."

Emma looked at her. "You don't agree?"

Lizzie shrugged. "I have no ear for music, apparently." She shut the door before Emma got a good look. "More interesting rooms ahead."

She led Emma upstairs to the first floor. "This is Lady Weston's apartment." She opened a door. "This is her dressing room, and her bedchamber is through there." Lizzie indicated the adjoining room, where Emma glimpsed a frilly, canopied bed.

Lizzie returned eager eyes to the dressing table. "Have you ever seen the like? There are enough lotions and potions to smooth the wrinkles from an elephant. Not that I've ever seen an elephant. But I have read a *few* books in my life."

Emma's gaze swept the dressing table with its three-paneled looking glass, swathed in lace and covered with cosmetics, hairbrushes and powder brushes with silver handles, flowers in a crystal vase, and another spray on the dressing chest. The room was very feminine, and very . . . frothy.

"Ought we to be in here?" Emma whispered.

"Why not? Don't you want to see what all her money buys?"

"*Her* money?"

Lizzie wagged her brows and grinned mischievously but made no answer. "Follow me." She turned and led Emma back into the corridor. But they had barely closed Lady Weston's door and taken three steps when that very personage appeared from around the corner and paused directly in their path.

"Lizzie. Miss Smallwood. What are you two doing, pray?" One penciled eyebrow rose high.

"I am only giving Miss Smallwood a tour of the place," Lizzie replied. "Thought someone should."

Lady Weston glanced from the girl's face to the closed door behind her. "Very good of you, I'm sure."

She swept past them, and the girls continued on their way. But Lady Weston's voice halted them once more. "Lizzie?"

Lizzie and Emma turned back.

Violet Weston's steely eyes looked from one young woman to the other. "Take care in wandering about the manor. Do remember the north wing is . . . better left out of your tour. It isn't safe or . . . well lit."

Lizzie's eyes glinted speculatively. "Is that so, my lady? I did not realize."

"Yes. It is so, Lizzie. Or I would not have said it."

"Then I thank you for your . . . concern."

Lady Weston looked at her pointedly. "Be careful, Lizzie."

"I always am."

Once Lady Weston had stepped into her room and closed the door, Emma whispered, "What was that about?"

"I'm not certain. But that reminds me—I want to show you something."

"But . . . Lizzie!"

Emma had to hurry to catch up with the younger girl as she trotted up the stairs to the next floor—the floor where Emma and her father had their rooms, as well as Julian and Rowan. At the top of the stairs, instead of going left or right, Lizzie stepped forward into a small alcove. There, lit by sunshine filtered through a stained-glass window, hung a portrait.

"I wonder if this is what she didn't want you to see. . . ."

Emma stepped closer, looking up at the oil painting in gilded frame. Autumnal-colored light shone on it from the stained-glass window, turning the subject's complexion golden. It was a skillfully painted portrait of a beautiful woman in her early twenties, with thick dark hair, thin, well-carved features, and Phillip Weston's blue eyes.

"It's the first Lady Weston," Lizzie breathed, almost reverently, Emma thought. "Phillip's mother. And Henry's."

"Yes, I would have guessed as much," Emma said. "I see something of both of them in her face—though, granted, I haven't seen either of them in years."

"You're perfectly right," Lizzie agreed. "Each of them inherited some of her features."

Emma nodded, captured by the image. "Why is it kept up here when most of the family have their rooms downstairs?"

Lizzie sent her a sardonic look. "Why do you think?"

Emma thought it wiser not to comment.

Lizzie continued, "I think she's far more beautiful than the second Lady Weston. But never tell her I said so. I should deny it to the death."

"I hardly think it would come to that."

"Don't be so sure. Now. Ready for the best part of the tour?"

Emma hoped it didn't include the off-limits north wing. "What is it?"

Lizzie wagged her eyebrows once more. "Phillip's and Henry's bedchambers." She tucked her hand in the crook of Emma's arm and led her back downstairs. "You've never been in a gentleman's bedchamber, I'd guess." She said it condescendingly, almost suggestively.

Emma was tempted to correct her, to tell Lizzie she had been in dozens. Of course the gentlemen had all been adolescents at the time. . . . But recalling Lizzie's confession that she didn't keep secrets, she decided not to say anything that might be repeated and misconstrued.

There was nothing remarkable about Phillip's bedchamber, yet Lizzie lingered. In Phillip's lengthy absence, the room had been kept tidy by dutiful housemaids, and the shutters left drawn against the damaging rays of the sun.

In Henry's room, books lay in piles on the writing desk and side table. Stacks of papers, spent quills, and inkpots littered every surface of the room. Emma wondered how the housemaids managed to dust in there.

Following her look of distaste, Lizzie said, "This is nothing. You ought to see his study."

Emma asked, "And what would Phillip or Henry say to finding you in their bedchambers?" *Not to mention me,* Emma added to herself.

Lizzie shrugged. "I don't think they'd care. Sometimes I think they look on me as an annoying little sister. Or a house-trained pug."

"And are they like brothers to you?" Emma asked.

Again that ill-bred shrug. "Perhaps. But I confess I flirt with all four of them shamelessly."

Emma tucked her chin in surprise. "Do you?"

"Why not? I wouldn't mind marrying one of them. Then the other three can be my brothers all they like."

"Any one in particular?" Emma asked dryly.

"I'm not particular, no. Though one professes to be in love with me."

"Good heavens," Emma breathed.

Lizzie glanced at her, waved a dismissive hand, and then amended, "But who can trust anything a man says?"

*I can,* Emma thought. She trusted her father's word, if not his capabilities. And she had trusted Phillip. She hoped she still could do so. Oh, if only it weren't so long until the term end.

Lizzie looked at her, then burst into giggles. "I am only teasing you, Miss Smallwood. You needn't look so scandalized." She slapped her thigh through her muslin gown. "If only you could see your face. The very image of a pursed-lip puritan!" She hooted in laughter, while Emma found it not at all amusing. But her censorious look only sent Lizzie into new heights of humor.

Emma wondered if she could trust anything Lizzie Henshaw said. She turned to leave.

"Oh, come, Miss Smallwood. Pray, don't be offended." Lizzie walked after her. "I don't know when I've enjoyed myself more. I've never had a female friend, so I am no doubt breaking all sorts of rules. I shall behave now." She placed a hand over her heart. "I promise. No more shocking talk. What say you to a game of battledore and shuttlecock instead? I long for a bit of exercise. Or we might walk into the village and look in the shop windows."

"No, thank you, Lizzie. I had better return to the schoolroom." Lizzie sighed. "Oh, you're no fun."

A thought struck Emma, and she turned back. "You have not shown me your room, Lizzie. That is one room I should actually like to see."

The girl's lower lip protruded and the sparkle faded from her eyes. "No you shouldn't. Nothing to see there." She shrugged. "But it's on the way to the schoolroom, so I can show you, if you like. Be prepared to be thoroughly unimpressed."

On the third level, a pair of oddly placed steps linked the floors of one addition with the next. Midway along the passage, Lizzie opened a door. The room was clean and sunny but fairly Spartan, with a plain single bed that had neither canopy nor bed curtains. The room held a simple washstand much like Emma's, though Lizzie also had a lady's dressing table, whereas Emma did not. And Lizzie had two large wardrobe cupboards bursting with gowns of every description.

"My goodness, Lizzie . . ." Emma breathed, taking in the colorful sight.

"Lady Weston likes me to dress well. Very concerned about appearances, Lady Weston is."

"So I see."

After that, the girls parted company. Emma spent the remainder of the day with her father in the schoolroom and later ate dinner with him and Mr. Davies.

That night before going to sleep, Emma added to the lists she kept in her journal.

> *Lizzie Henshaw: charming, amusing, nosy, fickle, hiding something.*
> *Lady Violet Weston: Proud, disapproving, cold, elegant, hiding something.*

Sometime after Emma had set aside her journal, blown out her candle, and fallen asleep, she awoke with a start. What had she heard this time? Not a howl. A hinge squeak? The click of a door latch? For a moment she lay there, unmoving, ears alert to any sound, eyes searching the darkness. Her room was black, save for the low glow of embers in the fireplace. The furnishings loomed as uncertain shapes in the shadows. Was that a figure near the wall or merely her wardrobe? Her heart rate accelerated.

She sat up and whispered, "Who's there?" She felt foolish even as she uttered the question.

Silence.

There was no one there, she told herself. And if there had been, it had only been a servant, come to check the fire, perhaps. She would not have expected such service while it was still night. But who else would come into her room?

Emma forced herself to lie back down, pulled the blankets up to her chin, and squeezed her eyes shut.

That was when she smelled it. She sniffed again. Shaving soap? Men's cologne? Good heavens, that was strange. She had not smelled it before.

She lay there, forcing herself to breathe deeply, to keep her eyes closed, to think of the book she was currently reading, and eventually managed to fall back asleep.

Emma woke again to find weak dawn light filtering through her windowpanes. The room was still, the fire had gone out. It must be early, for Morva had not yet made it to her room to lay another one. No doubt she and her father were low on the list, after all the family bedchambers had been seen to first. Emma was certainly glad it was spring and not winter.

Remembering her fright of the night before, Emma surveyed her room and found it apparently undisturbed. Of course, everything was as it should be. What had she been thinking last night?

Needing to use the chamber pot, Emma forced herself from the warm cocoon of her bedclothes, relieved herself, then stepped to the corner washstand to wash her hands and face.

As she turned back toward her bed, her bare foot landed on something sharp and hard.

"Oww . . ." she grumbled, and bent to retrieve the offending object.

In the dim light, the small article appeared a dull grey. She picked it up and carried it nearer the window to identify it. She blinked in surprise. A miniature toy soldier. Instantly, she was transported back to days of old at the Smallwood Academy when pupils were forever leaving small wooden balls, jackstones, and soldiers with pointy swords for her to step on.

Henry Weston, however, had been very particular about his collection of military figures, which he used to reenact historic or recent battles with the French.

A good thing he was away on family business at present, or she might have suspected Henry Weston himself had been in her room. She chuckled at the notion. It was far more likely that this soldier had lain hidden under the bed or carpets, long forgotten, only to be swept out in the hurried preparation for the unexpected Smallwoods. Yes, far more likely.

After Morva came in and helped her dress, Emma made her way downstairs for breakfast. She glimpsed Lizzie standing in the hall at one of the front windows.

"Good morning," Emma greeted.

Lizzie glanced over, but her gaze quickly returned to the window. "Yes, it is."

"You're up early." Curious, Emma walked to Lizzie's side and looked out the window to see what had captured her attention.

Past the garden wall, across the grassy expanse beyond, came a man riding a muscled black horse, its mane and tale flying on the wind as it galloped over the turf and leapt the garden gate with apparent ease. The rider sat the horse well, erect and confident, high boots in the stirrups, buff breeches snug to the horse's sides, riding coat sailing behind him, beaver hat brim shading his face.

As horse and rider trotted toward the stables, Emma recognized the man as Henry Weston. Her stomach clenched. Her palms became instantly damp.

"He's a bruising rider. . . ." Lizzie breathed, all admiration.

Emma frowned. "I had not heard he was expected this morning."

"He arrived late last night."

Emma stared at Lizzie, aghast. "Last night?"

Lizzie glanced over, clearly surprised at Emma's sharp tone. "Yes. It was after ten. You had already gone to bed."

Emma felt her jaw slacken. *Surely not. It must be mere coincidence.* Lizzie asked, "Did you hear it?"

"Hear what?" Emma thought of the unidentified sound that had woken her.

"The row. Between Henry and his father. Lady Weston too."

"No." Emma would not ask what the argument had been about; it was none of her affair. Nor Lizzie's likely.

Instead she asked, "Does he know I . . . that is, that my father and I are here?" Emma hoped that was not what they had argued about.

"I overheard Lady W. tell him last night." Lizzie snickered and then grinned at Emma. "Warned him, more like."

Offense and mortification shimmered up Emma's spine. Warned him indeed.

Intending to ask the boys about the toy soldier, Emma took it upstairs with her after breakfast. She placed it on the schoolroom desk and resumed her cataloging. She found herself reading too much and organizing too little but reminded herself there was no hurry. Kneeling before the schoolroom shelves, she spied a thin volume that had become wedged in the back of the lowest shelf. Since she was alone, she leaned forward to reach the book, her bum projecting in a most unladylike manner, to carefully extricate it without damage.

A dry chuckle disturbed her concentration.

"Well, well. Miss Smallwood. And just as I remember her."

Prickles of embarrassment and dread rippled through her. She recognized that voice. After so many years, she still did.

She flew to her feet, caught her slipper heel in her skirt hems, and nearly went sprawling as she spun to face him. In one hand she held the rescued book and raised it over her skittering heart. The other hand she lifted to her hair, fearing it was in as much disarray as her nerves.

Henry Weston stood there, leaning one shoulder against the doorjamb, his catlike eyes roving her burning cheeks, flicking to her hair, her gown, the book pressed to her chest like a shield, before returning to her face.

She swallowed convulsively and grasped for composure, reminding herself he was no longer a youth about to toss a mouse under her bedclothes. The thick dark hair framing his face was better groomed than she recalled, his features carved even more sharply than she remembered. Was that a smirk on his face? She coolly lifted her chin. "Mr. Weston."

He shook his head. "You have not changed one iota. Still the bluestocking with her nose in a book. Hidden away indoors on such a beautiful day."

Something about his smirk and the glint of challenge in his hooded eyes sent logic flying. And suddenly Emma was quite certain Henry Weston had, upon learning she was in residence last night, lost no time in returning to his old tricks.

She leveled him with an icy glare. "I am surprised you are not too tired to go gallivanting about today, riding and jumping and sneaking up on people."

One dark brow rose. "Tired? Why should I be tired?"

"You were up late last night."

Both brows lifted.

She added, "Up to no good."

His eyes narrowed. "What, pray, does that mean?"

"You know very well."

"If you are talking about my . . . disagreement with my father, that is none of your business."

"That is not what I am referring to, as well you know. And it *is* my business."

She set aside the book, snatched the tin soldier from the desk, and held it before him, pinched between thumb and index finger. "I found this in my room this morning. Did you drop it or leave it behind intentionally, like a calling card?"

He frowned at the figure, then reached out and took it from her—careful, she noticed, to avoid brushing her fingers.

She asked, "A bit old, are you not? To still be playing with toys?"

He said without expression, as if by rote, "It is not a toy. It is a miniature military figure."

How many times she had heard him say the same as a younger man.

He looked at her, eyes still narrowed. "You found this in your room?"

"Yes. As you no doubt intended."

He pulled a face. "You think *I* was in your room? That is an inconceivably ludicrous, not to mention scandalous, accusation."

Anger flared, but Emma kept her voice even by supreme effort. "I would have hoped it inconceivable, though you were certainly not above clandestine calls to my room at Longstaple."

He looked quickly over his shoulder, then stepped nearer. "You might wish to be careful when referring to our days at your father's academy, Miss Smallwood." He lowered his voice. "Have you any idea how your statement might be misconstrued by anyone who happened to overhear it?"

Emma felt her neck and cheeks heat as she replayed the words in her mind. But then she lifted her chin once more. She had done nothing wrong. "My lack of judgment in speaking of it is nothing to yours in doing it in the first place."

He chewed his lip as though he had not heard her. "Which room have they put you in?"

"As if you don't know."

His hard glare wilted her tart tone. She said, "The south wing. Around the corner, last room on the left." Why was she telling him where to find her if he had not, in fact, already been to her room?

He pulled another face as he considered her reply. "Lady Weston's idea, no doubt."

He looked at the soldier once more, then slipped it into his coat pocket. "Probably left behind by one of the boys years ago. That room hasn't been used in ages."

He eyed her again, then asked tentatively, "Or had you a particular reason for thinking someone had been in your room—besides the soldier?"

"Something woke me. I thought I heard someone. And I smelled . . . shaving soap, I believe. Or bay rum."

His eyes looked in her direction but were focused on internal thought. Then he straightened. "I promise you, Miss Smallwood, I did not come to your room last night. Most likely no one did. But please do let me know if anything like this happens again. As to what you heard . . . perhaps you did overhear me raising my voice. If so, I apologize."

She nodded in acceptance, but he was hiding something—she was sure of it. "I . . . do hope you were not arguing about my father and me being here."

He hesitated. "It was a disagreement about . . . family matters. Nothing you need be concerned about."

Emma said, "I regret we arrived at a bad time. We did write to let your father know when we were coming."

He lifted a hand in a vague gesture. "My father is not keen on details. It is why he leaves much of the estate management to Davies and me."

Emma twisted her hands. "Then . . . you don't mind our being here?"

Mr. Weston studied her, then looked away. "That has yet to be seen."

*Since the [ship]wreck at St. Minver . . . two
men who ventured too far into the sea to
secure a bale of bacon, were overwhelmed
by the waves and unfortunately drowned.*

—the *West Briton*, 1818

# Chapter 5

That evening, Emma, her father, and Mr. Davies were just fin-
ishing their dinner when Henry Weston knocked on the open
office door. Emma's body tensed as though expecting a blow.

Davies made to rise, but Mr. Weston raised his palm. "Don't get
up. I am only here to greet Mr. Smallwood."

Her father rose from the table. "Henry!" He beamed and strode
across the room, hand extended.

Ignoring Emma, Henry Weston walked forward and shook her
father's hand.

He looked very elegant in evening clothes, Emma noticed. Cravat and patterned waistcoat showed between the lapels of his dark
coat. A white shirt collar framed each side of his well-defined jaw.

Her fathered pummeled the younger man's shoulder good-
naturedly. "Good heavens, taller than I am. How are you, my boy?"

Mr. Weston said, "I am well. Though I regret I was not here when
you first arrived, and that your welcome was not all it should have
been."

"Now, now, not another word about that," her father said. "We are very happy to be here, Emma and I, especially now that you are among us." He turned to her. "Are we not, my dear?"

Emma's smile felt stiff. "Oh . . . yes."

Her father tilted his head back to better view Henry's face. "Seeing you again does my heart good."

A hint of a smile lifted Mr. Weston's mouth. "And mine. What good memories I have of my years in Longstaple with you." He looked at the steward. "Mr. Smallwood was my tutor before Oxford, Mr. Davies. Do you recall? Phillip's as well."

"I do recall, yes," Mr. Davies said dryly. "I sent the payments, after all."

If Henry heard this, he gave no indication, his eyes tilting upward in memory. "Happy days."

Emma nearly choked to hear him categorize them as such. Suspicion flared through her. What was he up to?

Her father went on to say he hoped they would be seeing a great deal of each other now that Henry had come home.

Mr. Weston, in turn, suggested they might play a game of backgammon of an evening, and her father heartily agreed.

Henry's gaze swept the table, avoiding Emma, before returning to Mr. Smallwood. "Well, I shall let you return to your dinner. Again, welcome to Ebbington Manor. If there's anything you need while you're here, please don't hesitate to let me know."

*As though he is the host,* Emma thought. Perhaps he was.

Her father smiled. "Thank you."

Henry gave a slight bow, nodded toward Emma without meeting her eyes, then turned and left the room.

Her father resumed his seat. "Well," he began, spooning into his pudding. "He has certainly turned out well, I must say."

A conclusion based on what? Emma wondered. A few polite words? It would take more than that to convince her he had changed from the churlish Henry of old.

After dinner, Emma went upstairs. It was still early, but she looked forward to writing in her journal and reading for several hours before she went to sleep. The image of Henry Weston's face, seven years older and apparently benign, made her suspicious. Had he set a trap in her room—did some prank await her? Was that what explained the pleasant looks and warm greetings?

*He's a grown man now, Emma,* she told herself. He would not do something so juvenile. She reminded herself how vehemently he had denied entering her room and leaving the toy soldier.

Stepping inside, she looked around. The room seemed as she had left it. She regarded her bed. Emma made her own bed every morning, before Morva had the opportunity. Was that a slight lump beneath the bedclothes, or only her imagination?

It was all too easy to recall that long-ago night when Emma had climbed into her bed at home, ignoring a small lump beneath her bedclothes. The lump that sprang to life as she pulled up the covers, clawing in desperation, scratching against her leg and squeaking piteously. Emma's skin crawled even now at the memory. She had screamed, she was embarrassed to recall. And Mrs. Malloy had come running with her stout candle lamp and threw back the bedclothes, exposing a writhing stocking—a mouse had been trapped inside and the end tied.

The boys had all been summoned and the responsible party asked to step forward. But the four boys with them at the time stood unified in their solidarity with protestations of innocence.

Emma knew very well it had been Henry Weston who had done it. But her father, partial to Henry, had not wanted to make a fuss. Henry was, after all, the eldest son and heir of Sir Giles, Baronet. It was a great privilege to have him at the Smallwood Academy.

Now unwilling to risk a surprise, Emma gingerly approached the bed. With an anticipatory shiver, she patted down the bedclothes, then folded them back for good measure. Nothing. Only then did she notice the freshly laundered smell of the sheets and realized the logical explanation. It must have been Morva's day to change the sheets, and in her hurry the housemaid had remade the bed in less than pristine fashion.

Emma shook her head at herself and began getting ready for bed, pulling the bell cord to summon Morva to help her undress. After the maid had done so, Emma settled into bed with her portable writing desk and journal.

*I saw Henry Weston today for the first time in nearly seven years. He has grown taller, his shoulders broader. His features are more defined than I recall, angling sharply from broad, high cheekbones to a jutting chin. He has thick dark brows and wavy collar-length hair. His eyes are deeply hooded and golden green. Cat's eyes.*

*Beyond his knowing smirk, I see little vestige of the youth who came to Longstaple years ago. He is all man now. All hard lines and confidence. I feared him as a girl, and the years have only served to make him more intimidating.*

With a little shudder, Emma laid aside her journal in favor of a book.

Later, when she lay tucked under the bedclothes in the dark, thinking over the events of the day and her encounters with Henry Weston, she tentatively sniffed the air but smelled nothing save lye and woodsmoke. She listened for any strange sounds, but nothing stirred in her bedchamber. Yet from somewhere, through floorboards or snaking through stairwells, came the distant sound of a pianoforte being played. There was one in the music room, of course. But she had yet to hear anyone play it and was surprised to hear someone playing now, so late at night.

She wondered who played. Lizzie, perhaps? She supposed a girl like her would count playing the pianoforte among her many accomplishments.

Henry crossed her mind—his return correlating with the sudden music. But she did not recall him ever playing their old harpsichord in Longstaple. During the tour of the house, Lizzie had mentioned that Julian and Rowan played. It was probably one of them.

Emma relaxed back against her pillows, telling herself it did not matter who played. It was a pleasant enough sound, from what she could hear of the faint melody. Mozart, perhaps? Whoever played did so well, it seemed, though she was no judge, and perhaps the distance filtered out any sour notes.

She would ask in the morning, she decided. And with that, she rolled over and went to sleep.

While Rowan and Julian took their Latin and Greek lessons from Mr. McShane the next day, Emma went looking for Lizzie.

She found the girl sitting alone in the drawing room with her embroidery. From the doorway, Emma noticed several details about the room she hadn't noticed the night of their arrival. The beamed ceiling showed this room had also once been part of the massive hall. Rich, dark tapestries graced the walls, and a watercolor of Ebbington Manor hung above the mantel.

Seeing no sign of Lady Weston, Emma felt comfortable stepping inside. She asked, "Was that you I heard playing the pianoforte last night?"

Lizzie looked up from her embroidery hoop. "Hm?"

"The pianoforte. I heard someone playing last night."

"Really? Wasn't me. I haven't played in an age. Though I should practice I know. Was the playing good or ill?"

"Good, I think."

"Then it definitely wasn't me." Lizzie chuckled.

Lady Weston entered the room, and Emma instantly felt out of place.

Lizzie said easily, "Hello, my lady. Miss Smallwood was just telling me she heard someone playing the pianoforte last night."

The woman paused, then slowly turned. "Last night? What time was this?"

"I don't know exactly," Emma said. "I had already gone to bed. Maybe ten thirty or eleven."

"So late . . ." Lady Weston mused. "And already in bed, you say? Perhaps you were dreaming."

Emma felt her brow pucker. "I don't think so. . . . No. I am quite certain I was awake."

"Hmm . . ." Lady Weston murmured. "Perhaps you only imagined it. Such odd noises this old house makes, especially when the wind howls. When you have been here longer, you shall grow accustomed to it."

Emma said, "I doubt the wind howls Mozart."

Lady Weston's eyes lit. "Mozart, was it? Then it must have been Julian. Such talent that dear boy has. Perhaps he slipped back down to play after he was supposed to be in bed. And who could reprimand him for that? When an *artiste* feels the muse, the muse must have its way."

"I did not realize Julian was so accomplished," Emma said. "I shall look forward to hearing him play again sometime."

Lady Weston traced a finger against her chin in thought. "Yes. In fact, that is an excellent notion. He should play for us all one of these evenings. I shall suggest it. It has been far too long since we have enjoyed any entertainment. An evening of music. How delightful. Lizzie may play as well."

"Oh no," Lizzie grimaced. "You don't want that, I assure you. I play very ill."

"Then practice, my girl. Did I not hire a music tutor for you only last year?"

"Yes, Lady Weston. And you were very good to do so, I am sure. Perhaps Miss Smallwood would play for us instead?" Lizzie turned eager eyes in Emma's direction.

"Thank you, Lizzie. But I don't play nearly as well as Julian evidently does. Perhaps his should be a solo performance."

"Apparently," Lady Weston said dryly. "Now if you girls will excuse me." She turned and left the room, seemingly forgetting whatever errand or purpose had brought her into the drawing room in the first place.

A short time later, Emma left the drawing room as Julian and Rowan exited the library with Mr. McShane.

The vicar hailed her, all smiles. "Hello. You must be Miss Smallwood. Allow me to introduce myself. I am Gerald McShane." He bowed.

Emma crossed the hall toward them. "How do you do." She returned the man's bow with a belated curtsy.

The clergyman's eyes shone. "Rowan and Julian told me about you and your father, and I have been eager to meet you."

"My father has gone for a walk but should be back directly. I . . . hope you don't mind us being here. We did not realize the boys already had a tutor."

He dismissed her concerns with a wave of his hand. "I have only been teaching them Latin and a bit of Greek. Attempting it, at any rate. I've told Lady Weston several times that I am not equal to the task of preparing these two for university. So I was quite relieved to learn a proper tutor had been engaged."

"I am glad to hear it."

"And your father? Was he unhappy to find an upstart had usurped two of his subjects?"

"Not at all. In fact, he plans to enjoy a long walk every time you come to teach."

Mr. McShane grinned. "Glad to be of service."

Emma turned to acknowledge the two young men. "Hello, Mr. Weston. Mr. Weston."

Julian said politely, "You may call us by our Christian names, if you like."

"Thank you, Julian. But I am afraid I must ask you to call me Miss Smallwood." Emma tilted her head to regard the smaller youth. "I understand you are a talented musician."

Julian tilted his head in mirror image to hers, one brow high. "You must have been talking to Mamma."

"Yes, but I heard you myself last night."

"Last night?"

"Yes, Lady Weston said it must have been you."

Julian and Rowan exchanged a look.

Julian said briskly, "Might have been. I don't recall."

*Don't recall?* Emma wondered—it had only been last night.

"He does sleepwalk sometimes," Rowan added helpfully. "Perhaps that explains it."

Emma looked quizzically from Rowan back to Julian. "Well. Whatever the case, I hope you will play again sometime when we are all of us awake to enjoy it."

Julian grinned wryly. "But what if I don't play half so well when I'm awake?"

"I'm sure you shall do very well." She turned to the vicar, hands primly clasped. "Forgive me, Mr. McShane, I did not intend to interrupt your lessons."

"Not at all. In fact, why do we not all go into the music room right now and listen to Julian play for us? I for one have had my fill of Latin verbs."

"Hear, hear," Rowan seconded.

Emma hesitated. "If . . . you are certain you don't mind."

Assurances were given, and Emma followed the three males down the hall and into the music room.

There Julian seated himself at the pianoforte. "What shall I play—any requests?"

When no one said anything, Emma suggested, "Perhaps the piece you played last night?"

Julian pulled a face. "I don't recall what I played. But here is Mozart's 'Turkish March.'" He launched into the piece with youthful vigor. The march was up-tempo, spirited, and boisterous. Julian's fingers flew over the keys, his skill evident.

Then why did Emma have the nagging feeling that he was not the musician she had heard the previous night?

Henry Weston strode into the room, expression tight. He looked from face to face, then visibly relaxed.

Julian looked up from the keyboard, brow quirked in question. Henry gestured for him to continue and sat next to Mr. McShane to listen.

As the last chord faded, Lady Weston walked in wearing a frown. She pinned Emma with a pointed look. "I said *I* would arrange a concert."

Emma swallowed. "I . . ."

"Forgive me." Mr. McShane rose, speaking up in her defense.

"It was my idea to ask Julian to play. Just a little diversion from our lessons."

"Oh. I see." Lady Weston gave the clergyman a brittle smile. "Well then. No harm done."

Hoping to avoid Henry Weston, Emma was the first to leave the music room a few minutes later. She made her way toward the stairs, glancing down the rear passage toward the tradesman's entrance. There she saw Mr. Davies talking quietly to an elderly couple. He gestured for them to wait where they were, then turned and walked into the hall. As Emma mounted the stairs, she glanced over her shoulder and saw Mr. Davies hail Henry Weston as he exited the music room.

"That couple is here. The Dykes," the steward said quietly. "Will you conduct the interview in my office or in your study?"

"Your office, if you don't mind, Davies. I think that would be more discreet."

"Very good, sir."

Emma wondered idly what that was about but decided it was none of her concern. Putting it from her mind, she retreated to the schoolroom and lost herself in a thick volume of Cornwall history.

She spent more than an hour reading about Cornwall, its rousing history of rebellions, battles, pirates, and shipwrecks, as well as its superstitions and legends—giants, piskies, mermaids, and ghosts. She came across an interesting chapter about the county's long tradition of smuggling and wrecking. One infamous smuggler was John Heale of Stratton. Was not Stratton a village nearby?

Her father and the boys came into the schoolroom before she could read further. She helped her father with the afternoon lessons, then returned to her book until it was time to dress for dinner.

She arrived at Mr. Davies's office early and was disconcerted to find Henry Weston sitting with his steward and two well-dressed gentlemen, going over drawn plans of some kind. She slipped from the room unseen, crossed the hall, and stepped into the library to wait until they had gone. Newspapers lay spread on the desk—both local and London papers. She glanced at the headings. Parliamentary news. Accounts of the ongoing social season. She had no interest in the latter but did wonder why the Weston family had not gone to London for the season. As a baronet, Sir Giles did not have a seat in parliament, but Emma would have thought Lady Weston would enjoy the whirl of social events anyway—and welcome the opportunity to meet prospective future brides for her sons or stepsons.

The door opened behind her, and Emma jerked back. Caught.

Sir Giles smiled benignly from the doorway. "Hello, Miss Smallwood."

"Sir Giles. Forgive me. I am only waiting for Mr. Davies and your son to finish their meeting."

"Ah yes. Meeting with Mr. Green and our surveyor, I believe. About plans for a new canal. Or was it reinforcing the breakwater? I forget which."

He glanced at the desk she was standing so near.

She hurried to explain, "I was just skimming the news. I haven't read any since leaving Longstaple and was curious to know what is going on in the world."

"You are very welcome to do so, my dear. In fact, help yourself to anything in here you find to interest you. I am afraid I am woefully out of date on current affairs myself. Can't conjure the interest I once did." He gestured for her to take a seat. "Make yourself comfortable. Or feel free to take the papers with you to read at your leisure. Henry is through with them."

"But if you mean to read them, I wouldn't want—"

"I don't mean to read them. There will only be more tomorrow." He turned toward the door.

"Please don't leave on my account," she said.

He lifted a staying hand. "No, no. I only came looking for Henry. I forgot about the meeting but will go look in now."

"If you are certain."

"I am. In fact, I will send in the hallboy to let you know when the meeting concludes and dinner is served. Might be late tonight, I fear."

Emma sat down. "That is very kind. Thank you. I do enjoy reading."

Sir Giles opened the door. "Yes," he said. "Phillip once mentioned you were very well-read."

Had he? Pleasure warmed Emma at the thought.

"Now, if you will excuse me."

Sir Giles took his leave, and Emma began reading. Late afternoon sunlight filtered through mullioned windows and onto the gleaming oak desk, making the library a cheerful, sunny place—perfect for reading. She began by perusing the *Royal Cornwall Gazette* and the *West Briton*.

In local news from a week past, she read of the ongoing investigation into a shipwreck earlier in the spring off the North Cornwall coast. The ship owners were complaining of missing cargo, despite dispatching agents to salvage the crates of tinware and silver cutlery.

She also found a mention of Henry Weston of Ebbington Manor traveling to Helston as guest of Mr. Trengrouse to watch a demonstration of a new invention—a rocket apparatus to shoot a lifeline out to ships in trouble. Emma wondered how the demonstration had gone.

In the current edition of the *West Briton,* she read a brief article about the Ebford village council voting down Mr. Weston's proposal to acquire a lifeboat from the Plymouth dockyard. She wondered why. One more article caught her eye:

### Wrecking at Godreavy

The brig *Neptune* was driven on shore in St. Ives Bay. Some of the ruffians who assembled under pretence of protecting the property actually robbed the captain of his watch and plundered all the unfortunate seamen of their clothes. One of the crew, who got on shore almost naked, saw a number of miscreants employed in carrying off some rope and remonstrated with them on the atrocity of their conduct. He was told that, unless he immediately departed and refrained from molesting them, they would strangle him on the spot.

Emma shivered. *"Uncivilized Cornwall" is right,* she thought, recalling Lizzie saying the phrase.

She set aside the local news and began reading the latest *Times.* In the advertisements, Emma skimmed past notices from milliners and modistes, but her gaze was snagged by a London auction house advertising the auction of a new shipment of tinware and silver cutlery. That was a strange coincidence. Or was it?

A knock interrupted her. She looked up, self-conscious to be found sitting at Sir Giles's desk as though some fine lady. She was relieved to see it was only the hallboy.

"Dinner is served, miss."

"Thank you." Emma rose, taking the London paper and one of the local ones with her, planning to read more later in her room.

She walked back down to the steward's office, relieved to find only Mr. Davies and her father within. Setting the papers aside, she joined them for a hearty meal of steak-and-kidney pie, green salad, fruit, and fig tart. While they ate, Mr. Davies told her father about the meeting that had gone later than planned. The men had met to consider plans to extend and reinforce the harbor breakwater. They had also discussed the idea of building a canal and sea lock, which would allow larger vessels to enter their port, regardless of tide levels. This would bring in much-needed trade for the area.

Emma listened with interest, impressed to hear Henry Weston was involved in such important projects, though she would have been loath to admit it aloud. She wondered if she would have the nerve to ask him about his various endeavors. Probably not. She had seen little of him since his return, and he seemed to prefer it that way.

During a lull in the conversation, Emma brought up what she had discovered in the library. "I was reading the newspapers earlier and noticed a strange coincidence—an auction notice for tinware and silver cutlery, less than two months after a ship's cargo of the same went missing here in Cornwall."

Mr. Davies looked at her sharply.

What had she said? She added with a lame little laugh, "Is that not interesting?"

Mr. Davies stared at her. "Why would you bring that up?"

Emma faltered, "I . . . was only making conversation."

Mr. Davies held her gaze. "Were you?"

"Yes. What else?"

Her father looked from one to the other, bemused.

The steward glanced at her father, then back at her. His Adam's apple bobbed. "Nothing. Merely . . . curious."

After the final course, Mr. Davies abruptly excused himself, and Emma and her father exchanged perplexed looks. She wondered why her comment had apparently offended the man. Did he think she was turning up her nose at the local people—by assuming a theft where there was likely no wrongdoing?

She and her father talked companionably for ten or fifteen minutes longer, discussing the day and their lesson plans for the morrow. When she rose to take her leave, her father remained behind, hoping Henry Weston might seek him out after his own dinner for a game of backgammon.

Newspapers under her arm, Emma left the office alone and crossed the hall. She saw Mr. Davies standing at the drawing room door, talking with Lady Weston. At the sound of her echoing footsteps, Davies looked over his shoulder and Lady Weston followed his gaze. They both sent her veiled looks, Davies's expression self-conscious, and Lady Weston's speculative. They ceased talking as Emma passed and began up the stairs, giving Emma the distinct impression they had been speaking about her. Their silence and watchful gazes pricked her spine with each step. She could not ascend from their sight quickly enough.

In the morning, Emma washed, cleaned her teeth, brushed and pinned her hair, and then made her bed while waiting for Morva. After the maid appeared and helped her dress, Emma took the newspapers downstairs, planning to return them to the library after breakfast.

When she arrived in the steward's office, she found Mr. Davies sitting at his breakfast, his own copy of the day's news spread before him. He looked up as she entered and began folding the paper aside.

"Don't stop reading on my account." She smiled, lifting her own copies of the *West Briton* and *Times*. "I have brought something to read as well. Sir Giles was kind enough to lend them to me."

Davis nodded and returned to his coffee without a word. She hoped he wasn't still upset about her comment last night.

Emma filled her plate and sat across from the steward. She thought him a nice enough man yet never felt completely at her ease in his presence unless her father was there to help carry the conversation.

She tried to read as she ate but felt self-conscious—every bite, every sip of coffee seemed loud and echoing in the high-ceilinged space. She had left the *Times* folded to the auction house advertisement, and she noticed the steward's gaze stray to it more than once. His eggs remained untouched, congealing on his plate.

Emma laid her index finger on the paper and slid it across the table. "I'm finished with this one. Would you like to see it?"

"Oh . . ." Mr. Davies puffed out his cheeks and fidgeted. "No, no. I have little interest in London news."

The silence between them lengthened awkwardly. Emma finished her breakfast and excused herself as quickly as she could.

Wanting to escape the tension in the manor—some of which she had inadvertently caused—Emma left the newspapers in the library and decided she would see what drew her father out of doors every day. Was the view from the cliff path really so appealing?

Her father had already left, being the early riser he was. But there was no reason she could not go for a stroll on her own. She returned to her room and pulled on a long-sleeved pelisse over her day dress, tied a bonnet under her chin, and tugged on gloves as well. For though it was early May, her father had warned her of the chilly winds blowing in over the ridgeline.

As she came downstairs, her father was just coming in through the rear entrance, cheeks ruddy, collar turned up. When she told him where she was going, he nodded approvingly, and then took himself into the steward's office for a second cup of tea and a biscuit. His appetite had certainly improved since coming to Cornwall. Emma categorized that as a good sign.

Emma ventured outside. Her half boots crunched over the pebbled drive and through the garden, its pathways lined with herbaceous borders, the stone walls hung with ivy and flowering vines. Clearly, spring came early in Cornwall, and the air smelled of apple blossoms, hyacinth, and lily of the valley. As she walked, Emma glimpsed many varieties they did not grow in Longstaple, like the fig and bay trees on the entrance drive—evidence of Cornwall's mild, semitropical climate, provided the trees had shelter from the wind.

Pushing through the garden gate, Emma left the manor grounds for the first time since they'd arrived. She crested a shallow rise, and the wind picked up, pulling at her bonnet. Yet the sunshine warmed her enough that the walk was pleasant. She breathed deeply the cool, fresh air and for a moment could understand why her father, why men like Henry Weston, were so often drawn out of doors.

Walking through long grass dotted with pink thrift and swaths of bluebells, she crossed the headland toward the horizon, where the land fell away and the sea faded into forever. Reaching the footpath paralleling the coast, she took a few tentative steps closer to the cliff's edge. Her heart gave a little thrill as she surveyed the sharp drop to jagged cliffs and rocky beaches below. Crashing waves struck jutting rocks in bursts of white mountains and flying spray. And beyond, sunlight shimmered on blue-green water.

Beautiful.

She looked farther out, ever westward, as far as the eye could see. Did the Americas really lie in that direction, far beyond her vision, her imagination? So she had read. How big the ocean must be. How small it made her feel.

Emma remembered reading that North Cornwall was one of the more remote parts of the western peninsula. Now she could see how true that was for herself.

"And what do 'ee think of our Kernow?" a gravelly voice asked from near her shoulder.

Emma started. Turning, she was surprised to see the red-haired man she had first seen in Mr. Davies's office. She had heard no one approach over the sound of the wind.

"I . . . I don't believe I've . . . heard that term before," she stammered, nervous to be alone with the man.

He nodded. "That's what we Cornish call this land. But the Westons don't consider themselves true Cornish folk. And nor do we."

"But the Westons have lived here for years."

"Sir Giles may live at Ebb-ton now, but his ancestors let it out to tenants year after year. Or came down only for summers, or on business—this is where they made their fortune in mining, after all. But they sold off their interests in the mines long ago."

Emma digested this, then rebutted, "The Weston sons have all been born and raised here at Ebbington."

"Perhaps. But the elder two were sent away to larn a *proper* accent."

"I assure you that was not in my father's syllabus."

He shrugged. "Hardly matters what they larned. They be gentlemen—others will do arl the work for 'em."

"And what is it *you* do?" Emma asked boldly, resenting the man's derision toward her hosts.

He replied as though she'd asked the question in earnest. "Most men hereabouts forge a living from the sea—working on sloops, or loading and unloading vessels in our harbor. Some are fishermen, or work in the pilchard salting sheds. A few work the lime kiln."

"And you, sir?"

He gazed out into the Atlantic, a hint of a smile playing on his lips. "I suppose 'ee could say I forge my living from the sea as well."

Though still uncertain of the man's connection to Ebbington Manor—let alone his name—Emma hesitated to pry further. Prolonging a private conversation with him did not seem wise.

Galloping horse hooves caught her ear, and she glanced over her shoulder. She felt both relieved and chagrined to see Henry Weston riding toward them, a scowl on his haughty face.

She glanced back at the red-haired man, but he was already walking away. He tipped his cap to her in profile but did not wait for Mr. Weston to join them.

Henry reined in his horse and glowered at the man's back before looking darkly down at Emma. "What were you doing talking to that man?"

Emma lifted her chin to look him in the eye. "*He* was talking to *me*. I was only being polite."

"Well, don't be. Do you hear me, Miss Smallwood? Stay away from him."

That evening, Henry David Weston stood, staring into the looking glass as his valet, Merryn, gave his tailcoat a final brushing. But it wasn't his own face Henry saw in reflection, but rather Miss Smallwood's.

He thought back to their conversation in the schoolroom two days before. He had lied when he'd told her she had not changed. For she had changed, at least physically, since he had last seen her some six or seven years before. She was still tall and thin, but her figure conveyed willowy elegance rather than the leggy colt clumsiness he remembered. Her face had thrown off little-girldom and become more defined, with high cheekbones and a good mouth. She held herself with a dignity and admirable posture—when she wasn't scuttling about on her knees on the schoolroom floor. He smirked at the memory of his first sight of her in Ebbington, her backside greeting him as she bowed down to her beloved books.

How strange that he still enjoyed provoking her. Perhaps it was because she had always been so dashed reserved, so in control of her emotions—assuming she had any. She guarded her reactions and words as though she wore bit and bridle and God himself held the reins.

Her hair was a bit darker than he remembered, golden brown and primly arranged in place of the stringy blond straw he recalled from her youth. And he'd been struck by her eyes. He'd forgotten they were green, like his. A soft green—when not snapping with irritation or challenge as they had today, when he'd rebuked her for talking to that man—a stranger to her—all alone on the point. Her irritation he did remember, and all too well.

He thought of Miss Smallwood's question—whether he minded her and her father being at Ebbington Manor. That he had answered truthfully. Normally he prided himself on making quick, sound decisions. A man of clarity and action. But he still wasn't sure what to think of their presence. Yes, his half brothers needed someone to take them in hand. Gerald McShane had done what he could, but Mr. Smallwood had far greater experience. Yet the timing was so dashed awful. What a week for his old tutor and his daughter to join them—with so many things up in the air. So many arrangements to be made. And Lady Weston still demanding utter secrecy. It was going to be doubly difficult to keep their secret concealed with Emma Smallwood under their roof. She had always been too clever for her own good.

Or his.

*Experience keeps a dear school,*
*but fools will learn in no other.*

—Benjamin Franklin

# Chapter 6

On Sunday morning, the Smallwoods were invited—or rather, expected—to attend church with the Weston family.

At the appointed hour, everyone gathered in the hall until the carriages and carts drew up outside. Everyone except Henry Weston. No one commented on his absence, so neither did Emma. Apparently he did not attend church with his family. *Why am I not surprised,* she thought, less than charitably. But then her conscience smote her. For the truth was, over the last two years she attended church only because it was expected of her. She and God had not been on close terms since her mother's death.

Emma wore her long-sleeved gown of deep blue with a high waistband and a gauzy fichu of white lawn tucked into its neckline. Glancing at the other ladies, she felt she had chosen well and in keeping with the modest gowns, capes, and bonnets Lady Weston and Lizzie were wearing. The men wore dark frock coats, sober waistcoats and cravats, and black beaver hats. Men had it so easy, Emma thought, when it came to dressing appropriately for any occasion.

Since there was no church in the small village of Ebford, the family attended services in neighboring Stratton. Sir Giles, Lady Weston, Lizzie, Rowan, and Julian crowded into the family's large landau, its hood up against the damp mist and driven by the well-dressed coachman.

Mr. Smallwood and Emma shared the rear of a two-wheeled chapel cart pulled by one horse, with Mr. Davies at the reins. Mrs. Prowse sat on the front bench beside him. Other servants—those whose Sunday in rotation it was to attend services—rode in the wagon driven by the groom.

As the cart rumbled along, the steward and housekeeper spoke quietly to each other, leaving Emma and her father to take in the passing countryside in peace.

Fifteen or twenty minutes later, they reached Stratton and soon arrived at St. Andrew's—an impressive grey stone church with a tall bell tower. They alighted and walked through a churchyard dotted with listing headstones and bright yellow daffodils. Entering the dim, echoing interior, Emma and her father sat several rows behind the Weston family, in the first unoccupied pew. Around them other people filled in, and Emma quietly surveyed the congregation by the light of candles and soft daylight seeping through stained-glass windows. A good-sized crowd, Emma thought, of all ages, from babbling children, to shushing mothers, to old men staring silently ahead. Some were well-dressed and others less so. The hats came off in church, but the coats remained, carrying the lingering smells of tallow, peat, and fish.

Lizzie, Emma noticed, was apparently lost in her own thoughts, for she made no effort to follow along in the prayer book. Emma recalled attending services with her father's pupils back in Long-staple. How many times had she glanced over at an adolescent Henry Weston and noticed he was not singing, not praying, and not reciting any of the readings. Apparently now, as an adult, he did not even bother to attend.

Mr. McShane mounted the stairs to the high pulpit, welcomed them, led them through the day's prayers and readings, then launched into a homily based on Matthew seven: *Judge not, that ye be not judged.*

Had Mr. McShane read her mind—her uncharitable thoughts

about Henry Weston? Emma shifted uncomfortably on the hard wooden pew.

Listening, Emma soon decided Mr. McShane was gifted in making sermons. Which was good, she thought, since she was less certain of his teaching ability.

After services, everyone thanked Mr. McShane as they filed out, and then the Westons and their party returned to Ebbington Manor in the same procession as they had arrived. The mist had cleared, but the day continued grey and cloudy.

Reaching the drive in their turn, Emma took her father's hand and he helped her down. Together they walked several steps behind the Westons as the family strolled sedately toward the house.

The sound of a cart, its tack jingling up the lane, sounded behind them. Already mounting the stairs, Lady Weston turned. Sir Giles, his hearing perhaps not all it should be, turned to see what had caught his wife's attention.

The same donkey cart that had first delivered the Smallwoods to Ebbington Manor now rolled up the drive. Emma's heart gave a little leap. For there on the back sat Phillip Weston—the one Weston she had looked forward to seeing. Pleasure and nerves quivered through her, and her stomach tightened. She hoped he would be happy to see her.

Phillip smiled and waved at them. At *her*? Did he even know they were there?

Sir Giles trotted back down the stairs in a spurt of youthful vigor. "Phillip! What in the world? We were not expecting you."

Phillip hopped off the back of the cart. "Hello, Father." He extended his hand, but Sir Giles pulled him into an embrace and soundly thumped his back.

Lady Weston descended the stairs more slowly, her expression inquisitive.

Phillip removed his hat. "Hello, Mother."

Emma wondered if Henry also addressed his stepmother as such. She had yet to hear him do so.

Lady Weston offered her hand, and Phillip pressed it briefly.

She asked, "Has Balliol burned down, or have they called a special recess?"

"Neither. But I heard that Mr. and Miss Smallwood had come, and I could not wait to see my dear old friends." He walked over and shook hands with John Smallwood. "What a pleasure to see you again, sir."

"Phillip." Her father beamed. "How well you look."

"Thank you, sir." Phillip turned to Emma, a smile dimpling his cheeks, eyes shining. "And Miss Smallwood. As lovely as ever. How are you, old girl?"

Emma bit back a retort at the word *old*. She was, after all, only a year older than he was. "I am well, Mr. Weston. Thank you."

Phillip's brows rose. "Mr. Weston? Now, now. We are old friends, are we not? You must call me Phillip, as always."

Emma glanced at Lady Weston but made no reply. She only smiled at Phillip, feeling her mood brighten. Seeing him on that grey Sunday was like seeing the first crocus poke its cheery face from the dregs of winter snow. His warm greeting a welcoming fire after Lady Weston's chilly reception.

Julian and Rowan came forward and shook hands with their brother. Behind them, Lizzie hung back, waiting her turn.

"Hello." Lizzie greeted Phillip almost shyly, followed by an awkward curtsy.

Apparently Lady Weston's presence could dampen even Lizzie's exuberant spirits. Emma certainly empathized, feeling self-conscious whenever the woman was near.

"Hello, Lizzie," Phillip replied, his reserve matching hers.

Emma studied him. In many ways, Phillip looked much the way she remembered. Mischievous blue eyes. Broad smile—his thin upper lip in such contrast to his full lower one. Yet his shoulders were broader than she recalled, and he was taller as well, a few inches taller than she. His brown hair seemed a shade darker, his face a bit rounder—she supposed with all his sitting and studying he had gained a stone. A few lines crinkled the corner of each eye and crossed his forehead. He seemed too young for such creases.

Were they new smile lines or evidence of worry or fatigue? She wondered if he found university difficult. Of the two, he had certainly struggled more with schoolwork than had Henry.

"How go the studies?" her father asked. "What have you decided to take up?"

Phillip grimaced. "I am reading law but confess I find it frightfully dull. I think a visit home is just what I need at present."

Lady Weston asked, "But will that not put you behind in your studies when you return?"

Phillip shrugged, apparently unconcerned. "Not insurmountably."

Henry Weston jogged down the stairs, a grin playing at the corner of his mouth. "Phillip! So you were the cause of all the commotion I heard."

"Hello, Henry." The two brothers shook hands. "Thank you for your letter."

"I thought you should know."

Lady Weston's brows rose. "Know what?"

The brothers' eyes met, and then once again Phillip beamed at Emma. "Why, that the Smallwoods had graced us with their presence, of course."

Lady Weston glanced at Emma, then Henry, before smiling stiffly. "Is that so?"

The woman didn't seem convinced, Emma noticed, and she wondered if Henry had written to Phillip for some other reason.

Sir Giles bustled forward. "Well, come in, my boy. Come in. You must be tired from your journey." He paid the driver and gestured everyone inside.

In the hall, Lady Weston inserted herself between Phillip and Emma. "His family has first claim on him, Miss Smallwood. You understand." She took his arm and escorted him into the drawing room.

Phillip sent her an apologetic smile over his shoulder. As the doors closed, he mouthed, *"See you later."*

And Emma found a small pocket of happiness in Cornwall.

In the dining room that evening, Henry noticed Phillip survey the candlelit table, from his father at the head, he and Phillip on either side of him, to his stepmother at the distant foot, her sons and Lizzie clustered around her, and all the empty chairs in between.

"Where are the Smallwoods taking their meals?" he asked.

"With Mr. Davies," Lady Weston replied, and added, "As befits their station."

Phillip frowned. "But we all ate together at the Smallwood Academy. This seems so dashed formal. So cold. If they take their meals separately, and are busy in the schoolroom all day, I shall hardly see them."

Lady Weston lifted her wine glass. Light from the candle chandelier glinted off her jeweled necklace and a ruby ring that had been his mother's. "Mr. Smallwood is hardly locked in the schoolroom all day. It seems to me he spends more time taking the air or playing backgammon with Henry than teaching the boys." She eyed Sir Giles pointedly. "Really, my dear, what are we paying him for?"

"I have never cared for brisk walks," Sir Giles confessed. "But Mr. Smallwood says he finds them invigorating to body and mind. So I cannot begrudge him his daily exercise."

Phillip persisted. "Why do we not ask them to join us?"

Lizzie's face brightened. "Oh yes. Let's do. I find Miss Smallwood quite diverting."

Lady Weston shot her a glare. "They do perfectly well with Mr. Davies."

With a glance at his stepmother, Phillip changed tack. "Might they not at least take breakfast with us? Surely we need stand on no formalities in the breakfast room. They would not disturb any order of precedence there."

"Would disturb me," Rowan muttered. "Trapped with that man enough as it is."

Sir Giles did not acknowledge the remark, though he no doubt heard it. Henry was disappointed his father did not reprimand

Rowan. He would never have gotten away with such disrespect at that age.

Instead, Sir Giles gently addressed his wife, "You know, my dear. As you take breakfast in your rooms most mornings, I hardly think it would inconvenience you."

"It is not about convenience," she snapped. "It is about propriety."

Their father gave Phillip an empathetic look, then said more firmly, "I would enjoy Mr. Smallwood's company and would use that time to keep abreast of our sons' progress."

Henry silently agreed, often wishing his father took a more active role in the boys' upbringing.

Phillip nodded. "Excellent notion, Father."

Lady Weston slanted Phillip a shrewd look. "And how would *you* use that time?"

"Very much the same way, I imagine. To renew my acquaintance with my old tutor, and Miss Smallwood as well."

Her eyes glinted. "I do hope you don't plan to flirt with her or raise her hopes, Phillip. You know she is not your equal. You and Henry are destined to marry fine, accomplished young ladies with good connections."

Phillip's lip curled. "And a shipload of money, I suppose? No pressure there."

Lady Weston smiled, unconcerned. "Family and breeding are of upmost importance, of course. And, fortunately, they are often accompanied by a generous dowry."

Phillip's eyes flashed and his jaw tensed—quite unlike his normal, easygoing demeanor.

Henry spoke up quickly. "I am sure Phillip has no improper intentions toward Miss Smallwood, Lady Weston. The two are of an age and were friends in their younger days. I am certain that is all it is."

Was he certain? No. But seeing the mounting annoyance on his brother's face, Henry thought it wise to defuse the tense conversation.

"I certainly hope that is all it is," Lady Weston said with an edge of warning in her cultured voice. She signaled the footman to remove the cover of the silver soup tureen, beginning the meal and ending the discussion.

After dinner, Lady Weston and Lizzie withdrew, urging Rowan and Julian to accompany them into the drawing room for a game of whist.

Henry remained where he was, idly rolling his table napkin and keeping his father and Phillip company as the two sipped port. He studied his brother closely and noticed his distracted look. "Phillip, why have you come home . . . really?"

Phillip stared back silently, downturned mouth lacking its usual smile.

Their father's bushy brows lowered. "What are you driving at, Henry? Phillip has told us why he's come. He was eager to see the Smallwoods again."

Henry's gaze remained on his brother. "So he said."

Sir Giles added, "Did you not write to him yourself to inform him they had come?"

"Yes, among other news I thought he should know. But I did not expect him to leave Oxford midterm. You gained permission from the dean, I trust?"

"My goodness, Henry," Phillip said dryly. "I have no need of two fathers, I assure you."

"Why do you doubt his word?" Sir Giles asked. "Phillip has always been fond of the Smallwoods."

"Far more so than you ever were," Phillip added, boldly holding his gaze.

Henry looked away first. "I don't doubt Phillip's affection for the Smallwoods. Or his curiosity about our other news. But I do doubt that those are the only reasons he is here. The Easter term ends on—what?—May twenty-fourth? Surely this little social visit—if that's what it is—might have waited."

Phillip made no answer.

Henry felt frustration rising. "Tell me you have not come to grief at Oxford. It was bad enough when Julian and Rowan were expelled from Blundell's."

"Julian was mistreated there," Sir Giles said. "That is why the boys came home."

Henry shook his head. "That is not what the headmaster wrote in his letter."

Sir Giles brushed his words away with a wave of his hand. "At all events, Lady Weston could not abide them being so far away from her."

"Tiverton is not so far."

"A good fifty miles."

"About the same distance as Smallwood's," Phillip spoke up. "I still don't know why you did not send the boys there."

"It was Lady Weston's preference," Sir Giles explained. "Strong preference, I might add."

Phillip asked, "What were the boys accused of doing?"

"Accusations are all it was," Sir Giles insisted. "Julian said Rowan was only trying to protect him."

"A fight, was it?" Phillip asked.

"Not . . . exactly," Sir Giles hedged.

Henry wished his father would not try to cover for the boys' behavior. But sensing his discomfort, Henry returned the conversation to Phillip. "How long will you be staying?"

"Have I overstayed my welcome already?" Phillip's eyes glinted, belying his grin. "I was under the impression this was my home as well."

"Of course it is, of course it is." Sir Giles patted his knee. "Henry didn't mean to imply otherwise."

Henry ran a hand through his hair. "But you do plan to return and finish out the term?"

Phillip shrugged. "I don't know. What I really want is a good long respite."

"Not now, Phillip," Henry said, trying to moderate the disapproval ringing in his voice. "Finish this term and the next, and then you shall have most of July through September for your *respite.*"

Ignoring Henry's counsel, Phillip said to Sir Giles, "I've been thinking, Father. Perhaps it is time we consider my grand tour."

"Your grand tour?" Henry's voice rose. "When I have yet to have mine?"

"That isn't my fault, is it? I want to live life, Father, not merely learn about it in the dusty, hallowed halls of your alma mater."

Their father's jaw tensed. "I always meant for you to have your tour after you earned your degree. That is the way these things are done, my boy—as well you know."

"But I think travel would give me the inspiration I need to return and finish strong."

Sir Giles shook his head. "I don't know, Phillip. This isn't a good time."

"Why? Do you mean because of him? Or because of the Smallwoods?"

Sir Giles looked at Henry, then replied, "Both."

"Personally, I think either is beside the point," Henry said. "You need to earn your degree, Phillip. Westons don't quit; we finish what we start. Have you not always said so, Father?"

"Have I?" Sir Giles looked troubled.

Henry nodded and said quietly, "You used to say it, when we were boys."

Sir Giles nodded vaguely.

Did his father not remember? He had certainly changed since he and Phillip were young.

Henry asked, "What does your Oxford tutor have to say about all this?"

"He will clear things with the dean, I know, if I ask him."

"Are you telling us you've come home without informing your dean?"

Phillip threw up his hands. "It was a spur-of-the-moment decision. But now that I'm here, I cannot stomach the thought of returning."

Sir Giles challenged, "Is all the money I've spent on your education to be wasted?"

"No," Phillip insisted, yet sullenly refused to look his father in the eye.

"Need I remind you, Phillip, that you are not my eldest and heir? I will make what accommodation for you I can, but you will need a profession."

"No, you needn't remind me, Father."

Over Phillip's bent head, Henry and his father shared bewildered looks.

Sir Giles sighed and heaved himself to his feet. "Let us speak no more of this tonight. We are all of us tired and frustrated. And I fear further arguing will only lead to words we might regret. Let us leave it for now. I shall write to your tutor and explain."

Henry erupted. "You ought not lie for him, Father."

"I don't intend to lie, Henry. I shall tell him the truth. That there are family troubles here at home and Phillip is needed."

"Family troubles?" Phillip echoed dubiously.

"That is true enough. And, now I think of it, Phillip may help you in our search. Perhaps he might have more success than you have."

Phillip looked worriedly at Henry. "I . . . I am happy to help, of course. But Henry is the best man for the job."

"That has yet to be proven."

Henry was about to protest when lightning flashed outside the window, followed by the rumble of thunder. He glanced at his father but saw no concern or even awareness there. With an inward sigh, Henry rose and quickly excused himself.

*An unlesson'd girl, unschool'd, unpractised;*
*Happy in this, she is not yet so old*
*But she may learn.*

—William Shakespeare, *The Merchant of Venice*

# Chapter 7

That evening, Emma sat with her father and Mr. Davies, lingering over tea, pudding, and guttering candles. Outside, thunder
rumbled and rain pelted the windows. There seemed no point in
going upstairs and trying to sleep until the rainstorm lessened.

The two men discussed recent parliamentary news, their aching knees, and several other topics, but Emma barely heard them.
Now and again she nodded or smiled when her father chuckled at
something the steward said, to give the impression she was listening,
but in reality her thoughts were of Phillip Weston. She remembered
how he had smiled at her, that familiar teasing light in his eyes as
he called her "old girl," as though he were seeing her again after an
absence of a few days rather than nearly three years.

As she thought back to Phillip's days at their academy, one long
ago Longstaple evening came to mind, and Emma recalled it in vivid
detail. Her mother had already left for a women's charity meeting
when her father decided to pay a call on the vicar. . . .

"I'll only be gone an hour or so," her father had said, wrapping a
muffler around his neck. "The boys are busy over a geography game
of my own invention. It should keep them occupied while I'm gone,

but if there is any trouble, just dash over to your Aunt Jane's. She knows I am popping out for a bit."

"Very well, Papa," Emma had said evenly, pretending not to care one way or the other. She would not admit she was wary of being alone in the house with her father's pupils, should one of them decide to tease her or pull some prank. She reminded herself that Phillip Weston was in residence, and she didn't mind his teasing and mischief quite so much. In fact, she secretly rather liked it. He was fifteen—less than a year younger than she was. And such an amiable young man. He would not allow the other boys to give her any trouble, she thought.

She hoped.

But her father had not been gone a quarter hour when the boys deserted their educational game around the table. It was winter and the sky had darkened early. Candle lamps had been lit for several hours by then, and the four boys shuffled and slid in stocking feet across the room and around the house, extinguishing candles and oil lamps as they went, laughing and jesting with one another.

Alarm needled its way through Emma. From the sitting room, she commanded, "Boys, stop that this instant."

"We needn't listen to you," one of the pupils, a Frank Williams, had said. "You're barely older than we are, Emma. So don't call us 'boys.'"

"I shall call you what I like, Mr. Williams." Emma sniffed. "And it is *Miss Smallwood* to you."

*Whoosh.* Someone blew out the lamp behind her, darkening the sitting room. Mrs. Malloy had not bothered to light the fire in there. Where was Mrs. Malloy? Emma was surprised their no-nonsense cook-housekeeper was not already scuttling about the house with a lit tinder, relighting the lamps and giving the boys a stern tongue-lashing, reminding them they were supposed to act like gentlemen, not wild animals.

But then she recalled that Mrs. Malloy spent Sunday evenings with her elderly mother, who lived in the High Street. Had Emma's father forgotten it was her evening off?

Emma stiffened her spine and drew her shoulders back, reminding herself that a cool, aloof tone had a way of making the boys give her distance, if not respect. She said in her most imperious, grown-up voice, "I insist that you light the lamps and cease running about the house."

"We only want to play a game of hide-and-seek," someone whispered near her ear. She started, then stilled when she recognized Phillip Weston's voice. "You won't deny us such an innocent pleasure, I hope?"

His whisper tickled the back of her neck, where she'd coiled her hair atop her head. "I . . ." she faltered, protest fading.

"Em-ma . . ." He drew out her name in two long, low syllables, his breath prickling her skin with gooseflesh. His warm hands touched her waist, and she jerked in surprise. His hands lifted, hovering near, whispering over the fabric of her frock. When she did not step away, they settled back on her waist.

In the passage outside, stocking feet thudded past on the floorboards. Emma stiffened, but whoever it was flew by, followed by a slamming collision of bodies.

"Found you, Frank!" a youthful voice called in triumph.

"Bowled me over more like."

"Frank's the seeker now!"

Phillip's hands tightened slightly on her waist. Although many layers separated their skin, the pressure sent a forbidden thrill through her. If anyone else had tried to touch her, she would have slapped him smartly and given him a setdown he wouldn't soon forget. But this was Phillip Weston. A friend who suddenly seemed like much more. How secret, how exciting, to stand there with him in the dark room, knowing they were surrounded by others who could not see them. Emma knew she should pull away, and she would. In just one minute more. . . .

"Emma, are you still in here?" Frank's voice, from the doorway. "I'll find you."

Phillip pulled her nearer yet, out of the path of the approaching figure. She turned toward her captor, unsure whether she ought to abrade him, or . . .

Releasing her waist, he pressed his fingers over her mouth and softly hissed in her ear, "Shh."

Footsteps passed inches from them.

Phillip's fingers moved tentatively from her mouth. When she inhaled to reprimand him, he pressed his lips to hers. She had no idea what to do, how to respond. Her first kiss. In the dark with Phillip Weston.

Somewhere in the house, a door closed. Light flashed in the passage.

"What is happening here?" Aunt Jane's voice, coming to check on them in her father's absence.

Emma lurched away from Phillip.

Aunt Jane called, "Emma?"

Emma didn't trust her voice. It would certainly give her away. Her aunt knew her too well. Emma stepped toward the door. Made it to the threshold just as Jane's light did.

Her aunt's wide eyes searched her face. "Are you all right?"

"Of course," Emma said, a bit too brightly, forcing a smile. "The boys insisted on a game of hide-and-seek. I tried to tell them to leave the lamps burning, but they would not heed me."

As her aunt stepped closer, the light of her lamp arced into the room behind Emma.

"Mr. . . . Weston . . ." Jane's eyes widened yet farther as she looked from the young man standing so near her niece, to her niece's no doubt blushing face.

"Good evening, Miss Smallwood," Phillip said, giving her aunt a little bow, as though nothing untoward had just happened.

Jane Smallwood's face stiffened. "I don't approve of young men and women being alone together in the dark, Mr. Weston." She aimed her words at him, though Emma felt the pinch of them far more than Philip did by the look of his cheerful face.

"You are perfectly right, Miss Smallwood," Phillip said. "I'm afraid Mr. Williams nearly knocked poor Emma over in the dark. But . . . no harm done. Thank goodness you came when you did."

Jane Smallwood eyed him skeptically. "I think it a very good thing I came when I did, Mr. Weston. And not because of Frank Williams."

Phillip said soothingly, "It was only a game, Miss Smallwood. No one was hurt. Nothing broken."

"Only a game, was it?" She arched one brow. "Whatever it was, let us have no more of it. Understood?"

"Perfectly."

Turning away, Aunt Jane began relighting the lamps and candles in the other rooms.

Emma turned to Phillip and tersely whispered, "Don't tell anyone, all right?"

He placed a hand on his heart. "You have my word. It never happened."

She believed him.

Later the words he had spoken registered more fully. *"It was only a game. . . . It never happened."* The truth of that left an odd prick of disappointment in her heart.

Sitting now with Mr. Davies and her father, Emma remained lost in reverie until running footsteps echoed in the hall beyond the office and tattooed up the stairs. She wondered what the matter was, but before she could rise to check, someone knocked on the doorjamb. She glanced over and felt her cheeks warm. For there stood the object of her reminisces.

"Pardon the intrusion, Davies," Phillip Weston said.

Mr. Davies waved the apology aside. "You are always welcome, Master Phillip. Come in."

Phillip stepped inside and beamed first at her, then her father. "Miss Smallwood. Mr. Smallwood. I hope you will do us the honor of joining the family for breakfast from now on in the breakfast room."

Emma stammered, "But . . . Lady Weston . . . that is, we are perfectly content here with Mr. Davies. Are we not, Papa? We don't want to be any trouble while we're here."

"Nonsense. You are no trouble," Phillip insisted. "I am delighted you are here. Please. I know Lady Weston is a stickler for certain formalities, and unfortunately I cannot ask you to join us for other meals, but she has agreed to your having breakfast with the family."

Emma bit her lip. "But if that is not her preference . . ."

"It is *my* preference," Phillip said. "As well as my father's, and even Lizzie's." He grinned. "You have made quite an impression on the girl."

"She is a dear, yes, but—"

"Please say you'll join us. If it makes you feel more comfortable, Lady Weston rarely ventures down before ten."

Her father interjected, "I for one would very much like joining you for breakfast, Phillip. Though I am an early riser, I fear, and may be off on my ramble before you raise your bonny head from the pillow. Never one to rise with the birds, if I recall correctly. I had to rouse you from bed myself on more than one occasion when Mrs. Malloy's attempts failed."

Phillip ducked his head, chuckling sheepishly. "I am afraid I have changed little in that regard, sir. Although if you two are at breakfast, I shall have incentive to rouse myself earlier." He smiled hopefully at her.

Emma exhaled and smiled tentatively in return. "Very well. If you are certain. It would be a pleasure for Papa, I know. For us both."

Phillip grinned. "Excellent."

Her father asked Phillip if he'd seen Henry lately, adding, "He usually joins me for a game of backgammon about now."

Phillip hesitated. "Ah. Well . . ." He grimaced toward the door. "With this storm he's already gone up, I fear. I don't imagine he'll be coming back down tonight."

Confusion passed over John Smallwood's face, but he was too polite to express any doubt over the unlikely excuse. "Well, what about you, Phillip. Will you join me?"

Phillip nodded. "Very well. If Emma will stay and cheer me on. Or at least console me when I lose."

Emma assured him she would be happy to do both.

Later, after the game ended and the rainstorm subsided, Emma took herself upstairs and rang for the maid.

Morva came in a few minutes later, muttering, "What a racket. Did 'ee hear it, miss?"

"The storm?" Emma asked.

Morva opened her mouth to reply, then seemed to think the better of whatever she'd been about to say. "Ess, that's what caused it."

The nimble housemaid helped Emma change into her nightclothes, and bid her good night.

Emma climbed into bed and wrote her impressions of Phillip in her journal, cataloging the changes in him. How his broad shoulders and height bespoke the man he had become. Yet how his boyish face and warm smiles reminded her of the lad she had once called friend.

She dipped her quill and paused, wondering if he remembered that night in the Smallwood sitting room in the dark. She hoped and feared he did.

She hoped and feared he did not.

When Emma finally blew out the candle and went to sleep, she dreamt they were all back in the Smallwood sitting room—her, Phillip, her father. Emma and her father sat reading while Phillip played the old harpsichord. His fingers drew reverberating, plucked-string sounds from the instrument as he attempted some piece she did not recognize. The sitting-room door opened, and her mother stepped inside. Emma expected Phillip to stop playing, but he continued on as though he had not seen Mrs. Smallwood enter. Emma shot him a look, tilting her head in her mother's direction. But Phillip only smiled at Emma and went on playing.

Did he not realize? There stood her mother, alive and well.

Emma rose and crossed the room, heart tingling with happiness to see her mother again.

Rachel Smallwood looked her up and down, shaking her head in exasperated admonition. "Stand up straight, Emma." She looked at the thick book in Emma's hand. "And why do you insist on reading scholarly books in front of Mr. Weston. You know he will never marry a bluestocking."

Mortification swept over Emma, drowning the happiness of a moment before.

She opened her eyes and the strange dream faded. Yet the sounds remained. Lying there, she stared into the darkness and listened. The music was real. Someone was playing the pianoforte in the distant music room. Julian again? Or was it Phillip at the keys, as in her dream?

The dream . . . Emma was disappointed her mother was not alive in reality but relieved she had not actually been so blatantly embarrassed in front of Phillip.

Too awake now to return to sleep, Emma slipped from the bedclothes, slid her feet into the slippers beside her bed, and pulled on her wrapper. She wondered if her hair was a mess. She told herself it did not matter. She would not let Phillip or Julian, or whoever it was, see her in her nightclothes. Though Phillip had certainly seen her in wrapper and unbound hair on any number of occasions when they were younger.

The small fire in her hearth had burnt itself out, so she took her unlit stubby candle with her, hoping the landing lamp would still be burning. She could light it there.

She inched open her door and slipped into the dark corridor. She rounded the corner, passed her father's room—still and silent within—and continued to the stairway. There the candle lamp guttered in a small puddle of wax. Lifting the glass, she tipped her candle into its dying flame, thankful when it flickered to life. The lamp wick glowed orange, then fizzled into a grey string of smoke, as though she had stolen its flame.

Emma replaced the glass, wincing as it chimed against the brass base. Hearing no answering noise, she turned and made her way gingerly down the stairs.

The sad music continued to weave its way up the stairwell, drawing her closer, kneading her heart like a needle-clawed kitten, pleasure pricked with pain.

Reaching the ground floor, she crossed the massive, echoing hall. Her candle flickered, casting strange shadows on the crossed swords and shields on the paneled walls. She wasn't sure what she should do when she arrived at the music room. Listen at the door, or step inside and confirm the player? If Julian—praise his playing and kindly admonish him to go to bed? If Phillip—take advantage of the tête-à-tête to speak to him alone? She wondered if their comfortable camaraderie would exist in private as it seemed to in the presence of others.

Reaching the door, she gingerly lifted the latch, slowly inching the door open. She paused, listening. The music had stopped. Just when, she could not say. Holding her candle before her, she stepped into the music room, explanation ready on her lips. *"I am sorry to disturb you. I only wanted to see who the talented musician might be."* Who would be staring back at her, a startled Julian or a smiling Phillip?

But when the candlelight swept the pianoforte, she found its bench empty. She blinked. Looked again. Stepped closer. No one sat before the keys. Feeling her brow pucker in surprise, she whispered into the dimness, "Hello?" Her voice caught in a shaky whisper. "Where are you? I didn't mean to disturb you."

No reply from the shadows. She turned in a complete circle, her candle's small flame faintly illuminating every corner of the room.

The empty room.

A chill prickled up Emma's spine, and gooseflesh curdled her skin. Had she only dreamt the music? *Foolish girl.* It wasn't like her to imagine things.

Ignoring a second wave of chills, she tiptoed out of the music room, crept up the stairs, and returned to her bedchamber as quickly as possible, shutting the door securely behind her and burrowing under the bedclothes.

In the morning, Emma rose at seven, wanting to arrive early for her first breakfast with the family. She hoped to be seated safely at the table with her father when the others began trickling in, thereby avoiding walking into an already crowded room, interrupting conversation and having every eye turn in her direction.

As she washed her face and cleaned her teeth, Emma regarded her reflection in the washstand mirror. She couldn't help but wonder what Phillip had thought upon seeing her again. Had he seen the same skinny, awkward girl he had known, or had he found something pleasing in the way her face had filled out—and other parts of her as well? It was vain and silly, she knew. But she hoped Phillip had been pleasantly surprised by her looks. Or at least, upon seeing her again in general. She thought again of the way he had smiled at her last night, when he had joined them in the steward's office. Yes, he had seemed pleased.

Morva bustled in, apparently taken aback to see her already up and midablution but pleased to find her so. "Yer up early, miss." Morva helped her into the stays and lavender frock Emma had already laid out.

As the housemaid did up her fastenings, Emma asked, "Morva, did you hear anyone playing the pianoforte last night, sometime after ten?"

"No, miss. Can't say I did. But I wouldn't, would I, being asleep in the attic by then."

"I thought I heard someone, but when I went down, the music room was empty."

Morva shrugged. "Master Julian, most like. Probably slipped out the back door when he heard 'ee comin'."

"There's another door?"

"Ess. The door we use. Leads on to the back stairs."

"Oh . . ." Someone *had* been playing but had slipped from the room through the opposite door just before Emma entered. Julian or Rowan most likely, hoping to avoid a scolding for staying up so late. How silly she felt for her fear of the night before.

Emma dressed her own hair while Morva tidied the room. Then she took a deep breath, told herself there was no reason to be nervous, and went downstairs. She paused in the threshold of the breakfast room, but no one was inside, save a footman standing at the ready near the rear servery door. The sideboard boasted a large silver spigot urn for coffee, several smaller teapots, and trays of assorted baked goods. Covered serving dishes likely held warm foods. The spread was similar to breakfasts in Mr. Davies's office but on a grander scale.

She wondered if her father had yet to come down or if he had already eaten and set out for his morning ramble.

Stepping inside, Emma poured herself a cup of coffee and eyed the sugar bowl but did not allow herself any lumps. The footman mentioned that she would find milk on the table for her coffee and offered to bring her freshly toasted bread or a muffin, if she liked. She agreed to his suggestion and took a seat at the empty table while he slipped through the servery door. It was too quiet. She felt more self-conscious eating alone and commanding the full attention of a servant than she would have felt in a room full of people.

She was relieved to hear voices in the corridor. Julian and Rowan came into the breakfast room, talking quietly.

Julian snickered at something his brother said. Then he saw her and drew himself up. "Ah. Miss Smallwood. That's right. You're to join us now. That'll be pleasant."

"Thank you."

She watched as the boys helped themselves to cups of chocolate and plates of hot food before they joined her at the table.

Emma began conversationally, "Was that one of you I heard playing again last night?"

The two boys exchanged a look.

"Wasn't me," Julian said.

Rowan held up his hands. "Don't look at me. I only play when forced."

"Must have been a ghost," Julian said, light blue eyes glinting. "The house is haunted, you know. Hasn't anyone told you?"

Emma shook her head. "I don't believe in such things."

Julian's eyes roved her face. A shadow of a grin lifted one corner of his mouth. "You will."

With a tolerant smile, she asked, "And what sort of ghost supposedly haunts Ebbington Manor—some ill-treated servant who died carrying water cans up the back stairs for ungrateful Westons of old?"

"No. Someone much closer to the family," Julian said. "The ghost of the dearly departed Lady—"

Phillip and Henry strode into the room, and Julian clamped his mouth shut.

"Good morning, Miss Smallwood," Phillip said cheerfully.

Henry hesitated at seeing her, then bowed tersely. He looked from her to his guilty-looking half brothers. "What have these two been telling you?"

"Oh, we were only teasing her," Julian said. "She said she heard someone playing the pianoforte last night and we told her it must have been a ghost."

Henry's dark brows rose. "Last night? When?"

Emma answered, "About ten thirty, I think. Did you not hear it?"

"I . . . was out." He stepped abruptly to the sideboard. He filled a coffee cup and then turned to his half brothers. "I don't want you two filling Miss Smallwood's head full of nonsense."

"I thought you might prefer a bit of nonsense to the alternative—in this instance," Julian said.

Henry glowered. "If you cannot say anything useful or kind, perhaps it would be better to say nothing at all."

Julian glared back. "Very well." He rose, dropped his table napkin on his chair, and marched to the door. There he paused, sending a pointed look at Rowan over his shoulder.

Belatedly taking the hint, Rowan popped half a sausage into his mouth, stood with napkin still tucked at his neck, and followed him.

They had barely left the room when the housekeeper, Mrs. Prowse, appeared in the doorway, brow lined in concern. "I am sorry, Mr. Weston. But might I have a word?"

Henry set down the coffee cup, untasted. "Very well. Excuse me."

Phillip sat across the table from Emma. He waited until Henry had departed, then quietly explained, "Henry gets angry when the twins talk about the ghost of the former Lady Weston. Our mother, you know. I don't like it either, but nor do I take it to heart. I don't remember our mother, you see. But Henry does. And he doesn't like that memory sullied." He chuckled. "Not even with foolish ghost stories of foolish boys."

Emma lifted her chin in understanding. "I should not like it either."

"Of course you wouldn't, Emma. And no one who knew your mother could think of saying a thing against her or her memory. She was always very kind to me."

Emma nodded. Yes, her mother had liked Phillip, while Aunt Jane had always preferred Henry for some reason.

Phillip reached over and patted her hand. "There is nothing to be frightened of, I assure you. The boys were only trying to scare you."

She liked the feel of his hand on hers, though she told herself it was only a friendly, comforting gesture.

"I know," she said.

They shared a little grin, and then Emma forced her attention to her meal.

When Emma left the breakfast room a few minutes later, she heard whispers from down the passage. She peeked around the corner and was surprised to see Henry Weston standing very near Mrs. Prowse, his head bowed like a sunflower, to better match her shorter stature. What could Henry Weston and the housekeeper have to whisper about so furtively? Surely not changes to the day's menu.

Having no other option than to pass by, Emma stepped purposely into the passage, humming as she went to warn them of her presence.

Mrs. Prowse looked up, blinking at her in surprise, and Henry straightened abruptly.

"Yes. That will be all, Mrs. Prowse. Thank you." He delivered the line in a stilted manner that left Emma quite certain they had not been discussing some common household situation.

But . . . ghosts?

*Come now, Emma Jane Smallwood,* she lectured herself. *You are made of more sensible stuff than that.* Ebbington Manor was beginning to affect her customary good sense. It was time to nip such foolish fancies in the bud.

With that in mind, Emma marched purposely up to the schoolroom to see how she might help her father prepare for an exhaustive lesson on logic and reasoning.

*Her heart became faint with terror. . . .*

—Ann Radcliffe, *The Mysteries of Udolpho*

# Chapter 8

The following evening, Henry sat with his brothers—Phillip, Julian, and Rowan—in the drawing room after dinner. They were sharing a rare jovial mood of relaxation and reminiscing, perhaps because Lady Weston had gone out for the evening to visit a friend, taking Lizzie with her. Sir Giles had eaten with them but then declared himself ready for bed. Henry suspected their father had not, in fact, gone directly to his own bedchamber. Or at least he'd hoped his father had a different destination in mind. But now Henry was sorry Sir Giles hadn't stayed. He would have enjoyed this—four of his sons talking together, jesting good-naturedly, and laughing about old times.

Phillip said to Julian and Rowan, "It really is too bad the two of you never attended the Smallwood Academy, as Henry and I did. Then you would know what we're talking about."

"Well, at least we've now met Mr. Smallwood and his daughter," Rowan said. "The rest we shall have to imagine."

"I feel I can almost see the Smallwood Academy," Julian mused, leaning back against the settee. "The small, damp bedchambers, the drafty schoolroom high in the rafters, Mr. Smallwood droning on in clumsy Latin—*vomō, vomere, vomuī, vomitus*. . . . Mrs. Malloy banging her pot to call you all to dinner—'Come on, ya dirty litt-ul mumpers. Wash yer 'ands, or I'll wash 'em fer ya.'"

Phillip burst into guffaws, and Henry bit back a grin. It was a fairly good imitation. But beneath the housekeeper's gruff exterior—especially when reading the riot act to new pupils—lay a warm, affectionate heart.

Phillip leapt to his feet. "There's Emma. Let's ask her to join us. She should be here to defend herself." Smiling, he hurried from the room before Henry could form a suitable protest.

Henry watched Phillip take Miss Smallwood's arm as she passed in the hall, tugging and cajoling her into the drawing room.

"There is no one here but us lads," Phillip teased. "And I know Miss Smallwood has never been intimidated by a roomful of rowdy boys."

She smiled but looked self-conscious nonetheless.

"We were just telling Julian and Rowan about all they missed by not attending the Smallwood Academy."

"Oh dear," she murmured.

Phillip began, "I remember one time when Mr. Smallwood left Emma to administer an examination, and—"

"Did he?" Henry interrupted. "Why would he do that?"

Phillip drew down his lips. "I don't know. He did so quite often when I was there. I sometimes think I learned as much from the daughter as I did the father."

"He did not do so while I was there."

Phillip shrugged. "Emma was younger then."

*And her mother's health had not yet declined—nor her father's spirits,* Henry thought. He considered pressing the matter but, noticing Miss Smallwood shifting and twisting her hands, decided to let the subject drop.

"At all events," Phillip continued, "Frank Williams—who's on his way to becoming a barrister, by the way—opened a jar of the foulest cheese you'd ever smelled, set it beneath his chair, and continued on with his examination without a word. Miss Smallwood, assuming what anyone would in a roomful of boys, calmly opened every window in the schoolroom without missing a single Latin conjugation."

The four Westons laughed. Even Miss Smallwood allowed a small chuckle.

Julian turned to him. "Henry, it's your turn to tell us a story—one of your notorious pranks."

Henry glanced at Miss Smallwood and hesitated. "I . . . don't know what you're talking about."

"Of course you do. You remember. Knocking on Miss Smallwood's door in the dead of night, then sneaking away before she answered. Putting the mouse in her stocking, and then in her bed . . ."

"And that love letter you wrote," Rowan added helpfully. "Signing it with another chap's name."

Emma Smallwood's eyes widened, and she turned to look at him, brows high.

Henry felt his neck heat. His cravat seemed suddenly far too tight.

"That's right," Phillip nodded as the memory returned to him. "Pugsworth, was it not?"

Julian grinned at Miss Smallwood, clearly enjoying himself. "Did you really think this Pugsworth fellow in love with you?"

Heaven help him, Henry hoped she wouldn't burst into disillusioned tears. Not all these years later. And *not* over Milton Pugsworth.

But Miss Smallwood remained her imperturbable self. "Goodness no," she said. "For all his faults, Mr. Pugsworth spelled exceptionally well and had the neatest hand I ever saw. Your brother, on the other hand, never did learn to spell. And I recognized his sloppy scratchings the moment I saw them."

Phillip gave her a long look of amused approval. "Bravo, Emma."

Miss Smallwood met and held Phillip's gaze with a smile as sweet and warm as honeyed tea.

Seeing it, uneasiness soured Henry's stomach. *Vomitus,* indeed.

A few minutes later, Mr. Smallwood joined them and shared reminiscences of his own. When the stories finally waned, Henry's old tutor slapped his legs and sighed. "Well, I think I'll turn in."

Miss Smallwood rose from the settee beside him. "I shall as well."

"Good night, gentlemen." Mr. Smallwood bestowed a general smile and wave to them all.

Henry stood. "I shall walk up with you."

At the landing, Henry lit a lamp and led the way. He spoke in low tones with Mr. Smallwood, but remained keenly aware of the man's daughter following quietly behind.

While he and Mr. Smallwood bid each other good night at the top of the stairs, Henry noticed Emma wander ahead into the alcove where his mother's portrait had been relocated.

When John Smallwood disappeared within his room, Henry could not resist the opportunity to speak with his daughter alone. He walked over and joined her as she stood looking up at his mother's portrait, lit by stained-glass moonlight and now his lamp as well.

He began quietly, "You recall, of course, that I won the Smallwood spelling contest every year I was there?"

"Yes, Mr. Weston," she replied evenly, eyes remaining on the portrait.

"And you might also recall that your father declared my handwriting the best he'd ever had the privilege to read?"

"Yes, Mr. Weston."

He looked at her composed profile and felt admiration fill him. When she said no more, he slowly shook his head, a small smile lifting the corner of his mouth.

"Well done, Miss Smallwood." He started to turn away but paused to add, "He did admire you, you know. He just didn't know how to show it."

She gave him an incredulous look. "Mr. Pugsworth?"

"Yes," Henry said, then walked away, thinking, *Him too.*

The following day passed uneventfully, taken up by lessons and a stroll with Lizzie. Emma saw neither Henry nor Phillip all day.

That night, Emma lay in bed reading by candlelight. The novel was *The Mysteries of Udolpho,* by Ann Radcliffe. It was a gothic romance—not her usual fare—set in a gloomy castle filled with supernatural terrors. Emma wondered why the brooding, haughty villain, Montoni, had Henry Weston's face. She had read the novel before, years ago. But it seemed more frightening now, here in Ebbington Manor, than it ever had in her snug home in Longstaple. She turned the page and read.

> Her heart became faint with terror. Half raising herself from the bed, and gently drawing aside the curtain, she looked toward the door . . . but the lamp that burned on the hearth spread so feeble a light through the apartment, that the remote parts of it were lost in shadow. The noise, however, which she was convinced came from the door, continued. While Emily kept her eyes fixed on the spot, she saw the door move, and then slowly open, and perceived something enter the room, but the extreme duskiness prevented her distinguishing what it was. Almost fainting with terror, she had yet sufficient command over herself to check the shriek that was escaping from her lips. . . .

*Creak.*

Emma's heart lurched. She froze, listening. A floorboard squeaked in the passage outside her room. It was only someone passing in the corridor, she told herself.

But . . . why would anyone be walking past her room, there at the end of the passage?

Emma picked up her chatelaine watch from the bedside table and peered at it by candlelight. Eleven. Surely too late for a servant to be up and about, sweeping floors or some such. The footsteps continued down the corridor and faded away.

She told herself to return to her book. Whoever it was had gone. Danger past.

Danger? How foolish. Her choice of reading material had definitely been unwise.

Emma laid aside the book, turned back the bedclothes, and sat on the edge of her bed. Curiosity nipping at her, she pulled on her wrapper and wiggled her feet into her slippers. Armed with her still-burning candle, she opened the door and listened. She heard the faint sound of retreating footsteps. Leaving her door ajar, she quickly tiptoed down the passage, trying to ignore the many pairs of eyes glaring down at her from the portraits of long-dead ancestors. She passed her father's room and paused at the top of the stairwell. Hearing nothing from below or above, she continued on, passing doors she had never ventured past before.

She reached the end of the corridor where it intersected with a perpendicular passage—the north wing Lady Weston and Mrs. Prowse had warned her to stay out of.

Heart pounding, Emma gingerly leaned forward and peered around the corner. She held her candle at waist level, too nervous to lift it high, uncertain what she might find.

Down the passage, she saw the retreating back of a man carrying his own candle. As he reached for the door latch of the last room, she glimpsed his profile by candlelight. Wavy hair, strong nose, high cheekbones—the unmistakable profile of Henry Weston. What was he doing? Certainly his room was not in the north wing.

His head turned in her direction. She jerked back out of sight and pressed against the wall. Had he noticed her light? Were footsteps now coming toward her? She turned and hurried away on the balls of her feet, quickly and quietly scurrying back to her room. Hopefully unseen.

⁂

Early the next morning, Emma again dreamt of Phillip. They were back in Longstaple, even though Phillip was too old to be her father's pupil any longer. He stood in the Smallwood sitting room as the man he was now—jawline and shoulders wide and masculine, brown hair thick, nose perfect, eyes still blue . . . and warm with admiration. The old affection she felt for him returned.

He stepped closer and wrapped his arms around her. How strong he was now. His gaze lingered on her face, looking at her fully, openly, nothing hidden, nothing to hide. Warmth and nostalgic longing filled her chest. Yes, this was how it felt to be with Phillip Weston. Good, yet wistful at once.

Then he leaned toward her and his eyes grew vague and unfocused, looking slightly past her, as if not wanting to see her reaction, in case she hesitated or outright refused. If he did not see it, he need not heed it. . . .

As his mouth neared hers, she thought, *Does he not realize how much older I am? That I am not that girl any longer? That we should not be doing this?* Yet she wanted him to kiss her, to feel his mouth on hers.

"Miss Smallwood?"

His lips whispered near.

"Time to rise, miss."

*Shh. No. I don't want to miss this. . . .*

*Click, clatter*—the shutters opening. Emma winced. Sunshine poured over her, chasing the dream away. She begrudgingly opened her eyes and saw Morva folding back the last of the shutters and going to her wardrobe to pull out the next frock in Emma's limited, predictable rotation.

Emma lay there a few moments longer, feeling the intoxicating pull of the dream fading but unwilling to miss a single moment. Like honey, sweet and sickening at once. How wanton she was, to wish the feelings to linger. That night in Longstaple was long gone. She could not kiss Phillip in real life. And likely he no longer wanted to do so. Was it so wrong to relish the feeling anyway? To enjoy the way it lingered, leaving her with a wistful awareness, a pleasant unease, as if she had forgotten to do something? Yes, it probably was wrong. But she did not wish it away.

Morva bent to pick up something from the floor and squinted at it. "Something for thee, miss. Slid under the door while thee slept, looks like."

*That's odd,* Emma thought, but held out her hand for the folded rectangle.

Morva gave it to her, expression expectant. Emma ignored her and focused on the letter. No seal marked its perfect fold. She turned it over. There was her name, clearly printed: *Miss Smallwood.*

Her curiosity trumped her qualms about arriving late for breakfast.

Might it be a kind word from Phillip? Or a word of reprimand from Henry, if he'd seen her about to enter the north wing the night before? She unfolded the single sheet, noticing the studied handwriting, its angles and descenders even and precise. She read:

> *Dear Miss Smallwood,*
>
> *I thought it was time you received a real love letter. I am too shy to speak to you of my feelings in person, but I want you to know how pleased I am you are with us. You have an ardent admirer here at Ebbington Manor.*
>
> *I will be watching you. For I could gaze upon your soft green eyes and sweet lips forever.*
>
> *Your Secret Admirer*

What in the world? Emma felt her stomach twist in alarm. Likely not the reaction the author had hoped for. Or was it? She reread *"your soft green eyes and sweet lips . . ."* and felt her cheeks heat. Who had written this? Was Phillip attracted to her as in her dream? He certainly made it clear he was delighted to see her again. But *ardent* admiration?

She did not recognize the handwriting. But three years had passed since she had seen Phillip's hand. Might he truly admire her?

Emma felt Morva watching her and quickly folded the letter. She rose and began washing for the day but was conscious of the housemaid's inquisitive gaze following her movements.

Morva helped her into a day dress of patterned muslin with green ribbon trim at neckline and sleeves, then finally took her leave.

Alone at last, Emma looked at the letter once more. She found herself transported back to Aunt Jane's house a few years ago, when she, then an adolescent with romantic ideals, had first seen the letter her aunt kept on her bedside table.

"Who's the letter from, Aunt Jane?" Emma had teased. "A secret admirer?"

"Yes, actually," Jane replied. "Though his identity is no secret.

His name is Mr. Delbert Farley of Bodmin." Jane nodded toward the letter. "You may read it if you like."

Emma had read the letter, expecting little. But she was impressed. "This is a good letter, Aunt Jane. A very good letter, indeed. How do you know this Mr. Farley?"

"I met him in the bookshop several months ago," Jane said. "I happened to be in the High Street and stopped in to poke around. I was skimming through a new volume on steam engines when I noticed a gentleman watching me. I feared he wanted the book for himself, so I offered it to him, but he said he was only interested to know why a 'lovely lady' such as myself should find such a book interesting."

Jane's dimple appeared at this.

"I explained that I was a teacher interested in many things. He told me he was in town visiting his cousin. You know Mr. Gilcrest who bought the forge?"

Emma nodded. "Vaguely."

"Mr. Farley came to help him bring the old place into good working order. At all events, we talked for some time and I soon found myself agreeing to take tea with Mr. Farley before his coach departed." Jane's dimple deepened. "He asked the innkeeper for tea for himself and his 'learned colleague.'"

Emma's eyes widened. "What did Mr. Pruett say to *that*?"

"Not a word. Mr. Farley was obviously known and respected by the Pruetts, as well as several others in the inn. I felt no qualms about being in his company."

Emma exclaimed, "Why did you not tell me this before?"

"I did not want you to follow my example of talking to strange men! It is one thing at my age, but not at yours."

"Oh, Aunt Jane. You are not old!"

Jane sighed. "Well, on that day, I had never felt younger. Or more interesting. Mr. Farley told me about his china clayworks; I told him about my school. We discussed favorite books. . . . I have rarely enjoyed myself more. When he left, I thought that would be that. But a week later, I received a parcel—the very book I had been skimming." Jane ran a finger over the volume on her side table. "I knew immediately who had sent it. Perhaps I should not have accepted the gift, but I hadn't the heart to return it."

"Did you ever see him again?"

"Once. He returned for Mr. Gilcrest's wedding. He married Alice White, you may recall, and I had been invited to the wedding breakfast. I don't know if Mr. Farley arranged the invitation or not. But either way, I enjoyed seeing him again."

Emma asked eagerly, "And then he wrote you this letter, asking to call on you formally?"

Jane nodded, her eyes far away.

Emma looked at the date of the letter and saw it had been written more than a month before. "Have you answered him?"

Jane shook her head.

"Why not?"

Her aunt shrugged, sad but resigned. "Mr. Farley lives in Bodmin, Emma. Nearly thirty miles from here. It seems silly to contemplate uprooting my life, giving up my established school here—my livelihood—for the mere *possibility* of romance."

Now Emma grimaced and pressed a hand to her brow. The memory of her aunt's practical response to her own "love letter" prompted Emma to be realistic about hers. She likely had no secret admirer. The letter was probably a joke, though a joke in bad taste.

She recalled the Westons reminiscing about boyhood pranks the previous night, and her stomach soured. Apparently, one of them had decided to poke fun at her—the sure spinster.

Emma thought of the footsteps she had heard outside her room last night—delivering this letter, she guessed. Whoever it was had probably stifled laughter all the way back to his room. Had Henry Weston delivered another forged love letter, an encore of his long-ago prank? Or had one of his brothers done so in his stead?

A chill swept over her. She stepped to the wardrobe and wrapped a lightweight shawl around her shoulders, pinning it across her bosom with an old fleur-de-lis brooch of her mother's. The pin would not cooperate, or perhaps it was her trembling fingers, but her watch read two minutes after the hour by the time she was ready to go downstairs.

How should she react? She would not. She would not tell anyone. She would handle this herself, as she handled most things in her life. She would act as though nothing had happened. After all, nothing *had* happened. No harm had been done.

Looking about the room, Emma lifted the lid of her bandbox and stuck the letter under the hat within. She did not want Morva to be tempted to read it. Then, brushing her hands together, she left her room and made her way down to breakfast.

Emma hesitated in the threshold to survey the scene within the breakfast room. Henry Weston, Sir Giles, and her father sat engrossed in conversation over coffee as the footman cleared away their used plates. Phillip stood at the sideboard, poking through an assortment of breads with silver serving tongs.

He glanced over. "Ah, Miss Smallwood. Good morning."

Hearing this, the other gentlemen rose and looked her way. Feeling self-conscious, she dipped her head in acknowledgment and stepped inside.

The gentlemen returned to their seats and their discussion. But Phillip waited for her to join him at the sideboard, an expectant expression on his boyish face. Thinking of the morning's dream, and the letter, Emma could not quite meet his eyes.

"And how are you this morning, Emma? I wonder if you slept as poorly as I did, hearing every breeze whistle through the window frames and the whole place shudder every time one of its occupants turned on his bed?"

For once she could not return his playful grin. "I slept well enough, thank you."

He shot her a look of surprise at her officious tone but made no comment as he returned his attention to the breads and muffins.

Even though Emma had all but convinced herself the letter was insincere, she found her gaze drifting furtively to Phillip as she picked up a plate and helped herself to several items, not paying much attention to what she selected. He seemed the same as yesterday. She did not detect any hidden meanings in his words or looks.

He glanced over—from her plate, to her face, then back again. "Hungry?"

She looked down at her plate as though through a fog. It came into focus, and she was chagrined to find it piled high with several types of sausages. Her cheeks heated. "My goodness," she murmured. "I am not as awake as I thought."

He surveyed her no-doubt troubled expression. "Everything all right?"

"Hm? Oh yes. Everything is fine. I'm fine. Why should I not be fine?"

Phillip's lips puckered into an uncertain grin. "No reason. You look fine. Perfectly fine. I'm sorry if I implied otherwise."

His eyes sparkled. He was teasing her. *"You look fine. Perfectly fine."* What did he mean by that? Was it a veiled reference to the letter, to the compliments about her appearance—her eyes and lips? *Emma!* She silently scolded herself. *Stop being ridiculous.*

Phillip stepped to the unoccupied end of the table and pulled out a chair for her. Dumbly she went forward, feeling slightly ill at ease about sitting next to him. She noticed Henry Weston looking at her. She forced herself to meet his gaze and nod before returning her attention to her meal.

Rowan and Julian entered the breakfast room, and Emma was relieved to have the attention redirected toward them. Julian looked at her and bowed. He elbowed his brother beside him, and Rowan halfheartedly followed suit.

Julian smiled. "Good morning, Miss Smallwood."

Emma dipped her head. "Julian. Rowan."

"And good morning to you too," Phillip said dryly.

"Oh, hello, Phillip," Julian obliged.

Rowan had already made a beeline for the sideboard. Not only was Rowan several inches taller than his twin but at least a stone heavier as well. He'd recently had a growth spurt, she'd overheard

Lady Weston say, assuring Julian he would no doubt catch up with his brother soon.

Emma felt someone watching her and glanced over to find Henry Weston's eyes shifting from her to Phillip and back again. When she met his gaze once more, he looked away first.

Emma suddenly wished Lizzie was not so fond of sleeping late. How self-conscious she felt, the only female in a room of six males. She ought to be used to it, having grown up in a house full of men. But then, her mother had been there, and the men had been boys. And none of them had written to her under the guise of a secret admirer. Well, except for Henry Weston, writing as poor Milton Pugsworth.

After breakfast, Emma helped her father administer an examination covering significant events of the first century. Both Rowan and Julian performed very well, which was a relief to Emma and her father, not to mention the boys themselves. Apparently, examinations at the "West Country school" their mother had chosen had not gone as well.

Later that afternoon, Emma went for another walk, and Phillip jogged out to join her. Emma was pleased but reminded herself it was probably just a friendly gesture. It meant nothing. Together they strolled through the garden, Emma admiring the stately old rhododendrons, clumps of primroses, and camellia bushes with dark pink blooms. She asked Phillip to identify species unfamiliar to her, but he was unable to name more than a few.

They walked in silence for a time, and then she began gently, "I was surprised to hear the boys had been sent away to school. I had thought you might have recommended Smallwood's."

"I did. I do! But it was Lady Weston's decision to send them to Blundell's. I don't know why."

Emma said, "Lizzie mentioned Lady Weston wanted them to attend a 'good, old-fashioned West Country school.'"

"That sounds right. Lady Weston is West Country born and bred, after all. Unlike Father."

Emma remembered what that red-haired man had said about Sir Giles not being considered "one of them" by the villagers.

She asked, "How long were the boys at Blundell's?"

"I don't know exactly. I was not home at the time. Three or four months, I think."

Emma nodded. "Lizzie mentioned they did not like the school. Something about the schoolmaster and other students treating them unkindly."

"So they say. I gather the schoolmaster maintained a different version of events. Something about bad behavior and fighting."

"Fighting?" she echoed, recalling how Rowan had stepped between Julian and Mr. McShane.

"Well, don't quote me on it. Father said, 'not exactly fighting.' Apparently, Julian insists Rowan was only trying to protect him."

"I wonder if it is difficult, being so much smaller than his brother."

"Yes . . ." Phillip mused. "It certainly can be."

Was he referring to himself and Henry? Henry was taller, certainly. But there was not the glaring gap between them as between Rowan and Julian.

She offered, "At least the disparity is likely only temporary."

His eyes sparkled. "Whereas the disparity between Henry and me is permanent?"

She tucked her chin, regarding him in bemusement. "I never meant to suggest any such thing." Did Phillip feel inferior in some way to his elder brother? She could not credit it.

He flicked a playful finger under her chin. "I should hope not. I always rather thought you preferred me to Henry."

Emma's nerves crackled to life. She took a long breath and told herself to stop imagining references to that cursed letter. She swallowed and answered diplomatically, "You and I, being so close in age, naturally became friends. Henry and I did not."

He gave her a crooked grin and tweaked her chin once more. "That's what I like to hear."

Emma's heart gave a little flutter. His manner toward her was certainly warm. But warm enough to indicate romantic feelings?

She wasn't sure. Pulling her gaze from his, Emma looked beyond the garden wall, across the expanse of grassy headland to the horizon, to where the land faded into the greenish-grey sea beyond. "Shall we venture out to the coast path?" She lifted her face to enjoy the warm sun on her skin. "It is such a lovely day."

Emma felt his gaze on her profile and glanced at him.

Phillip smiled. "It is indeed." He opened the garden gate for her, and together they set off toward the ends of the earth.

A few minutes later, they reached the footpath worn in the grass along the cliff's edge—near but not too near. The wind swirling all about her, Emma looked out at the endless sea beyond and then down to the rocky beach below. They walked northward until the path widened and began its descent to the harbor and village. For a moment they stood at the northwestern-most point, looking down at the harbor intersected by a narrow river making its way out to sea. In the late afternoon sun, the golden sand of the harbor looked damp and wrinkled. The tide had gone out, leaving puddles of trapped water behind and revealing dark rocks usually covered by the sea. One large rock reminded her of a majestic lion lying at rest, from its great head to its low rock paws resting on the sand.

Around the harbor huddled cottages of grey stone with roofs of mossy slate. And there, set apart from the others, one whitewashed house wore a thatched roof like a boy with thick straw-blond hair.

Where the bottom of the cliff met the beach, a rocky peninsula fingered into the sea, forming a natural breakwater for one side of the harbor. An octagon tower stood at the peninsula's end.

"What is that building?" Emma asked.

Phillip looked in the direction she pointed. "That is the Chapel of the Rock."

"It looks dangerous, out in the sea like that."

"It is. When big storms blow in, the chapel is sometimes flooded."

"Who built it there of all places?"

He shrugged. "I don't recall much about it, actually. I am sure I've heard the story a hundred times but paid little heed. You might ask Henry. He has always been more interested in local history than I have."

Emma nodded. She would perhaps, if she ever found herself in conversation with the man and had nothing else to fill the awkward silence between them.

"Well." Phillip pulled his hat down more snugly against the buffeting wind. "Let's head back. You're not dressed for this biting wind, and neither am I."

He offered her his arm, which surprised her, and after a moment's hesitation, she took it. The ground *was* spongy and uneven, she reasoned, and she had no interest in turning an ankle.

As she and Phillip returned to the gardens fronting the estate, Lizzie and Henry stepped out of the manor together, engaged in conversation. When Lizzie noticed them, she smiled, waved, and walked toward them. Henry, however, nodded brusquely and continued on his way to the stables without a word.

As Lizzie neared, her gaze dropped from Emma's and Phillip's faces to their joined arms. Suddenly self-conscious, Emma extracted her hand from the crook of Phillip's elbow.

Lizzie looked shrewdly from Phillip's easy smile to Emma's no-doubt-embarrassed face. One of her dark brows rose.

Phillip cleared his throat and looked over at Henry's departing figure. "You know, I have a sudden hankering to ride."

"So late in the day?" Lizzie asked.

"Yes. Please excuse me, ladies." He bowed and quickly turned.

Lizzie lingered beside Emma, and together the two young women watched Phillip hurry toward the stables.

"You like Phillip, don't you," Lizzie said, turning an expectant gaze her way.

Emma replied, "Of course I like him. We became friends when he lived with us in Longstaple." Seeing the speculation sparkling in the girl's eyes, she added quickly, "But only friends."

"I am glad to hear it. For I don't have to tell you Lady Weston would be none too pleased about a romance between one of her sons and the tutor's daughter."

"Even her stepsons?" Emma asked before she could think the better of it.

"Especially her stepsons. She expects them to marry for money or connections. She reserves thoughts of happiness and love for her own sons, I imagine."

"And what does she expect of you?" Emma asked.

Lizzie looked at her, surprised by the question. "Not a thing." She looked away, muttering, "Except to keep my mouth shut."

Surprise flared through Emma, but she saw the hardening of Lizzie's jaw and thought better of asking what she was supposed to keep quiet about.

Instead Emma said, "May I ask, Lizzie, how you came to be Lady Weston's ward?"

Lizzie bowed her head for a moment, and Emma feared she had broached a sad subject.

"I'm sorry. I don't mean to pry."

Lizzie looked over the garden wall toward the sea. "It is only natural you should be curious."

Emma waited several moments, but Lizzie said no more. Emma asked gently, "Is Lady Weston some relation to you?"

Lizzie hesitated. "Only very distantly."

Again Emma waited for the girl to explain.

Glancing at Emma and seeing her expectant expression, Lizzie went on, "Lady Weston introduces me as her ward, the daughter of a distant cousin."

"I see. And your parents . . . ?"

Lizzie winced. "Must we talk about that?"

Guilt swamped Emma. "No. Not if you don't want to. But I have lost my mother too. So I can guess how you might feel."

Lizzie lifted her chin. "You still have your father."

"Yes." Emma nodded. "I do." She imagined Lizzie had lost both of her parents and Lady Weston had taken her in, perhaps because the ailing father or mother had asked it of her on his or her deathbed. That seemed likely, but she reminded herself not to judge anyone too quickly, for the better or worse, until she had all the information.

Lizzie picked a primrose and idly twirled its stem in her small fingers. "How long has your mother been gone?" she asked.

Emma swallowed the lump in her throat. "Nearly two years now."

Lizzie tossed the flower aside and said darkly, "Mine has been gone far longer." Suddenly Lizzie brightened and turned to Emma. "What say you to tea and cakes? I could eat a whole plateful myself, and I imagine you are hungry after your walk. Shall we go in and see what we might find?"

Emma blinked at the girl's sudden change of mood and topic. "Of course. If you like." And she followed Lizzie into the house.

That evening, Emma made her way downstairs to the steward's office for dinner—late again, for Morva had forgotten to come and help her change. As she passed, she heard voices coming from the drawing room.

Sir Giles's voice. "Any success, Henry?"

"No. Not yet," Henry replied.

"Surely there must be someone," Lady Weston said. "I still don't understand what was wrong with Mr. and Mrs. Dyke."

Intrigued, Emma paused, ignoring a twinge of guilt for eavesdropping.

"They were too severe and too . . . cold."

"I think you are being purposely obstructive. You simply don't *want* to find a suitable person."

"I don't see any point in hurrying only to regret our choice later."

"Do you not? With the Smallwoods under our roof, and the Penberthys invited to visit?"

"No. And I still don't understand the need for all the secrecy."

"Nor I." Phillip's voice.

"You *ought* to understand," Lady Weston argued. "Both of you. It affects you two more than the rest of us. Why should it always fall to me to be the keeper of the Weston family honor? It ought to rest on your shoulders, Giles, or yours, Henry, as eldest son."

"As you have soundly placed it, madam," Henry said dryly. "Whether I agree or not."

*Good heavens,* Emma thought, continuing down the passage. She knew she ought not to have listened. And now that she had, she ought to forget what she heard. Instead her inquisitive mind began trying to figure out what in the world was going on. And what the secret was. Emma had guessed Lady Weston was hiding something. She had been right.

Again.

*In the Early Christian period, the Tower of
the Winds was converted for use as a chapel
or the baptistery of a nearby church.*

—Athens: From the Classical
Period to the Present Day

# Chapter 9

I t was there waiting for her when she returned to her room after
dinner the next evening. In her hurry, she almost stepped on it. She
hesitated, at first thinking it a fallen scrap of paper, one she'd used to
mark her place in the book she was reading. But as she bent to pick it
up, she saw it was a folded rectangle—another letter. Instantly, both ea-
gerness and dread filled her. Unfolding the letter with fingers not quite
steady, she took it to the window and read by evening's waning light.

*My dear Emma,*

*How sweet to be under the same roof once more. It reminds
me of our days at the Smallwood school, when you and I would
sit outside and gaze up at the stars, you reminding me of all their
names and me gazing at you. Do you recall that time I sneaked
into your room late one night? And what we did? I am thinking of
that now, as I write this note and prepare to sneak down to your
room in a few minutes. As you read this, know that I am thinking
of you. When you next see me, please acknowledge this note by
pulling on your earlobe. Your delectable earlobe.*

*W.*

Emma felt a hot flush creep up her neck. *W . . .* for Weston? Which Weston? She and Phillip had studied astronomy together, true. But the only time he had come into her room was to leave flowers on her birthday. She could not imagine either Henry or Phillip writing something so suggestive. More likely it was Julian or Rowan, playing a trick on her. But how would they know about the stargazing?

She tried to look at the handwriting objectively. It seemed to be in the same hand as the first letter. She had not seen Phillip's or Henry's handwriting in years, but she had seen Julian's and Rowan's—in their examinations and essays. The hand did not look exactly like either of theirs, she did not think. Perhaps it had been disguised somehow. Yet there was something familiar about the penmanship. What was it?

She looked at the individual letters, their shape. She noticed the *t*'s had tall ascenders and were crossed with excessively long horizontal lines that intersected the two letters to the right of it as well. But that was not so uncommon.

She decided she would take the letter up to the schoolroom in the morning and compare it to the handwriting in the assignments kept there. She tucked the letter away for the time being, and pulled out her journal.

> *Tonight I received a second unexpected missive under my door. Signed only by W. I don't know precisely how to take it. Its words are complimentary for the most part, if presumptuous. But I cannot help suspect a prank at the root of it. For once upon a time a certain Weston brother taught me to suspect even apparent acts of kindness from his hand, and old ways die hard.*
>
> *Yet, I own a small part of me wonders, dare I say hopes that the letter and its sentiments are sincere. Even I, it appears, am not immune to feminine vanity. It reminds me of the letter Aunt Jane keeps from her former admirer. I suppose it is natural for a young woman (and I am still that, though no longer in the first blush of youth) to long to receive love letters at least once in*

*her life. To experience that heart-racing rapture of romance and poetic nonsense.*

*However, in this second letter, the writer mentions an occasion when "he" sneaked into my room one night back in Longstaple. And refers to "what we did." This confuses me. For I don't recall Phillip ever coming to my room at night. Only one of my father's pupils ever dared do so.*

Emma lifted her quill and paused as the memory of that odd night returned to her. . . .

Illuminated by moonlight, Henry Weston stood a few feet from her bed, staring down at her. She was startled, of course, to awaken to find someone in her room. And once she recognized Henry Weston, she was frightened as well, for it would not be the first time he had sneaked up on her with foul intentions.

What had he in mind this time?

She lay oddly frozen, not able to call out or flee, just waiting for him to say or do something.

He stood there, hesitating. Finally he whispered, "Are you awake?"

Silently she nodded, trusting the moonlight to reveal her answer.

He took a step closer. "I leave on the morrow."

Again Emma nodded.

Another step brought him to the edge of her bed. What final prank had he planned? Did he mean to go out with a bang, a climactic culmination of all the lesser mischief of the last few years?

"Emma . . ." he whispered, face somber.

Her throat went dry. Good heavens, what did he intend to do?

But he did nothing. Instead he turned on his heel and retreated. At the door, he turned back. "I am sorry. For everything."

And he was gone.

In the morning, Emma walked down to the breakfast room feeling more anxious than usual. Would he, the letter writer, the author of *"Please acknowledge this note by pulling on your delectable earlobe,"* be watching her? She plastered on a prosaic expression and stepped inside.

Henry Weston sat alone at the table with a newspaper spread before him and a cup of coffee at his right hand. He glanced up as she entered and politely folded the paper and set it aside. "Good morning."

"Morning," she murmured and took a plate from the sideboard. She bypassed the eggs and sausages, which looked greasy and unappealing to her agitated stomach. Instead she placed a muffin and a spoonful of fruit compote on her plate. She took a seat on the opposite side of the table from Henry—not rudely distant, but not too close either.

Phillip came in, beamed at her, bowed, and then went to the sideboard. Emma's ear began to itch. Her hand was halfway to her earlobe when she felt Henry's watchful gaze. Had he written the letter after all? Her hand paused midair. Now what should she do with it? She feigned a wave at Phillip's back. "Good morning," she said belatedly and foolishly, trying to ignore the heat creeping up her neck.

Phillip turned, smiled, and echoed the greeting.

From the corner of her eye, she noticed Henry look from her face, to Phillip, and back at her. He frowned. "Are you all right, Miss Smallwood?"

"Quite all right, Mr. Weston. And you?"

"I own myself confused."

"Ah. Well. Such is life." She did not offer to enlighten him but instead sipped her tea, wishing her earlobe would cease its maddening, prickling itching. She longed to angle her head and rub it against her shoulder, but doubted she was limber enough to accomplish the feat. And how unladylike would that appear?

She set down her teacup with a *clank* and stood abruptly.

Henry's eyebrows rose. Phillip turned from his place at the sideboard.

"I find I am not hungry after all. Please excuse me."

Emma was already out the door when Phillip's hiss reached her.

"Henry," he scolded, "what did you say to her?"

"Nothing."

Emma did not pause to hear the rest of the conversation. Instead she scratched her ear and marched up the stairs, passing Julian and Rowan coming down.

"Good morning, Miss Smallwood." Julian's lips curved into a knowing grin. Had he seen her scratch her ear?

"Good morning," she replied briskly, without pause, and continued on her way to the schoolroom. There, winded, she strode directly to the desk and opened the side drawer. She sat in her father's chair and began flipping through the papers there—essays and examinations the boys had written. Within one of the essays on first-century events, the *t*'s struck her. Tall ascenders, crossed with long horizontal lines that marred the letters to the right of it. Just as in the "love letter" she had received. The name at the top of the paper?

Rowan Weston.

Emma frowned, feeling little satisfaction at the discovery. Someone might be mimicking Rowan's hand, she realized, or perhaps all of the Westons crossed their *t*'s in such a way.

Continuing her search, she next glanced through the verses she had assigned the boys to write after a lesson on classical poetry. She had yet to read them. As she skimmed through them, one brief stanza caught her eye.

> *I could gaze upon her sad green eyes*
> *And winsome figure endlessly*
> *I pretend to attend well my studies*
> *But in reality, I am studying she.*

It was signed with only—*W.*

The poem certainly seemed to be about her, but here the *t*'s were not crossed in that exaggerated fashion.

Emma was tempted to ask her father for his opinion, but she

didn't want to worry him. She thought of asking Mr. McShane about the cryptic letter, since he had known the boys, and their handwriting, far longer. But how embarrassed she would be if he laughed and assured her it must be a prank. She guessed that was the case but blushed at the thought of having the vicar declare it obvious. How mortifying that would be. No. She decided she would ask no one. She would figure it out and handle it herself. As she did most things.

She wrote objective comments on the poems and other papers, and returned them to Rowan and Julian when they entered the schoolroom a few minutes later, followed by her father.

Afraid her words—or itching ear—might give her away, Emma decided to retreat from the schoolroom.

Going outside, she wandered through the walled garden alone, glad to be apart from all possible letter writers, so she could think. She watched a tiny olive-brown warbler flitting among the branches of a flowering hawthorn, singing *chiff-chaff, chiff-chaff* and searching for insects.

A door opened and Henry Weston strode out of the house.

Emma looked away, but not before she saw Mr. Weston raise a hand in greeting. She suppressed a groan. It would be rude to pretend she had not seen him.

She waited as he crossed the garden toward her, broad shoulders squared, stride long and confident.

"Hello. It's good to see you out-of-doors," he said. "Do you mind if I speak with you a moment?"

Instant alarm flared through her. "I . . . no. Of course not."

He stepped nearer and said confidentially, "I noticed you seemed a bit . . . em . . . distracted at breakfast. Is everything all right?"

She hesitated. If he had written the letter—in jest, of course—she would not give him the satisfaction of admitting she had given it a second thought. If Phillip had written it—in sincerity—then that was her secret to relish close to her heart. And if Rowan or Julian had written it . . . Did she really want to get either young man in trouble with his stern, older half brother?

No.

"Everything is fine." She swung her gaze from his discerning eyes to the colorful garden. "I only wanted a bit of fresh air."

His gaze remained on her profile. She could feel his scrutiny.

In the distance a dog barked. An unseen insect tickled her ear, and it began to itch all over again. Still she felt him watching her.

She remembered thinking that, if she ever found herself in awkward conversation with Henry Weston, she would ask him about the chapel to fill the silence between them. She did so now.

"Might I ask, Mr. Weston, about the Chapel of the Rock? Phillip mentioned you were something of an expert in local history."

His brows rose at the sudden change of topic. "I wouldn't say 'expert,' but I am interested in history, yes."

Relieved his gaze had at last wavered from her face, she continued, "Have you ever been in the chapel?"

"Of course. Would you like to see it?"

Emma glanced at him in surprise. "Go inside, you mean?"

He nodded.

"I thought Phillip said it was unsafe."

"It is. Unless you are very familiar with the tides at every season and have become somewhat of an expert at predicting the weather—or at least at noticing the approach of storms."

Emma said, "And you are expert on both tides and the weather, I suppose?"

He pursed his lips. "I am, yes. And before you accuse me of being boastful, remember I have lived here my entire life, save my few years at Longstaple and then at Oxford."

"Phillip has lived here most of his life as well, and he has never ventured down there, I don't think."

"I believe he may have gone out there once as part of some boyhood dare, but yes, he has always been leery of the water, and I don't blame him. However, while Phillip has little interest in his environment, I am something of an enthusiast."

Yes, she did recall his interest, the books he'd read, the weathervane he'd built in Longstaple, the rain gauge he'd placed in their garden.

He gestured with his hand. "Here, come with me up to my study, and I shall prove it."

She swallowed, hesitant yet undeniably curious. "Very well."

He led the way up to the first floor and along the corridor to a room she had never entered. He opened the door and gestured her inside before him.

"You go ahead," she murmured. She hovered in the threshold as he stepped inside a modest-sized gentleman's study, lined with books and dominated by a cluttered desk.

He strode to the desk—she would have it put to rights in two shakes were it hers—and from one of several piles pulled a red leather-bound notebook. He flipped open the cover and leafed through its pages.

"Here we are. Week-by-week predictions of daily low and high tides, based on previous data and the known cycle. I've hired a local lad to report the high-water marks in the harbor. I periodically check these and revise the estimates, if necessary. Factors like spring tides or neap tides affect water levels, but barring storms, this gives me an accurate forecast of when it is safe to visit the chapel."

Emma tentatively walked over to the desk. He turned the book toward her, and she glanced at the dates and times in orderly columns with rows for estimates and actualities. *Impressive.*

"So." He looked at her expectantly. "Shall we go?"

Emma blinked. "Now?"

"Did you not say you would like to see inside?"

"Well . . . yes. If you are certain it is safe."

"Perfectly safe." He extracted his pocket watch and glanced at it. "That is, for the next four hours."

Emma followed him to the door, twisting her hands. "Should we not at least let someone know where we are going? Just in case?"

"Ever the prudent Miss Smallwood." He inhaled and drew himself up. "No. You are quite right. I shall inform my father and you inform yours." He tilted his head in thought. "And perhaps you would be more comfortable if someone accompanied us?"

Emma swallowed. "Perhaps."

He nodded. "Phillip might oblige. He seems to seek out your company at every opportunity."

Had everyone noticed? Emma wondered. "I don't know that he would enjoy going down there. Perhaps Lizzie?"

Henry shrugged. "As you like."

They found Lizzie in the drawing room, working on needlepoint chair covers with Lady Weston. Emma would not have braved entering on her own, but Henry showed no such hesitance. At Henry's invitation, Lizzie quickly agreed to accompany them, pinning her needle into the coarse fabric and rising with apparent relief.

Lady Weston's eyebrows rose over the spectacles she wore for close work. "Why anyone would want to go to that damp old place is beyond me." She looked at Lizzie shrewdly. "Unless it is to get out of work one finds tedious."

"It is only that I long for fresh air," Lizzie said. "But I shall return soon and finish. I promise."

Looking unconvinced, Lady Weston nevertheless dismissed the girl and sent her on her way.

The ladies retrieved their cloaks and bonnets and, together with Henry, left the grounds. They followed the coast path, turning at the switchback as it descended toward the fishermen's cottages, harbor, and beach below.

Lizzie accompanied them as far as the strand, but when they reached the place where the beach gave way to jutting rock, she hesitated, then stopped altogether. "You two go ahead. I shall wait for you here."

"Do come, Lizzie," Emma urged, reluctant to go out alone with Henry. "Mr. Weston says it is perfectly safe. And it is such a fine day—barely a cloud in sight."

Lizzie looked out at the ancient chapel. The sun glinted off the choppy water, causing her eyes to squint into mere slits. The wind was stronger beside the sea and blew thin coils of black hair across her face.

"No, that's all right," she said. "You two go on. I'll be all right here on my own."

"Very well. We shall meet you back here shortly," Henry said, and gestured for Emma to precede him.

With a last beseeching look at Lizzie, Emma turned and stepped out onto the rocky peninsula. It rose several feet above water level and was dry and sound. She kept her eyes focused on the uneven rocks, making sure of her footing. She did not wish to trip and make a fool of herself in front of the man behind her. The wind, though not overly strong, made all but the most basic conversation difficult, and Emma decided to save her questions until they arrived.

The chapel had been built upon a level of rocks several feet higher than the path they now trod. A series of rock steps, worn narrow and slick by time and waves, led up to the higher level. Passing her, Henry loped up the few stairs, then reached back down to offer a hand.

She ignored it. "I can manage. Thank you." She lifted her skirt hems slightly so she would not trip and carefully navigated the steps.

Reaching the top, she paused, gazing up at the tall sandstone octagon with a wooden door and a cross on its roof.

Henry said, "The original door rotted away years ago. I replaced it with this one myself."

"Yourself?"

"Well, the estate carpenter helped me hang it. It's a two-man job."

"I'm surprised you would know how to do such a thing."

"You would be surprised by many things about me, I think."

For a moment she met his gaze, wondering what he meant. Then self-consciousness crept in, and she returned her gaze to the building. "I feel as though I have seen something like this before."

He nodded. "It was built to resemble Greece's Tower of the Winds."

"Ah. Yes," Emma said. "I have seen drawings in Father's books. But why would anyone build a chapel here?"

"Hundreds of years ago, this was part of a larger seaside church," Henry explained. "A chapel-of-ease for the local people, where the vicar from Stratton would hold services once a month. But the years and the waves eroded all but this side chapel and the peninsula we're standing on. The village council plans to reinforce and extend the causeway into a more effective breakwater, and the surveyor proposes pulling this old place down to accomplish it. But I hate to see it go."

At that, Henry lifted the latch and opened the door.

"It isn't kept locked?" Emma asked.

He shook his head. "I have the key in my study, but I don't think it right to lock the door, as though I own the place. It belongs to the whole village, though I seem to be the only person who comes here with any regularity." He preceded her inside, as if to demonstrate his confidence in the safety of entering.

Tentatively, she stepped in after him. She hoped this wasn't one of his tricks and resolved to remain between him and the door. Her half boots scraped against the paving-stone floor. The interior was cool and dim but not dark. Sunlight sliced into the tower from four narrow slit windows—in every other of the eight stone walls. She glanced around the octagon, perhaps twenty-five feet across. At the far end stood a modest, moldering altar and the remnants of a few sagging, rotting pews. To one side of the altar stood an old baptismal font—a stout waist-high pillar with a recessed basin for christening babies. In the wall behind the font, Emma saw the outline of an arched doorway now bricked over and sealed.

Henry followed the direction of her gaze. "That doorway led to the nave before it was washed away."

Emma nodded her understanding. She stepped to one of the high open windows—the one facing west—and craned her neck to peer out at the sea beyond. It gave one a feeling of lostness, of panic, seeing no land. Just endless miles of sea.

From behind her, Henry said, "History has it that in the fifteenth century, a monk lived here. He kept a fire constantly burning in this window to warn boats of the rocks beneath."

Emma shivered involuntarily, thinking a fire sounded very good at the moment. She moved away to inspect the font instead.

Henry continued, "The monk lived here well into his nineties, long after the chapel had fallen out of church use. Then came a day when fishermen foretold of a terrible storm coming. They warned the monk, but he refused to leave. The fishermen were right, as it turns out. Ebford was hit by the worst winter storm known before or since. The sea rose and covered the causeway, and the water became too rough for any boat to reach him. They say that old monk did not fight his fate. He calmly kept his light burning as long as he could, ready to meet his maker. The rest of the church was washed away, and the monk with it. Only this tower remained."

Emma shivered again, and Mr. Weston noticed.

"You're cold. Here, take this."

He began to peel off his greatcoat, but she stayed him with a hand to his sleeve. "Don't. I'm fine."

Realizing she had touched him, she snatched back her hand and forced a chuckle. "It is only your gruesome story."

"I don't find it gruesome at all. I admire that old monk. This was his home, and he was devoted to it. This is where he worshiped God and served mankind. He lived a long, full life and died without fear, knowing heaven awaited him."

Emptiness gnawed at Emma. Could *she* face death without fear? If she were to show up at heaven's door tomorrow, would God even recognize her, when it had been so long since she'd bothered to call on Him?

Henry stepped to the west-facing window she had abandoned and looked out. "I like coming here to think now and again. To pray. Sometimes looking through these windows, I see more clearly. And am able to focus on what is truly important."

Emma turned to look at him, surprised by his earnest words. "And what is truly important, in your view?"

He glanced at her, gave a sardonic chuckle, and then returned his gaze to the sea. "I don't presume you'd care to hear it."

"I would."

For several moments he said nothing, and she began to think he would not answer. Then he said quietly, "Each of these four windows faces one of the cardinal points of the compass." He pointed to the window to the right. "When I face north I think of God, the Almighty, the North Star. When I face east, I see the village and think of the people who live and work there. My duty toward them. And when I look south, toward Ebbington Manor, I think of the family God has given me, with all its blessings and trials. . . ."

His words trailed away, and he seemed lost in thought.

Emma prompted, "And west?"

He made no answer, simply staring out at the sea beyond. She thought he had not heard her, or had no intention of answering. But then he said, as if to himself, "All my life might have been."

Emma blinked. Had she heard him correctly? How had Henry Weston, heir to Ebbington Manor, been disappointed in life? Unsure of what to say, she instead glanced up at the figures carved above each window. She knew her Greek mythology. She had even taught a course on it last year in her father's stead.

She gestured to the largest winged figure. "That is Boreas, the Greek god of the north wind. His three brothers are . . ." She pointed to the second figure, then the next, pivoting as she faced each direction. "Zephyrus, the west wind. Notus, the south wind. And Eurus, the east wind."

Henry nodded. "That's right. Your father taught us Greek mythology when I was in Longstaple."

Emma's mind was busy recalling what she'd read on the subject. "Unlike the kind Zephyrus, Boreas was known for his fierce character and terrible storms. But when Boreas fell in love with the beautiful Oreithyia, he left behind his fierce character to win her over."

"Stuff and nonsense, of course," Henry said with a sardonic grin.

But Emma paid him no heed, suddenly struck by an ironic thought. She said, "Four brothers. And four very different Weston brothers. How interesting."

He scowled. "Not true."

Her head reared back. "Which part?"

He made no answer, but his scowl remained.

Emma said evenly, "I did not mean to imply that I saw in you the fierce character of the north wind."

He crossed his arms over his chest and slanted her a dark look. "Did you not?"

She lifted her chin. "I have not had sufficient time to determine which brother best matches the character of each wind."

He pulled a face. "I would not waste your time. Besides, we both know which of us you view as the kind Zephyrus."

*True,* Emma thought. But she deemed it wiser to neither confirm nor deny his supposition. Instead she drew herself up and consulted her chatelaine watch. "Well, I had better be getting back. I usually help my father tidy the schoolroom about this time." Actually, she had plenty of time to return, but she was suddenly eager to leave the tower and return to the open skies.

"Very well."

Remembering her resolve, Emma led the way to the door, lifted the latch, and opened it, allowing light and breeze to enter, and tension to flee.

Emma started picking her way toward the stairs. A light sunshower began to fall, making the rocks slick.

"Miss Smallwood, wait."

She turned as Henry shut the door and obliged by waiting for him to join her.

He reached her side and offered his hand. "Please. Allow me."

This time, she hesitated only an instant before placing her gloved hand in his.

He helped her down the stairs, and together they crossed the causeway. Emma wondered if it was her imagination or if the water surged nearer the walkway than it had on their way out. Either way, she was relieved to step back onto the sand.

Looking up, she saw Lizzie talking to a man on the beach. A man too well dressed to be a passing fisherman. As they neared, Emma recognized him as the red-haired man who had spoken to her on the point, and in Mr. Davies's office.

Emma wondered if Lizzie knew him or if he had taken it upon himself to strike up a conversation as he had with her. Emma certainly hoped she and Henry had not exposed Lizzie to harassment by leaving her alone. Yet Lizzie's posture as she stood near the man spoke of familiarity. Though perhaps not a friendly familiarity, for both wore somber expressions.

Lizzie glanced up at them, and for a moment her face fell, as if chagrined to be found with the man. She had obviously not seen them coming. But in the next second Emma wondered if she had only imagined the expression, for Lizzie brightened, smiled, and waved. She walked abruptly away from the man, hurrying over to meet them.

"I am so glad to see you two. You were gone an age."

"Are you all right?" Emma asked. "Was that man bothering you?"

"Him? Heavens no." She flopped her hand in a dismissive gesture. "We were just passing the time."

Emma glanced at Henry and noted the tightening of his jaw. Perhaps he did not approve of Lizzie speaking with the man either.

He asked, "What did Teague want with you?"

Lizzie gave him a look of surprise. "Do you know him?"

"I know *of* him. And if half of what is said of him is true, I don't . . . But I should not malign a man I barely know."

Lizzie looked at him shrewdly. "I believe you just did."

"You're quite right. I beg your pardon," Henry said. "Shall we go?"

He offered an elbow to Lizzie, then turned and offered his other arm to Emma. Together they began the long walk back up the steep cliffside path.

When Henry joined his family in the drawing room before dinner that evening, Lady Weston, in a low-cut evening gown better suited to a younger woman, turned on the settee to regard him.

"I must say I was surprised to see you walking arm in arm with Miss Smallwood this afternoon. I would expect such a thing of Phillip, perhaps, all harmless flirtation and boyish charm. But you . . . ? Good heavens."

Henry frowned and glanced at Phillip, seated behind Lady Weston. Phillip lifted his hand in a helpless gesture but said nothing.

Nearby, Julian and Rowan shared knowing grins.

Forcing a neutral expression and casual tone, Henry said, "If you were watching from the window, my lady, then you no doubt saw that I had offered an arm to both Miss Smallwood *and* Lizzie. Considering the rain and slippery footing, I thought it the gentlemanly thing to do."

Lizzie spoke up. "That's right, my lady. Henry offered us each an arm on the way back from the chapel. Very gentlemanlike, I'm sure."

Sir Giles lowered his glass. "The chapel? Good heavens. What were you doing down there?"

"Showing it to Miss Smallwood. She wanted to see it."

"Yes . . ." Lizzie nodded, appearing distracted. Henry noticed she did not mention she hadn't gone inside with them, nor her conversation with Derrick Teague.

Phillip said, "Are you certain that was wise, Henry? It isn't safe."

"Perfectly safe. I checked the tide tables first, of course."

Sir Giles nodded, and swirled the brandy in his glass. "Just so, my boy. Very proper."

Lady Weston smiled thinly. "Be that as it may, we would not want Miss Smallwood to misconstrue an innocent act of mere chivalry, would we?"

Henry was tempted to ask what she thought of Phillip's far warmer behavior toward Emma but held back the petty comment.

Julian, however, showed no such restraint, saying, "I'm surprised you are not more concerned about Phillip, Mamma. He's far more friendly with Miss Smallwood than Henry is."

"Of course I am," Phillip said. Then, with a glance at Lady Weston's disapproving face, added, "We are old friends."

Lady Weston inclined her head and replied as if Phillip had not spoken. "I cannot say I'd look kindly upon an alliance between any Weston and the tutor's daughter, but worse for Henry, as the eldest son."

Henry grimaced. "Eldest . . . Really?"

Sir Giles cleared his throat. The footman pulled opened the door, announced dinner was served, and the matter was dropped.

But, Henry knew, not forgotten.

*Govern thy life and thoughts as if the whole*
*world were to see the one, and read the other.*

—Thomas Fuller, seventeenth-
century author and preacher

# Chapter 10

Before blowing out her bedside candle that night, Emma pulled out her journal, hoping to put her thoughts about the visit to the chapel, and the unexpected conversation with Mr. Weston, into perspective.

> *I confess myself astonished. Who would have guessed such serious, thought-provoking words could emerge from Henry Weston? Not I! I actually enjoyed my outing with him and Lizzie today—except for the uncomfortable moment when we came upon her speaking with that strange man.*
>
> *And my mind is still engaged with the interesting if futile question of which Weston brother is most like each of the four winds. Henry is cold Boreas, to be sure, though I denied thinking it when he asked. And yes, kind Phillip very well suits the image of mild, friendly Zephyrus.*
>
> *But what about Notus, the south wind who brings heat and fog, who means well but occasionally blows overzealously? And which is Eurus, the east wind with his violent and disorderly personality who likes to create storms?*
>
> *Is Rowan, mature for his age and perhaps the author of a*

*love letter in jest, more like Notus or Eurus? And what of boyish, talented Julian?*

*Of course there is no logical reason the four Weston brothers should represent the four winds, but I find I rather like the notion. I will continue to observe the brothers and draw my own conclusions.*

The following morning, a Sunday, Emma found herself alone at breakfast. Her father, Sir Giles, and Henry Weston had already eaten and returned to their rooms, according to the footman she'd asked. Her father and Sir Giles were both early risers, so an early breakfast for them was commonplace. But she was rather surprised to hear Henry Weston had already eaten and taken his leave. She hoped he hadn't eaten early to avoid her.

She was taking her last sip of tea when Phillip and Julian entered together, dressed in Sunday best, laughing and joking about something. Rowan followed after, quiet and brooding. Perhaps he shared his eldest brother's temperament more than she'd originally thought.

Phillip greeted her with his customary warmth. Julian with polite interest. And Rowan with a mumbled "Morning" that sounded little more than a grunt. She thought again of the letter and Rowan's crossed *t*'s. If Rowan's apparent indifference to her was an act to cover a secret calf love, he was certainly convincing. More likely, she'd been wrong about the handwriting.

"We heard you went down to the chapel yesterday," Julian said, eyes alight. "What did you think of the old place?"

"I found it quite fascinating, actually," Emma said, studying each brother surreptitiously, still formulating her four-brothers/four-winds theory.

"Did it not frighten you, being surrounded by all that water?" Phillip gave a little shudder.

"A little, yes. But it was worth it."

"I am surprised Henry could be prevailed upon to lead such an expedition," Phillip mused. "He was his usual stern self, I trust?"

She looked at Phillip over the rim of her teacup with a small smile, not sure how to describe how Henry had been. Or even if she wanted to try.

"What's put that secret smile on your face?" Phillip asked, a teasing light in his eyes. "Don't tell me Henry was actually pleasant company."

"He was," Emma allowed. "Very knowledgeable."

Julian said, "What did you do out there all that time—that's what I'd like to know." He leaned back in his chair and watched her face with a knowing smirk. "Lizzie said the two of you were alone out there for quite some time."

"Oh?" Phillip asked, clearly surprised. "And what did you find to talk about with our laconic Henry?"

"Greek mythology, mostly," Emma said casually, wanting to end any romance rumors before they might begin. "I found it very interesting."

"You would," Rowan muttered.

Emma noted Rowan's foul mood with interest, and then glanced at inquisitive Julian.

Regarding her, Phillip slowly shook his head, a bemused smile playing on his lips. "How you look at us. If I didn't know better, I'd guess you were plotting something."

"Me?" Emma asked, all wide-eyed innocence. "Not a bit of it."

The truth was she was doing one of her favorite things. Beginning a course of study on a new subject. Or in this case, four subjects.

After breakfast, Emma returned to her room, eager to add her latest observations about the brothers into her journal. She still had half an hour before it was time to leave for church. She glanced about, surprised not to see the green leather volume on her side table, where she thought she'd left it. Had she put it in the drawer instead, wanting to conceal it after writing personal things about the Westons? She dug through the drawer but found no journal among her handkerchiefs and other belongings. Then she sifted through the volumes stacked atop the side table. Not there.

Had it fallen? Emma looked under the bed, under the table,

among the books atop the dressing chest. Nothing. She looked atop the washstand. At the bottom of the wardrobe. Nothing.

She stopped, pressing her eyes closed in concentration. Where had she put it? Had she taken it up to the schoolroom? No. Down to the breakfast room? Never.

Her stomach twisted in mounting panic. She, who had a place for everything and put everything in its place, had not mislaid it. Not something so personal and private.

*Heaven help me.*

Someone had taken her journal.

She stood stock-still as a chill passed over her. Who would have done such a thing? A nosy maid? Unlikely. Lizzie? She had seemed curious about it, but Emma did not want to believe Lizzie capable of such a breach of privacy. One of the boys? She did not think it wise to accuse anyone, especially not Lady Weston's sons.

She rang for Morva a second time, which she had never done before.

The maid entered ten minutes later, flushed and rushed. "You rang, miss?"

"Yes. I am sorry to disturb you, but I didn't know where to find you this time of morning. I am wondering if you happened to see my journal—a green leather book about so big? It isn't where I left it."

"No, miss." Morva's eyes widened. "I didn't take it, if that's what 'ee think."

"No, of course not. Why should you? I only hoped you'd seen it when you tidied up."

"No, miss. But if I do see it, I shall let 'ee knaw directly."

Emma thanked the offended maid and distractedly began gathering her pelisse, bonnet, and gloves. It was almost time to depart for church.

She went downstairs, heart hammering, afraid to ask, but more afraid of remaining silent while another person read her most private thoughts.

The family was gathering in the entry hall, awaiting the carriages and carts that would deliver them to Stratton. Sir Giles and her father stood speaking in low tones. Lizzie stood talking with Julian, Rowan, and Phillip. Lady Weston came down the stairs a minute or so after Emma, resplendent in an ivory gown with a high neck of lace, a red cape with stand-up collar, and matching hat with jaunty feather. Only Henry was not among them. She would not have a better opportunity.

Glancing around the assembly, Emma resolved to keep her tone casual, took a deep breath, and asked, "Has anyone seen my journal? It seems to have gone missing. Green leather. Quarto sized?"

Her father asked, "Have you searched your room, my dear?"

"Of course. It is not there. I think someone might have . . . inadvertently . . . taken it."

Lady Weston frowned. "Taken it? How silly, Miss Smallwood. No one took your journal. You simply misplaced it. That is all. These things happen all the time."

Lizzie added with a wink, "Probably lost among your many books Morva complains of having to dust."

Julian wagged his eyebrows. "Or the Ebbington ghost took it. Quite the greedy thief, that ghost."

"Now, Julian," Lady Weston said tolerantly. "I know you are only teasing, but really. Ebbington Manor is *not* haunted."

"Only the north wing," Rowan whispered to his brother.

Emma overheard him. But no ghost had taken her journal.

"I wish it back," she said in uncharacteristic sharpness. "I don't care to cast blame. I just want it back. It is, after all, my personal property. Not meant for anyone else to read."

"Full of juicy secrets, is it?" Julian asked, eyes glinting. "About you? Or about all of us?"

"Perhaps I shall have to track down this ghost and claim the journal myself," Rowan said. "Sounds like interesting reading."

Emma lifted her chin. "I assure you, you would find it frightfully dull."

"Your blush tells a different tale." Julian smirked.

Phillip sighed. "If one of you has taken Miss Smallwood's journal, pray return it this very day."

"Why do you accuse one of us?" Julian complained.

Phillip began, "I am not accusing—"

But Lady Weston cut him off. "Phillip, you know very well my boys would never do such a thing. Why should they care a fig about the scratchings of a woman they barely know? I must ask you to apologize."

"Now, my dear," Sir Giles gently interceded, "I don't think Phillip meant any harm. He is only trying to come to Miss Smallwood's aid." Sir Giles looked at Emma kindly. "I shall have a word with Mrs. Prowse. Ask the staff to keep a sharp look out for it. Green leather, you say? Never fear—we shall find it."

Emma felt uneasy. "I don't wish to put anyone to extra trouble."

"A bit late for that," Rowan muttered, and he and his brother shared a private chuckle.

Emma felt indignant and embarrassed both. The conversation had certainly not gone as she'd hoped, and she dreaded having to go through the same awkward explanations with Henry when next she saw him.

After the service concluded, Lizzie walked beside Emma through St. Andrew's churchyard, entwining her arm through hers. Emma took pleasure from the act of warm companionship. She'd had so few female friends in her life.

"I hope you don't think I took your journal," Lizzie said in a vulnerable little voice.

It had crossed her mind, but Emma suddenly felt guilty for the disloyal thought. "I don't mean to accuse *anyone*, Lizzie. I simply wish it back."

Lizzie squeezed her arm. "Of course you do. I cannot imagine how you must feel. You didn't write anything too embarrassing, I hope."

Emma sighed. "It isn't that I wrote anything so terribly embarrassing. But I certainly never meant for any of it to be read by anyone else."

"Then why write in the first place?" Lizzie asked. "Seems like a lot of time and bother. I recall when my old schoolmistress made me write a long letter all over again, so I might learn to write more neatly. And what did I gain for my trouble? A pain in my neck and ink-stained fingers."

Emma chuckled. "I enjoy writing in my journal. It's like having a very close friend with whom I can share my thoughts without fear of censure."

"Why not tell a real friend?" Lizzie looked at her and asked gently, "Have you no friends, Miss Smallwood?"

"Not really. Not growing up in a boys' school."

Lizzie nodded. "You were probably more accomplished and clever than the other girls. Which made them jealous. And, I imagine, intimidated the boys at the same time."

Emma felt tears prick her eyes at Lizzie's insight. She inhaled deeply and turned away from the girl's direct gaze. "If so, it was never my intention. There were times I would have traded years of book-learning for one honest-to-goodness friend."

She sensed Lizzie's look of surprise in her peripheral vision but kept her own face turned away. She had surprised herself with the admission. Embarrassed herself too.

Lizzie squeezed her arm once more. When Emma dared glance over, she glimpsed tears sparkling in Lizzie Henshaw's eyes.

"I shall be your friend," she whispered. "If you'll have me."

❧

The rest of Sunday passed slowly. A roast beef dinner with Mr. Davies and her father. A letter to Aunt Jane. A thorough search of the house by Morva and Mrs. Prowse—to no avail. The housekeeper promised to conduct a search of the washhouse as well in case the journal had gotten into the laundry somehow.

Emma resigned herself to wait. Or so she told herself. Inwardly, she paced and worried, cringing every time she recalled something she had written about Lizzie or one of the Westons, imagining the reaction of the reader, whoever he or she might be.

She didn't see Henry Weston all day. And she fought against the nagging image that kept forming in her mind: of him ensconced in a public house somewhere with candle lamp and pint, reading page after page of her journal. Perhaps even reading bits aloud to his companions, all of them guffawing over her foolish feminine trifles, the pitiful thoughts and dreams of a bluestocking on her way to becoming a spinster. Emma shuddered at the thought.

In the evening, while searching her room yet again, Emma came across the small wooden chess set she had brought with her to Ebbington Manor, figuring she and her father would need some amusement to help them pass solitary evenings. But they had yet to use it. Her father evidently preferred to spend evenings in the company of Sir Giles, Henry, or one of his many books.

The old set was incomplete. The white queen had been missing for many years—since Henry Weston's days at Longstaple. She'd always suspected he'd taken it.

Whenever she and her father had played at home, they'd substituted a small figurine of a lady in court dress. A gift her mother had received as a girl, after her own presentation at court. But Emma had not wanted to risk breaking the delicate porcelain figurine and had left it at home, thinking she would find some suitable replacement once at Ebbington Manor. Now she selected a thimble from among her things. It would suffice, though some of the elegance of the game would be lost with it.

She found her father and asked him to play, thinking it would distract her. Since Henry had not appeared for their nightly backgammon match, her father agreed. They set up the pieces on the small table between two cushioned chairs in her father's room, which was quite a bit larger than her own.

He smiled thoughtfully at her. "This reminds me of all those times you and Henry played chess back at home."

Emma made her opening move, sliding a white pawn forward two squares. "That was a long time ago. And he was certainly not a very cheerful opponent, I can tell you."

"It was difficult for him," her father said. "The first of his family to be sent away to school. I believe he was homesick." He moved his own pawn forward. "I remember he became especially cross when the other boys received letters from home. He so rarely did. Now and again Sir Giles would scratch a few lines, but not often."

Emma glanced fondly at her father. "You always did make allowances for him, Papa."

He nodded. "I understood him, I suppose. I was the first in my family to be sent away as well. You can be thankful you have little notion of what that's like, Emma—being sent off alone, from all you've known, at a tender age."

Emma doubted Henry Weston had ever been *tender* but refrained from saying so. They played for several minutes longer, but it was obvious her father was having difficulty concentrating.

He sat back, wincing. "I am sorry, my dear. It's this dashed headache."

She studied his face in concern. "You ought to have said so, Papa. We needn't have played." She began sliding the pieces back into the box. "May I bring you anything?"

"No, sleep is all I want."

"Are you certain? You have been doing so well since we arrived. . . ."

"Don't fret, Emma. It is only a headache, I promise you. Not a harbinger of one of my black moods."

"I didn't mean . . ." She let the words trail away. It was what she had been thinking. She said instead, "It has been a great pleasure to see you thriving here, Papa."

His eyes sparkled, despite his pain. "We were right to come, weren't we?"

"Yes," she agreed. It didn't solve the problem of what they would do when they returned home, but she had no wish to add to his headache.

"I shall check on you later. Good night, Papa. Sleep well." She kissed his brow and let herself from the room.

In her own bedchamber, Emma tried reading and list writing to distract herself but could concentrate on neither. She gave up and decided to go to bed early as well, hoping to escape into the forgetfulness of sleep. She rang for Morva, who came in nearly a quarter of an hour later, muttering about how they were all running behind these days, what with Mrs. Prowse so often busy abovestairs.

"Have you seen Henry Weston this evening?" Emma asked as Morva hung up her gown. Noticing a flicker of interest in the housemaid's eye, Emma hastened to add, "He is the only one of the family I have not yet asked about my journal. I have not seen him all day."

"As a matter of fact, I heard he just come home. Michael—he's the groom—was called out to tend to his horse a few minutes ago."

Emma nodded. "Thank you."

Morva returned and began unlacing Emma's stays. Now Emma regretted getting undressed. She couldn't very well go down and demand the return of her journal in her nightclothes.

After Morva left her, Emma pulled a wrapper over her nightdress and slipped down the passage, thinking only to check on her father and see if he needed anything for his headache. But hearing voices from the floor below, she crept past her father's room to the top of the stairwell.

Sir Giles's voice. "Any success, my boy?"

"Perhaps. I'll need to check his background first. Find out more about his character and conduct. I think I'll ask Mr. Bray what he knows about him."

"My goodness, Henry," Lady Weston said. "The man's not running for political office."

"There is every reason to be cautious, madam. To choose wisely."

"Well, then do so. As long as you choose before the Penberthys arrive."

It was the second time Emma had heard the Westons talking about a potential candidate. She wondered what position they were hiring for and why Henry had been tasked with the duty. A new valet, perhaps, or man of business? Whatever the case, she would have to wait until the next day to ask Henry about her journal.

She returned to her father's door, opened it a crack, heard his soft snore, and closed it once more.

At breakfast on Monday morning, Emma saw no sign of Henry Weston. After she ate a few bites she barely tasted, she went directly to the schoolroom, hoping to immerse herself in some productive pursuit to subjugate concerns about her journal. At least for a while.

When she entered, she was surprised to see Rowan already in the room, bent over a sketchbook, drawing pencil in hand.

"Might I see what you are drawing, Rowan?" Emma asked.

He shut the sketchbook and leaned back in his chair. "We all have our secrets, Miss Smallwood."

"Oh. Well, if your sketches are private, you needn't show me."

He thrust the sketchbook toward her. "Only joking, Miss Smallwood."

Uncomfortable now, she hesitantly accepted the sketchbook. Her father and Julian came in, and Emma feigned a smile and greeted them both. She carried the sketchbook to the small table she'd placed near the dormer window, set apart from the boys' table and her father's desk. Her own little space to read and review assignments.

There, she opened the sketchbook. She didn't know what she had been expecting, but it had not been this. His sketches were really quite good. Landscapes mostly, of the rocky coastline, of the harbor framed by jutting cliffs, of Ebbington Manor itself. And finally, several sketches of the Chapel of the Rock. Rowan had captured not only the detail and perspective, but also the lonely, mysterious mood of the place, with the grey sky and foaming sea behind.

Her father assigned the boys a passage to read. He then excused himself to return to his room for a volume he'd forgotten. Emma offered to go in his stead, but he insisted it would be easier if he went himself, for he knew right where it was. Did he fear she might lose the book as she had "lost" her journal?

When her father had left, Emma glanced over at Rowan and found him watching her. He ducked his head, feigning interest in the passage he was supposed to be reading.

"These are very good, Rowan," she said. "I am impressed."

He looked up, self-conscious pleasure for a moment overtaking his usual sarcastic nature. He looked younger. More like Julian. He bit his lip, trying to hide a smile.

Emma asked, "Who taught you to draw?"

Julian piped up. "No one taught him. He's a natural."

Rowan shook his head. "I did have a few lessons from that drawing master."

"Before he ran off with the governess, you mean. All that man taught us was how to flirt with older women."

Emma tried not to react to the inappropriate comment, steering the conversation back toward art. "Do you draw as well, Julian?"

Julian shrugged. "Nothing to Rowan here. He's the only one in the family with any true artistic ability."

Rowan frowned at his brother. "No. Did you not see—"

"Shut up, Rowan. Henry's sketches hardly count. You are too modest. I've always said so."

*Henry's sketches?* She didn't recall Henry or Phillip displaying any particular artistic skill.

But her father returned at that moment, and her chance to inquire further had passed.

He said, "All right, gentlemen. I trust you have read the assigned passage and are ready to state your views?"

The young men exchanged looks of exasperated injustice.

Emma spoke up. "I am afraid we began talking of other things. Art and such. My fault, Father. Might you give them a bit more time to read?"

He pulled a face. "Oh, very well. But please try not to distract my pupils, Emma."

Emma felt her ears heat to be corrected by her father. Especially in front of Rowan and Julian. But when she risked a glance at the boys to see if they were smirking, she saw Rowan bent diligently over his text and Julian looking at her with empathy.

He mouthed, "Thank you."

And she felt better immediately.

Emma did not see Henry Weston the rest of that day. How long did it take to check a candidate's character and qualifications—whatever the job? The only news came from Mrs. Prowse, who reported nothing had been found in the laundry. Biting back a groan, Emma resolved to push the matter from her mind, reminding herself worry never solved a single problem.

That night, when she returned to her room after dinner, she found a cheerful fire snapping in her hearth.

*Thank you, Morva,* she thought. Emma wondered if the warm fire was a guilt offering. Perhaps Lizzie had confessed she'd let slip the maid's complaints about having to dust Emma's many books.

Emma took a tinder from atop the mantel and tipped it into the flames. This she used to light her bedside candle. She sat wearily on the edge of her bed, slid the shoes from her feet, and bent to remove her stockings. That's when she saw it. Stocking forgotten, she leaned forward. There in her bedside stack of books, a flash of green caught her eye. Midway through the pile, a green leather cover stuck out askew from the otherwise straight stack. She rose quickly, lifted the other volumes, and revealed the cover in all its familiar glory. She ran her fingers over the grainy surface, to assure herself it was real.

She picked it up, opened the cover, saw the inscribed starting date and her name in her own hand. Relief rushed through her. *Thank you!* she thought, not pausing to consider whom she was thanking.

The relief was quickly followed by a sour tangle of less pleasant emotions—had it been there all along? Had she simply misplaced it, as Lady Weston asserted? Had she blamed Lizzie, Julian, Rowan, Henry, even Morva in her heart and all but accused someone of stealing something that had been there all along? Mortification heated her neck and curdled her stomach. She would have to apologize. Admit she had been wrong—that somehow she had overlooked it there on her bedside table. She did have a great deal of books. Though it was very unlike her to leave the stack disorderly, Morva might have jostled the pile while doing the dreaded dusting or, in a subtle act of rebellion, left the stack in disarray.

Emma detested the thought of having to admit she had been wrong. But she would.

She flipped through the journal, skimming the entries with two minds: one, relief that perhaps no one had read these private words after all, and two, how embarrassed she would be if someone had read and returned the journal. But to take it and return it the next day? It hardly seemed worth the trouble. Perhaps her impassioned plea yesterday morning had affected its hearers more than she'd believed.

Suddenly Emma stopped. She reread the last line at the bottom of the left-hand page, then moved up to the first line of the next— a new, unrelated sentence. Her heart began beating oddly. Nerves jangling, she bent the binding open more widely, peering into the inner spine. Yes, faint ragged edges remained.

A page was missing.

Someone *had* taken her journal, as she'd thought. Taken and returned it. But not before they had torn out a page.

Good heavens . . . Why in the world would anyone do that?

She tried to recall what she had written on that page—both sides of the missing page. . . .

She read the last few lines before the torn page once more.

*I am very much enjoying conversing with Phillip Weston again. In his company, the intervening years fly and we speak with the camaraderie of old friends. Yet at the same time, I am very aware that he is a boy no longer. Still, I found it surprising he was reluctant to venture out to the Chapel of the Rock.*

*How different he is than his brother Henry. . . .*

*Oh no.* She had been writing about Phillip and Henry Weston, comparing the two. How each had changed since she had seen him last. Her pleasure at spending time with Phillip again. Her surprise at Henry Weston's words within the chapel. Perhaps even her strangely pleasant reaction to putting her hand in his . . .

She squeezed her eyes shut and groaned aloud. "Oh no . . ." Who had the page now, and why had he or she taken it—for what purpose? Emma looked at the page after the missing one, and read the first line.

> *Not that I have any romantic feelings for Phillip Weston. It is only a relief to have a friend here at Ebbington Manor.*

Irony soured her mouth. Of course, that line would be separate. Without it—out of context—she feared how what she had written on that loose page might be misconstrued.

In the morning, Emma rose early and, after Morva helped her dress, went in search of Phillip. She longed to speak to a friend, and not with an audience. But when she peeked into the breakfast room, she glimpsed only Julian, Rowan, her father, and Sir Giles within. Where would Phillip be at this hour? Still abed? Or had he gone for an early ride with Henry?

She turned, crossed the hall, and stood at the front windows, looking out through the wavy glass past the drive and into the garden beyond. There she was surprised to see Phillip standing beside a shaped yew talking with Lizzie. A minute later, the girl turned and stalked away. Had they quarreled?

Lizzie passed by the front of the house on her way to the side door. Hoping to speak to Phillip alone, Emma stepped outside.

As she crossed the drive, Henry came sauntering over from the stables, riding boots gleaming with each confident stride. His tousled wavy hair danced over his collar and across his forehead in the breeze.

Now what? Should she turn back? But a glance at Phillip told her he had already seen her.

Phillip lifted a hand in greeting. "Hello, Miss Smallwood. Any sign of your journal?"

Was it odd that he should ask about it? Had he some reason to know it had been returned? *Now, Emma,* she corrected herself. *He is merely showing polite concern.*

She stepped nearer. "Yes, actually."

His brows rose. "Excellent. Where did it turn up?"

"In my room."

"Ah. There all along, was it? Not like the champion of order to mislay something." He winked, then patted her shoulder. "Don't feel bad. We all of us misplace things from time to time."

"That's what I thought at first. But then I discovered a page is missing."

Henry joined them as she spoke the words.

Phillip nodded to acknowledge his presence, then looked back at Emma. "Fell out, did it?"

"No," she insisted. "Someone tore it out."

From the corner of her eye, she noticed Henry frown.

Phillip rocked back on his heels, chewing his lip in thought. "I don't suppose it would be gentlemanlike to ask what was written on that page?"

*You will only make it worse by blushing and faltering*, she warned herself, uncomfortable with both brothers staring at her. *Speak matter-of-factly. There is nothing for you to be embarrassed about.* Even as she admonished herself, she felt her cheeks heat and struggled for words. "I . . . No. It was nothing. Just . . . observations."

Phillip grinned. "About what? Or shall I say . . . whom?"

Henry Weston crossed his arms, brow furrowed. "Someone tore a page from your journal?"

"Yes. The journal was taken from my room, then returned last night, minus one page."

At her words, Henry's thin nose belled out into flaring nostrils. Ah yes, she remembered those flaring nostrils. And the anger darkening his green eyes.

He asked, "When did you first notice the journal missing?"

"Sunday morning. Before we left for church."

"Was it there before you went down to breakfast?"

"I am not certain. But I wrote in it the night before, so I know it was there then."

"Julian blamed the Ebbington ghost," Phillip quipped.

Henry's earnest gaze remained fixed on Emma, ignoring his brother's comment. "I am very sorry this happened, Miss Smallwood. I will do everything in my power to see that your missing page is returned and such a thing never happens again."

"How on earth can you do that?" Phillip asked, incredulity ringing in his tone. "Unless, perhaps, you know who took it?"

Henry hesitated, then pierced his brother with a look. "I have an idea." With that he turned and strode away, greatcoat billowing in his wake.

*I beg your pardon that I did not write to*
*you from Tunis . . . but the heat there was so*
*excessive, and the light so bad for the sight,*
*I was half blind by writing one letter!*

—Lady Mary Wortley Montagu, 1718

# Chapter 11

Henry had felt guilty walking through each of his brother's rooms, looking on tabletops and in drawers for the missing journal page. Two of the bedchambers had been occupied when he'd gone in. One brother had given him a look of confusion during his search, the other a sullen glare. He did not bother to explain what he was looking for and was relieved not to find it. Granted, he had not torn the rooms apart in an exhaustive search. The most likely culprit would probably not have bothered to hide it well. Giving up, Henry returned to his own room.

He did not often allow himself to withdraw the cigar box from the bottom of his wardrobe. He had to stop and think before he could recall the last time he had examined its contents. It had been his first night at Oxford, when he was feeling homesick. And before that, at the Smallwoods', where he often felt homesick, especially that first year. How he'd resented being sent away from home.

The day had turned grey and drizzly. And somehow that dreary afternoon seemed the perfect time to open the box again. He lit a candle, sat on his bed, and lifted the lid. That smell—her smell—wafted out, enveloping him in a faint embrace as he began sifting through the items within.

163

He first extracted a half sheet of paper, and unrolled a child's pencil sketch—stick figures of a man, a woman, and a snake. He knew the small ovals with stick legs below were supposed to be leaves, meant to hide the figures' nakedness. But he doubted anyone else looking at the unskilled drawing would recognize them as such. The snake was a bit better. Curved and complete with eye and forked tongue. For years he had been uncertain why he felt such nostalgic fondness for this drawing. Now he knew why.

A sudden burst of curiosity filled him, and at its impulse he tugged back the sleeve of his frock coat. He held his wrist close to the flickering candle lamp and inspected it. After so many years, and now camouflaged by dark hair, the scar was barely noticeable. Like the leaves in the old drawing—probably only recognizable by him.

Repositioning his sleeve, Henry moved on to happier memories. He unfolded a piece of paper, carefully ruled by hand. The handwriting upon it was straight and precise. It looked very much like young Emma Smallwood's hand. Upon it were written the words:

EMMA LIKES MILTON PUGSWORTH.
EMMA LIKES MILTON PUGSWORTH.
EMMA LIKES MILTON PUGSWORTH.

Over and over again as though an exercise in penmanship. Only it was not Emma Smallwood's handwriting. It was his own, written carefully to mimic hers. And left in her primer as a joke. She had not found it at all amusing. But the other pupils had.

Beneath the ruled sheet lay another stiff rectangle of paper. This one *was* in Emma Smallwood's hand, written during his second year at Longstaple. It was a carefully-lettered notice which had once been tacked to her bedchamber door:

BOYS, KEEP OUT

And in smaller characters:

Yes, Henry Weston, that means you.

It gave him a chuckle even now, years later. She ought to have known a boy like him could not have resisted such a challenge.

Beneath the notice lay a chess piece. A queen. He picked it up, remembering. He had only taken it to vex her. *Not* because he was angry she had beaten him that last time. And *not* as any sort of foolish, fond memento.

How Emma Smallwood could not stand for anything to be out of order. She had a place for everything and put everything in its place—as she often proudly repeated. She had no pity for any pupil who lost his glove or drawing pencil or primer. So he had taken one of her carefully stored chess pieces merely to draw a reaction from her, which was dashed difficult to do. For Emma Smallwood prided herself on her composure nearly as much as her order. He had been tempted to take one of her prized books, but in the end, could not do so. That, he knew, would have truly wounded her.

Beneath the chess piece lay his only mementoes of his mother. He did not count the portrait tucked away in the alcove upstairs, which jibed only vaguely with his memories of his mother's face. It had been painted when she was quite young, before marriage and childbirth had softened her figure, added lines to her face, and sadness to her eyes.

Henry set the chess piece aside and lifted a dainty handkerchief, yellowed now with age, and fingered the embroidered initials— M.W. Margaret Weston. Wrapped in the handkerchief was a slender green vial of perfume. He pried up the tight-fitting stopper, held the vial near his nose, and closed his eyes. The scent struck a chord of memory and conjured fleeting images of his mother. A tender touch on his arm. A sad smile. Large eyes meeting his in a bond of empathy. His cheek against her soft bosom, wrapped in her arms and the scent of lily of the valley.

Just as quickly the image began to dissolve and fade away. He could no longer hear her voice. And without the aid of the perfume, he could barely conjure her face in his mind's eye. Increasingly, it was that stranger, the young woman in the portrait who appeared when he beckoned his mother. Not a satisfactory replacement. How thankful he was that the few remaining drops of perfume worked like an elixir that allowed him to summon her dear face once more.

He recapped the perfume and unfolded the final memento. A small rectangle of fine stationery upon which she had written her last words to him.

*Be brave, my dear boy. And remember.*

It had been neatly torn from a longer letter—a letter written to his father, Henry supposed. He vaguely remembered Sir Giles handing him the strip of paper. He had been old enough to read by then and would've liked to have read the whole letter. But perhaps final words from wife to husband were too private for young eyes. He'd asked to see it once long ago, but Sir Giles had gently refused. Perhaps he would ask again. Henry decided to leave the perfume atop the cigar box on his side table, to remind himself to do so.

He wondered if Phillip had any mementoes of their mother. Unlikely, being so young when she died. He considered showing Phillip his, though the notion embarrassed him somehow. He would have to think about it.

※

For several years now, Emma had been teaching her father's course on *Geography and the Use of the Globes*. She had read many travel diaries and books by world explorers and loved little more than perusing the latest maps from the cartographer in Plymouth. Her father's knowledge of the classics—Greek and Latin—far exceeded hers, but he was welcome to the ancient world. Emma was drawn to the present one, with all its unexplored wonders.

Her father conceded her superior knowledge of geography, at first reluctantly but eventually with barely concealed pride. Unlike her mother, he had never worried about Emma being labeled a bluestocking.

At present, Julian and Rowan sat, chins on hands propped on elbows, eyes unfocused, glassy stares.

Emma realized it was time to liven things up a bit. "Let's play a game," she announced.

Julian straightened and said, "I like games."

Was that innuendo in his young voice? Emma hoped she was mistaken.

She gave the globe a hearty spin on its stand. "One point to whichever of you can name the location where my finger lands. Extra points for anything you can tell me about the country's landscape, history, language, or religion."

Her finger landed first on an island in the Indian Ocean off the southeastern coast of Africa. "What is this place called?" She left her finger where it was, covering the tiny print which might otherwise reveal the answer.

"No one knows," Rowan said. "Or cares."

"That's not true. I care."

She identified the island as Madagascar, then spun the globe again, her finger landing on the continent across the Atlantic Ocean from England.

That they named easily, but further spins were less successful.

Rowan complained, "Nobody knows all of these places."

"I do," Emma said.

"Prove it," Julian challenged.

Emma hesitated. Would it help? She didn't know but decided it was worth a try. "Very well. You may test me. You point to the place and see if I can tell you anything about it."

Turning the tables on her seemed to appeal to the young men. Eagerly, they took turns spinning the globe and trying to stump the tutor's daughter—Greece, the Canary Islands, Lithuania, *Terra Australis*—to no avail.

Rowan sat back, shaking his head in wonder. "Have you been to any of these places?"

"No. I am afraid I've not had that privilege."

Julian said, "Too bad women aren't allowed grand tours as young men are."

"Only wealthy gentlemen, to be fair," Rowan amended. "Or those who don't have responsibilities tying them down. Look at Henry. He's never gone anywhere either."

Emma remembered Henry's words in the Chapel of the Rock. *"All my life might have been."* Had he been referring to the places he'd never seen?

She said, "Some women have traveled widely on their own. And published accounts of their journeys. I have read them."

Rowan smirked. "Fictions, most likely."

"Not at all. Vivid accounts of beautiful, historic places . . . Here, I shall show you."

She walked to the bookcase and surveyed the top shelf, where she had lined the volumes they had brought from home. She selected one and began thumbing through its well-worn pages. "This was written by Lady Mary Wortley Montagu nearly a hundred years ago." She found a favorite excerpt and read.

"August 28, 1718. Genoa.

I am now surrounded by subjects of pleasure, and so much charmed by the beauties of Italy, that I should think it a kind of ingratitude not to offer a little praise in return for the diversion I have had here.

Genoa is situated in a very fine bay; and being built on a rising hill, intermixed with gardens, and beautified with the most excellent architecture, gives a very fine prospect off at sea. The street called Strada Nuova is perhaps the most beautiful line of buildings in the world.

But I am charmed with nothing so much as the collection of pictures from the pencils of Raphael, Paulo Veronese, Titian, Michael Angelo, Guido, and Correggio. . . ."

"Michelangelo, Guido, and Correggio . . ." Rowan echoed wistfully. "Does she write of Guido Reni or Guido Cagnacci?"

Emma replied, "Reni, I imagine."

Rowan nodded. "Yes, very likely, since she was writing from Genoa. . . ." His eyes glowed in soft awe.

Julian asked, "Where would you go, Miss Smallwood, if you could travel to just one country in the whole world?"

"Delightful question." She considered, and the image on her mother's teacup appeared in her mind. "If I had to choose one place, I suppose I would choose Italy."

Rowan nodded again. "So would I."

An idea came to Emma. She pondered it briefly, then said, "I would like each of you to pretend you are soon to embark on your own grand tour and begin planning your ideal itinerary. You may use any of my books here, the maps, and any other sources you can think of—newspapers or books in your father's library. Write down where you would go, how you would get there, how long you would stay in each place, and what you would see and do there."

Emma would enjoy such a project herself. She looked at the boys, waiting for the scornful look or groan. Instead, she saw the faintest spark of interest in their eyes. She hoped the assignment would arouse their interest in the world beyond Cornwall.

Henry, standing outside the schoolroom, overheard the last few minutes of the conversation within. He was moved by the restrained passion in his half-brother's voice. He really ought to see about engaging another drawing or painting master for Rowan, to help him hone his natural talent.

He was also surprised to hear of Miss Smallwood's desire to see Italy. He would not have guessed long-distance travel—with its inherent risks, unavoidable delays, heat, dirt, and fatigue—would appeal to her practical, orderly nature.

*Interesting,* he thought.

He guessed she would find the reality of such travel less pleasurable than reading about it from a comfortable armchair in a snug English parlor. But he would like to be wrong.

He regretted never being able to take his own grand tour. Soon after he had returned from Oxford, his father had asked him to oversee the day-to-day management of the estate, working with

Mr. Davies in Sir Giles's stead. But even if his father had not asked, Henry doubted their finances would have borne the expense of a lengthy tour. They were in somewhat better financial position now. Even so, Henry knew there was little chance of him getting away anytime soon. Besides, with the recent newcomers to Ebbington Manor, he had little desire to be anywhere else.

In bed that night, Emma drifted to sleep thinking of her Aunt Jane, how they had enjoyed reading travel diaries together, looking at maps, and planning a "someday trip" of their own. Not that either of them believed they would actually make such a journey, but nonetheless it had been enjoyable to think about it, to plan—if only in their imaginations. To dream.

Emma awoke with a start. Was that a footstep near her bed? She'd heard no click of a door latch. Had she dreamt it? She lay there, pulse pounding, ears alert, searching the darkness in vain.

If someone had come in to play a prank, she would not simply lie there as a victim and await her fate.

She sat up. "Who's there?" she whispered, her voice a girlish squeak.

*Silence.*

Feeling foolish, part of her certain she was conversing with mere air, *or ghost,* she forced her voice into the calm, firm tones she always used with recalcitrant pupils. "Please leave my room this instant."

A squeak of a floorboard. A shuffle. A creak. Good heavens, someone really was there. Her heart pounded in her throat, stifling the cry before it could emerge.

A latch clicked, and silence returned. Not the pregnant, expectant silence of a few moments before, but a calm, static nothingness—except for her own erratic heartbeat. She felt certain whoever had been there had heeded her command and fled.

What did she do now? Alert her father . . . or Henry? Why had she thought of him? Surely she had meant Phillip or Sir Giles.

But she didn't want to accuse without proof, not after the doubts raised by the "missing" journal. Nor did she want to worry her father.

She climbed from bed. There was no lock on her door. Should she slide a chair in front of it? She thought for a moment, then crossed the dark room and fumbled for her drinking glass beside the pitcher and basin. She carried it over and knelt down, propping it against the door. It would not stop anyone, but she would certainly hear if anyone tried to enter her room again.

Rising to her feet, Emma hesitated. What was that smell? A pronounced aroma lay on the air. Not shaving soap or bay rum this time, she did not think. She closed her eyes and focused on the fragrance . . . a sweet floral scent—a woman's perfume.

A woman?

Who wore such perfume? She did not recall smelling it before. Lizzie? Lady Weston? One of the servants? That seemed unlikely. At least the idea of a woman in her room was less frightening than that of a man. Thoughts of the Ebbington ghost drifted through her mind, but she blinked them away.

Emma forced herself to lie back down, pulling the bedclothes up to her chin. She decided she would pay attention on the morrow and discover which woman in the house wore perfume.

And then what? She had no idea.

Emma must have fallen asleep, for when she opened her eyes again, wan dawn light seeped through her windows. The room was still, peaceful.

Needing to use the chamber pot, Emma forced herself from the warm bed, relieved herself, and then stepped to the corner basin to wash her hands and face. Drying her hands, she looked at herself in the mirror . . . and saw a handprint on the glass—fingers spread wide.

Her heart beat dully at the sight. It had not been there when she'd cleaned her teeth the night before. Surely she would have noticed it. *Maybe not,* she told herself. Perhaps it had not shown by candlelight, and only the natural light of dawn revealed it. She extended her hand toward the image. She had rather long fingers for a female, and whoever left the print had a similar-sized palm but slightly shorter fingers. Too large to belong to the diminutive Morva, she believed. Perhaps the footman had been in to help lay the fires—a footman with smallish hands?

A creak startled her, and she gasped, whirling about. Her drinking glass clinked against the wooden floor and rolled several feet before coming to rest against a chair leg.

There in the doorway, a perplexed Morva looked from the glass up to Emma, no doubt wondering why a water glass announced her arrival.

Emma offered no explanation. Instead, she pointed to the hand-print on the mirror. "This is not your hand, I take it?"

Morva held up her right hand. "No. *This* be my hand," she said dryly.

Emma rolled her eyes. "I meant . . . well . . . I was surprised to find it there, and wondered who left it."

Morva shrugged. "I can't get every dust mote and smear, miss. Can I? Not with all the extra people in the house."

"I am not criticizing, Morva, only wondering who has been in my room."

Morva lifted her chin, eyes flinty. "Lots of us come and go, trying to keep thee and thy father tended."

Emma looked down, torn between feeling chastised or offended, but determined to keep a civil tongue.

"Sorry, miss." The maid's voice gentled. "I'm worn off my feet, but I ought not snap at thee."

Emma nodded. "I understand."

Morva stepped to the mirror and studied the handprint. Then she held her own hand up to it. As Emma had thought, the house-maid's hand was smaller.

"Perhaps 'ee left it by chance," Morva suggested.

Emma shook her head. "My fingers are longer."

The housemaid shrugged. "Could be anybody's." She said it dis-missively, but a wary light in her eyes caused Emma to wonder if Morva knew . . . or feared . . . who had left the mark.

Emma lingered over breakfast that morning, hoping Lizzie and perhaps even Lady Weston might join her.

Eventually, Lizzie wandered in, yawning. She saw Emma and smiled. "Good morning. I didn't expect anyone to still be in here. I do hope the coffeepot isn't empty."

The footman near the wall straightened to attention. Lizzie walked to the spigot urn, picked up a coffee cup, and tried the spout. Dark, aromatic liquid flowed. "Yes . . ." she murmured in triumph.

The footman relaxed.

Lizzie sat beside Emma, pouring cream from a tiny pitcher on the table and asking Emma to pass the sugar bowl.

Lizzie added several lumps and stirred, yawning yet again.

Emma took advantage of the girl's weary state to lean close and . . .

Lizzie jerked back. She stopped stirring and stared at Emma with a startled frown. "Did you just . . . smell me?"

Emma stammered, "I . . . no . . . I didn't mean to. I—"

"Do I smell?" Lizzie turned her head toward her shoulder and sniffed.

"No, of course not. I was just . . . wondering if you wore perfume."

"Are you suggesting I should?" Humor glinted in the girl's eyes.

Relieved, Emma replied, "No, I meant nothing by it. I was only curious. I smelled something flowery earlier and thought . . ."

"Isn't me. Unless it's my talcum powder. I don't wear perfume anymore. I did when I first came here, a little bottle of *eau de cologne* I received as a gift. But it made Lady Weston's eyes water and her nose itch, so I returned it."

"So Lady Weston doesn't wear perfume either? Or was it just your particular scent that irritated her?"

"Everything irritates Lady Weston," Lizzie said wryly. "Or hadn't you noticed?" Lizzie sipped her coffee and shrugged. "She doesn't wear scent either, as far as I know. Though her complexion cream has a citrus fragrance, I think."

Citrus? No, Emma hadn't smelled lemons or oranges.

Emma thought of the small bottle of *eau de cologne* Phillip had given her. Thankfully she had yet to use it. She said, "Then I had better refrain from wearing scent as well."

"You learn fast." Lizzie sipped again at her sweet, creamy coffee. "Phillip said you were clever."

Emma nodded vaguely, lost in thought.

Lizzie eyed her over the cup. "What is it? What's got your nerves in a bunch?"

"Nothing. I . . . was just wondering about the smell. That's all."

Lizzie's focus sharpened. "Where did you smell this perfume?"

"Apparently I imagined it. For I thought I smelled it in my room."

Lizzie's thin brows rose. "Did you indeed? Then perhaps the Ebbington ghost paid you a visit."

"Don't tell me Julian and Rowan have you believing their ghost stories too."

Lizzie shrugged. "Perhaps." She glanced at the footman, then leaned near and whispered, "I used to think all their talk of a ghost was pure stuff and nonsense. But lately I have heard a few things that cause me to fear they might be right."

"What sort of things?"

Lizzie's dark eyes widened. "Footsteps where there ought not be any. Voices too. And that strange music at night . . ." Lizzie shivered theatrically.

Emma said, "The boys are probably trying to scare us."

"Then they're doing a bang-up job of it."

Emma found herself silently agreeing.

Lizzie looked over her shoulder, then continued, "They say it is the ghost of Lady Weston herself—the former Lady Weston, I mean. Henry and Phillip's mother."

An illogical chill crept up Emma's spine. "I heard that as well," she acknowledged. "But it's only foolishness. Why should she want to haunt the place?"

Lizzie said, "Maybe she wasn't happy about Sir Giles marrying again, and so soon after her death. Henry certainly wasn't."

"Lizzie." It was Emma's turn to glance toward the door. "You ought not to say such things."

"Don't you believe in ghosts?" Lizzie asked.

"No," Emma said resolutely, recalling the oddly comforting image of the handprint on her mirror. A handprint left by someone very much alive.

*While she . . . had been planning a most
eligible connection for him, was it to be
supposed that he could be all the time
secretly engaged to another person! Such a
suspicion could never have entered her head!*

—Jane Austen, *Sense and Sensibility*

# Chapter 12

Henry sat at the desk in his small study, adding his latest observations of the day's weather and tide levels. These he checked against previous readings.

A quiet knock interrupted him. He looked up, surprised to see Emma Smallwood at his door. She held herself rigid, clearly uncomfortable in his presence. His fault, he knew. He still regretted how he'd treated her. All these years later, he still cringed at the memory of overhearing her tell her mother, *"He's no gentleman. He certainly does not act like one."*

He slid his quill back into its holder and rose. "Come in, Miss Smallwood. What may I do for you?"

"Not a thing," she said briskly. "But perhaps you recall, after I found the . . . em . . . miniature military figure in my room, you asked me to let you know if anything like that happened again."

Henry stiffened, as though bracing for a blow. "Yes?"

She stepped nearer and stood before his desk, hands primly clasped. "It isn't my intention to complain, or accuse anyone, but I do think someone was in my room again last night."

He arched one brow high. "Another toy soldier?"

"Toy?" she echoed. Humor sparked in her wide eyes, but he did not respond to the bait. He merely stared at her, waiting.

She sobered. "Em, no. Nothing . . . physical. That is, no object was left behind. But I did find a handprint on my mirror, and a strong scent lingered."

"Bay rum again?" he asked skeptically, for he wore that particular men's cologne, and wasn't the only Weston to do so.

"No, not this time. It smelled like a woman's perfume. Very flowery and sweet."

Henry snapped to attention but kept his voice level. "Not yours, I take it?"

She shook her head. "And Lady Weston, I understand, does not wear scent. Lizzie either."

"Hmm . . ." Henry twisted his lips in thought. Then he asked, "May I see it?"

Miss Smallwood blinked up at him. "The handprint?"

He nodded.

"Oh. Of course."

But he did not miss the hesitation in her voice.

Emma felt self-conscious about taking a gentleman to her bedchamber, but she nevertheless turned to lead the way. She reminded herself it was his home, after all, and his intentions were not only honorable but impersonal. Official.

As she mounted the stairs, she was conscious of him close behind her and resisted the urge to reach back and smooth her skirts. They did not speak as they walked down the corridor and around the corner. When she reached her door, she opened it and stepped inside, leaving the door open for him. She crossed the room toward the mirror but noticed he hovered in the threshold.

Emma stared at the mirror—the perfectly clear mirror—and sighed. "It appears Morva has already polished the glass." How foolish she felt for not foreseeing that.

In the mirror's reflection, she saw Henry grimace and inhale his disappointment.

She turned toward him and said, "I can tell you the palm was about the same size as mine, though the fingers were somewhat shorter." She held up her hand, fingers pointed toward the ceiling.

Stepping toward her, he raised his left hand, mirroring her right, close but not quite touching. His palm was bigger, his fingers thicker and longer than hers.

He asked wryly, "Am I exonerated?"

She swallowed. "In this, yes."

He cocked his head to one side, mouth twisted in an ironic grin. "Will you never forgive me the rest?"

For a moment, Emma held his gaze. Then she looked away first, suddenly unaccountably nervous. "If not for the handprint," she said, "I might be tempted to think Julian right about the ghost. A female ghost with a fondness for perfume."

His grin faded. "The ghost of my mother, I suppose?"

Emma's stomach fell. "Forgive me. What a thoughtless thing to say."

His face hardened. "Julian is wrong, Miss Smallwood. There is no ghost—as much as some members of my family would like you to believe otherwise."

She dared a look up into his stony face. "Why should they want me to believe that?" She forced a lame chuckle. "Are they trying to frighten us away?"

"No. That is not what I meant." He expelled a frustrated breath. "Forget I said that. I know you've never cared for foolishness."

"True. But I like intruders even less."

"You have nothing to fear, Miss Smallwood."

She looked at him coolly. "I am not afraid."

His gaze brushed over her countenance. "Good. For I don't believe you are in any danger."

"And if you are wrong?"

He ran a hand through his wavy hair. "Then lock your door."

She gestured toward it. "Mine hasn't a lock."

He stepped to the door and jiggled the latch. "I shall have to see to that." He looked at her once more. "I will look into the matter, Miss

Smallwood. Thank you for telling me. Please . . . do not mention it to anyone else. If you want to tell your father, of course you must, but—"

"The housemaid saw the handprint, and I told Lizzie I'd smelled perfume, but otherwise I have not said a word, nor shall I."

"Thank you." He gave a curt bow. "Now, if you will excuse me."

She dipped her head in acknowledgment, but he had already turned and left the room. She listened to his purposeful strides echo down the corridor, intent on a mission of his own.

Henry took himself directly to his bedchamber. He crossed the room to the bedside table, where he'd left the perfume and cigar box instead of returning them to their usual place in the wardrobe. He didn't see the slender green vial atop the box, where he thought he'd left it. He flipped back the cover and rummaged through its contents in vain.

Then he sat on the bed, pulled the box onto his lap, and dug deeper. He found his mother's handkerchief. The empty, limp handkerchief. But the perfume was gone, as he'd feared. So was the chess piece. Who would have taken them? A greedy housemaid? His valet?

The more likely answer lurked at the back of his mind, but he chose to ignore it. He thought about going to question his brother— several brothers, perhaps—but remembered his interview in Stratton. Questions would have to wait.

In the drawing room that evening, Lady Weston announced that her friend, Mrs. Penberthy, and her charming daughter had accepted her invitation to visit Ebbington Manor.

Standing there, hand against the mantel and staring into the fire, Henry listened to his stepmother's plans with disinterest, which twisted into annoyance and then ire the longer she droned on.

The Penberthy family had been guests at Ebbington Manor a few times before, and on those occasions Henry had enjoyed talking with *Mr.* Penberthy. In fact, doing so was often the sole bright spot in an entire visit from that family. More than once Henry had cloistered himself away with Sir Giles and Mr. Penberthy in the library, or lingered overlong in the dining room after dinner, even when politeness dictated they ought to join the women in the drawing room. The man had been good company. But Mr. Penberthy had died more than a year ago. And Henry dreaded the upcoming visit from his widow and daughter.

Whenever Lady Weston and Mrs. Penberthy were together, they chirped on like exotic birds in a London aviary. All colorful plumage and constant, inane, headache-inducing chatter. Not to mention the preening.

Tressa Penberthy was quieter than her mamma, Henry allowed, which was a point in her favor. She was not unattractive, he supposed, but he was certainly not attracted to her himself. She was a stout, ginger-haired girl, her gowns unbecomingly tight. That he might have overlooked. That, and the crooked teeth. But the young woman was as dull as his grandmother's letter opener. As smooth and uninteresting as a beach rock, worn featureless by the constant tide of her mother's foolish banter.

Phillip, he gathered, didn't mind simpering, insipid creatures who batted their lashes and hung on his every word, forming no reply more interesting than "Oh my. You don't say."

But Henry did mind.

Worse yet, Lady Weston had made it clear she expected one of them to marry Miss Penberthy. How kind of her to let them decide the particulars among themselves, when she would have preferred to choose for them and post the banns herself.

But even that was not what had Henry growing increasingly vexed until he barely managed to keep hold of his temper and his tongue.

Lady Weston said, "Mrs. Penberthy, dear friend though she is, has a . . . shall we say, superstitious streak. Very keen on lineage. An outspoken proponent of character and traits being passed from one generation to the next."

"Like her daughter inheriting her bad teeth?" Rowan asked with a snort.

Lady Weston silenced him with a glare.

"And so, with that in mind," she continued, "I expect each of you to demonstrate your good breeding, talents, and intelligence. She must have no doubts about the Weston family, or the benefits of joining its ranks. I understand the girl was interested in the heir of the Nancarrow estate. But when Mrs. Penberthy learned of a cousin with a club foot, she called the whole thing off, to my great relief. Therefore, I must ask you to keep certain things to yourselves, as we have been doing."

Lady Weston glanced at him. "I know you don't approve, Henry. But I must insist. During their visit, we will not speak of our added residents, certain Westons being sent home from school, nor any other unpleasantries."

Henry could hardly believe she tossed their "added residents" in the same lot as Julian and Rowan being expelled from school.

But Lady Weston hadn't finished. She skewered Phillip with a sharp look. "And, Phillip, come up with a plausible excuse for being home midterm. I won't have Mrs. Penberthy thinking you've come to grief at Oxford." Next she turned to Rowan and Julian. "And by all means, you two, no tricks or fighting while they're here. Do I make myself clear?"

"Perfectly," Julian drawled.

"Good."

Lady Weston paced before them. "Westons are keen, moral, healthy young gentlemen, among whom Mrs. Penberthy will find a suitable, nay, a superior match for her only daughter."

Henry wondered if he or Phillip were supposed to marry the girl and only afterward air the family secrets. How dishonest. How mercenary. Henry felt his father grip his tense shoulder or he likely would have snapped out some cutting remark. He glanced over at him.

His father's hound-dog eyes pleaded with him. *Please, this is important to her,* the look said. *It's only a few days. Can it really make such a difference, after all this time?*

Henry sighed and held his peace.

A few hours later, Henry stood in his room, dressed only in trousers and shirtsleeves. He'd already dismissed his valet, after Merryn had helped him off with his coat and taken his shoes and boots away to polish.

Drying his face at the washstand, Henry heard footfalls outside in the corridor and stiffened. He had lately heard too many accounts of uninvited nighttime visitors for his comfort. Tossing the towel aside, he stepped to his door and swiftly opened it. But it was only Phillip, fist raised to knock, startled expression on his handsome face.

"Expecting someone?" Phillip asked.

"No. Heard footsteps. Thought it might be someone else. Come in."

His brother did so. Considering the subject of the earlier family meeting, Henry was not surprised to see him.

"Have a seat." Henry removed the discarded towel from the chair and returned it to the washstand.

"I'm too worked up to sit," Phillip said, running a hand through his straight brown hair.

"Very well, I'll sit." Henry gestured to the carafe on his side table. "All I have to offer you is water."

At the word, Phillip hurried over, poured water into the single glass, and drank it down in one long swallow.

Henry said sardonically, "Make yourself at home."

Phillip paced across the room, turned, and paced back again.

Henry prodded gently, "Has this something to do with our little family meeting—Lady Weston's edict?"

"Yes, of course it has. And I can't do it. I know she means for me to, but I can't do it."

"Slow down," Henry soothed. "Can't do what—marry Miss Penberthy?"

"Don't be an idiot. What else would I be talking about?"

Henry leaned back, crossing his arms. "Why do you assume she means for you to do it? Here I've been fearing the task shall fall to me."

Phillip turned toward him. "She'd like that. Thinks you'd have the best chance with her, being the eldest."

Henry frowned, and then opened his mouth to protest.

"Don't scowl." Phillip huffed. "You know what I mean. But I expect she believes you will refuse simply to vex her."

"Yes, you have always been more malleable in her hands than I."

It was Phillip's turn to frown. "Well, not this time. You will have to do it."

Henry regarded his brother closely. "Why?"

"Because . . . because I am in love with somebody else; that's why."

Henry raised his eyebrows. "Are you indeed? Pray, who is the fortunate creature?"

Phillip grimaced. "I shan't tell you. You'll only ridicule me over it."

"Why should I?"

"Because you will no doubt think her no more suitable than Lady Weston would."

Henry's mind ticked through the possibilities, avoiding the conclusion that nipped at his breastbone, pestering him for acknowledgment. *Not yet.*

"Why would I think her unsuitable?" he asked tentatively, dreading the answer.

"Because she hasn't any money, of course. She is a lovely girl, but her circumstances are humble, I admit."

"Someone you met in Oxford?" Henry asked, on a thread of foolish hope.

"No. Someone I've known a long time. Why do you think I am here?"

Why should it feel like a kick to his gut? He should not care, but he found he cared very much indeed.

Henry gripped the chair's armrests and forced a casual tone. "We are both probably worrying over nothing. Likely Miss Penberthy shan't want either of us. She has never shown any partiality before—at least not to me."

Phillip turned away, but not before Henry saw discomfort pinch his face.

"Oh dear," Henry murmured. "As bad as all that?"

"No," Phillip defended. "I was simply polite to her—that's all. Something you rarely bother to be."

Henry had never seen his usually cheerful brother so upset. "Well then," he said. "This time I shall be on my best behavior for your sake, if not for her."

Henry did not specify whether the "her" he referred to was Miss Penberthy or Lady Weston. In either case, the sentiment would be the same.

After morning lessons the next day, Emma's father confided his intention to retire to his room for a nap, but Emma felt too restless to remain indoors. Longing for a bit of fresh air, she tied on her bonnet and cape, and trotted downstairs.

When she passed the drawing room on her way outside, Lizzie saw her and hurried out to join her.

She whispered, "I hear you found a mysterious handprint in your room yesterday."

Emma looked at her sharply.

"Morva told me," Lizzie explained. "She tells me everything. So if there is anything you don't want me to know, don't tell her."

Emma feared Henry would think she had reneged on her promise of secrecy and judge her an untrustworthy gossip. "I shall remember that in future," she said.

It was Lizzie's turn to give *her* a sharp look. "The tutor's daughter has secrets, has she? My, my."

"That is not what I meant."

Lizzie eyed her bonnet and cape. "Where are you going?"

"For a walk." Emma hesitated, then added, "Would you like to come along?"

Lizzie smiled, apparently pleased to be asked. "I would, yes. Just let me run and gather my wrap."

Lizzie returned a few minutes later, wearing a straw sun hat with a lacy scarf over the crown and tied in a bow under her chin. She wore a short spencer over her dress but no gloves.

Emma bit back a maternal admonition. She wore gloves whenever she ventured out-of-doors, a practice ingrained in her since childhood. But it was not her place to advise Lady Weston's ward.

They strolled outside, through the garden and past its gate, toward the coast. The chilly wind made Emma's eyes water, the streaks of tears warm on her cool cheeks.

Ahead of them, out on the headland point, stood a figure, his back to them, an easel before him. Rowan.

Emma wondered if he would mind being disturbed. She and Lizzie exchanged a look, then approached him tentatively.

Emma said, "Hello, Rowan."

He glanced over, expression guilty. Was he so self-conscious about his work?

"Miss Smallwood. I . . . Am I late for afternoon lessons?"

"Not at all. Forgive us. We did not mean to disturb you."

"That's all right. It's nothing important."

Emma glanced from the painting on the easel to the actual scene before them. The calm sea shimmered blue-grey in the sunshine, and upon it floated a green sailing vessel, white sails unfurled and taut, rigging rattling in the wind, approaching the waiting harbor north of them.

Emma looked back toward the painting once more. Rowan had painted a nighttime scene. A dark, stormy sea capped with ominous waves and a red sloop tilted dangerously on its side, breaking up on jagged rocks beyond the mouth of the harbor. A tiny figure of a man, mouth agape, stretched his arm toward the viewer, begging for help.

Emma blinked. She asked tentatively, "Is this . . . from your imagination?"

Rowan shook his head, eyes on his painting. "From memory."

Emma stared at his profile. "You witnessed a shipwreck?"

"More than one. There are many wrecks along this coast."

"Are there?"

He nodded.

Lizzie said, "Approaching an exposed coastline like this is always dangerous. But the natural breakwater there"—she pointed to the rocky peninsula, jutting partway across the harbor, the chapel at its tip—"narrows the entrance and increases the risk."

Emma was surprised the girl would know anything about it.

Rowan nodded his agreement. "Many a ship has struck those rocks. And many a man drowned just beyond the safe haven of the harbor."

Emma shivered at the thought of going under those icy waves. She gestured toward Rowan's painting. "When did this happen?"

"Early this spring."

"Did the crew survive?"

Rowan shook his head. "Not one."

"Was there nothing to be done?" Emma asked.

His lip curled. "Do you mean, besides wait for the bodies and cargo to wash ashore?"

Again Emma shivered. "Yes, before that."

Rowan shrugged. "John Bray tried. He always tries."

"Who is John Bray?"

"Local constable and salvage agent."

Lizzie sniffed. "I hear the man causes more trouble than he solves."

Rowan shot her a dark look but made no reply.

Emma gazed at the painting once more. "Well . . . it is really quite good, Rowan."

A voice came from over her shoulder. "It is indeed."

Emma whirled around, surprised to see Henry Weston standing there, looking from the painting to his brother with a gleam of nearly paternal pride in his eyes. She had not heard him approach over the wind.

"Not as good as it could be," Rowan began. "Not even as good as—"

"No rebuttals, Rowan," Henry interrupted. "Miss Smallwood is not one to hand out compliments lightly. If she says the painting is good, then it is indeed."

A look passed between the brothers, some undercurrent Emma couldn't place. Henry turned to her. "You have a good eye, Miss Smallwood."

"Um . . . thank you," Emma murmured, consternated by Henry Weston's praise. "Were you here when the shipwreck occurred?"

Henry looked at the painting once more, eyes suddenly fierce. "Unfortunately, I was not." His face contorted. "Poor souls."

A moment of wind-strummed silence followed.

Henry inhaled and drew himself up. "Well, I'm off to check the water levels and visit the chapel." He tugged on his hat brim, turned his face into the wind, and strode away.

Watching him go, Emma was relieved he did not ask her to accompany him again, for she would have demurred.

Lizzie took her arm. "Let's leave Rowan to his painting, shall we? You promised me a walk, and I long to stretch my legs."

Still gazing after Henry's retreating figure, Emma shook herself mentally awake. "Of course."

They bid Rowan farewell, and the two young women continued their walk along the coast path.

But Emma's thoughts remained on Henry Weston. "I find it interesting that Mr. Weston is so drawn to that abandoned chapel when he doesn't even attend church."

"Oh, but he does," Lizzie said, looking at her askance. "He usually attends with the family in the morning, and then goes to an evening service at the Wesleyan chapel in Stratton."

Emma was astonished. "Does he?"

Lizzie's look of confusion cleared. "That's right. He hasn't gone with us since you arrived. Two weeks ago, I believe, a traveling preacher was in the area for some special early meeting Henry didn't want to miss, so he went there instead of St. Andrew's. I don't know where he was this last Sunday. Gone somewhere on more family business, I think."

Emma realized she had simply assumed Henry Weston was an unbeliever—though come to think of it, he *had* spoken of God in the chapel. Guilt pinching her, she asked, "Does his family mind?"

"Lady Weston doesn't approve of him associating with dissenters, but when have those two ever seen eye to eye on anything?"

"And Sir Giles?"

Lizzie shrugged. "I've never heard him object. I think he's just relieved Henry still attends St. Andrew's with the family."

"I see . . ." Emma digested this new information.

They walked on for a few minutes more, listening to the wind, the surf, and the sea gulls.

Then Lizzie asked, "Have you heard we are to have visitors, Miss Smallwood?"

"Oh?"

Lizzie nodded. "Mrs. and Miss Penberthy." She began parroting Lady Weston's affected voice, "The *dearest* friend, and her *most* eligible daughter." Then Lizzie added almost glumly, "We're even to have a party with dancing in her honor."

Lizzie's dour tone surprised Emma, considering how little amusement life at Ebbington Manor usually afforded the young woman.

"You should enjoy that," she said gently.

Lizzie frowned and shook her head. "Not likely."

"Why not? What is the matter?"

"Oh, Emma. May I call you Emma?"

"Yes, if you like."

"I am so worried, and I have no one to confide in. May I tell you my troubling secret?"

Emma hesitated. She had no wish to place herself in an awkward position between ward and host family.

Apparently noticing her hesitation, Lizzie said, "I shan't use names, if that will make you feel better. That way, if asked, you can say you truly didn't know. Please, Emma. I must tell someone or I shall burst. I can't eat. I can't sleep for worrying."

Vaguely in the back of Emma's mind, a verse she had heard as a child whispered to her. *"Cast all your cares upon Him for He cares for you."* But she did not say the words aloud. After all, as distant as she had been from God since her mother's death, who was she to offer pat religious comforts?

Instead Emma said quietly, "Very well. But no names."

Gratefully, Lizzie nodded, and led the way to a bench overlooking the sea. She plopped down and Emma sat beside her, carefully arranging her skirts.

"You see," Lizzie began, "Lady Weston hopes, or should I say plans, that one of the Weston brothers should marry this Miss Penberthy. She is apparently quite the little heiress. Her father made a tidy fortune in tin mining, I believe. Lady Weston would very much like to see her friend's daughter marry into the family—and bring along a good deal of money into the marriage, of course. Very fond of money, Lady Weston is."

Emma waited, wondering and fearing what Lizzie's interest could be in all of this.

Lizzie gripped her hands together and looked out toward the horizon. "You see, I have formed a secret . . . attachment to one of the Weston brothers. Foolish, I know. But this was several months ago, before—" She was about to say a name but corrected herself. "Before *he* came home. And now I regret that foolish promise I made to . . . shall we say, a younger Mr. Weston. For since then I have fallen hopelessly in love with . . . an older Mr. Weston. And now I fear that Lady Weston means for *him* to marry Miss Penberthy with her five thousand pounds, and where shall that leave me?"

Emma's mind whirled. She didn't want to know whom Lizzie spoke of, yet found herself drawing conclusions even as she told herself not to. Younger brother . . . Phillip? Older brother . . . Henry?

Had Phillip actually formed an attachment with Lizzie Henshaw? Is that really why he had left Oxford and returned to Ebbington—to see Lizzie, and not Emma and her father as he'd protested? Emma hoped it wasn't true. But nor did she like the thought of her dear friend having his heart broken if the girl he loved had transferred her affections to his older brother.

She wondered which man Lady Weston had in mind for this Miss Penberthy. Henry, the eldest son? Or Phillip, whom Lady Weston clearly preferred?

Emma asked carefully, "Does this . . . older brother . . . return your affection?"

Lizzie's eyes were wide and plaintive. "I think so. Oh, I dearly hope so."

*Did* Henry Weston love Lizzie Henshaw? It was difficult to believe. Yet Emma had certainly noticed his kindness, his politeness to his stepmother's ward. If it was more than that, Emma had seen no indication. But then again, neither had she seen any hints of romance between Lizzie and Phillip—other than, perhaps, seeing them talking together in the garden. But they might have been discussing any number of unromantic topics.

Had Lizzie, with her charming looks and neglected education, really managed to turn the heads of both Phillip and Henry Weston, leading her to disappoint one of them?

Emma supposed some young women lived for such romantic ideals. But personally, Emma would find it loathsome to put herself and two brothers in such a predicament.

Lizzie said imploringly, "You see now why I'm upset? Why I'm worried?"

Emma nodded. She did indeed.

*As dancing is the accomplishment most
calculated to display a fine form, elegant taste,
and graceful carriage to advantage . . . [beauty]
cannot choose a more effective exhibition.*

—The Mirror of the Graces, 1811

# Chapter 13

Mrs. and Miss Penberthy wrote to inform the Westons they would arrive on Friday and depart on Sunday afternoon. Lady Weston had hoped for a longer visit but consoled herself with the notion that it would be easier to maintain an unwavering picture of familial perfection during a shorter interval.

The Penberthy ladies would reach Ebbington Manor late in the afternoon, in time to dress for dinner, followed by cards and an early evening as they were sure to be tired from their journey.

On Saturday, each young man would be given an hour to entertain Miss Penberthy and demonstrate his virtues. Even Julian and Rowan, though too young for twenty-year-old Tressa, would have their chance to impress, for Lady Weston would not miss the opportunity to display the superior talents and charms of her natural sons.

Henry had overheard Lady Weston tell Lizzie, "How could any woman regard my accomplished sons and not imagine her own future offspring painting and playing with such skill if only she were to marry a Weston?"

Henry was to take Miss Penberthy riding, and Phillip was to give her a tour of the estate. Nothing too lengthy, for they would all need time to prepare for an early dinner followed by an evening party, complete with dancing and a midnight supper afterward. A small private ball, just like those Violet Weston remembered so fondly from her youth.

Mr. Davies had arranged for musicians from the village to play. And, wishing to have sufficient couples for a proper ball, Lady Weston had even invited Miss Smallwood to join them. Altogether then, there would be five gentlemen and five ladies: Sir Giles, Henry, Phillip, Rowan, and Julian. Lady Weston, Mrs. Penberthy, Miss Penberthy, Lizzie, and Miss Smallwood.

Overhearing the guest list, Sir Giles protested, "But, my dear, you have forgotten Mr. Smallwood."

Lady Weston wrinkled her powdered nose. "Mr. Smallwood shall take his dinner with Davies, as usual."

"But surely we might at least ask him to join us for the party afterward?"

She protested, "But then we should have an uneven number of men and women for dancing."

"I don't care for dancing, my dear, as you know. And Mr. Smallwood as I recall is an excellent dancer. Mrs. Penberthy is out of mourning and may wish to dance. We don't want her monopolizing the eligible gentlemen, do we?"

She considered this. "I suppose you have a point, my dear."

"And might it not look well, my love, that we have our own private tutor in residence?"

Lady Weston narrowed her eyes in shrewd contemplation. "Very well. Mr. Smallwood may join us."

She turned and leveled first Phillip, then Henry with a stern glare. "But we shall hear no tales of boyhood escapades with the tutor's daughter. Do I make myself clear?"

Friday afternoon arrived, and with it their guests. The Penberthys were warmly greeted by Lady Weston and Sir Giles and shown to their rooms to rest and change before dinner.

Henry's valet helped him dress for the occasion. For once, Henry did not urge the exacting fellow to quit fussing and make haste. Henry was in no hurry. He dreaded the upcoming dinner—the awkward conversation and pointed expectation.

Merryn began tying Henry's cravat in the simple barrel knot Henry usually preferred.

Seeing his valet's long-suffering expression, Henry suggested, "Perhaps the waterfall tie tonight?"

Merryn's fidgeting fingers paused, and he stared up at his master with wide eyes, which brightened from shock to extreme pleasure in a heartbeat. "Yes, sir!" He pulled the cravat from Henry's neck, retrieved a longer one from the cupboard, and began the process all over again, tying and arranging the white linen until it cascaded over his waistcoat. Henry felt the dandy, but Merryn assured him he looked very elegant.

Finally Henry could put off the inevitable no longer. He thanked Merryn, took a deep breath, and steeled himself to join the others.

Trotting down the stairs, Henry prayed for patience, for the grace to treat their guests kindly, and for much needed self-control to hold his tongue.

A few minutes later, Henry took his chair in the candlelit dining room. He noticed that Miss Penberthy had been seated directly opposite him and next to Phillip.

Her appearance was better than he recalled, he admitted to himself. Her ginger hair, well dressed atop her head, flattered her round face. Her brown eyes were large and pleasing, her complexion and figure tolerable. She fawned over neither Phillip nor Henry himself. Instead, she directed most of her attention toward his father, politely asking about his health in the most respectful tones. Another point in her favor.

Henry asked himself for the tenth time if it was his duty to try to woo this woman, to help Phillip and his family? Marriage to an heiress like Tressa Penberthy *would* help the Westons greatly. And the reality was, neither he nor Phillip could hope to achieve a more advantageous match. Especially since their present financial situation did not allow them the expense of London seasons and the inherent "marriage market" they offered.

In many ways, it was unfortunate that both he and Phillip preferred someone else. Still, Henry decided he would be polite and do his best to keep an open mind about Miss Tressa Penberthy.

On Saturday morning, Henry and Miss Penberthy rode together, the lady looking undeniably smart in a sleek burgundy riding habit and jaunty hat. During the ride, Henry chose several less-than-smooth tracks but did not provoke complaints from the heiress as he'd expected and perhaps secretly hoped. Instead, Miss Penberthy demonstrated a stoic endurance. He even saw a knowing gleam of challenge in her eyes, as if she knew what he was up to.

She spoke little, now and again asking a question about the property—where the estate boundaries lay, how old the house was, and so on. But, not wishing to usurp Phillip's assigned role as tour guide, Henry answered her only briefly, not expounding as he might have done otherwise.

He did answer more fully the questions Phillip was unlikely to address—the routes he usually rode and the history of the village. She seemed mildly interested, though not necessarily impressed. Still, he was relieved she didn't ramble on or flirt with him as he'd feared.

When they returned to the stable yard an hour or so later, he was forced to admit that it had been a reasonably pleasant experience, as much as it galled him to give any merit to his stepmother's machinations.

Duty dispatched, Henry went up to his room to change from his riding clothes and assumed Miss Penberthy did the same. Afterward, he retreated to his study to focus on the more pressing matters of the breakwater and plans to construct a warning tower at the point. In fact, he had a meeting scheduled with the surveyor later that afternoon.

He spent the next few hours writing letters and drafting plans.

Then he turned to his weekly review of the estate ledgers and was relieved but perplexed to see a better balance of income to expenses than he'd expected. He checked the amounts in the income columns, the rents and interest paid, and other incomes from the estate. Something didn't add up. He'd have to check with Davies. He supposed Lady Weston had provided another transfusion of capital from her marriage settlement. That was how Davies had accounted for it before when Henry had noticed other such discrepancies.

At the scheduled time, Henry went outside to meet the surveyor at the point. He saw Phillip and Miss Penberthy returning from their walking tour of the estate. The young woman now wore a promenade dress of apple green, a broad hat, and carried a parasol. At the front steps, she smiled and thanked Phillip for the tour and excused herself to rest and dress for dinner.

Phillip bowed but remained outside with Henry. The two men stood silently and watched her depart. If Henry was not mistaken, the smile on Miss Penberthy's face and the warm looks and thanks she had bestowed on Phillip were evidence of the young woman's marked preference for his brother. Henry found himself relieved, though it was a blow to his male pride. If not for his presumed position as heir, he supposed no woman would prefer him to his amiable, blue-eyed brother. He wondered if—hoped—Phillip had revised his opinion of Miss Penberthy as well.

When the doors closed behind her, Henry asked, "Well? How did it go?"

Phillip shrugged. "Fine, I suppose. I don't know why I had to give her the tour when you know so much more about the estate and its history than I do. Still, I think it went tolerably well."

Watching his brother's face, Henry said, "I believe Miss Penberthy has improved since we last saw her."

Phillip's fair brows rose. "Do you think so?"

"Yes. Don't you?"

"I . . . own I have rather steeled myself against her. Though I hope I was polite."

Henry studied his brother's agitated countenance. "I am certain you were. You are always unfailingly polite, Phillip."

*If not wise,* Henry added to himself.

---

For that evening's formal dinner, Henry's valet had been pressed into serving duty along with the footman. Merryn bore the indignity of livery and powered wig with long-suffering aplomb. Henry bit back a smile and avoided the man's gaze, not wishing to add to his mortification.

It gave Henry an unexpected sense of satisfaction to see Miss Smallwood seated at the dining table with his family. She wore an evening gown of pale tea-leaf green, simple and elegant. The color made her eyes dance like polished jade in the candlelight.

Inwardly he chided himself. What was he now, a poet?

He looked instead at Miss Penberthy. She was a good rider, he reminded himself. He admired that. Miss Smallwood did not ride, he knew. Of course, she'd never had the opportunity. He wondered if she'd like to learn.

Henry regarded his brother Phillip over the rim of his glass. He answered Miss Penberthy's questions and engaged her in conversation but appeared distracted and ill at ease. Was it because he was aware he sat under the watchful and exacting eye of Lady Weston? Or because he sat there ostensibly flirting with one woman, while the woman he loved sat at the very same table?

Several times he noticed Phillip's gaze straying to the far end of the long table, where Miss Smallwood sat speaking animatedly with Sir Giles and Lizzie. Emma smiled as she listened to his father relate some tale in dramatic fashion. She looked to be genuinely enjoying herself, apparently unaware of the tension, the expectation in the room.

Henry's gaze skimmed past Lizzie but then returned. He was surprised to see the normally chirpy creature looking subdued and unhappy. As if sensing his scrutiny, Lizzie glanced up at him and their gazes caught, but she reddened and returned her attention to

Sir Giles. He wondered what was amiss and guessed the girl resented any female who diverted attention from her.

A burst of laughter at the foot of the table drew his attention next. There, Lady Weston and Mrs. Penberthy sat, heads near, talking and laughing like schoolroom misses. Their collective gazes now and again slid conspiratorially toward Phillip and Tressa, engaged in dutiful conversation. Soon to be engaged to marry, the two mammas no doubt hoped.

Poor Phillip. Poor obliging Phillip. Always eager to gain Lady Weston's fragile, flighty affection. Would he once again choose his stepmother's approval over his own happiness?

Perhaps Henry should have tried harder to turn Miss Penberthy's head. But it was dashed difficult to conjure the enthusiasm when his interest was otherwise engaged.

Now and again, Emma glanced surreptitiously down the length of the candlelit table, past the many serving dishes and fruit and flower arrangements to observe Phillip, Henry, and the elegant Miss Penberthy. She admired the woman's hair, her gown, her poise. Did the men admire her as well? They certainly paid her every attention. Poor Lizzie. Emma glanced at the girl's glum face and felt pity for her. Yet, if she no longer wanted Phillip for herself, might it not be a relief if he formed an attachment with someone else? Or, did she worry Henry might admire their guest?

After dinner, Emma followed the others into the drawing room, where her father joined them. Three musicians with fiddle, flute, and pipe played a quiet melody as the company filed in. The carpets had been rolled away and the chairs and small tables arranged around the perimeter of the room to allow for dancing. Sir Giles went immediately to claim his place in one of the armchairs near the fire. Mrs. Penberthy followed. Her father took a step in their direction, but Emma hooked his arm, halting his progress.

"Perhaps, Papa, you and I ought to sit over there with Rowan and Julian."

Their eyes met, and for a moment she feared she'd offended him, but then he patted her hand and walked with her to the game table where the younger Westons sat, idly shuffling cards and looking bored.

"May we join you?" Emma asked.

Rowan shrugged. "If you like."

Julian waved to Lizzie, beckoning her to join them as well, but she turned as though she had not seen him and laughed at something Miss Penberthy had said. Julian rolled his eyes. "Lizzie seems to be ignoring us."

After a few minutes of conversation and a halfhearted game of whist, Lady Weston stood and clapped her hands, gaining everyone's attention.

She addressed the musicians. "Now, let us have something lively the young people might dance to."

"What's your pleasure, madam?" the fiddler asked.

Julian stood abruptly and called, "The Eightsome!"

The Eightsome was a lively Scottish reel, perhaps not the best choice to begin with, especially after such a large dinner. But Lady Weston voiced no objection, so no one else did either.

Julian crossed the room and claimed Lizzie for his partner, which was not surprising, Emma thought, since Lizzie was the female closest in age. Phillip dutifully asked Miss Penberthy to dance, though Emma imagined he would rather dance with Lizzie. And Henry bowed and asked Mrs. Penberthy if she cared to dance.

The widow appeared taken aback but then smiled up at him. "Why not, Mr. Weston. Why not."

Emma did not miss the look of surprise and perhaps even approval shared by Lady Weston and Sir Giles.

Lady Weston looked imploringly at her husband. "Come, my dear. Just one dance?"

"Perhaps, my love, but not this jig. It should be the death of me."

Emma thought of prodding her father to the task but instead tapped Rowan on the arm and nodded toward his mother.

"What?"

Again she nodded.

"Must I?"

"It would be the kind thing to do."

He heaved himself to his lanky height with a sigh. "Oh, very well."

Lady Weston accepted Rowan with a beaming smile of satisfaction.

Her father leaned near. "I'm sorry, my dear, but I don't think I am equal to a Scottish reel either."

"That's all right, Papa. I am not certain Lady Weston really wishes us to dance—unless, of course, we are needed to complete a set."

After the first dance, the older women excused themselves to catch their breaths and have a glass of punch.

Rowan snagged Lizzie's hand, which earned him a glare from Julian. Then cheeky Julian butted past Phillip and asked Miss Penberthy to dance the next with him. She agreed with an indulgent smile, to which Julian reacted with a barely concealed scowl. For Julian detested being treated as a boy. He did in fact dance with excellent address and elegance, twice that of any other gentleman there. But some of the effect was lost, since he had to strain to reach high enough to turn his partner under his arm.

He looked around the room. "Come on, somebody. We ought to have at least one more couple."

Henry, standing near Phillip, turned toward her. "Perhaps Miss Smallwood would care to dance?"

"I . . . would be happy to oblige. If I am needed."

Henry said to Phillip under his breath, "Shall you do the honors, or shall I?"

Emma heard it and for some reason the words stung. Apparently Henry Weston did not wish to dance with her. By "honors," did he mean duty? A duty he preferred to delegate to his younger brother? Ah well, she told herself, at least she did not have to dance with her own father while two single gentlemen stood idle.

"Perhaps Mr. Smallwood would like to dance with his daughter," Lady Weston interjected, as if reading her thoughts.

Mr. Smallwood hesitated, glanced at Emma, then wisely replied to Lady Weston, "I cannot pretend to be half the dancer either of the accomplished Weston brothers are."

Henry and Phillip looked from Emma's burning face to each other. Henry stepped forward, but Phillip laid a hand on his arm. "It would my great pleasure to dance with you, Emma. If you would oblige me."

Relief filled her. She could always rely on Phillip to be unfailingly kind. She rose and accepted the hand he offered.

Together she and Phillip danced the Sir Roger de Coverley. What fun it was to move to the jaunty music. To smile without self-consciousness into Phillip's face, which mirrored her own grin back at her. To take his hands, to skip, turn together, to clap. She felt eyes watching her and glanced over, chagrined to see both Lady Weston and Henry observing them, smiles *not* mirrored on their faces. Lizzie, too, was looking at her strangely.

But then Phillip took her hands once more, and she forgot about everyone else but him.

When the dance ended, Phillip pressed her hand. "That was great fun, Emma. Do say you'll dance with me again."

She nodded in happy agreement.

But then the fiddler called the Lancers Quadrille, and Lady Weston abruptly stood. "Phillip, you know how much I adore dancing the Lancers. You must accompany me."

"Oh . . . of course." He looked apologetically at Emma, then sent a meaningful nod toward his brother.

Henry Weston stepped forward to fill the gap as bid.

*How awkward,* Emma thought, reminding herself it was not as though she had been begging a partner. Yet she felt very much like the last player picked for a cricket team. The spinster on the shelf— and everyone quite content to leave her there.

Henry bowed formally before her, his face a mask of neutrality. "Miss Smallwood, may I have this dance?"

"If you like."

He stretched out his hand and she placed her gloved hand in his.

Waiting for the introductory music to pass, Emma recalled the last time she had danced with Henry Weston.

He had been forced to dance with her then, as now. The old dancing master, visiting the Smallwood Academy, asked a then seventeen-year-old Mr. Weston to partner a fourteen-year-old Emma in the positions of the French and German waltz. She still recalled the embarrassment of seeing him hesitate, his face falling into lines of evident displeasure.

Emma's face burned anew even now as the memory revisited her. Did he find her person so disgusting? Apparently. For his hand on her waist all those years ago had been the merest whisper of contact, his other hand beneath hers, only the barest of holds. She had felt the rough spot on one of his fingers and at first assumed it a callous.

Then later, whilst joining hands once more as the dancing master commanded, she'd noticed the rough spot looked more like the remains of a fading wart. She looked up from the offending bump to his face. Saw him realize she'd noticed. A part of her wished to hurt him back, to sneer, "And you don't wish to dance with *me?*" Or, "And you think *I* am disgusting?"

But in that flash when their eyes met, she saw a flicker of self-consciousness there. Of vulnerability. And she could not do it. She knew many boys were afflicted with skin eruptions of all sorts and were embarrassed by them, especially when fellow pupils teased them in front of a *girl.*

So instead, and without flinching, Emma had placed her hand squarely in his.

As they danced, Henry Weston recalled a particular visit from the dancing master at the Smallwood Academy. The "caper merchant," as the boys called him, had asked young Emma to demonstrate the female steps and partner the pupils. She had obviously done so before and had learnt the steps thoroughly, though her form was a bit ungainly—a colt still trying to master long, wobbly limbs. She stepped precisely where she was meant to step, raised her arms at the correct angle, yet her movements at fourteen had lacked the fluidity, the feminine grace, she now possessed.

In place of the self-consciousness he recalled, her pleasure in dancing with Phillip earlier had been evident, though it appeared to him she tried to mask her enjoyment by suppressing the rogue smile that continually teased her mouth. She was not, perhaps, the accomplished dancer Miss Penberthy was, but he doubted Emma Smallwood had nearly as much opportunity to practice.

He still felt a prick of embarrassment over the memory of the last time the dancing master had called him forward from the line of male pupils to dance with the tutor's daughter. He had suddenly recalled the fading wart on his left ring finger. It had yet to disappear completely and left him with a rough scaly spot which anyone taking his hand would surely feel and likely see as well. How he hated the thought of her face wrinkling in disgust, reluctant to place her lily-white hand in his, or refusing to do so altogether. The other boys were watching. And he, as the eldest student, felt obliged to appear in possession of superior confidence and ability. His reputation was about to be tainted if not ruined altogether.

So he'd taken her hand with the barest touch of his fingertips, hoping she would not notice. In his discomfort, he barely knew what steps he was meant to be doing and dropped Miss Smallwood's hand as soon as the pattern was completed. The dancing master frowned at his faulty performance and told them to start over. This brought a few titters from the younger boys. Feigning nonchalance, he once again extended his hand toward her—and that's when she noticed. He saw it in her eyes and steeled himself for her reaction.

For a moment she simply looked at him, a dozen thoughts and emotions flickering through her wide eyes. Here was her chance for retribution for all his pranks and taunts. He'd handed her the opportunity with his own hand. His own marred flesh.

But instead of wrinkling her nose, or announcing his flaw, or saying anything at all, she had simply laid her hand fully, squarely, in his. At that moment, he'd felt a flicker of admiration for her. Of brotherly affection. He might have embraced her but for the onlookers, and his fear of her reaction. He settled for placing his hand on her waist, that time as firmly as she had placed her hand in his.

At present, Miss Smallwood looked less eager to dance with him than Henry might have wished. He was tempted to show her both palms, blemish free and perfectly smooth save for a riding callous or two. But he resisted and ignored the little pinch of disappointment that she would prefer to dance with his brother. Of course she would—had not Phillip intimated he was in love with her? Or was she as yet unaware of his feelings?

Henry was careful not to stand too close, and to keep his touch brotherly. He had never had a sister, true, but he had certainly had to dance with many women in his life for whom he held no romantic feelings.

He focused on the steps, strangely unable to begin the shallow chatter expected in such situations. The silence between them stretched awkwardly.

Finally she said, "You are a very good dancer, Mr. Weston."

Did she feel the need to encourage him as though he were one of her pupils—as she had sought to encourage young Rowan? He found it both sweet as well as irritating.

"Thank you. I had a good partner at the academy I attended as a young man."

Her brows rose. "Did you?"

"I did. And she, too, has become quite an accomplished dancer, I see."

"I doubt that. I've had very little practice outside the schoolroom."

"Have you never been to a ball?"

"Not a formal ball, no. Though Aunt Jane did take me to the public dances in Plymouth a few times. Her idea for a "coming out," of sorts. Though a shabby one, in hindsight."

They joined hands and turned around each other. "I remember your Aunt Jane. A fine woman. I liked her a great deal."

She looked up at him in surprise. "Then you are a very fine judge of character, Mr. Weston. For she is the best of women. The best of friends."

He tilted his head to look at her more closely. "You miss her, I think."

"I do. But we write to each other."

The dance separated them as each turned to face his "corner." When they were close enough to speak again, he said, "You ought to invite her to come and visit while you are here. Perhaps during the summer or Christmas holidays?"

Her mouth opened again in surprise. He was getting reactions from her at last, as he had long tried to do in Longstaple through pranks. Perhaps he ought to have tried kindness sooner.

"Do you really think so?" Her sudden smile died midbloom. "Oh. You are simply being polite. You cannot want—"

"I was not being polite," he insisted. "Though in retrospect I should speak to Lady Weston and my father first, make certain it would not conflict with any of their plans. I shall let you know."

"That is very kind," she said evenly. But her expression said, *"I won't hold my breath."*

He didn't like the polite reserve between them. On a whim, he decided to toss pride aside and try transparent honesty instead.

"Do you recall the last time you and I danced? I am afraid I was rude to you."

She ducked her head, embarrassed. "You didn't like being forced to dance with me then any more than now, I imagine."

It was his turn to be taken aback. "Miss Smallwood, you are mistaken. I am very much enjoying dancing with you. I only hesitated because I thought you would prefer to dance with Phillip."

She stole a glance at him from under her long lashes. "And the last time we danced?"

She hadn't denied that she would prefer to dance with his brother, he realized. He grimaced, almost wishing he hadn't brought up the past. "I had a dashed wart on my hand and was afraid you'd be repulsed."

She looked up, a grin quivering on her lips. "That was all?"

"That was enough. Dashed embarrassing."

Her grin widened. He wasn't sure if he liked her reaction or not. She seemed to be enjoying his mortification a bit too much.

She said, "You might simply have said so."

"In front of that lot? Never. Probably would have given me the nickname *Wart*son before the day was up."

A burst of laughter escaped her, and hearing it caused his heart to warm and swell. Her face shone, her eyes sparkled, her lovely smile and inviting mouth beckoned. Perhaps mortification was a small price to pay.

He felt Lady Weston's frown and Phillip's questioning look but paid neither any heed. He decided to forget his resolve to remain aloof and simply enjoy himself. After all, who knew when or if he would ever have the chance to dance with Emma Smallwood again? The truth was, he liked the woman. Though there was precious little he could do about it.

*I cannot command winds and weather.*

—Horatio Nelson

# Chapter 14

Emma had barely fallen asleep that night when a piercing cry awoke her. She sat straight up in bed, ready to bolt to the aid of whichever pupil was in distress. Who was it?

Then her mind caught up with her pounding heart and whirling thoughts. She was not in Longstaple with pupils under their roof. She was in Ebbington Manor. Not quite a guest, not quite a servant, and certainly not family. And, unless it had been her father crying out—and it had not—it wasn't her place to take care of the crisis, whatever it was.

For a few moments she sat there, listening. Waiting to see if a second cry would follow the first, or if it had been the single cry of one waking from a nightmare.

Lightning flashed beyond the window. In the flurry of extra work for the party and the added guests, no one had come in to close her shutters, nor had she bothered when she'd gotten into bed. Outside, thunder rumbled, and lightning lit up her room. Was someone in the house afraid of storms? She could not imagine Julian or Rowan at nearly sixteen being afraid, nor Lizzie a year older, though immature for her age. Emma hoped no one was ill. Especially on the Penberthys' last night.

Knowing she would not sleep until she reassured herself all was well—or at least that there was nothing she could do, Emma rose, pulled her wrapper around herself, slipped her feet into her shoes, and opened the door.

The cry ripped through the house once more, freezing Emma to the spot and sending shivers down her back. The poor thing, whoever it was. She heard distant footsteps. Good. Someone was on his or her way to help, to comfort.

Emma rounded the corner, planning to press an ear to her father's door and, if all was silent, allow him to slumber on, undisturbed. If anyone could sleep through such a noise, it was her father—which was no doubt the reason she had become trained to leap from bed in response to the rare cry back at their boarding school.

As Emma stood there, still and quiet at her father's door, a figure appeared at the top of the stairs, candle lamp in hand.

Henry Weston, in shirtsleeves and trousers. Henry Weston, who swung his light in her direction, as if to assure himself no one was about, and who obviously did not see her in the recessed threshold of her father's room.

He turned and crept down the corridor and at its end turned, disappearing from view into the north wing. It was the second time she'd seen him venture there at night.

Emma wondered where they had put the Penberthys. Surely Henry was not on his way to Tressa Penberthy's room. Not dressed like that. Besides, though she could have been mistaken, the cry Emma had heard had not sounded female to her.

Emma carried no candle and hoped she would run into no unexpected obstacles. Especially one named Henry Weston.

At the end of the corridor, she turned. There the passage darkened, cut off as it was from the candle lamp on the stairway landing.

*What am I doing?* Emma wondered, nerves buzzing. *I am only seeing if any help is needed,* she told herself. *Then I shall return to my bed.* The rational thoughts did not quite trump her irrational fear of the dark passage, the off-limits wing of the house, and Henry Weston.

The wind howled, and the house shuddered under its sway. An answering cry rent the darkness. To her it sounded like a terrified child. But there were no children at Ebbington Manor. Perhaps it was the youthfulness of the cry that lent her the courage to continue down that dark corridor, the smell of dust and disuse heavy in the air.

She sneezed, then paused, fearful a door would open and footsteps pursue her. . . . But she heard no one, her sneeze likely lost in the wind and thunder. Another sound caught her ears. A banging—the cracking of wood on wood.

As she neared the end of the corridor, the sound grew louder. Faint light seeped from beneath the last door. Other noises accompanied the louder banging. *Whap-whap-whap* punctuated by a "No, no, no," in monotonous drone. What in the world? Was someone being beaten? Surely not. Whatever she had thought Henry Weston guilty of in his youth, she would never have believed him capable of such violence.

Ready to defend the child, whoever he was, Emma pushed open the door. The creaking of the hinge was swallowed in the cacophony of howling wind, banging, slapping, and crying.

It took Emma's eyes a moment to adjust to the candlelight and understand the scene before her.

Henry Weston rushed from window to window, frantically tossing aside billowing draperies and banging shutters to reach the open windows beyond. Why in the world were the windows open on such a night? The *crack-crack* of wooden shutters lessened as Henry pulled in one window after another and then hurried to the next.

On the floor sat a figure huddled tight. Legs bent, ankles crossed, chin tucked, elbows framing knees and hidden face, cupped palms hitting his own ears—*whap-whap-whap*. A slight young man from what she could see of him, in a long dressing gown. His "No, no, no" high-pitched—though he was not a child, as she had guessed.

She wanted to go to him, to comfort him, but decided it would be best to first help stop the racket, which clearly distressed him.

She ran to the far window, slid beneath the flying veil of gauzy drapes, and felt for the sash.

Henry snarled, "Why she insisted on putting him in this room with all these dashed windows, I'll never know. And why on earth are they open during a storm?"

Emma pulled the window closed and secured the latch. Deprived of billowing wind, the drapery fell flat, and she emerged from behind it.

Henry glanced over and froze. He had obviously assumed she was someone else. A maid, perhaps, or one of the family come to help.

"Miss Smallwood . . ." he murmured, stunned.

"I shall get the last one. Go to him," she commanded, cool and officious.

He hesitated only a moment, then turned and crossed the room. She hurried to the last window and secured it, then began to close the wooden shutters over the windows, which would further muffle the storm and block the flashes of lightning. She glanced over her shoulder as she worked. Henry sat on his haunches before the young man, close but not touching, speaking in low, soothing tones.

The slight man continued to cup his ears, but the force of the blows lessened. Emma finished as quickly as she could and then tentatively approached them. Now that the shutters were closed and the storm noises subdued, she could hear what Henry was saying.

"It's all right now. I'm sorry about that. Did you open the windows yourself?"

No answer beyond the "No, no, no . . ."—quieter now.

Emma knelt beside the young man. She caught a glimpse of his face tucked between elbows—a grimace of fear, or pain? Impulsively, she reached out and laid a gentle hand on his arm. "It's all right. You're safe."

He jerked away from her touch as though burned and began beating his ears in earnest once more, his "No, no, no . . ." becoming a panicked wail.

She gaped at Henry. "I'm sorry! I only meant to comfort him."

"I know. It's not your fault. He doesn't like to be touched."

Henry began soothing him with gentle words once more. "This is Miss Smallwood. She did not mean to upset you. She has helped us close all those dashed windows and shutters. Was that not kind of her? Miss Smallwood is very kind, you will see. You have nothing to fear from her."

Henry glanced over at her meaningfully, as if willing his words to be true. "You are not to be here, you know."

"I heard him cry out. I could not sit by and do nothing."

He gave a sardonic grin. "Of course you could not. Others, it seems, had not the same problem."

It was indeed surprising that no one else had come to check on the source of the alarm.

The young man quieted, whether from Henry's reassurances or the peace of the room, she did not know.

"Adam, did you open the windows yourself?" Henry asked again.

*Adam.* Who was Adam? Emma wondered. She didn't recall the Westons mentioning anyone by that name.

The young man made no reply and his face remained hidden in his arms, but a convulsion, a slight shaking of his head, apparently signaled *no*.

"Then who opened them?"

When he made no answer, Henry patiently prompted, "Mrs. Prowse?"

Adam shook his head.

"One of the boys—Julian or Rowan?"

A hesitation. A momentary stillness. Then another slight shake of his head.

Emma wondered what it meant.

"Well, we'll talk about it tomorrow," Henry said, rising. "For now, let's get you back into bed. All right? You must be tired. I know I am."

When Adam didn't respond, Henry urged gently, "Come on now. On your feet." He didn't reach out to cup the young man's elbow but extended his own hand in an offer of assistance. For a moment Adam looked up at Henry's hand from under a fall of wavy brown hair, and then finally he reached up and gripped it. Henry pulled him easily to his feet.

Emma had her first full glimpse of Adam's face. Thin and pale, yes, but quite pleasing. He reminded her of a Raphael painting of a soulful young man she had seen in one of her books. Ethereal, yet clearly male. There was also something vaguely familiar about him, though she was certain she had never before laid eyes on him.

While the young man climbed into bed, Emma remained where she was.

Henry waited until Adam was situated on his pillow, arms straight at his sides, before pulling up the blankets to just under his chin. "All right?" he asked.

A little nod, eyes staring up at the ceiling as though waiting for sleep to fall on him from above.

Emma waited to speak until Henry had retrieved his candle, preceded her into the corridor, and quietly closed the door behind them.

There she whispered, "Who is he, poor creature?"

"He is not a poor creature, Miss Smallwood," he said. "He is my brother."

Her eyes flew to his face in the flickering candlelight. "Brother?" she echoed, mind whirling. A brother named Adam? Why on earth had she never heard of him? In a moment she answered her own question. Recalling the scene, the posture and behavior in which she had first seen Adam, she thought she had an inkling of why they had never been introduced.

Henry ran a hand over his face. "I will explain it to you, Miss Smallwood. You have my word. But not tonight. It's terribly late, and I'm exhausted."

"I understand."

"If you would be good enough to keep this to yourself . . . for now? Lady Weston is most adamant that the Penberthys not learn about Adam during their visit."

Emma wondered how Lady Weston planned to keep such a thing quiet if Miss Penberthy was to marry into the family, but said only, "Very well," and turned.

"Miss Smallwood?" His voice turned her back around. "Thank you for helping. For understanding."

"You're welcome. Good night."

Emma retraced her steps to her room. Thoughts and questions

still churned in her mind, and she knew she would not find sleep for several hours.

❦

Lady Weston had decided to end the Penberthys' visit with an afternoon concert. So after church, a buffet meal awaited them at home: breads, cold meats and cheeses, salads and desserts.

Then they all adjourned to the music room, where Mr. and Miss Smallwood joined them at Lady Weston's behest, to add to the illusion of a proper audience. It irked Henry to see the respected tutor and his lovely daughter seated at the back of the room.

Julian took his place on the bench. He announced, "Beethoven's *Pathétique* Sonata in C Minor."

He struck the jarring opening bars.

The music hit Henry like fists to his heart, followed by softer, apologetic caresses. Then the dramatic notes spun away in a bright, whirling dance, rising to a fevered pitch, so loud it nearly hurt Henry's ears. Again and again Julian reached a reverberating crescendo, only to fall away into a gentler refrain. It put Henry in mind of delicate flower petals laid on an anvil, struck again and again by a merciless hammer.

The sonata was not to Henry's taste, but he knew he was no great judge of music. He glanced over and noticed Mrs. Penberthy exchange a suitably impressed glance with Lady Weston. Her opinion being all that mattered, Henry sat back to endure the rest of the performance.

After Julian finished and accepted their applause, Lady Weston suggested, "Perhaps now Miss Penberthy will favor us with a piece?"

"If you like," Tressa said, rising. "Though I fear I play very ill compared to young Mr. Weston there."

Julian smiled thinly at the compliment wrapped in a remark about his age.

"Perhaps Phillip will be so good as to turn the pages for Miss Penberthy?" Lady Weston looked significantly at Phillip, who reddened but rose dutifully.

Julian said, "I shall do it, Mamma. For I am right here already and am far more familiar with music than Phillip is."

Lady Weston's smile tightened. "No doubt, Julian. But oblige me and allow Phillip to assist Miss Penberthy."

Julian scowled and flopped into a nearby chair, crossing his arms over his narrow chest.

Miss Penberthy played, and very accomplished she was. Henry did notice one slightly off-key note and told himself they ought to get the old thing tuned one of these days.

When Miss Penberthy finished her piece, he joined the others in polite applause.

"Well"—Mrs. Penberthy rose—"this has been quite a pleasant visit. Tressa and I thank you all for your kind hospitality, but I am afraid we must excuse ourselves to prepare for our departure."

Lady Weston rose as well. "So soon? How quickly the time has flown. But isn't that always the way it is when friends meet? You and I were already friends, and I hope the same may be said of our children, now that other bonds of . . . affection . . . have been formed."

Henry noticed Mrs. Penberthy did not quite meet Lady Weston's eager gaze when she replied, "Well, of course we are all now better acquainted."

Lady Weston smiled. "And hopefully you will both visit us again soon?"

As the women spoke about vague future pleasantries, the others began rising and funneling from the room through its double doors. Henry followed suit and brought up the rear of the party.

Suddenly from behind him came the sound of a key being struck, once, twice, three times. The same key. Henry turned and saw with dismay that Adam now sat at the pianoforte, head bent, hitting that single off-tune key. C, C, C. . . . C, C, C. . . .

Where in the world had he come from? Henry had not heard the rear door open. Had he been hiding in the room all along? Henry hoped, for his stepmother's sake, that the Penberthy women would exit the music room and be on their way without hearing or investigating this latest "musician."

But Miss Penberthy turned in the threshold, looked at Adam, then to Phillip expectantly, waiting for an explanation or introduction. Phillip reddened once more and smiled inanely as though he did not understand her meaningful look.

Mrs. Penberthy, perhaps not finding her daughter at her side, stepped back into the music room.

Henry groaned. *Thunder and turf....*

"My dear, we must be going...." Mrs. Penberthy hesitated at seeing the young man at the pianoforte. "Who is that, pray?" she asked, chuckling uncertainly at the repetitive note, as though it were some sort of joke.

Lady Weston stepped to her side, stiffening at the sight of Adam. She sent a thunderous look toward Henry, then smiled benignly at her friend. "Come, my dear. You don't want to be late in departing. You have a long journey ahead."

"Yes, I know. But who is that young man?"

Henry stood where he was, ready to introduce his brother, waiting for a sign from Lady Weston as to how she wanted to handle the situation. Surely she would not lie directly to her friend and deny knowledge of who Adam was. Claim he was a servant or some such. Watching Violet Weston's face, he thought he detected a parade of possible explanations passing behind her eyes.

Finally she settled on one. "Oh, that is a relative of my husband's. Staying with us for a few days. He doesn't like company or I would have introduced him."

"Oh? Who ... ?"

"Come, come, my dear," Lady Weston insisted, taking her friend's arm. "I hear the carriage outside. Come, Tressa, your mother was most adamant about an on-time departure, and I won't be blamed for any delays."

Violet Weston shepherded her friend from the room with a firm tone and a firm grip. The others followed, as did Miss Penberthy, but Henry did not miss the suspicious glance over her shoulder as she quit the room.

*Crisis averted,* Henry thought dryly. He crossed the room to where Adam was still tonking away at that single note. "Where did you come from, Adam?"

Adam tilted his head, listening intently as the note reverberated through the instrument.

Henry said, "I didn't see you here when we all came in."

"I hid."

"Where?"

Adam glanced over to a long-skirted table against the nearby wall, upon which a row of marble busts was lined.

"I see." Henry winced at the increasingly irritating repetition of the off-key middle C. He asked gently, "It's out of tune—is that it?"

Adam nodded and struck the key again, ear bent near.

"You have a good ear, Adam," Henry said. "I shall ask Mr. Davies about arranging for a piano tuner, shall I?"

Suddenly Lady Weston's voice slapped the air. "Well. That was the outside of enough."

Henry turned, steeling himself and telling himself to remain calm.

She stood inside the door, hands on her hips, in high dudgeon. "I asked you to keep him out of sight for two days. Two days. And you cannot even manage that." She looked past Henry toward the pianoforte. "Where has he got to now?"

Henry looked at the empty bench, then glanced at the skirted table. The curtain ruffled slightly, but he made no comment.

Lady Weston pointed an angry finger at Henry. "Tell me you did not arrange this little drama to vex me—to scare away Miss Penberthy. The most eligible young woman any of you are likely to meet."

"I did not."

"It was bad enough last night with that infernal crying and banging. Fortunately I had arranged to put the Penberthys as far from that room as possible. And though I feared otherwise, they both assured me they enjoyed an undisturbed night's sleep. You see, when I manage something, it is done and done correctly."

Henry gritted his teeth.

"I told you we ought to have locked his door," she continued.

"For all our sakes. That way there would have been no chance of our . . . inconvenient . . . secret coming to light, today of all days."

Righteous indignation boiled through Henry's veins. "He is not some dirty little secret, Lady Weston—not an unwashed stocking to be kicked under the bed when polite company arrives. He is a human being. And he has done nothing wrong nor hurt anybody. I will not stand by while you speak of locking him up as though he were a criminal. Do you understand me? Adam is my brother. My *brother*."

Sir Giles strode into the room, followed by Phillip.

"I say, what's all this, then?" his father asked, looking from his wife to Henry.

Henry inhaled through flared nostrils. "Lady Weston is upset because her precious friend got a glimpse of Adam. She had hoped to keep him hidden until after the vows were said."

"Vows? What vows?"

"Aren't you keeping up, Father? Lady Weston plans for Phillip or me—it doesn't really matter which—to marry Miss Penberthy. And only after it is too late will the poor girl learn that we all have deceived her by keeping this particular member of our family secret."

Phillip, still standing in the threshold, said nothing, but with a glance over his shoulder, he discreetly shut the door.

Lady Weston lifted her chin. "Why does she ever need know? You've never told any other young lady you admired, I don't imagine. Why should now be any different?"

"Because I didn't *know* before. That's why."

Lady Weston barely blinked. "Once he is installed with a replacement guardian, all shall be as it has been for the last twenty years. Why should things change now?"

Sir Giles must have seen the dangerous fire in Henry's eyes, for he wisely steered the conversation to safer ground. "My dear. Henry. Let us not be at one another's throats. Please do remember, Henry, that Lady Weston deserves a respectful tone from you, even when the two of you disagree." He laid a hand on Henry's shoulder. "Your mother and I did what we thought was best for you. For everyone."

"For me? It's my fault somehow?"

"Don't be ridiculous. Of course it's not your fault. You were only a child. But we were worried about you—and Phillip. How living with such a . . . different . . . boy might affect your development, your intelligence and learning. And we feared keeping him here would put you both in danger. He was so changeable. His fits, so violent."

"So it was all for us." Henry could not keep the sarcasm from his tone. "Not to avoid embarrassment on your part?"

"Of course we were embarrassed," Sir Giles snapped. "Our first-born son. Not right. How we thanked God when you showed no signs of the same. How we prayed for you."

"Did you pray for him too?" Henry challenged.

Sir Giles frowned. "Why are you so angry, Henry? I might understand if Adam resented us, but why should you feel this so personally, so intensely?"

"Because you sent him away. Let me believe he died."

Sir Giles raised a finger. "I never said he died."

"'Gone' was the euphemism you used, Gone and not coming back. What else was I supposed to think? I was too young to press you. Too young to doubt my own father."

"That's right—you were young," Lady Weston interjected. "Too young to remember."

Henry clenched one fist but kept his gaze trained on his father. "I remember I had a big brother." He clapped his other hand to his chest. "Not clearly. But enough to know I have missed someone all my life."

"You're thinking of your mother, surely."

"I miss her, too, of course. But no, it was Adam I've missed all these years." Henry shook his head. "All these years thinking he was dead, and there he was, living not twenty miles away from us the whole time."

"Oh, come now." Lady Weston huffed, gesturing emphatically. "You were only—what?—four at the time? You no doubt forgot all about him until you read that letter."

Henry's voice quivered in anger. "Do not presume to tell me what I do and do not remember, madam."

She continued undeterred, "I still don't understand what you were doing poking about the estate ledgers in the first place, not to mention reading your father's correspondence."

Phillip sent him a beseeching look, but Henry ignored it. "What I was doing, madam," he ground out, "was trying to make sense out of this family's precarious financial situation."

"I did ask him to take it in hand, my dear," Sir Giles swiftly added. "The tangle was beyond me, and he agreed to do so, when he no doubt had plans of his own that had to be set aside."

She sniffed. "Be that as it may, I still maintain Henry is making too much of this. Why could he not leave well enough alone?"

"Well enough? Well enough!" Henry's voice rose. "Adam's guardian dead, left in that damp cottage all alone . . . If I had not gone and fetched him when I did, who knows where he would be by now?"

"Anywhere but here would have been preferable these last two days."

"The workhouse would be preferable?" Henry thundered. "For Father's eldest son?"

Lady Weston shook her head. "I don't mean the workhouse, of course. But he does not belong here, as I—"

From under the skirted table rose a muted litany, "No, no, no. . . ."

*What a fool I am,* Henry chastised himself. He'd forgotten about the very person he'd been trying to defend. Of course harsh words and arguing would upset him. A very real storm in the room he occupied as unwilling witness.

Henry hurried to the table, lowering himself to his haunches. He drew the curtain aside, revealing Adam in a fetal position, cradling his ears, and repeating his chant of distress.

Lady Weston took one look at him and threw up her hands. "Oh yes. Ready to meet the queen, he is." She stalked past Phillip and out of the room.

Henry turned back to Adam. "Sorry about that. We are all through arguing. All done." He heard his father's footsteps retreat as well.

Henry ignored the sting of rejection and continued, "All is well. Shhh . . . You are not in any trouble. You're all right," he said, grimly determined to make certain that was true.

Phillip followed along as Henry escorted Adam upstairs to his room a few minutes later. When they reached the north wing, Phillip preceded them down the corridor and opened the door for them.

Inside, Henry led Adam to his favorite chair while Phillip stepped to the washstand and poured a glass of water. When Adam was seated, Henry laid a lap robe over his knees and Phillip handed him the glass of water.

"Thank you," Adam whispered, his chin still quivering.

Henry noticed Phillip staring at his eldest brother. A person he had never seen in his life before returning from Oxford.

"I still can't quite get over it," Phillip said. "That there is another Weston. Another son of our mother and father."

Henry nodded. "I know."

Phillip's gaze remained on Adam. "His features are so familiar. His eyes are like mine, are they not?"

Apparently aware of their scrutiny, Adam's innocent blue gaze skittered from one to the other before landing on a book on the side table. He picked it up and placed it in his lap, running his hands over the cover again and again as though drawing comfort from its texture, its familiarity.

"Yes," Henry acknowledged. "You look more like Adam than like me. Lucky devil."

Phillip did not acknowledge the compliment. He was busy staring at Adam. "He looks so . . . normal."

"I know," Henry agreed. "When I look at him, I see a little of you, a little of Father, and now and again, in one of his rare smiles . . . a little of our mother."

Phillip said quietly, "I don't remember her."

Henry opened his mouth to reply, but Mrs. Prowse knocked and entered with Adam's dinner tray. A second plate—hers—joined his. The kind housekeeper often shared her mealtimes with Adam. It warmed Henry's heart to see it. He owed the woman so much.

They greeted her, thanked her, saw the two of them settled contentedly together, and then Henry and Phillip excused themselves.

Together they retreated slowly from the north wing. As they reached the main corridor, Henry glanced at his younger brother. "Phillip, I'm sorry. I know I lost my temper downstairs."

"No need to apologize to me."

Henry shot him a look. "If you're hinting I need to apologize to Lady Weston, that will need to wait. I am not yet calm enough to attempt it."

"No doubt. I haven't seen you that upset since they announced you were being sent away to school."

Henry snorted. "Remember that, do you?"

"Impressed on my ten-year-old mind forever." Phillip shuddered theatrically, then sobered. "It still bothers her, you know."

"What does?"

"That you've always refused to call her Mother."

Henry expelled an exasperated breath. "Everything I do, or don't do, seems to bother her."

Phillip continued as though he'd not heard his protest. "Is it because you remember our own mamma?"

"I suppose so. That and the fact that Violet Weston and I have never liked each other."

"I don't think it's so much that she does not like you, Henry," Phillip said quietly. "It's that you never let her forget she is not your mamma and never shall be."

His brother's words, gently spoken, stung Henry's heart with conviction. He wanted to dismiss them but could not.

When they reached the top of the stairs, Henry turned in to the alcove and stood before the portrait of their mother.

Staring at it, Phillip inhaled deeply. "I wish I did remember her. How weak you must think me for trying to gain Violet Weston's affection all these years."

His brother's downcast expression stung Henry's conscience

once more. "Not at all, Phillip. Good heavens, you were only a toddler when Mamma died. Of course you needed a mother."

"And you did not?"

Henry looked away from his brother's knowing blue eyes.

Phillip let the subject drop. "Father used to tell me Mamma called me her 'little pip.' But when I try to remember, all I see is this portrait of her, with the mouth moving and father's voice speaking in falsetto, 'my little pip.'"

Henry chuckled. "I know. I can't remember her voice either. And her face . . . The older, dearer face I knew is fading more and more into this"—he nodded toward the portrait—"less familiar one."

Phillip looked at him. "What do you remember about her?"

Henry thought. He did *not* remember her sending Adam away. Had he so idealized her as the perfect person no one was? He said, "I remember her reading to me. And her sad smile. Her large, kind eyes. The way she smelled—like lily of the valley. But of course that memory has been renewed by the occasional sniff of her old perfume bottle." He glanced at his brother sheepishly. "And now you will think *me* the weak one."

"Never." Phillip paused. "I don't suppose I might take a sniff?"

Henry's lips parted in surprise. "Of course. It has recently gone missing, I'm afraid. But as soon as I find it again, I shall bring it to you. How selfish I've been to keep it to myself. I didn't think you'd remember."

"I don't," Phillip said. "But I'd like to."

*We have this comfort, he cannot*
*be a bad or a wicked child.*

—George Austen (Jane Austen's father)
writing about his son raised elsewhere.

# Chapter 15

The next afternoon, Lizzie found Emma in the schoolroom just after the boys had been dismissed for the day. She held a battledore under her arm and a shuttlecock in her hand. With her free hand, she thrust a second racquet toward Emma. "Do say you'll play, Emma."

Emma stared down at the offered racquet with resignation but little pleasure. She had refused the girl too many times to do so again. Besides, the thought of fresh air and sunshine appealed to Emma more than usual. She was eager to leave behind the tense confines of the manor and her relentless questions about Adam.

"Very well. I shall." She accepted the battledore. "But I warn you—I play very ill."

At least Emma assumed she did. She had not played in years but accepted the fact that she was not athletic in general. She had long avoided any activity involving fast-flying objects.

After Emma retrieved bonnet and gloves from her room, the girls went downstairs and outside. As they walked to an open area of the lawn, Lizzie asked, "Did you hear what happened yesterday, after most of us left the music room?"

Emma shook her head. "No."

Lizzie explained, "After the Penberthys departed, I asked Julian what all the fuss had been about. Apparently Miss Penberthy saw a stranger playing the pianoforte, but Lady Weston passed him off as a distant relative. Like me. Really, it was a fifth Weston brother. They've been keeping him in the north wing!" Lizzie shook her head in wonder. "It was the first I'd heard of him. I told you they don't trust me to keep a secret." She looked at Emma accusingly. "I suppose even you knew about Adam Weston before I did."

Emma soothed, "I only learned of him Saturday night. I heard him cry out during the storm."

Lizzie nodded in relief. "I went up to see him this morning." She darted a sly smile at Emma. "He is quite good-looking, isn't he, for all his odd ways?"

"Yes, I suppose he is."

Lizzie stepped several yards away and faced Emma, shuttlecock held in her fingertips over the battledore, poised to serve. "I wonder about Henry. If he'll still be heir and all. Julian says they'll likely have Adam declared incompetent to inherit or something like that."

"I wouldn't know," Emma said, though she imagined Julian was probably right.

Lizzie struck the feathered shuttlecock, and it lofted in the air in Emma's general direction. As Emma tried to follow it, the sun got in her eyes and she blinked. The shuttlecock fluttered to the ground.

"Sorry." Emma bent to retrieve it, tried to mimic Lizzie's method of serving, missed the feathered object altogether, and had to retrieve it once more.

She groaned. "I told you I was out of practice."

Unconcerned, Lizzie said, "Lady Weston is sorely vexed. She fears Adam has spoiled their chances with the Penberthys."

Emma swung hard, sending the shuttlecock high. Too high. The wind caught it and carried it far out of Lizzie's reach.

"Sorry!"

As the girl hurried after it, Emma thought back to the ball. If she had read Miss Penberthy correctly, the young woman preferred Phillip. Though it was less easy to tell if either Phillip or Henry admired her. Emma found she felt no jealousy where Philip was concerned. For all his warmth, Emma had come to realize he felt only platonic friendship for her.

When Lizzie returned and prepared to serve, Emma asked, "Do you mean that Lady Weston hoped for an attachment between Miss Penberthy and Phillip?"

Lizzie snapped her head up. "Why would you say Phillip?" She frowned. "Why should it be him and not Henry? He is the eldest after all, if one doesn't count Adam, and Lady Weston certainly does not."

Emma felt her brow pucker. Had she misunderstood Lizzie's declaration of love for an "older Mr. Weston," or had Lizzie changed her mind? She sputtered, "I don't know. I—"

Lizzie smacked the shuttlecock hard and it flew right toward Emma's face.

Emma squealed and ducked. When she looked up, she saw Lizzie roll her eyes.

Emma picked up the shuttlecock and positioned it. But a glance told her something else had caught Lizzie's attention from across the stable yard.

Head turned, Lizzie said, "Here come Phillip and Henry now. They went to interview another possible guardian for Adam, I believe." She slanted Emma another of her sly looks. "Or so I overheard."

The two brothers came striding across the lawn, coattails billowing in the breeze. Henry wore his customary intense look, topper pulled low. Phillip's sat a jaunty angle, but even he appeared uncharacteristically sober.

Lizzie hurried toward them and thrust her battledore at Henry's midriff. "Henry, do be a dear and take over for me with Miss Smallwood. I need to ask Phillip something."

Emma was offended and embarrassed all at once. Lizzie had all but begged her to play, only to abandon her when they had barely begun? And worse—handed her off to Henry Weston? That man would not relish the notion of playing any sort of sport with her. Making sport *of* her, yes, but not playing an actual match. Nor did she want to play with him. How intimidating to face off against the man with all his masculine athletic prowess.

Henry looked down at the battledore in his hands as though unsure how it suddenly appeared there. He glanced to the side, where Lizzie had taken Phillip's arm and was all but tugging him away.

Phillip looked at them over his shoulder with a self-conscious shrug.

Lizzie said, loud enough for them all to hear, "I have vexed Lady Weston yet again. You must advise me. You always know just what to do to regain her favor."

Emma wondered if that was really what Lizzie wanted to talk to Phillip about. She had said nothing about Lady Weston being vexed with *her*.

Henry looked from the battledore to Emma, then strode slowly toward her.

"You needn't play, Mr. Weston," Emma said. "I only agreed to play for Lizzie's sake, so . . ."

"Oh, come, Miss Smallwood. Please tell me you don't shun all things athletic as you did as a girl." A teasing light shone in his eyes. "Afraid you'll lose?"

Emma huffed. "I am not afraid to lose. I know I shall. This isn't chess, after all."

One eyebrow rose. "Oh, ho! A shot to the heart. The lady recalls soundly trouncing me, I see. Then you must give me a chance to redeem myself." He set aside his hat and adopted a ready stance, bouncing lightly from foot to foot. He looked fifteen years old all over again.

Emma felt a grin lift a corner of her mouth. "Oh, very well. But promise not to laugh too hard."

"I promise."

She positioned the shuttlecock, concentrated, and swung her battledore. *Thwack.* A satisfying echoing snap, and the shuttlecock lofted in a graceful arc. Henry leapt to the side and smacked it back. Emma stepped backward, raised her racquet, and miracle of miracles, made contact with a hollow plunk. The shuttlecock flew, and Henry ran forward and tapped it lightly at her. The shuttlecock rode the soft breeze slowly enough to give Emma time to judge distance and react. Much easier than a fast-flying ball. She hit it again, hard, and since Henry had run forward to return her last hit, he had to quickly backpedal. She thought—hoped—he might miss it, but the man had the wingspan of a wandering albatross. He reached back, back and whacked it high overhead. Emma was determined not to waver for a second or blink in the sun as before. She would not mortify herself in front of this man if humanly possible.

Eye on the shuttlecock, she ran forward, raised her battledore high, and slammed right into Henry Weston's chest.

The wind knocked from her, Emma lost her balance and might have fallen had not Mr. Weston's arms shot out and caught her about the waist and shoulder.

"Oh," she cried, embarrassed to have plowed into the man. Embarrassed to find his arms around her.

Embarrassed to find she liked it.

"I'm so sorry," she blurted, pushing away from him.

"Don't be. I admire your singular focus. My goodness, Miss Smallwood, where is the timid little creature who flinched at every flying bird as though it were a cricket ball headed for her nose?"

Emma straightened and righted her off-kilter bonnet. "I was determined not to embarrass myself," she admittedly breathlessly. "Only to do just that."

He chuckled, and their eyes met in a moment of shared levity.

Then he sobered. "Thank you for the laugh, Miss Smallwood. Just what I needed after yesterday."

"Then I am happy to oblige. Lizzie told me a little of what happened after I left the music room. Is your brother . . . Is Adam all right?"

"Yes, I think so. Lady Weston less so." He told her briefly what had happened, then held out his hand for her battledore. "Shall we walk instead, Miss Smallwood?"

She surrendered her racquet. "Yes, thank you. I am a far more accomplished walker."

Henry laid both racquets along with the shuttlecock on a garden bench, retrieved his hat, and then gestured for Miss Smallwood to precede him out the garden gate. He walked beside her, near enough to talk easily but not too near.

When their footfalls left crunching gravel for spongy turf, Henry began, "I had hoped now that the 'awful secret' was getting out, she might ease up a bit. Instead she's in high dudgeon, pushing for Phillip and me to find another place for Adam. But my heart's not in the search, I own. I've only just been reunited with Adam; I'm not ready to send him away again."

Beside him, Miss Smallwood nodded in empathy, then said gently, "I don't recall either you or Phillip mentioning an older brother."

Henry grimaced. "I only recently learned about him—that he was still alive."

"I don't understand."

"Adam looks young, I know. But he is actually four years older than I am. When I was not yet four, and Phillip a newborn, Adam disappeared. There one day but not the next. When I asked, I was told he was gone and not coming back. I was too young to fully understand, or to question. And as time passed and no one spoke of him, my own memories began to fade. My mother died a few years later. After that loss, I retained vague recollections of a playmate named Adam but little else."

Henry squinted out toward the distant horizon. "I asked once or twice when I grew older. But my father told me only that there had been another child, but he'd gone long ago. And in those days, when child mortality rates were even higher than they are now . . . well, no one questioned one more child apparently dying. My mother had lost an infant before Adam was born, I have since learned. But when I saw the little nameless marker in the churchyard, I thought it Adam's."

Miss Smallwood considered this. "Why would they want you to believe he'd died?"

Henry shrugged. "Perhaps they thought it easier than trying to explain why my brother lived elsewhere. Probably thought I'd never stop pestering them to bring him home." He exhaled a dry puff of air. "They'd have been right."

She asked, "When did Adam return to Ebbington?"

"The night before you arrived. And with very little warning."

"Good heavens," Miss Smallwood breathed. "No wonder Lady Weston and Sir Giles seemed, well, disconcerted by our coming when we did."

Henry nodded.

"When did you find out he was still alive?" she asked.

The dreaded question. Guilt filled him instantly. "After I took my degree and returned home, my father asked me to take the place in hand. One day, when I reviewed the estate ledgers, I saw a monthly fee sent to a Mr. and Mrs. Hobbes in Camelford. When I asked Davies about it, I learned that Mrs. Hobbes was none other than Miss Jones—my old nurse before she married. It didn't really explain why we were still paying her, but I didn't question it for several months. We had far larger amounts to worry about."

In his mind's eye, Henry saw again the thick ledger, the many expenses documented in painful detail in their columns, and the occasional large deposit listed without explanation. Davies said it was a portion of the money Lady Weston had brought into the marriage, which she put into the estate when funds ran low. It had irked Henry—more reason to feel beholden to the woman. It had also irked him that he could not balance the books, for all his Oxford education.

Henry took a deep breath of salty air. "When I finally asked my father about the payment to our old nurse, he told me it was a pension he'd decided to grant her, in consideration of her 'exceptional care' for his offspring. We did not pay other servants after they left our employ, but I supposed a favorite nurse was a worthwhile exception and went away reasonably satisfied with his explanation.

"Then one day, village business took me to Camelford. I was curious to see my old nurse and, I admit, curious to see how she spent the money we sent. I asked around and easily located her home. Instead of the pleasant surprise I expected, Mrs. Hobbes came to the door dressed in black and seemed very nervous to see me. At first I thought she feared I had come to tell her there would be no more pension. Then I heard a commotion in the next room. Someone crying 'No, no, no' over and over again. Mrs. Hobbes explained that her husband had recently passed on, and their son was deeply unsettled by his death.

"I asked if there was anything I could do to help. But she was clearly eager for me to go. I was about to oblige her when something crashed in the next room. She ran in and I followed her. I saw a young man sitting amid broken glass, banging his head and muttering nonsense. It was clear he was not right in his mind. I was repulsed, I admit, and quickly took my leave."

Henry shook his head in regret. "I should have suspected. Guessed. But I did not. Perhaps I simply did not want to acknowledge the evidence of my eyes."

He paused to gather his thoughts. And to swallow his guilt once more. "I put it from my mind, and years passed. But then, three or four weeks ago, Mrs. Hobbes wrote to my father. I've been handling all of the estate correspondence for some time, so I read the letter myself. In it, Mrs. Hobbes acknowledged she had agreed to care for Adam discreetly, as her own. But she could not do so much longer. She was dying."

Henry risked a glance at Miss Smallwood and saw her listening intently, fern green eyes large and sad. He continued, "The name Adam struck a chord with me. And I realized the young man Mrs. Hobbes referred to—the young man I had seen—was my older brother, whom I had assumed dead. I was shocked, as you can imagine. And yet . . . not completely. Lingering questions and memories surfaced, and began snapping into place like puzzle pieces.

"In her letter, Mrs. Hobbes also referred to my visit a few years before and explained that I had seen Adam at his worst. Any change unhinged Adam, and Mr. Hobbes's death was a big one. She insisted Adam was usually quite sweet-natured, but she worried what her imminent death would do to him.

"I confronted my father with the letter, and he admitted the truth. He wanted to wait, to try to find another caretaker elsewhere. But Mrs. Hobbes had asked us to come quickly, for she feared what the local authorities might do with Adam after she died. Her last wish was to make certain Adam was never sent to a lunatic asylum or workhouse.

"So I went charging off to make certain that didn't happen. A man with a mission at last. I even took a physician friend of mine with me. I was glad I did, for we found Mrs. Hobbes already dead and ended up having to sedate Adam to remove him from the house after she had been buried.

"I brought him home to Ebbington. I wanted to put him in his old room and arrange a caregiver for him. But Lady Weston insisted that he be kept in the little-used north wing away from the family. She wanted him to be locked in as well, but I battled against that. She relented on that point but still insists another situation be found for him, and that he not be kept at Ebbington Manor a day longer than necessary. And so, on that errand, I asked Mrs. Prowse to oversee Adam's care and left for a few days, to close up the Hobbes's house and interview possible replacements for the kindly couple. To no avail. When I returned, I was baffled to discover you and your father installed in the house. And my stepmother none too pleased about it either."

"She made little secret of that fact," Miss Smallwood said. "Now at least I understand why."

Henry sighed. "I have judged my father as unfair and unfeeling, but I know he did what most upper-class people would do in this situation. There are no decent institutions for people like Adam. And a lunatic asylum, workhouse, and poorhouse are grim fates indeed. We can be glad Adam was spared any of those."

"Yes." Miss Smallwood nodded, then looked upward in thought. "I still wonder about the open windows in his room the night of the storm. Mrs. Prowse wouldn't have left them open."

Henry agreed. "I have been thinking about that too."

She squinted in concentration. "Surely whoever it was could not have known what it would do to Adam—how it would throw him into a fit."

Henry frowned. "Or perhaps they did know. And did it for precisely that reason."

"But why?"

"To scare off the Penberthys, perhaps."

"But who would want to do that?"

He shook his head regretfully. "I can think of several possibilities, unfortunately."

Miss Smallwood nodded. "So can I."

*Care killed a cat.*

—Shakespeare

# Chapter 16

Emma, regretting her first meeting with Adam Weston had been an unhappy one, decided to brave the north wing again, this time by daylight. She wanted to take him something as an olive branch. A token of friendship. Acting on a hunch, she brought down a tin of ivory dominoes with ebony pips from the schoolroom. She wondered if he might play a game with her, or at least enjoy playing with them on his own. She had seen little source of diversion in his room, though, of course, she had not checked every drawer and cupboard.

She made her way to the end of the north wing and knocked softly on his door. A sound from inside suddenly ceased. A rocking chair? The door opened a few inches, and the housekeeper, Mrs. Prowse, appeared. Emma realized she had barely laid eyes on the woman since she and her father had first arrived. Now she knew why.

"Ah . . . Miss Smallwood. How did you know where to find me? You're not to be in here."

"It's all right, Mrs. Prowse. I know about Adam."

Her eyebrows rose. "Do you now? Then I suppose you'd better come in." Mrs. Prowse held the door for Emma, then shut it quietly behind her.

Adam was sitting in an armchair near the window. She was surprised and pleased to see him reading a book. He glanced up timidly when she entered but, after apparently assuring himself that she meant no harm, resumed reading.

Emma quietly explained to Mrs. Prowse about the storm, hearing Adam's cries, and coming to investigate.

The housekeeper nodded, mouth downturned. "Yes, Master Henry told me about that night, though he didn't mention your part in it. And sorry I was to hear it too. I've been looking after Adam as much as I could amidst my other duties, but then my father fell ill, and I had to go and see him."

"I am sorry to hear it. How did you find him?"

"Very bad, I'm afraid. Had an apoplexy, poor soul. But at least I was able to see him and help a bit."

Emma nodded her understanding.

"That's why I wasn't here that night, " the woman continued. "Had I been, I would have come to check on Adam and sit with him during the worst of the storm."

Emma lifted the tin in her hand. "I brought some dominoes for him. Unless . . . Has he a set already?"

Mrs. Prowse turned to look around the room. "Not that I've seen. Don't know as he'll have any interest, but kind of you just the same." The housekeeper hesitated. "You . . . know not to say anything about him, right?"

"I do. Though I think it a pity."

"As do I." Mrs. Prowse inhaled deeply. "I knew Mrs. Hobbes very well, though she was Miss Jones when she worked here. We stayed in touch over the years. Very fond of Adam she was. Like a son to her and Mr. Hobbes. God rest their souls." Tears brightened her eyes.

Emma felt she ought to squeeze the dear woman's hand but hesitated, and the moment passed.

Mrs. Prowse wiped at her eyes and drew back her shoulders. "Well, I had better go down and check on things."

Emma nodded. "I'll see you later."

When the door closed behind the housekeeper, Emma stood with the tin in her hands, observing Adam, waiting for him to look up at her.

He did not.

She looked around the room instead, noticing several drawings pinned to one wall. Battle scenes. Soldiers engaged in hand-to-hand combat. Gruesome yet impressively realistic. Had Rowan done these or had Adam?

Gently, she said, "Good afternoon, Mr. . . ." She paused. She wanted to treat him with all the respect she would give any other Weston. But did he even recognize that surname as his, or had he grown up as Adam Hobbes? She decided to use his Christian name, something she would not usually do, at least until invited. "May I come closer, Adam? I have brought you something."

Finally, he looked up, his blue eyes skittering from her face to the tin in her hand.

"Biscuits?" he asked hopefully.

A little bubble of mirth tickled her stomach. "Do you like biscuits?"

He nodded.

"Perhaps next time I shall bring you some. But today I've brought dominoes. Have you ever played?"

Slowly, she crossed the room, watching his face to make certain he showed no signs of alarm. His expression remained rather static, so it was difficult to tell what he was thinking or feeling, but she saw no obvious distress. Emma walked to a small table and chairs placed beneath another window. A stack of drawings lay there, similar to those on the wall. She set the tin on the table beside them.

"Come and see," she offered, keeping her gaze on the tin, removing the cover and setting it aside.

Adam appeared beside her, staring down at the tiles. "Bone sticks," he murmured.

"Dominoes," she corrected.

"My pa, Mr. Hobbes, likes to play bone sticks."

He slid into a chair and began pulling from the tin domino after domino, lining them up in ascending order: 0–0, 0–1, 0–2, 0–3 . . . then moving on to the 1–1, 1–2, and so on, until all twenty-eight were arranged.

"Shall we play?" Emma asked, but he didn't appear to hear her.

As soon as he had arranged all the dominoes once, he began rearranging them, this time in ever-widening rows, like the branches of half an evergreen tree: the blank domino followed by a row of two dominoes (0–1 and 1–1). Below that a row of three (0–2, 1–2, 2–2), and so on.

Watching Adam Weston, head bent, tongue tip protruding, fingers flying, Emma felt a smile quiver on her lips. Noticing his small hands, she wondered if Adam might have been the one to come into her room and leave behind the handprint. If so, she could understand why Henry Weston had told her she needn't be afraid.

After observing Adam a few minutes longer, Emma gave up on playing a game but left content, hearing the *click-click* of ivory tiles follow her from the room.

Standing in the drawing room that afternoon, Henry ran frustrated fingers through his hair. "I don't understand why he has to remain in his bedchamber."

Lady Weston looked up from her customary chair. Phillip sat nearby, fiddling nervously with the antimacassar on the arm of the settee. Across the room Rowan and Julian sat at an inlaid game table, playing draughts.

She said, "And I don't know how to make myself any clearer. I do not want him growing accustomed to the place. To life here. It will only make it that much more difficult for him when he leaves for his new situation, which will be very soon, I trust. I am only thinking of him."

"Only him?"

"Well, of course I am concerned for Rowan and Julian. That's why I have asked them not to spend time with this particular half brother. They are not so young that I fear they might come under the influence of his less-developed behaviors, but I have every right to be concerned for their future prospects. The longer he is here, the more likely it is that the whole parish—nay, the whole county—

will know of him, and that, I assure you, will not help any of your marriage prospects."

"But most of the servants must know by now, I imagine, which likely means it's halfway across the county already."

"Only Mrs. Prowse and your valet are allowed in his room. Both very trustworthy and discreet. Mr. Davies knows, of course. The other servants have merely been told that an ailing relative has temporarily come to stay. But if he were to begin roaming the house and the grounds . . . ? Besides, I don't want Lizzie finding out. You know that girl can't keep a secret."

Lady Weston turned toward Julian and Rowan. "Nor do I want either of you telling Mr. Teague. He would find some way to use the information against us and to his profit no doubt."

Henry frowned, perplexed. "What has Teague to do with Rowan and Julian? With any of us?"

She lifted her chin. "He is about the place a great deal. An acquaintance of Mr. Davies, I believe."

"Davies? I thought he had better sense."

Lady Weston narrowed her eyes. "There is no call to criticize. What we need is to take care of this situation—and quickly, before it gets out of control. Later, if you and Sir Giles decide to bring Adam back here after all four of you boys are married, I shall raise no objection, I assure you. But until that time, I really must insist."

Julian spoke up from across the room. "I'm afraid Lizzie already knows."

Lady Weston shot him a fiery look. "Does she? How?"

"I told her after the Penberthys left. I didn't think it was still such a secret. Especially since Lizzie is practically one of the family."

Lady Weston gave an unladylike snort. Seeing the males of her family gape at her in astonishment, she quickly yanked a handkerchief from her sleeve and dabbed at her nose. "I beg your pardon."

That evening, Henry ate an early dinner with Adam in his room. Mrs. Prowse served them before going downstairs to her own meal.

Henry confided in the housekeeper that he had hoped Adam might begin taking his meals with the family but Lady Weston had refused.

Mrs. Prowse considered, then replied gently. "It's probably for the best, sir. I don't think he'd like it, sitting there in that big echoing place, at that long table, with everyone staring at him, and with so many forks to choose from, so many rules, so many courses and different foods. Really, he prefers the same dinner over and over again: Soup, bread, chicken or fish. . . ."

"Peas," Adam said. "I like peas."

Mrs. Prowse nodded. "Right, love. Peas." To Henry, she said, "I think it would upset him, his order of things, truth be told."

Henry sighed. "You are probably right. Still, I hate the thought of him being cooped up in here all day. Alone, except for you and me."

"And the occasional visit from Miss Smallwood," Mrs. Prowse added, sending Henry a telling look. "I take it Lady Weston doesn't know about that?"

He shook his head.

The housekeeper nodded. "And a good thing too, I imagine."

Emma strolled with Phillip through the garden the next morning after breakfast. The garden was even more colorful now in late May, with more flowers blooming almost daily it seemed. Birdsong beckoned amid the morning-fresh air, damp with dew. White mayflowers clustered shyly, while poppies tilted their bright orange bonnets, coyly waiting to be admired.

She pointed out a red bell-like flower and asked Phillip to identify it.

But he only murmured, "Hm? Yes . . . beautiful."

How quiet and distracted he was. This wasn't the Phillip she knew. The easygoing friend of old. Emma no longer harbored any romantic notions about Phillip, but still she hoped nothing was seriously wrong.

Taking the matter in hand, she said gently, "I can't imagine what it must be like, to learn you have an older brother you never knew."

Phillip turned toward her, a deep crease between his brows. "Oh. That's right. Henry mentioned you knew."

Emma didn't like Phillip's look of displeasure—or the fact that she had put it there. She added, "I haven't told anyone. Not even my father."

Phillip grimaced. "Lady Weston had hoped to limit the news to family. And a few trusted servants."

Emma said quietly, "And I am neither."

He looked at her quickly, regret wrestling with discomfort. "Forgive me, I didn't mean . . ." He sighed. "This has all been very difficult. Very unexpected and strange. It should be a happy time, reuniting with one's long-lost brother. And it is for Henry, in a way. But I never knew Adam. And Lady Weston and Henry have gone to war over what should be done about him, and I . . ."

"You feel trapped in the middle."

He looked at her, relieved at her understanding. "Yes."

"What does Sir Giles say about it?"

Phillip bleakly shook his head. "Very little. He is caught as I am. Trying to appease Lady Weston and make peace with Henry. A nearly impossible task. Mostly Father retreats to his library and drinks brandy."

Emma thought of her own father and his former lethargic melancholy—which was lifting, thankfully, since coming to Cornwall. She wondered what it would take for Sir Giles to find his way again as well.

Emma returned to Adam's room that afternoon. She knocked softly on his door and was surprised when it was opened not by Mrs. Prowse, but by Henry Weston.

"Oh. Hello."

"Miss Smallwood. Come in." He opened the door for her. "Adam is enjoying the dominoes you gave him. As you see."

She glanced over and saw Adam at the table, head bowed in concentration. She said, "I am glad of it. I brought a little something else, if you don't mind."

"Not at all." He gestured her inside.

She slowly approached the table where Adam sat, his hands moving over the rows and columns of dominoes. He wore a different waistcoat or she might have thought he'd remained in the same position since she'd last seen him.

"Hello, Adam. You mentioned you liked biscuits. So I've brought you mine from tea."

She unwrapped a small cloth bundle and set it on the edge of the table, out of the way of the dominoes. His eyes landed on the two ginger biscuits, and his hand, fluttering over the tiles, hesitated. He looked up at her in question.

Sitting there in the sunlight from the window, his eyes shone china blue, his pale skin was smooth, his features delicate—high cheekbones, straight nose, full mouth.

"For me?" he asked shyly.

"Yes."

"Don't you want them?"

"I don't eat many sweets. You go on. I brought them for you."

He reached for a biscuit and then, as if suddenly remembering something, looked back up at her—not quite directly but almost. "Thank you, Miss . . . ?"

"Miss Smallwood. Or you may call me Emma, if you like. Since I've been calling you Adam."

"Emma . . . That's my mar's name. Emma Hobbes. Pa calls her Emma or Em or sweetheart."

It was as many words as Emma had yet heard Adam speak all together. She noticed Adam spoke of the woman in the present tense and wondered if he understood his mar was gone for good. She hoped the mention of his adopted mother's name would not upset him or spur another fit.

But as she watched him nibbling on one of the biscuits, he seemed perfectly at ease.

"Emma. Emma . . ." He said it with no apparent distress, not as a chant, but rather as though he were tasting each ginger-spiced syllable—"Emm-ma . . ."—and finding it delicious.

She glanced up and found Henry Weston looking at her. Their eyes met and held in a moment of mutual relief and pleasure.

Someone knocked softly on the door, and Henry tore his gaze from Miss Smallwood's.

Mrs. Prowse entered, carrying her mending basket. "Oh, hello, Miss Smallwood. Mr. Weston." She hesitated. "I was just coming to sit with Adam for a while." Her uncertain gaze shifted to Miss Smallwood. "But if . . ."

"I was just leaving," Miss Smallwood said, answering the woman's unspoken question.

"Thank you, Mrs. Prowse." Henry smiled reassurance at the woman. "Your timing is perfect, for I was about to leave as well." They both bid Adam farewell, and then Henry walked Miss Smallwood to the door and opened it for her. "Where are you off to now?" he asked her, oddly reluctant to part company.

"To the schoolroom."

He nodded and walked beside her down the passage. "And how are Julian and Rowan getting on?"

"Very well, I think."

They walked together as far as the stairs. Down the corridor, Mr. Smallwood stepped from his room, wrestling a stack of books into one arm, freeing his hand to shut his door.

Before Henry could react, Emma said, "Excuse me," and hurried toward her father. He really should have helped, but instead he watched her go. Despite his best efforts, he could not help but notice the subtle sway of her hips as she strode away with her long-legged stride—head high, shoulders back. What excellent posture. What a long, elegant neck.

*Henry . . .* he silently warned himself, such thoughts catching him unaware. He recalled the scene in Adam's room. Of seeing his brother smile shyly up at her. His heart warmed at the memory. And the gift of dominoes—how had she guessed he would so enjoy them?

Miss Smallwood relieved her father of several books to lighten his load. He said something to her, and she smiled in return. She had good teeth—a charming smile.

Henry would like to make Emma Smallwood smile like that. He would have to make it his aim next time they were together.

But then he remembered Phillip, his confession of love for a lovely girl of humble circumstances, someone he had returned to Ebbington to see. Henry sighed and tried to swallow the bitter lump of disappointment lodging in his throat.

Later that afternoon, Emma sat in the lone chair in her room, reading her volume of Cornwall history.

A knock sounded, and she called, "Come in."

Lizzie opened the door and poked her head in. "May I join you? I long for female company—preferably a female who doesn't require me to go blind over needlework all the day long."

Emma nodded and rose, offering Lizzie the chair. "You may read with me, if you like." She gestured toward the stack of books on her side table, crowned by her teacup and the *eau de cologne*. She'd only recently set it there, deciding that since she was not able to wear the scent, the bottle should at least serve a decorative purpose.

Lizzie crossed the room, pulling a quarto-sized periodical from behind her back. "I feared you might be reading. So I've come prepared." She held forth the latest volume of *The Lady's Magazine, or Entertaining Companion for the Fair Sex, Appropriated Solely to Their Use and Amusement.*

Emma rolled her eyes but could not help sharing the impish girl's grin. She sat on her made bed and leaned over to pick up a travel diary. "At least tuck it inside this, so I can pretend you are reading something worthwhile."

"Don't be a snob, Emma," Lizzie said, in mock severity. "This very respectable periodical contains foreign news, home news, and poetical essays."

Emma quirked one brow. "Yes, but do you read any of that?"

Lizzie shuddered. "Heavens, no. I only read it for the fashion copperplates. Oh, and the descriptions of what the royal princesses wore on the queen consort's birthday."

Amused, Emma lifted her own book. "I have been reading about the history of Cornwall. Twice now I've come upon the name John Heale of Stratton. Apparently an infamous smuggler." Emma chuckled. "Lady Weston's maiden name was Heale, was it not? I wonder if she is related to him."

Lizzie snapped, "Better not let her hear you say that."

Emma was stung by the girl's sharp tone. She had thought Lizzie would enjoy the little joke, since she was forever taking jabs at Lady Weston. Now her conscience chastised her. She ought not to have lowered herself to common gossip.

"You're right. I'm sorry."

Lizzie forced a little laugh. "All that reading will be the death of you."

"What?"

The girl's hard demeanor melted, and her dark eyes sparkled playfully. "Oh, Emma. You know how much I like to tease you. Your reactions are priceless, honestly. If only you could see yourself!"

How changeable Lizzie Henshaw was, Emma thought. She wasn't sure what to think.

Voices from outside snaked in through the open casement window. Curious, Emma rose and crossed the room. Looking down, she was puzzled to see Julian in the rear courtyard talking with the red-haired Mr. Teague. What could he have to talk about with that man?

Lizzie tossed her magazine onto the chair and joined her at the window, wearing a mischievous grin. "Are we spying?"

But when she looked down, her grin fell away. She murmured, "Foolish fellow."

Emma wasn't positive which male she referred to, but Lizzie didn't clarify.

Emma whispered, "I was not spying. I heard voices and simply wondered who it was."

Abruptly, Teague glanced up. Seeing her in the window, he

stopped speaking midsentence, and raised a hand to halt Julian's reply. Julian followed Teague's gaze as the man stared up at her with narrow, menacing eyes.

Lizzie tugged her away from the window. "Careful, Emma," she said under her breath. "Care killed a cat."

Shaken by Teague's malevolent glare, Emma slowly registered Lizzie's words. "That's . . . from *Much Ado About Nothing*, I believe. Have you . . . read Shakespeare?"

Lizzie sent her a sidelong glance. "What do you think?"

Emma sat back on her bed, but Lizzie wandered idly across the room. She picked up Emma's teacup from its place of prominence on the side table. "Why do you keep this here?"

"It was a gift from my mother," Emma replied, then added tentatively, "Did your mother leave you anything?"

"My mother? *Pfff.*" She muttered under her breath, "Not unless you count *him.*"

"Pardon me?"

"It's pretty, to be sure." Lizzie set down the cup, her eye drawn to something else. For a moment her hand hovered midair above the table. Then she picked up the decorative bottle of *eau de cologne* sitting as unused as the cup.

The girl said, "I had one very like this. Given to me as a gift."

Emma mused, "I suppose it was a popular scent and all the shops carried it."

Lizzie stared at the small bottle of yellow-green liquid. Quietly, she asked, "Did Phillip give this to you?"

Emma hesitated. She did not want to lie, but nor did she want to give Lizzie the wrong impression. "Yes, but only as a parting gift. A token of friendship. Nothing more."

"Yes," Lizzie murmured, eyes vaguely focused. "Phillip is thoughtful that way. . . ."

Emma added, "Of course I have not worn any scent—not since your warning about Lady Weston's nose."

Lizzie nodded, eyes lingering on the bottle. "Yes. One must be very careful what one does under that particular nose."

*This is the time, yours is the happy*
*hour, Improve your minds from*
*learning's pleasing flow'r. . . .*

—John Fenn, schoolmaster, 1843

# Chapter 17

The next day, while her father lectured on Homer, Emma noticed Julian's and Rowan's eyes glazing over. She found her attention wandering as well. She thought about what else she might give Adam to help him pass the time, to help her establish a friendship with him, and to learn what his other interests and capabilities were. She knew he liked to read, and wondered if any of the books they had brought along might appeal to him.

She rose and ran her fingers across the spines of their books on the schoolroom shelf. One slim volume caught her eye. It was a recently published diary of a soldier who'd served with Lord Wellington during the Peninsula War. She had read it because she enjoyed the author's descriptions of Spain and Portugal, though Adam might find the battle details more interesting.

But then she recalled the fits Adam sometimes experienced. The violent beating of his own head. Might he damage other things when upset? She would have to ask Henry. For now she would hold off on giving him a book.

She thought next of her chess set with the missing queen. In the midst of cleaning out the schoolroom cupboards, she had found a marble-and-ivory chess set, dusty from disuse. She considered taking him the entire set, but its thick marble board and stout ivory pieces were very heavy. Besides, she wasn't sure the family would approve of her moving valuable things about the house. Instead, she decided to borrow only the white queen to temporarily complete her set. She left a neatly penned note in the schoolroom cupboard, explaining where the borrowed piece had gone and promising to return it. A queen I.O.U.

With eager anticipation, Emma excused herself, taking the queen with her. She went down to her own room to retrieve her chess set, and then carried both to Adam's room.

Reaching it, she knocked and, hearing a vague reply, tentatively pushed the door open with the chessboard. Adam, she saw, sat reading in his armchair.

She crossed the room, placed the game on the table, and began setting up the white pieces. Adam came over and watched with interest, but his attention was immediately snagged by the mismatched queen. He picked it up and set it aside.

"I'm sorry, Adam. But we need that."

He shook his head. "Not the same."

"I know. I'm afraid the original queen was lost."

Adam sat down in the chair opposite and began gathering up the black pieces. She wondered if he already knew how to play. Perhaps Mr. Hobbes had been a keen chess player as well as a "bone stick" player, but somehow she doubted it.

She watched Adam's intent movements as he picked up each piece and then placed it with those it matched. A pawn with other pawns. Two rooks. Two knights. The king and queen. But instead of the customary positions for the game, he set the eight pawns into two ranks of four, flanked by the knights and bishops.

Battle lines.

At the rear, king and queen stood surrounded by their rooks. Safe within their castle walls.

Emma bit her lip, not wanting to criticize. She asked, "What sort of game are you playing?"

"War," he said. Then Adam stunned her by launching into stilted narration. "The allied army marched west along the north bank of the river, right into the mousetrap set by the French commander, cutting the allies' line of retreat . . ."

Adam moved the pawns and knights forward; then he grabbed the king and placed him at the front. "The allies tried to form an advance," he recited. "Suddenly, the king's horse ran off with him." Adam moved the king in a violent lurch.

"Moving a king to the front?" Emma asked skeptically.

"King George the Second. The last British monarch to lead his troops into battle."

"I see." Emma sat back in her chair. "My goodness. I had no idea you were so keen on military history."

But Adam continued to move pieces and narrate battles without taking much notice of her. Emma glanced over at the battle drawings she had seen there before. Perhaps she should have guessed.

Giving up on the notion of a formal game, Emma left him and wandered downstairs, thinking to help herself to a cup of coffee from the urn in Mr. Davies's office.

She nearly ran into Lizzie coming in the rear door, wearing no gloves as usual and flushed as well. "Oh! Hello, Emma," she said, louder than necessary.

Emma caught the door as it closed and glanced out. She saw a man retreating behind the stables—though which man she could not tell—and in front of the stables, Henry Weston dismounting his horse.

She looked back at Lizzie in concern. "Are you all right? You look"—*Nervous? Guilty?* Emma settled for—"upset."

"Do I?" Lizzie fumbled with the ribbons of her bonnet. "I'm fine, I assure you. A bit of an argument with the twins. Nothing new there."

Emma glanced at Lizzie's bare hands. "You really ought to wear gloves." She looked more closely. "You've got something beneath your nails."

"Have I?" Lizzie stretched the small palms and short fingers before her, then turned them over to regard her fingernails. "Probably just a bit of dirt. I was . . . cutting flowers for Lady Weston earlier."

It didn't look like dirt to Emma. It appeared more red in hue. But then, she was unfamiliar with Cornish soil.

Lizzie looked up and said brightly, "Well, I had better go wash them then." She turned to go.

At that moment, Henry came in the rear door, breeches and hessians splattered with mud. Not reddish at all, Emma noticed.

"Hello, Miss Smallwood," he said.

"Mr. Weston. Good ride?"

"Excellent."

"Good." She added, "By the way, I hope you don't mind. I took a chess set to Adam."

"Chess? Really?" His lip protruded in thought. "I would have guessed that game beyond his ability."

"Actually, I think the game well within his grasp but outside his interest. He transformed the pieces into battle lines and acted out the battle of Dettingen."

"The battle of Dettingen?" Henry repeated, frowning in thought.

Emma nodded. "Seeing him reminded me of your toy sol . . . I mean, your miniature—"

"Miniature military figures," he supplied. "I wonder . . ." He winced as though in pain. "I have a vague memory of playing soldiers with someone when I was young. I see pale fingers lining tin soldiers one after another in rows. I don't think it was Phillip. He never cared for war games. Perhaps it was Adam."

"What age would Adam have been?"

"Six or seven, maybe. And I must have only been two or three. And a child of that age has no interest in neat rows of soldiers; only in dashing them about or putting them in his drooling mouth. How that must have vexed him."

Henry shook his head, then snapped to attention, looking at her with eyes alight. "Thunder and turf. I'll wager those soldiers were Adam's to begin with. Why on earth did they not send the things with him? He might have had that pleasure at least."

"I don't know . . ." Emma murmured, at a loss.

"Come with me." Henry turned abruptly and strode toward the stairs.

She followed after, hitching up her skirt hems and trotting up the stairs to keep up with him.

One flight up, Henry turned down the corridor. At a door midway down, he stopped. "Wait here."

She was glad she warranted enough propriety to be asked to wait outside. Yes, Lizzie had shown her Henry's room briefly on her "tour," but mere tutor's daughter or not, it would not do for her to enter a man's bedchamber with him inside.

*Would it not?* her mind whispered, thinking of how freely she had entered Adam's room. But somehow entering Henry's would be a different matter entirely.

Henry reappeared in his threshold a moment later, allowing the door to swing open behind him. The faint scent of bay rum came with him. She glimpsed mahogany furniture, a massive four-poster bed, burgundy bed curtains, and as much clutter as when she had seen the room last.

In his hands, he held two rectangular cases she recognized. He'd brought them with him to Longstaple and had insisted no one touch them. Now he handed her one of the cases eagerly. "Let's take these up to him."

From within the bedchamber, an affronted valet beseeched, "But, sir, your clothes . . . the state of your boots!"

Henry looked down at himself, as if suddenly recalling his muddied state. "Dash it, you're right. I've no doubt spread more than enough mud about the place already." He looked at Emma. "You go up, and I shall join you as soon as I can."

She shook her head, handing back the case. "I would not give these to him without you for the world. But I should like to be there to witness it."

"Of course you shall. All right. Give me twenty minutes."

His valet protested, "Half an hour, at least!"

Henry rolled his eyes. "Half an hour, then. Meet me outside Adam's door. All right?"

"I look forward to it," she said evenly, though inwardly she felt as giddy as a girl on her birthday, anticipating a special treat.

He smiled at her, and her elation increased severalfold.

Emma floated away down the corridor. When she reached the stairwell, she was startled to find Lizzie lurking on the steps.

Lizzie peered over Emma's shoulder, then looked pointedly at Emma's no doubt flushed face. "I saw you talking to Henry. What were you two doing up here?"

"Hmm?" Emma murmured. "Oh, nothing, really." Emma licked dry lips and changed the subject. "Did you get your hands clean?"

Lizzie eyed her speculatively, but Emma made an effort to keep her expression impassive. Looking everywhere but the girl's too inquisitive gaze, Emma lifted one of Lizzie's hands to inspect it.

"It's clean now," Lizzie said, pulling her hand away. She curled her hand into a fist as though to keep the offending fingers from view. Sheepishly, she said, "It was only a bit of rouge."

"Ah." Emma lifted her chin in understanding. "You don't want to get that on your white frock."

"No," Lizzie agreed. "Don't mention it. All right?" She added on a little laugh. "I want him to think me a natural beauty."

"Who?"

"Why, everyone, of course!" Lizzie grinned.

What a singular creature the girl was. Emma was more accustomed to young men, with their more straightforward manners and easygoing ways. Though there were always exceptions. Henry Weston came to mind. No, he had not been easygoing, not an easy pupil to share a house with at all.

Emma hoped Lizzie would leave now that she'd satisfied her curiosity. But the girl remained where she was and asked, "And what are you going to do now?"

Before Emma could answer, Phillip's voice called up the stairwell, "Lizzie? Are you coming?"

His footsteps tattooed up the stairs. "There you are."

His gaze landed on Emma. "Oh . . . and Miss Smallwood. Perfect. Mother longs for a game of whist. Will you be our fourth?"

Emma's mouth opened, but she hesitated to reply. Had Phillip wanted to ask her, or did he feel obligated to because she happened to be there? Emma had enjoyed spending time with her old friend, but at the moment the prospect held little appeal. Partly because she was intimidated by Lady Weston, and partly because she would rather not jeopardize her meeting with Henry and Adam. A game of whist could easily last longer than half an hour.

"Thank you, Phillip, but I cannot join you now. You two go on. No doubt Julian or Rowan would be happy to play."

A crease appeared between Phillip's brows. "They are still in the schoolroom."

"Oh. Right. Well, I am on my way there now. I shall see if they are finished for the day and send them down as soon as may be."

It was not a lie. She *was* on her way to the schoolroom—but only for a few minutes to check on her father before meeting Henry.

Lizzie continued to watch her, something very like suspicion glittering in her eyes. "Perhaps I shall come up with you," she began. "Unless . . . you don't wish me to?"

Emma forced a smile. She knew, instinctively, that to refuse Lizzie would only fan her suspicions. "Of course you may come along. Though I thought you found the schoolroom a dead bore."

Lizzie said, "True. But Julian will be happy to see me. Rowan too, of course, if he isn't in one of his dark moods."

"As you like," Emma said officiously, hoping to hide her disappointment. Emma was surprised at herself, how unwilling she was to share the upcoming rendezvous. Though neither Lizzie nor Phillip had shown a great deal of interest in the newfound family member.

Emma turned and started up the stairs. Lizzie followed.

Phillip called after her, "Don't be long, Lizzie. You know Mother will be vexed if we keep her waiting."

"Yes. I do know," Lizzie called back.

The girl kept pace beside Emma, up the many stairs to the school-room, chatting about some new paisley shawl Lady Weston had ordered for her.

Emma barely heard her, thinking ahead to how she might slip away, so she could meet Henry alone as planned.

They entered the schoolroom quietly and found the boys writing away on some assignment.

Julian turned as they entered and smiled at Lizzie.

"Shhh," Mr. Smallwood urged from his desk. "Julian and Rowan need to finish their essays."

Emma nodded in acknowledgment and led Lizzie to one of the schoolroom cupboards. She whispered, "Lizzie, I need to carry these old primers up to the attic storage room. You may help me, since you're here."

Lizzie wrinkled her nose at the stacks of dusty volumes. "No, thank you."

Rowan looked over at them as he dipped his pen. "Lizzie is quite averse to anything resembling work, you'll find, Miss Small-wood."

"And why should she not be?" Julian defended. "A young lady like her, bound to marry a gentleman one day. The only work she's accustomed to is needlework."

Lizzie pulled out a dainty handkerchief and touched her small nose. "I would help, Emma. But you heard Phillip. Lady Weston longs for a game of whist." She turned to the boys. "Miss Smallwood refuses to oblige us, so one of you will have to come down as soon as you've finished."

"I shall come right now," Julian said, rising.

"Ahem. Mr. Weston?" her father interrupted. "I trust your essay is completed, then?"

Julian dipped his pen once more and scrawled a large *The End* with a flourish. He smirked. "It is now."

And knowing Julian, he probably had written twice the essay Rowan would manage—in half the time. Even so, Emma did not like Julian's attitude. It lacked respect for her father. But she held her tongue. It was not her place to say anything. Besides, she was only too glad for Julian to finish and go downstairs.

As long as he took Lizzie with him.

At the appointed time, Emma met Henry in the corridor outside Adam's room, and together they carried in the cases.

Mrs. Prowse sat near Adam in companionable silence, she mending and he reading.

Henry said kindly to Mrs. Prowse, "We've brought a few more things for Adam. So if you'd like to have your tea, or check on things . . ."

"I would indeed, sir. Thank you." Mrs. Prowse rose. She eyed the cases—and Emma—with curiosity but made no comment. No doubt a housekeeper of her experience knew better than to question her masters.

After the housekeeper took her leave, Emma set the first case on the table. Henry squeezed the second between it and the chessboard.

Henry's hands shook a little, she noticed, surprised and touched. Was he nervous, excited, or both?

Adam clapped eyes on the first case, an odd wrinkle of concentration forming between his brows. *Oh dear.* Emma hoped nothing would upset him. Did he remember the case? Surely not.

"Well, Adam," Henry said. "Would you like to open it, or shall I?"

"What's inside?"

"Open it and see."

Adam didn't seem the type of person to enjoy surprises, and she feared he might refuse, but instead he came forward tentatively. He laid one finger on the lid of the first case, surveying its two latches. Then he lifted a hand to each latch and flipped them open in a single snap. Slowly, he lifted the lid on its hinges and stared at its contents.

No change in expression followed. No comment or question. For several moments he just stood there, staring. Then his finger cautiously touched one soldier within, as if it were a fragile bubble, testing it to see if it would pop, dissolve, and disappear.

He swung his gaze to Henry, mouth ajar.

"They're yours, Adam," he said.

"Mine?" Adam stared into the case.

Henry nodded. His voice thick, he said, "Yes. Yours. I'm sorry they've been kept from you all this time."

Adam said, "I had one. But I lost it."

Henry glanced at her, then slowly pulled from his pocket the soldier Emma had found in her room. "Like this?"

Adam looked up. "Yes." He accepted the soldier from Henry and laid it with satisfaction next to a matching one in the case. Then Adam's focus shifted to the second case. He moved around the table and opened its lid as well.

Henry said, "Those are newer. I received them after you . . . had left."

"Yours?" Adam asked.

Henry shrugged, looking uncharacteristically uncomfortable. "Ours," he said.

If Henry was waiting for an invitation to play with his brother, it appeared he would be disappointed, for Adam sat down and began digging through the pieces and lining the soldiers into ranks with relish.

He pushed aside Emma's chess set, her gift forgotten in the shadow of a superior diversion. But seeing Adam's rapt attention— and the tears brightening Henry Weston's eyes—she did not resent it for a moment.

*A little learning is a dangerous thing. . . .*

—Alexander Pope, 1709

# Chapter 18

E mma awoke the next morning with a lingering feeling of contentment. She thought of the previous day and felt a smile tugging at the corners of her mouth. She had found interacting with Adam quite satisfying. And if she were honest, she had also enjoyed her time with Henry Weston, and his warm looks of approval.

She rose from bed and stretched her arms above her, feeling her chest rise, her spine lengthen, her muscles ease.

"Ahh . . ." she murmured with pleasure.

Then she saw it and frowned. Something had been slid under her door again—a piece of paper, quarto sized and lightly lined, but not folded as a letter this time. Emma moved quickly from full extension to crouch and felt something wrench in her neck. But when she picked up the paper she forgot about her momentary discomfort. For the piece of paper was the missing journal page.

Recognizing her own handwriting, she read a few lines to confirm what it was:

*Henry is cold Boreas to be sure, though I denied thinking it when he asked. And yes, kind Phillip very well suits the image of mild, friendly Zephyrus.*

Emma cringed anew at the thought of anyone else reading her foolish fancies.

Then she noticed color showing through the paper from its other side. That was odd. She had written only in blue gall ink. She turned it over and froze.

There on the back, over the lines she had written, someone had drawn a picture. In bold black ink and red paint. A chess piece, a white queen, with her head . . . severed. Blood flowing from her jagged neck.

Emma's stomach turned. Who had drawn this? Was it a threat?

The door opened and Emma gasped, whirling to face it.

Morva paused in the threshold, gaping at her. "Are you all right, miss?"

"Yes, I'm fine. You startled me—that's all."

Morva look at the painting, eyes wide.

Following the direction of the maid's gaze, Emma quickly set the page on her side table, drawing side down. "Let me hurry and wash," she said. "I am a bit behind schedule this morning."

After the maid had helped her dress and taken her leave, Emma picked up the drawing once more. This time she tried to study it objectively, without the personal offense she had initially felt.

At first glance, it had appeared haphazardly drawn. Bold, brash strokes of quill and paintbrush. The work of a nasty boy. But on closer inspection, the finer lines caught her attention. The detail of the drawing clearly depicted a chess piece, complete with carved feet flat on the rounded base. The static posture showed it was not a living person, but an object. Or was she reading too much into it? Yes, skill was involved, she decided, even though the crude spurt of blood marred its lines, giving it an initial amateurish appearance. Rowan was an artist who both drew and painted. . . . Might he have done this?

But she could not ignore the fact that the drawn figure was a chess piece and she had recently given Adam Weston a chess set. And had she not wondered if Adam had been the person sneaking into her room? But why would he draw such a horrid thing? Would he repay her gift in such a crude manner?

And then something else struck her. She looked more closely at the queen itself—the detail of the robe, the facial features and crown on the disembodied head. Unless she was mistaken, this looked very much like the white queen from her chess set, the piece that had been missing for years. So how in the world could someone draw it so exactly? For the set had been somewhat unique in that the white king and queen looked distinctly different from their dark counterparts. The white had facial features from the Orient in contrast to the African styling of the dark pieces. She supposed someone who saw the rest of the set could carry over the style to the missing piece. But so accurately? True, she was relying on memory, but there was no denying how familiar the drawn piece looked. She *recognized* it.

That brought Henry Weston to mind. For she had always suspected he had taken the white queen as some sort of revenge after she had beaten him that last time. But even if she was right, that piece would be long gone—he probably would not have kept it. Nor would he have been able to recall it in such detail. But who else could have drawn it? Rowan, Julian, and Adam had never even seen the original piece. Phillip either. It was already missing when he'd come to Longstaple.

Looking at the beheaded queen, a chill prickled over her. Did Henry Weston still carry such a grudge against her? Had it intensified over the years? She could hardly believe it, especially since she had noticed a lessening of old tensions, and since Adam, the beginnings of a tentative friendship. But perhaps she had misread the situation. Fooled herself.

Emma shook her head. Her mind could not wrap itself around the idea that, for all his past mischief and hot temper, Henry Weston would draw such a thing—even if he somehow still resented her. She must be mistaken at how exact a copy the queen was. It likely had been drawn by someone who had never seen the original. It still could be Adam, she told herself. Although he did not seem capable of such crude symbolism or cruelty, perhaps something more dangerous hid beneath his innocent, childlike appearance.

She wondered what she should do. Should she show the drawing to anyone? She didn't want to show her father. He might think they had offended someone, or even worry for her safety. Who else could she show—Lizzie? Phillip? Dare she show Henry?

Emma quailed at the thought of Lady Weston's face puckering in disapproval and accusing Emma of having an overactive imagination. Or seeing her rise up in maternal defense of her "delicate" boys. Nor did Emma want to cast blame on Adam, whom she wanted, in her heart of hearts, to believe as innocent as he appeared.

Emma thought back to all the little pranks boys had pulled on her over the years at the Smallwood Academy. She had learned early on that the best course was usually to ignore such behavior. Deprive the boys of the girlish shriek or cry of feminine outrage they sought, and the pranks soon lost their appeal. She would try the same approach now.

Emma tucked the drawing back into her journal and finished getting ready for the day.

Going downstairs a few minutes later, Emma ate a quick breakfast and was about to head up to the schoolroom when Lizzie caught her on the stairs.

"Oh good. I found you. Please walk into the village with me. I simply must show you a new bonnet I have my heart set upon—say you will."

"I cannot go now, Lizzie. I am needed in the schoolroom." Seeing the girl's crestfallen expression, Emma added, "Perhaps later."

Lizzie's eyes brightened. "When?"

"I don't know. Ten or eleven?"

"Very well, I shall wait." Lizzie pouted. "But do hurry. Why your father can't tutor without you, I shall never know."

Emma went up to the schoolroom and there assisted her father as he attempted to explain the significance of Copernicus's theory, which changed the face of astronomy forever.

Then they moved on to the explorer James Cook, also something of an astronomer. At her father's invitation, Emma took over at that point, outlining the explorer's significant contributions and his major expeditions, tracing his voyages on the schoolroom globe. The man had seen so much of the world, sailing from England to South America, Africa, Antarctica, and more. What a life. Though, Emma acknowledged, it would be negligent not to include the cost of that adventurous life—Cook's death at the hands of Sandwich Islands natives in 1779.

After the lesson, Emma left the schoolroom to meet Lizzie. On her way downstairs, Emma detoured toward her own room for her cape, bonnet, and gloves. She also thought she would tuck her journal into the dressing chest, out of sight. No use in inviting any further "borrowings."

Emma opened her bedchamber door and stepped inside. She drew up short at the sight of Lizzie sitting on the edge of her bed, Emma's journal open in her hands.

"What are you doing?"

Lizzie snapped the journal shut. "I'm sorry, but I was bored. I've been waiting here an age."

"Has no one ever told you it isn't right to snoop about in other people's things?"

Lizzie shrugged. "Only Henry." She extracted the torn-out page with the horrid drawing and waved it like a flag. "What is this?"

Emma walked forward and snatched it from her, then took the journal from the girl's other hand. "None of your business—that's what it is."

"Looks ghastly. I confess Morva mentioned it to me and I had to see it for myself. Will you show Lady Weston?"

"I had not planned to, no."

"But this is your missing journal page, is it not, returned to you?"

"As you see."

Lizzie's dimples appeared. "I found what you wrote about Henry and Phillip rather surprising. Most interesting, really."

Emma felt her cheeks heat in a combined flush of indignation and mortification. "You ought not to have read it at all. How would you feel if I read your private journal?"

"I don't keep one," Lizzie replied. "I'm not fool enough to record my secrets for anyone to find and hold against me."

What secrets did Lizzie have? Emma wondered. Beyond the one she had already confided about the Weston she loved, and the younger Weston with whom she had an understanding?

"Do *you* know who drew it?" Emma asked.

Lizzie looked up at her sharply. "Don't you?"

"No. Though I have an idea." To herself, Emma added, *Several ideas, actually.*

"It seems obvious to me," Lizzie said.

Emma blinked. "Does it? Whom do you mean?"

Lizzie shook her head. "Oh no. You won't hear me accusing anyone. Not in this house. I already told you I'm no fool."

Emma was tempted to refuse to accompany Lizzie into the village after the girl's breach of privacy. But in the end, she went. She went because she had said she would. She went because she found Lizzie Henshaw intriguing: a puzzle she had yet to figure out. Emma hoped she did not go merely because she was desperate for companionship. But whatever the case, Emma found herself walking beside Lizzie down the steep path into Ebford, listening to the girl's incessant chatter, wondering how Lizzie felt about the things she had read in her journal. And worse, if she would repeat them to anyone.

Reaching the small ladies' shop in the High Street, Lizzie pointed out the cherished object in the bow window: a small cap-like bonnet trimmed with ribbon, lace, and a wreath of roses. Emma conjured apropos admiration for the longed-for bonnet and joined Lizzie in bemoaning its extravagant cost. Then they indulged in another hour of looking in windows and poking around shops before heading back.

Leaving Ebford, the steep path passed along the back of the cottages bordering the harbor. There Mr. Teague stood in the weedy garden of a white, thatched-roof cottage, set apart from the others and the nicest in the row.

He was cleaning fish on a stump but paused in his task to hail them. "'Ark, what brings such *fine* ladies down to our humble village?" His tone was mocking, derisive.

Lizzie glanced at Emma, then lifted her chin. "A bit of shopping, that's all."

"Shopping for more newspapers, miss?" He smirked at Emma. "I hear thee be fond of the news. And other things what don't concern 'ee."

Trepidation needled Emma. She had no idea what to say.

"We were looking at hats, if you must know," Lizzie blurted, taking Emma's arm. "Come along," Lizzie hissed, and urged her more quickly up the path.

Emma glanced back over her shoulder at the man.

Boldly meeting her gaze, he chopped off the head of the fish.

Later that evening, when Emma passed the drawing room on her way to the steward's office, Lady Weston beckoned her inside.

Sighing, Emma pasted on a smile and entered. She glimpsed Lizzie on the settee with a magazine in her hands. Both ladies, she noticed, were already dressed for dinner.

At the center of the room, Lady Weston sat on a high-backed armchair, as regal as any queen. "Miss Smallwood, Lizzie tells me your missing journal page has been returned to you."

Caught off guard, Emma glanced at Lizzie, who ducked her head, feigning interest in an article.

"Yes," Emma acknowledged.

"I should like to see it, if you please," Lady Weston said, holding out her hand as though Emma carried the page on her person.

Phillip had entered the room unnoticed and here interrupted. "Why should you want to see Miss Smallwood's journal, Mother?" He chuckled nervously. "Young ladies intend such things to be private, I believe. Not read aloud in the drawing room."

Lady Weston's lip curled. "I assure you, Phillip, I have no interest in Miss Smallwood's private thoughts, whatever they may be. However, Lizzie tells me the page was returned with a drawing upon it. A 'not very nice drawing,' she said. And she thought I should see it."

Phillip looked at Emma, eyes wide in concern. "Is this true, Emma?"

"Yes. But I had no intention of showing it to anybody."

He came forward. "But we must know if someone under our very roof is damaging your personal property."

Emma squirmed. She did not want Phillip Weston, and certainly not Lady Weston, seeing that particular journal page. She said, "It was nothing but a harmless prank, I am sure."

"Was it Henry, do you suppose?" Phillip asked.

It was not surprising he might assume so, since Phillip knew about Henry's more notorious pranks at the Smallwood Academy.

"I don't think so, no. I am not accusing anyone."

"Show me the drawing, Miss Smallwood." Lady Weston held out her hand once more. "I know everyone in this house quite well and will no doubt be able to identify whoever drew it."

Perhaps noticing Emma's discomfiture, Phillip asked gingerly, "The drawing is not of you in a . . . shall we say, embarrassing state. Is that why you don't wish us to see it?"

Lady Weston blanched. "Good heavens, Phillip. What a thought!"

"No," Emma rushed to say, cheeks heated. "Nothing like that. More violent than embarrassing."

"Violent?" Phillip repeated, brows furrowing. "Dash it, Emma. Now you really have me alarmed. No one's threatened you, I hope."

"No. I . . . I'm quite certain nothing was meant by it."

"Gave me the shivers," Lizzie said, half under her breath but loud enough for everyone to hear.

Phillip frowned at the girl. "And what were you doing looking at Miss Smallwood's journal? I doubt she showed it to you."

Lizzie ducked her head, but Emma saw the dark flush rising. It was the first time she had seen the girl look repentant for anything.

Phillip looked at her earnestly. "Emma, I'm afraid I must ask to see this drawing. I promise not to look at the words you wrote, if I can avoid it. Otherwise I shall worry about you. Please?"

Emma huffed. "Oh, very well. I shall bring it down."

A few minutes later, Emma left her bedchamber with the folded journal page and started back down the corridor, hands damp. She knew Phillip would be true to his word about not reading the words beneath, at least not intentionally. But she had no reason to expect the same discretion of Lady Weston.

She met Henry coming from the north wing. "Miss Smallwood, Adam is asking for you." He said it with a touch of wonder in his voice. "Will you come and say hello?"

"Oh. . . . I would like to see him, but I am afraid I can't at the moment. I am . . . requested in the drawing room."

His head reared back. "Requested? By whom?"

"Lady Weston. And Phillip."

He studied her face. "Is everything all right? You don't look happy about it. In fact, you appear to be on your way to your own execution."

She sighed. "I . . . didn't plan to tell anyone about this drawing. But Lizzie saw my missing journal page and told Lady Weston. And now I've been asked to produce it."

He frowned, trying to follow her convoluted explanation. "You found the page?"

"It was returned to me. Under my door."

His eyes narrowed, measuring her words. "I don't understand. Why should Lady Weston want to see it? Or Phillip for that matter?"

Again Emma sighed. Unfolding the paper, she said, "Please don't read the words themselves." She held up the page, drawing side facing him.

He stared at it, brows drawn low. "Who in the blazes did this?" He snatched the paper from her and brought it closer to his face.

Not him, apparently—unless he was a better actor than she gave him credit for. The longer he stared at the page, the more Emma fidgeted. "I asked you not to read it. Please give it back. It's not meant for anyone else to see."

"A bit late for that, is it not?" he said, scowling over the drawing.

Tentatively, she reached for a corner of the page and tugged it from his grasp. "Excuse me. They are waiting for me in the drawing room."

It was his turn to sigh. "I shall go with you."

She trotted lightly down the stairs, and he followed behind her. When they reached the drawing room, he opened the door for her and gestured her inside, closing the door behind them.

Phillip looked up in surprise. "Henry, what brings you down early?"

"I happened upon Miss Smallwood in the corridor. She told me what was happening."

"Have you seen this supposed drawing?" Lady Weston asked.

"Only a moment ago."

Again Lady Weston extended her hand. But this time, Emma held on to the page firmly. "I shall show it to you, my lady." She stepped forward and held it for Lady Weston to see, but not too close.

Phillip came and stood at his stepmother's shoulder to view the drawing as well. "What on earth . . . ?" he muttered.

"Pish." Lady Weston huffed. "Much ado about nothing. It isn't even a drawing of you or even a person at all. It is simply a chess piece. A challenge to a rematch, I'd wager."

Henry's jaw clenched. "A chess piece doesn't bleed, madam."

Lady Weston frowned at him. "Surely you don't read a threat into this amateurish drawing?"

"It is not an invitation to a tea party," he retorted.

Lady Weston looked from Henry to Emma, dark eyes simmering. "You are not accusing one of the boys, I hope."

Emma said, "I am accusing no one, my lady."

"I should hope not. Besides, Julian and Rowan both draw far better than that. I should know if one of them had drawn it—I would recognize their work."

She looked up, lips parting as a new thought struck her. "Of course. It is suddenly quite obvious who drew this. Who in this house is capable of such a childish act, such unskilled scrawling?" She sent Emma a guarded glance, then continued in vague terms. "Nothing like this ever occurred here before . . . a certain someone arrived. Missing journals, nighttime wanderings, beastly sketches. I told you, Henry, we ought to have kept the door locked, but you would not listen to me."

"He did not draw this," Henry insisted, nostrils flaring.

"How do you know?" Lady Weston challenged.

"It is not in his nature."

"Excuse me, Henry," Lady Weston said, "but you have known this person for little more than a month. You can hardly call yourself an expert on what he is and is not capable of. You cannot know he did not draw it unless you drew it yourself."

"Did you?" Phillip asked quietly.

Henry huffed. "No, I did not."

Lady Weston went on before Henry could say more. "For all we know he is capable of far more besides. Mark my words, if you do not begin keeping him to his room, we shall all live to regret it. Miss Smallwood, perhaps, most of all."

Henry gaped at her. "Miss Smallwood? Are you threatening Miss Smallwood?"

"Am *I*?" Lady Weston touched the lace at her throat. "Good heavens, what a notion. I am not the one sneaking into Miss Smallwood's bedchamber at night, nor leaving her frightening pictures."

Emma wondered who had told her someone had sneaked into her room at night. She said, "I don't think Adam means me any harm."

"Adam? Since when is the tutor's daughter on a first-name basis with him?" Lady Weston's voice could have curdled cream. "Was I not clear in my instructions as to how and why he was to be kept apart?"

*Oh dear.* Now she had done it. Exposed the visits to the off-limits north wing. Exposed Henry's part in it as well.

"I have only met him a few times, my lady," Emma hurried to say. "I meant no harm, only heard him calling out and went to see what the matter was."

Lady Weston studied her, expression skeptical. "And based on these brief meetings, you also claim to be an expert on what he is and is not capable of? Even though Sir Giles felt he had no choice but to send him away for the other boys' safety? But you have decided he is incapable of harm? Are you a soothsayer, Miss Smallwood? Are you God?"

Emma's stomach twisted. "Of course not. I never meant to imply—"

At that moment they were interrupted by Sir Giles, Julian, and Rowan coming in together, laughing at some tale of mishap from the day's shoot.

"I say," Rowan proclaimed, surveying the assembled company. "What a lot of gloomy faces."

"What is it, my dear?" Sir Giles asked his wife.

Lady Weston pointed at the page hanging limp in Emma's hand. "Someone has left a rude drawing on a page from Miss Smallwood's journal."

"Oh?" Sir Giles turned to look at Emma, and she obliged him by lifting the page before him.

"I haven't got my reading spectacles, but badly done, whichever of you did it."

"Don't blame Rowan," Julian said quickly. "Just because he's the artist among us and keeps paints in his room. Why, I sneaked a peek into ol' Adam's room and he's got drawings of dead soldiers and other gruesome things in there. I imagine it was him who did it."

Significant looks were exchanged around the room.

Henry appeared as though he would launch into another defense of his elder brother, but the footman came in and announced dinner.

Eager for escape and realizing she was late for her own meal, Emma excused herself and hurried to join her father and Mr. Davies, taking the journal page, folded safely away in her pocket.

At dinner, John Smallwood asked Mr. Davies about his boyhood education.

Mr. Davies wiped his mouth with a table napkin before answering. "Piecemeal, it was. My parents put me at a school kept by a poor blind woman, and then with a man ninety years of age if he was a day. Don't laugh—it's true."

"A blind woman? But how could she judge your handwriting, your compositions?"

The steward's eyes lit with memory. "Lots of reciting aloud, as I recall. And she kept a scullery maid who could read—she'd check our work now and again, read it back to the mistress, and woe to any pupil caught reciting what he hadn't written down proper."

Mr. Davies noticed her father's skeptical look. "You shake your head. But she was twice the teacher the old man was. And far kinder."

Emma finished eating and then excused herself as the men continued their good-natured sparring about education in its various forms.

Crossing the hall, she saw Henry starting up the stairs. She called to him and he paused, waiting for her to catch up.

As they climbed the stairs together, she said confidentially, "Do you think Lady Weston has a point? That we don't really know what Adam is capable of? For all his sweet temper, his behavior can be a bit, well, unpredictable."

Henry made no answer, apparently lost in thought.

Emma continued, "I don't want to believe it either. But he does have small hands, like the handprint left on my mirror. And he admitted he lost a soldier like the one I found. At the very least, it seems likely he has entered my room on two different occasions. If not more."

"That I might believe of him. It was his old room, after all."

"Was it? Goodness. I had no idea."

"I wonder if he remembers," Henry murmured.

"I imagine he does—that must explain it. At least why he may have wandered in."

"Perhaps," Henry replied. "Though someone has taken things from my room as well."

At the landing, she turned to him in concern. "Really? What?"

He hesitated, appearing almost sheepish. "A small bottle of my mother's perfume."

She stared at him. "Perfume?"

He defended, "I have very little of hers. To remember her by."

She rushed to say, "I was not mocking you. I have kept a few things of my mother's as well. I was only remembering the perfume I smelled in my room after one of those nighttime visits."

"Yes, I have thought of that too," he said as they continued up the stairs. "I didn't see it in Adam's room. But I admit I have not asked him about it. Nor anyone else for that matter."

"I wonder if it was Adam playing the pianoforte at night. . . ." Emma mused. "Lady Weston insists it must have been Julian, but he seems less certain."

"Was the playing good?"

"Very."

"Have you seen any evidence of musical ability in Adam?"

She thought. "No . . ."

"And hitting one key repeatedly is hardly a promising indicator."

"True," she allowed, recalling Henry's version of the scene. "But we do know he likes to draw . . . violent . . . things."

His brow puckered. "Yes."

Emma continued, "But the queen in the drawing looks exactly like the one missing from my set. And no one here could have seen it. Except . . ."

"Except me."

"Yes. I'm sorry, but—"

"Don't be. I am the one who is sorry. I did take it. I've had it all these years. In the same box of mementoes as my mother's perfume. Unfortunately both went missing about a week ago."

Emma was stunned by his confession. She also realized it meant anyone might have drawn the queen. Timidly, she asked, "Why did you take it?"

"To vex you. It was wrong of me, I know. I hope you will forgive me."

"Very well."

He bowed his head, then glanced up at her from beneath a fall of dark hair. "Did you really think I might have drawn that picture?"

Emma swallowed a self-conscious lump in her throat, then lifted her chin. "I own the notion did cross my mind. But can you blame me? After all, you knew what the piece looked like and you gave me prodigious cause to suspect you in the past."

He inhaled deeply. "I suppose you are right. But that was a long time ago. I have no interest in tricking you now. Nor in frightening you, nor any other dishonorable motive, I assure you."

The warm tenor of his voice did odd things to Emma's stomach. She blinked, unable to meet his gaze.

"Emma, look at me."

She forced herself to meet his remarkable green eyes and saw the sincerity burning there.

He said, "You have my word, Emma. I did not do this."

He had called her Emma. She liked the sound of her name on his lips. Nodding, she said, "I believe you."

"Good." He exhaled. "Now let's figure out who did."

Henry began by continuing on to Adam's room alone. But instead of the casual visit he'd intended, he decided he needed to ask Adam about the missing things and . . . possibly the other wrongdoing as well. He hated to accuse Adam of anything. But it could not be helped.

Henry knew he should have admitted to Miss Smallwood earlier that he had taken the chess piece. But he had put it off. She had just begun to trust him, and her faith in him was still a shaky, newborn thing. He had hoped he might figure out who was to blame before handing her the perfect reason to blame him. Ah well, it was a relief to have the confession over and done.

When Henry opened Adam's door, his brother looked up at him from a line of soldiers.

"Adam. I am missing something and I wonder if you can help me find it. Have you seen a slender green bottle about so big?"

Adam ducked his head, and his telltale look of guilt made Henry's stomach fall. Adam rose and minced across the room to a small valise on his side table—the belongings he'd come with—and opened the lid.

His back to Henry, Adam asked, "It was hers? Our mother's?"

*"Our mother's . . ."* A shaft of pain and satisfaction pierced Henry to hear another human being say those words.

"Yes."

Adam turned, the vial of perfume clutched in both hands. "Smells like her."

"I know."

Adam handed it back. "Sorry."

Henry wanted to quickly tell Adam all was forgiven and to think no more about it, but he bit his tongue, determined to learn all. If Adam had taken one thing, might he have taken the other? Adam did, after all, possess the rest of the chess set. And if he was capable of taking the perfume—petty theft though it was—what else might he be capable of?

"Thank you," Henry said. "Phillip wishes to see it. But then I shall return it to you. All right?"

Adam nodded.

Henry sighed. "I hate to ask, Adam, but did you also happen to take a chess piece from my room? The white queen that matches the chess set Miss Smallwood lent you?"

Adam looked up at him, blue eyes wide. "That piece is lost, Emma says."

"Yes, well . . ." What a hypocrite he was, accusing Adam of anything! "I meant to return it to her . . ." *Seven years late.* "But it seems to have gone missing from my room. You haven't seen it?"

Adam shook his head. So immediately, so guilelessly, that Henry wanted to believe him.

He glanced at the drawings pinned to the wall and stacked neatly on the table. He paged through several. It was difficult to tell if they were of the same style as the decapitated queen.

He forced himself to ask, "Just one more thing, Adam. I know you are fond of drawing. Did you happen to, um . . . give . . . one of your drawings to Miss Smallwood?"

Adam's brow puckered in confusion. "Does Emma want one?"

"No. That is . . . Never mind."

Henry thanked Adam again, then excused himself to return to his own room.

*The Cornish Peninsula . . . that old death
trap of sailing vessels, with its fringe of
black cliffs and surge-swept reefs on which
innumerable seamen have met their end.*

—Sir Arthur Conan Doyle

# Chapter 19

From the schoolroom window two days later, Emma watched the activity going on in the distance along the coast. Henry Weston stood talking with Mr. Davies, the two of them consulting a large roll of paper—building plans she assumed—while several workmen unloaded lumber from a donkey cart. She wondered what they were doing. She had overheard Mr. Davies tell her father of Mr. Weston's plans to build something on the point, but he had not mentioned the details.

Her father finished the morning lesson, and excused the boys for a few hours' respite. Julian went off in search of Lizzie, and Rowan declared the light was just the sort he liked to paint by and would be going outside.

Feeling peckish, Emma went downstairs to the steward's office, hoping the coffee urn and cheese biscuits might still be out for tradesmen's morning calls.

Strolling down the passage, she drew up short at finding the room occupied. A man sat drinking tea and reading the newspaper. Emma had seen Davies outside with Henry—otherwise she would not have barged in.

"Pardon me," she said, recognizing red-haired Mr. Teague.

He lifted his chin in acknowledgment and took a long swallow of tea.

"If you are looking for Mr. Davies," she said, "he is outside working on something with Mr. Weston."

"Fool's errand, that's what," he said.

"Is it? I don't know what they are doing. Building something from the looks of it."

"Aye. Buildin' an eyesore and a problem."

"I am certain Mr. Weston would build neither."

Teague shook his head. "He would indeed and congratulate himself for doing so. Youth and money don't mix, I always say. Too much self-righteousness in the young."

Emma blinked and tried not to frown. She wasn't sure what the man referred to but resented the unkind remark about Henry Weston.

Mr. Teague went back to reading the paper. Not the news page, she saw, but the advertisements and notices.

Curiosity nipped at Emma. She said boldly, "We have never been properly introduced. All I know is your name—Mr. Teague. And I am Miss Smallwood. My father tutors the younger Westons here at Ebbington, and I assist him."

"I knaw who thee bist." His tone was not complimentary. He did not, as Emma had hoped, return the favor by explaining his connection to the family or what he was doing there now.

Hunger forgotten, Emma was suddenly eager to be anywhere but in that room, with that rude, unpleasant man. "Well, if you will excuse me," she said, "I think I shall go and see what the men are building."

"Trouble, that's what they're building. It won't last, I can tell 'ee."

Emma collected her pelisse, bonnet, and gloves and went back downstairs and outside. She let herself out the garden gate and strode across the grassy headland. The sun was warm, but a cool wind yanked at her bonnet strings.

Ahead of her, she saw Rowan had already set up his easel and was uncorking his paints. The wind knocked the easel over, and he scrambled to pick it up and reposition it once more. She hurried over and caught the canvas as it tumbled across the grass.

"Hello, Rowan," she said, handing it back. "What will you paint today?"

"The men working on the bell tower, I suppose."

"Bell tower? Out here?"

"Some sort of warning bell, I gather."

"Oh." Emma looked toward the workmen as they sank the first post in its foundation hole. "Well, perhaps I shall take a closer look and leave you to paint."

He nodded, and she walked toward the point. The workmen set the second post and carried over a crossbar. Looking up from the plans in Davies's hands, Henry jogged over and held the crossbar in place while the estate carpenter hammered it to one post, then the other.

Emma watched for several minutes as they repeated the process with the third and fourth corner posts. The crewmen paused to wipe their brows, and Henry stepped away. Seeing her, he lifted a hand in greeting and walked over to join her.

"Hello, Miss Smallwood. What brings you out on such a windy day?"

"I was curious to see what you were doing."

"Ah. We are building a warning tower. From this height we are likely to see a ship in trouble before anyone down in the village. Sounding the alarm might give the port crews more time to mount a rescue effort." He stepped over to take the plans from Davies and unrolled them, showing her a scaffold-like tower, railed observation deck, and bell.

"I have been campaigning for an official rescue service for the harbor for several years," he continued. "But my efforts have come up against resistance from fishermen, villagers, and landowners alike—each for his own reasons. After the shipwreck earlier this spring, I decided I was done waiting. So for now, this is something I can *do*."

Henry excused himself a moment. He called off work for the day, thanking the men and asking them to resume first thing in the morning. As the men began gathering their tools, he rejoined Emma.

"I admire your efforts," she said. "But I must say I am surprised something like this is so important to you."

"Then I shall tell you why—though it's not a story I'm proud of. In fact, the memory plagues me." He gestured for her to take a seat on one of the pathside benches. He remained standing, looking toward the sea and gathering his thoughts.

"I was home from Oxford for the Easter holidays some five years ago, and I witnessed a shipwreck from this very spot." He pointed to teethlike rocks jutting from the sea some distance from the breakwater. "I saw a brig, her sails in tatters, strike the rocks there. I tried to shout, but no one could hear me from this height, not with the near-constant wind. So I ran down the cliff path. But by the time I got down to the harbor and managed to rouse the port crew, the ship was breaking apart."

He winced. "It was an Irish brig, I later learned, laden with butter bound for France. As soon as the vessel struck rock and grounded, one of the lads stripped off his outer clothes and jumped overboard. Usually that's the end of a man. Few can swim strong enough to overcome the undertow. Indeed, we lost sight of him beneath the waves and thought we'd seen the last of him. But then he popped up and swam to shore, like a duck in a pond. The rest of the ship's company, however, remained on board.

"Seven or eight men and boys stood on deck, too afraid to jump overboard. And with good reason. The poor souls screamed for help, but no one on shore gave them the least assistance. They were too far out for any rope to reach them, and no boat could have made it out of the harbor over the high surf—even had some brawny sailor or Mr. Bray been on hand to try. Or so I told myself—as did the old fishermen and the crews on shore leave that night. That's how we all justified and comforted our aching consciences as we stood there and watched men die."

He shook his head, eyes far away in memory. "When a part of

the ship broke off, the poor men would climb atop it, until a wave washed them off. At last the mast fell, and it was soon over, all the crew drowned. But that was not the end, no. Cargo and parts of the ship began washing up on shore. One of the unfortunate men had lashed himself to the mast and the rope had cut him in two."

He grimaced. "No one should ever have to see what I saw that day wash up on the beach as if so much flotsam. I ducked behind an overturned fishing boat and retched, sick and ashamed. Casks of Irish butter split open all about us, mingled on the sand with . . ." His words trailed away, and he swallowed. "To this day, I cannot stomach butter."

Emma felt bile burn her own throat.

"Sea gulls began circling and swooping down to take what they might," Henry continued. "Then the wreckers began to appear, like sneaky crabs creeping forward on the sand, rejoicing at gold coins found in a corpse's pocket, a silver watch, or a gold ring wrenched from cold fingers."

Again Henry shook his head. "Agents were dispatched and were soon busy saving as much of the cargo as possible—and staving off the attacks of the wreckers. About a thousand casks of butter were gathered and locked into our local fish cellars. Mr. Bray arrived and stood guard as our acting constable. Eight stout men approached and said they came for butter, and butter they would have. They were all noted wreckers, Derrick Teague among them. A fight broke out.

"I was worried about the one lad who'd survived, for because of him the butter washed ashore was not fair game under the common law. So I grabbed his arm and half-dragged, half-carried him up to the house." He exhaled roughly. "It was the worst night of my life."

Emma ventured quietly, "You saved him, at least."

"That's all I did." Henry's mouth twisted. "I should have done more."

Her heart ached for him. "But you were young," she soothed. "Only a lad yourself."

"No, I was nineteen. A man. Or at least, I should have been."

"But you said yourself there was little anybody could do. To risk your life under those odds . . ."

"We all of us die, Miss Smallwood," he interrupted. "But we don't all of us make our lives count for something. How much better to die saving another soul than to stand safe on shore and do nothing while others perish? I promised myself then and there that the next time I was in that situation—and I knew there would be a next time, living here at a place infamous for shipwrecks—that I would not hesitate to act."

Emma's gaze remained glued to Henry Weston's profile, fascinated and moved by the emotions playing over his face. "Well. You are acting now. And I for one am very impressed."

"Miss Smallwood, impressed?" He gave her a sidelong glance, green eyes shining. "That is one for the history books."

The next day, Henry was surprised but pleased when Miss Smallwood came out again to view the work on the warning tower. She was followed by Rowan and Julian, who had the day off from their studies because their tutor had gone with the vicar to a lecture sponsored by the Royal Geographical Society of Cornwall. Of the young people at Ebbington, only Phillip and Lizzie were not among them. And Adam, of course. How he wished Lady Weston would relent and allow his older brother a bit of freedom. Henry would not give up until he had convinced her, or at least his father, to do so.

For now, however, he would be satisfied with the progress on the tower. The risers, supports, and observation deck were finished, and the estate carpenter was busy fashioning the railings.

"Good morning, Mr. Weston," Emma greeted him. "How goes the work?"

"Very well, thank you. I have ordered the bell from a nearby foundry, but it is not yet ready. Otherwise, we are on schedule for completion by week's end."

She smiled at him. "Excellent."

Her praise lengthened his spine, and her smile did strange things to his heart.

Beside her, his half brothers squinted up at the bell tower with distaste.

"Looks like a guillotine frame to me," Rowan said.

Julian added, "Or a hangman's gibbet."

So much for praise. Yet Henry had to acknowledge the justice of their comparisons—there were fundamental similarities. The structure was fairly rudimentary: a tower of wooden scaffolding, with a ladder to reach its deck ten feet from the ground.

When the bell arrived, he would mount it on the deck in a rocker stand. Henry pointed upward and explained where the bell would be positioned and how it would be rung.

Rowan asked, "Why not just run a rope to the ground?"

Henry had considered that. He explained, "I want a person standing on the observation deck to be able to sound the bell from up there as well. But perhaps I shall bore a hole and run a rope down so it might be rung from either the deck or the ground. Good idea, Rowan."

Rowan lifted his hands in defense as though accused of wrongdoing. "Wasn't my idea."

"Don't make the rope too long," Julian said darkly. "Or you'll hang us all."

Henry was taken aback. From the corner of his eye, he noticed Miss Smallwood frown. He asked, "What do you mean by that?"

Julian shrugged. "You know there are some who won't take kindly to the idea."

"Wreckers, you mean?"

"Many of our neighbors view shipwrecked cargo as their right."

"I realize that, but lives are more important."

Julian sniffed. "Depends on whose life, I suppose."

Irritation shot through Henry. He scowled at Julian. "How so? In God's eyes all lives are equally important."

"That's one interpretation," Julian said. "I just hope you don't bring down trouble on the rest of us with that contraption."

Henry was jolted by his brother's words. He hoped they weren't true. Noticing Miss Smallwood's troubled look, he said, "If there are consequences, I hope they shall fall on me alone and not the rest of you."

Julian slanted him a look, the sunlight glinting off his eyes turning them icy blue. "Be careful what you wish for."

Rowan, his gaze trained on the tower, said, "You are familiar with the other name for a gallows?"

Henry frowned at this apparent change in topic. "Which name are you referring to?"

Rowan made no answer, but Miss Smallwood quietly supplied, "A derrick."

*Derrick* . . . the word resonated in Henry's mind. The given name of the area's most infamous wrecker. Derrick Teague.

A short time later, Julian and Rowan announced their intention to make the most of their day off by jaunting into the village. They invited Emma to join them, but she politely declined. The two strolled eagerly away, leaving Emma and Henry standing in awkward silence, watching them go.

Emma was about to excuse herself and return to the house when the donkey cart rumbled up the cliff road. As it passed the boys, Rowan turned and pointed in their direction. The driver waved his thanks and steered toward them, carrying neither passenger nor visible delivery.

Henry called out, "What is it, Tommy?"

The young man pulled a letter from his pocket and waved it in the air. "A message for a Mr. or Miss Smallwood."

As the youth reined in the donkey, Emma stepped forward. "I am Miss Smallwood."

He handed down the note, and Emma instantly recognized the handwriting.

"It's from Aunt Jane."

Henry withdrew a coin from his pocket and handed it to the driver.

"Thank you," Emma acknowledged, her eyes glued to the message as she unfolded it. "I shall repay you as soon as I retrieve my reticule."

"No matter. I hope everything is all right."

Emma skimmed the letter and looked up at him in astonishment. "She is at the Stratton Inn this very moment. Good heavens."

As the donkey cart rattled away Emma read the letter again more slowly.

*Hello my dears,*

*I have made an unplanned trip into Cornwall, to escort one of my pupils home (her mother is ailing and sent for her). As I was in the area, I thought I would attempt to see you.*

*I understand from your letters that unexpected guests are not always welcomed at Ebbington Manor, so I have decided it would be unwise to arrive unannounced. Therefore I shall await you here. My return coach departs at two this afternoon. If you are unable to get away, I shall understand perfectly. But if you are able, I should dearly enjoy seeing you for even a brief visit. Either way, know that I am well and missing you both.*

> *All my love,*
> *Jane*

Henry asked, "Why did she not come here?"

"She did not wish to arrive unannounced. To presume . . ."

"Meaning you told her how you and your father were received when you arrived?"

Emma bit her lip. "I am afraid so."

"Jane Smallwood would be very welcome, I assure you," Henry insisted.

"Thank you." Emma consulted her chatelaine watch and frowned. The lecture her father had gone to with the vicar was several hours away. They would not return until late that afternoon. "Her coach leaves in three hours," Emma said. "If I wait for Father to return, I shall miss her."

"Come." Henry gestured. "Let's make haste to the stables. We shall go in my curricle."

Emma began to protest, "That is very kind of you, but—"

"No buts, Miss Smallwood. You must see your aunt. In fact, I would very much like to see her again myself. If you don't mind, I shall stay just long enough to say hello, and then leave you ladies to visit."

"Of course, if you like. I am certain she would be happy to see you as well."

A short while later, Emma and Henry were on their way to Stratton in the open, two-wheeled curricle pulled by a pair of sleek roans. Ten or fifteen minutes in the smart, lightweight carriage brought them to their destination.

At the inn at the top of the High Street, Henry gestured for a hostler to take the reins and hopped down to give Emma a hand.

Behind them, the door to the inn opened, and Jane Smallwood stepped outside, apparently having seen them arrive. "Emma!" She beamed and walked forward, arms outstretched.

Emma entered her embrace and felt tears prick her eyes. She had not realized just how much she missed her aunt.

Aware of Henry behind her, Emma turned. "And you remember Mr. Weston."

"Of course I do." Jane Smallwood smiled. "How good to see you again, Henry."

"And you, Miss Smallwood. You are looking well, I must say. How are you?"

"Very well, I thank you. Better now that I am with my dear niece again. Thank you for bringing her."

"My pleasure. I am only sorry Mr. Smallwood has gone out for the day. Can you not stay longer? You would be most welcome at Ebbington Manor...."

"Thank you, no. I've left the other girls in the care of my maid and Mrs. Malloy—you remember Mrs. Malloy?"

"Yes, a very capable woman."

"Indeed. But she has her duties as cook-housekeeper for my

brother's tenants, so I cannot ask her to stay on longer. But thank you just the same."

"Very well. I will leave you two to visit." Henry turned to Emma. "And, Miss Smallwood, do feel free to tell your aunt about Adam. I trust her discretion." He drew himself up. "I shall return at two o'clock to see you off and collect Emma."

Jane smiled once more. "That is very kind of you, Henry. Thank you."

Her eyes shone with speculation as she watched the tall young man walk away.

"Well. What a pleasant surprise."

"Yes," Emma said. "Mr. Weston is full of surprises."

"Is he?" One of Jane's thin brows rose high.

Emma hurried to explain that she was merely referring to all of Henry's endeavors, describing his warning tower and his work with the village council.

"Very impressive, yes," her aunt agreed, opening the inn door for Emma. "The two of you are getting on better than you predicted, I take it?"

"Yes, I suppose we are."

The two ladies entered the inn and took seats at the table where Jane had left her carpetbag and cloak. Jane ordered refreshments from the innkeeper, then asked Emma, "And who is this *Adam* Henry mentioned?"

Emma leaned close and confided all she knew about Adam Weston. She ended by saying, "I thought of writing to tell you about him but was not sure I should, in case the letter might be misdirected. I haven't even told Father."

Jane nodded. "I am surprised Lady Weston thinks they shall be able to keep him a secret after everything that has happened."

"It is unfortunate she wishes to do so."

"Yes. What does Phillip say about it?"

Emma had mentioned in one of her letters that Phillip had returned from Oxford. She replied, "He says he feels trapped between what Henry wants for Adam and what Lady Weston wants."

Jane's eyes were distant in thought. "I can imagine. How strange to be reunited with a brother he never knew."

The two Miss Smallwoods went on to speak of other topics. Emma shared details about her father's marked improvement in spirits, and Jane, in turn, shared news from Longstaple—their tenant, Mrs. Welborn, had asked her unmarried sister to stay with her, to help with the children. And Mr. Gilcrest had sold the forge for a larger one in Plymouth.

"I am sorry to hear it," Emma said, thinking that with his departure went any hope of his cousin and Jane's former admirer, Mr. Farley, returning to Longstaple. How unfortunate.

The innkeeper brought tea and a light meal, and their discussion moved on to other things. The time flew quickly, and all too soon, Jane's coach was called.

Henry appeared as promised and carried Jane's bag out to the coach. "I was telling Emma she ought to ask you to Ebbington Manor whenever you might be at liberty to visit. Please do consider yourself invited, Miss Smallwood. You would be most welcome."

"Thank you, Henry. I shall consider it."

Jane hugged Emma and climbed inside the coach. The few outside passengers took their seats, the guard climbed up on the rear and blew his long horn, and the horses pulled in tandem. As the coach moved down the lane, Jane waved from the window and Emma waved back, tears blurring her vision.

She stared after the coach until it disappeared, aware of the man waiting patiently beside her but unwilling to turn until she had blinked away all her tears.

Finally, Emma sighed and turned, forcing a smile. "Shall we go?"

Henry laid his palm before her, and she placed her hand in his. And unless she was mistaken, he held her hand several moments longer than absolutely necessary to simply help her into his curricle.

*When a wreck took place—it might be within*
*a stone's throw of the land—in many cases*
*the sailors perished beneath the very eyes of*
*those on shore who could do no other than*
*stand as helpless witnesses of the tragedy.*

—A.K. Hamilton Jenkin,
editor, *An Account of Wrecks*

# Chapter 20

The next day, a fine June morning, Emma decided to join her father for his early walk along the coast and tell him all about her visit with Aunt Jane. When she went downstairs, however, Mr. Davies informed her she had just missed her father, but if she hurried, she might yet catch him. Thanking the steward, Emma hurried out into the passage and nearly ran into Henry Weston in riding clothes.

"Good morning, Miss Smallwood," he said, removing his hat. "Where are you off to in such a hurry?"

"I was hoping to catch my father and join him for his walk."

Henry opened the door for her. "I shall walk with you as far as the stables."

As they crunched across the gravel path, Mr. Weston turned his head to look over the garden wall toward the coast. He stopped in his tracks.

Emma turned, following his gaze. "What is it? What's wrong?"

Henry pointed to the horizon. A horizon no longer broken by a wooden tower.

His jaw clenched. "Pardon me." He turned and strode out the garden gate and jogged across the headland. Emma hitched up her skirt and ran after him.

Winded, sides aching, she caught up with him as he neared the tower. Or what was left of it.

Splintered posts and planks lay haphazardly on the ground.

Surveying the damage, Emma panted to catch her breath. "Did the wind knock it over?"

Henry kicked at a fallen post. "See this? Marks from a saw. No wind did that. Unless it was one of your nefarious wind gods."

Emma shivered. "Why would anyone do such a thing? Simple vandalism, or . . . ?"

Henry shook his head, expression hard. "No. Other motives were at work here."

"What motives?"

"Greedy wreckers, I'd wager." He yanked off his hat and ran an agitated hand through his hair. "You heard what Julian and Rowan said yesterday."

Heavy dismay filled her at the loss of all his work and plans. "Yes, but I still can't believe anyone would truly object to saving lives."

"Remember that cargo from wrecks is often considered free for the taking when there are no survivors. So any effort to save life is viewed by some as depriving the poor of what is regarded as God's grace to them."

"Can people really be so heartless, poor or not?"

He picked up a severed chunk of wood and hurled it off the cliff. "Apparently."

Taking in the stern set of his jaw and the fire in his eyes, she asked tentatively, "What will you do?"

Henry Weston inhaled through flared nostrils, clearly trying to master his anger. "I shall report this to our constable, Mr. Bray. Though I doubt there is anything he can do. Then I will rebuild."

News spread quickly across the estate. Members of his family and clusters of servants and tenants ventured out to see the damage, going away with somber faces, whispered warnings, and "Did I not tell you this would happen?"

Henry had sent a groom with a message for Mr. Bray. The grey-haired constable rode his horse across the headland an hour later. Reaching the point, he dismounted and grasped Henry's hand. He surveyed the scene, shook his head, and said he would do what he could, though he offered little hope of the perpetrators being identified or brought to justice.

When the constable turned to remount his horse, Miss Smallwood walked over and stood beside Henry.

He glanced down at her, self-conscious to have her witness the failure of his project he'd been so proud of the day before. He'd not thought to post guard. He had truly believed Julian and Rowan had exaggerated the risk. He looked away from her concerned, gentle eyes. Instead he watched Mr. Bray ride away toward the cliff path. He nodded in the man's direction. "There goes the bravest person I know."

"Oh? How so?"

"I told you that most people believe it's too dangerous to enter the breaking sea to try to rescue sailors. But Mr. Bray has done so numerous times."

Together Henry and Miss Smallwood watched the man as he disappeared down the path. There was nothing about the man's average size or grey head that made him an obvious candidate for such feats of bravery.

She asked, "What did he say about the tower?"

Henry exhaled. "He will make inquiries. But even if he learns who did it, it will be difficult to prove, and more difficult to find a jury to convict those responsible."

Miss Smallwood opened her mouth, closed it, and then said, "How well do you know Mr. Teague?"

He turned to look at her. "By reputation mostly. Why?"

"I met him in Mr. Davies's office when you were building the tower. He predicted it would not last long."

Henry tucked this away for later consideration. He said judiciously, "An accurate prediction doesn't make him guilty. Julian and Rowan said basically the same thing to me, as did Lady Weston. We all knew it would not be a popular project."

She nodded. "Does this alter your plans to rebuild?"

He shook his head. "We shall reconstruct the original tower for the time being. But I think I shall also hire a stonemason to design and build a tower as sturdy as the Chapel of the Rock. Let's see the greedy curs knock *that* down."

The two of them stood in silence for several minutes. Above them seabirds floated in twos and threes above the cliff tops, and the sun shone cheerfully, at odds with the dismal scene. Behind them the other onlookers lost interest and returned to the house.

Henry inhaled. "May I tell you my favorite shipwreck story?"

She looked up at him. "Of course."

Thinking of his last gruesome story, he said, "Don't worry, this one has a mostly happy ending. And a moral."

"A moral?" she asked in surprise. "Is it a made-up story, then, like one of Aesop's fables?"

"No. It is a true story. Told to me by Mr. Bray himself."

"Go on."

He nodded and gathered his thoughts. "A ship from America, laden with salt fish and oil, wrecked right there off the Chapel of the Rock." He lifted his chin toward the distant landmark below.

"At the moment the ship struck, the captain and his wife were at prayer in the cabin. One of the sailors saw them and asked, 'Is this a time for you to pray? You had better save your lives.' And he swore at them bitterly."

"Soon the bottom of the ship parted. The cabin drove farther in on the rocks, and the masts fell toward the chapel, so that the captain, his lady, and many sailors were able to crawl across the masts and onto shore. Most everyone was saved—except for the bitter sailor who'd rebuked the captain for praying. He was drowned, and a stout lad also."

Emma nodded. "Yes, I can see how a praying man like yourself might like that story."

Hearing her defensive tone, he looked at her. "It is a *true* story." Slowly, her averted face and rigid posture registered in his mind, and he felt his brows rise in question. "Do you not pray, Miss Smallwood?"

She avoided his gaze. "No."

"God is speaking to you every day," he said softly. "You might return the favor."

She raised her chin. "I don't hear Him."

"Do you listen?"

She looked at him, clearly offended, then turned away again. "I used to pray, until I found God was not listening, at least not to my prayers."

Henry heard the inner voice of caution but barreled ahead. "He *was* listening. But He doesn't always answer the way we would like Him to."

She turned to him, eyes flashing. "And what about that stout lad who drowned? Did he swear at the captain for praying too? Is that why he died?"

Henry shook his head sadly. "Probably not."

"Then why did he die?" she challenged. "No doubt he had a mother somewhere, praying for him. Or a sister."

Henry saw her chin quiver and realized she was thinking of her own mother. A sheen of tears brightened her eyes, but she fiercely blinked them away, clearly determined not to cry in front of him.

"It's a fallen world," he said gently. "Sometimes bad things just happen."

"Yes," she breathed, staring off into the sea, "they do."

He pressed her hand briefly, then drew himself up. "Forgive me, Miss Smallwood. Your prayers or lack thereof are between you and God and are not for me to mettle with or judge."

Looking up at him from beneath damp lashes, she slowly shook her head. "You have certainly changed, Mr. Weston. In Longstaple, you all but slept through Sunday services."

A humorless chuckle escaped him. "I was not a complete heathen, Miss Smallwood. Simply a bored adolescent."

"Lizzie tells me that nowadays, after you attend church with your family, you also go to a Wesleyan preaching service. May I ask what draws you there?"

Henry nodded. It was a question he'd had to answer before. "The lively singing and preaching. The extemporaneous prayers. I feel . . . awakened there, after years of . . . as you say, being asleep. I have become more grateful for God's pardoning love. More aware of my need of Him." Henry stopped and pulled a face. "Sorry. I am sounding like a preacher now. You must make allowances for a well-meaning muttonhead."

She braved a wobbly grin. "Must I?"

"No." He smiled ruefully. "But I would sincerely appreciate it."

That night Emma awoke to gentle strains of music in the distance. It struck her as a pleasant surprise. It had been too long since she'd heard it—since the Ebbington "ghost" had favored them with a song. She recalled her discussion with Henry Weston about whether or not Adam might possess any musical ability. Henry had doubted it, but Emma was not convinced. Maintaining her theory of the identity of the "ghost," she felt no alarm, only the desire to verify her supposition. And to hear the music better.

She slid her arms into her wrapper and pulled on stockings, deciding to forgo shoes.

She crept quietly past her father's room and down the stairs. She knew her way around the house better now, so this time, she lit no lamp to light her way, and in her silent stocking feet, she hoped to give no advance warning of her approach.

Tiptoeing across the hall, she paused before the music room. . . . Yes, the "ghost" was still playing. Gently, tentatively, she released the door latch with a gentle click and paused, listening.

Relief. He had not heard it over the music, for the playing continued. She ever so slowly inched open the door, then slipped inside. Her heart thumped loudly in her ears as she pressed her back against the wall and stood still in the shadows.

As her eyes adjusted, she saw that moonlight from the transom spilled weakly onto the pianoforte and its player. Emma's heart exulted. It was Adam, as she'd thought. She wondered how he read the score, for he had no candle and certainly the dim moonlight was insufficient to read music by.

As her eyes adjusted further, she could better see his face. It appeared as though his eyes were closed as he played. Was it only a trick of the shadows? From where she stood she could see no sheet music, but perhaps it was her angle and the poor lighting.

Soon she gave up wondering and simply absorbed the gentle, sweet melody. She did not know the piece or its composer. But she did know she liked it. So much more pleasing than the banging, dramatic pieces Julian favored.

Emma listened for a few more minutes. Then, turning, she was startled to see a figure leaning against the shadowy back wall on the opposite side of the door. Her heart raced. But then she recognized Henry Weston and expelled a sigh of relief.

He glanced over and silently opened the door for her. She slipped out of the room, and he followed, quietly closing the door behind them.

As they crossed the hall together, Henry said, "You were right again, Miss Smallwood."

She liked hearing those words more than she should have, she knew. She cherished praise of her intelligence like some women cherished compliments on their beauty.

She whispered, "I wonder if Lady Weston was so eager to credit Julian because she wanted to hide Adam's existence, or if she truly believed such talent could only come from her own child."

"Both, probably."

At the foot at the stairs, she turned to Henry and gripped his arm. "Let's not tell anyone. Not yet."

Henry looked down at her expectantly, and Emma suddenly realized she was still gripping his forearm. And that he wore only shirtsleeves. She felt thick, ropey muscles beneath her fingers. She swallowed and pulled her hand away.

Embarrassed, she risked looking up into his face by the moonlight leaking in through the hall's unshuttered windows. Was it a trick of the shadows or did his eyes darken? Did he lean closer?

Her heart thumped. *Goodness.* She was standing alone with Henry Weston late at night, him in his shirtsleeves and her in her nightclothes. With her in stocking feet, he loomed even taller than usual. He would have to lean down to—

"Have you something in mind?" he whispered, his face suddenly very near hers. She smelled bay rum cologne. Felt his warm breath.

"Yes," she murmured, her gaze drifting to his mouth.

"Some . . . plan?"

*Plan?* She blinked. *Oh, right—Adam.* She took a shaky breath and stepped back. "Not yet, but I am working on it."

After breakfast the next morning, Emma went up to the school-room for some old sheet music she had seen in the cupboard. Then she went to visit Adam.

He recognized her now and seemed at his ease in her company, or at least not distressed by her showing up at his door. He sat in his armchair with a pad and drawing pencil, sketching a new battle scene, but glanced up as she crossed the room.

Softly she began, "I heard you playing the pianoforte last night."

He looked up at her, stricken. "I'm not to leave my room."

"That's all right. I was glad to hear you. You play very well."

Adam set aside his drawing. He rose and went to the table, pulling the chess board front and center.

"Adam," Emma asked, laying a piece of sheet music on the table before him. "Do you read music?"

He shook his head. "I read books."

"I know you do. But not music?" She ran a finger over the score. "Does this mean anything to you?"

His glance skittered from the score to the chess pieces. "My mar looks at pages like that when she plays."

Emma's eager mind and curiosity were roused. "May I ask . . . how do you play the pianoforte if you cannot read music?"

He shrugged, sliding the music back toward her, off the chessboard. "I play what I hear."

"What you hear?"

He nodded.

"So . . ." She tried to keep the incredulity from her tone. "You heard music played, remembered it, and now can play the piece by ear?"

His focus remained on the chess set as he set up the pieces. "I play with my hands, Emma. Not my ear."

"Of course. I meant . . . how?"

Again the unruffled shrug. "I don't know."

"And where did you hear the music you were playing last night?"

Adam thought a moment. "The village hall. My par, Mr. Hobbes, takes me there to hear music sometimes."

She shook her head in wonder. "That is quite a memory you have. A gift."

Adam did not seem as impressed as she was but finished setting up the chess pieces.

"Do you ever play the music you hear Julian play?"

He looked up at the ceiling. "Is he the one who plays very loud?"

"Yes," she allowed.

"It hurts my ears."

Emma smiled. "Mine too."

She glanced down at the chessboard. For the first time she noticed Adam had set up the pieces in correct position for a proper game. "Who taught you to set up the pieces like that?"

"Henry."

That's when she saw it. For a moment she thought it was a trick of the light, or her imagination. But then her hand reached out of its own accord and touched it, and it didn't disappear. She picked it up, astonished and disconcerted. The white queen with oriental features—the one depicted in the bloody drawing. The original from her own chess set that Henry had taken years ago but said had recently gone missing.

"Adam, where did you get this?" she breathed.

"It matches."

"I know. But where did you find it?"

He turned and pointed to a valise on the side table. "In my case. Yesterday."

Emma's mind reeled. How had it ended up in Adam's room? Glancing around at the violent battle scenes pinned to the walls, she swallowed the queasy dread rising in her throat.

Had Adam drawn the beheaded queen after all?

A chill passed over her at the thought.

Emma wondered whether or not Henry knew Adam had the queen. If he already knew, why hadn't he said so?

That afternoon, Lizzie came to Emma's room and asked her to take a turn with her in the garden. The girl was already dressed for the out-of-doors, her large straw hat tied with lace beneath her chin. She stuck out her hands. "Look, I am even wearing gloves."

Emma agreed to join her, pulling on a bonnet and gloves of her own.

As they passed the drawing room on the way to the side door, they heard Henry and Lady Weston arguing within—Lady Weston recommending an acquaintance in Falmouth to care for Adam, and Henry rebutting that a distance of more than fifty miles was too great to allow for regular visits.

Lizzie tugged Emma's arm, pulling her more quickly toward the door, out of earshot of the tense conversation.

"He really vexes her, you know," Lizzie said, shaking her head.

Emma extracted her arm to shut the door behind them and then followed Lizzie into the garden. "Who does . . . Adam?"

Lizzie turned to wait for her, brushing a breeze-blown curl from the corner of her mouth. "Well, yes. Him too. But I meant Henry. Always refusing to call her Mother, going against her wishes by bringing Adam here, and now refusing to find a place for him."

Lizzie took Emma's arm again. Pea gravel crunched under their slippers. Sunlight shone on orange-red poppies, steel-blue globe flowers, and violet clematis, intensifying their vibrant colors.

As the girls strolled through the garden enjoying the sunshine and sweet smells, Emma commented on the first vexation in Lizzie's long list. "I suppose since Henry remembers his real mamma, the one who birthed him, he finds it difficult to call another woman by that name. It's only natural he should miss her and want to remember her. I can understand that, having lost my own mother. Certainly you can as well."

"Why should I understand it?"

"Well . . ." Emma faltered. "Because you lost your mother too."

Lizzie snorted softly. "Wouldn't say I lost her, exactly. Though I suppose my father did. Lost her to the excise man."

Emma frowned. "I don't understand. I thought both your parents were gone."

Lizzie pulled her arm from Emma's and bent to pick a spent bloom. "I never said so. You simply assumed."

"No. I distinctly recall you saying your mother had been gone far longer than mine."

"Gone, yes. But not dead. At least as far as I know."

"And your father?"

Lizzie sighed. "I never knew my father, but I had a stepfather. Briefly."

"Oh. Is he . . . ?"

"Alive and well and pulling all our strings."

Emma gaped at the girl. "But . . . I thought you were here because . . . that you were Lady Weston's ward because she had taken you in after . . ." She let her words trail away.

"Lady Weston did take me in 'after,'" Lizzie said. "After my mother took up with another man, left me with my new so-called stepfather, and *he* saw fit to be rid of me." She tossed the spent bloom to the ground. "How naive you are." She gave Emma a look of world-wise superiority. "You assumed I was an orphan and *kind* Lady Weston took me in out of the goodness of her heart?"

"Well . . . yes."

Lizzie shook her head. "That is a fiction. You read too many books, Emma. I have always said so."

Emma stared at the stranger before her. She barely recognized this Lizzie Henshaw with the blazing eyes, curled lip, and sharp tongue.

"Put that in your journal, why don't you," Lizzie snapped. She whirled away from Emma, pointing over the garden wall toward the fallen tower, where workmen were already beginning repairs. "And as to the warning tower, Henry went directly against Lady Weston's wishes in having it built."

Emma blinked and thought quickly to follow this lurch in topic. "But why should she object to that? Henry told me about the villagers' rights to the cargo if there are no survivors, but why should Lady Weston care about that?"

Lizzie slowly shook her head, eyes glinting. "And here I thought you were clever."

*Eternal Father, strong to save,*
*Whose arm hath bound the restless wave . . .*
*Oh, hear us when we cry to Thee,*
*For those in peril on the sea!*

—William Whiting, 1860

# Chapter 21

After her disconcerting talk with Lizzie in the garden, Emma returned to the house.

Desiring a more pleasant encounter, she decided to seek out Henry Weston. She wanted to ask if he knew about Adam having the queen. She knew Henry wouldn't welcome any additional black marks against the brother he did not wish to send away. She would have to make it clear casting blame was not her intention. Perhaps Henry himself had found the piece and placed it in Adam's room to complete the set. Though it was odd that he had not mentioned it.

The drawing room was silent—Henry and Lady Weston were no longer there. Might he be in his study? She went upstairs, but that room was empty as well.

He might be with Adam, Emma thought, and began climbing the stairs. As she reached the top floor, she told herself not to get her hopes up. Henry could as easily be sequestered with his father or Mr. Davies over some estate matter.

She anticipated she would find Adam alone, bent over the tin soldiers with as much singular focus as he had given the dominoes and chess pieces.

But when she reached Adam's door, she heard voices coming from the other side. Two voices.

Slowly, she inched the door open and peered in. There sat Adam and Henry, not at the table but on the floor. Coats discarded, knees bent, reclining casually like children in their shirtsleeves. The table must have been too small to contain the large battlefield they had created with many regiments of soldiers, as well as objects placed hither and yon to represent terrain. Perhaps that hat was a hill? And that hand mirror a lake?

Emma watched a few moments longer, the scene gladdening her heart. Deciding not to disturb them, nor to bother Henry about the queen, she slipped silently from the room.

Henry looked at his older brother, more talented than he. More troubled. More vulnerable. He thought of the upheaval Adam had experienced, losing his mother, his home, his entire family. Though Mr. and Mrs. Hobbes had apparently treated him well, Henry wondered if Adam felt abandoned, or bitter, or betrayed. He also wondered if the Hobbeses had taught Adam about God. If they had taken him to church and prayed with him, or if he had been isolated from those experiences as well.

Henry moved a major forward on their pretend battlefield and quietly asked, "Adam, what do you believe about God?"

"God?"

"Yes. You know—our creator. 'Our Father who art in heaven . . .'?"

Adam nodded. "Mar and Par told me about God. We went to visit him at church."

"Ah. Well . . . good." Henry recalled his conversation with Miss Smallwood and determined to tread more carefully. He said, "And do you ever pray?"

Again Adam nodded. "Mar says it is good to pray."

Henry wondered if prayer was more than a rote act for him. He fumbled for words. "Do you . . . believe God hears you?"

Adam shrugged and moved an ensign forward. "I talk and that is all."

"You don't . . . feel God's presence?"

Adam's face wrinkled. "I don't know what that means. I don't feel . . . that."

Henry felt his own brow crinkle in concentration. It seemed as if he were trying to explain an abstract thing—faith—in a foreign language, and one he had only a rudimentary understanding of himself. He said, "It is all right if you don't feel it. Faith is far more than emotion. More than feelings."

Adam's expression remained flat. Unimpressed.

Henry inhaled deeply and turned his head to look out the window for inspiration. He saw the tallest branches of the turkey oak bending in the southwest wind. He unfolded his long legs, lumbered to his feet, and stepped to the window. "Adam, would you please come here a moment?"

Adam rose and joined him at the window.

Henry asked God to give him the right words. He said, "We cannot feel the wind from here. So how do we know it is real?"

Adam thought. "We see it."

"You see the wind? What good eyes you have, Adam. Where?"

Adam pointed out the window. "I see it blowing the branches."

"Right. We can't feel it from here or see it directly. But we know it's there because we see its effects. What it does."

Adam said nothing, nor did his expression light with understanding as Henry had hoped.

Henry tried again. "Do you see that cedar—that stout tree overshadowing the courtyard?"

Adam shifted his focus and nodded.

"It was planted the day our grandfather was born. For its age, it should be twice the height it is now. But its top has been blasted out by the prevailing winds blowing over the ridgeline. So it has grown out instead of up. The trees have all been shaped by the wind."

Adam nodded.

Henry continued, "Like you, Adam, I don't always *feel* God listening or speaking to me. But I have seen Him answer my prayers and the prayers of others—though not always as I would like, nor as quickly as my impatience desires. But I have *seen* the effects of prayer."

Adam said suddenly, "I asked God to forgive me for all the bad things I've done."

Astounded, Henry studied his brother's profile. "What bad things could you have possibly done?"

Henry wondered if Adam had done more than sneak into Miss Smallwood's room at night. More than helping himself to their mother's perfume and perhaps the chess piece, though he'd denied the latter, saying it appeared in his valise sometime after Henry had asked him about it.

"You know." Adam's glance slid to Henry, then away again. "You were there."

"Was I?" Henry asked, confused.

Adam returned to the soldiers and sat back down on the floor. "They sent me away after."

Henry stared. "I was not yet four when they . . . when you went to live with Mr. and Mrs. Hobbes. I don't remember very much of those days."

Adam looked up, his eyes taking on a distant gleam. "We were in Mar's sitting room. Though she was not my mar yet. She had a kettle on the fire for tea. She was called away and was a long time coming back." Adam shook his head. "I wanted to help her, so I tried to pour. But I spilt it on your arm. How you cried. Mrs. Hobbes said it was a blessing—for if you drank boiling water you'd have burned your innards. Might have died."

Henry sat down across from Adam and looked at his own arm. The small patch of slightly scarred skin began itching at that moment as if provoked by the memory. "I am fine, Adam. As you see. Fine."

Impulsively, he reached over and laid a hand on Adam's arm. Adam stiffened, and Henry quickly withdrew it. "It was an accident, Adam. You were only a child."

And while that accident might have been the final straw, Henry guessed the reasons for sending Adam away were far more complicated.

"I am sorry," Adam said, as if a line in a script.

"You have nothing to be . . ." Henry began, then thought the better of it. Clearly this had been bothering Adam for years. He said firmly but gently, "Adam, look at me."

Adam's gaze flickered up toward Henry but quickly skated away.

"Adam, I forgive you. Do you believe me?"

"Yes."

Henry's heart ached. He said hoarsely, "Adam, will you forgive me?"

Adam darted a look at him, and before he looked away again, Henry thought he saw a hint of surprise there. "What did you do?"

Looking at his brother's profile, a lump rose in Henry's throat. "Nothing. For far too long."

The following week, while Henry was out on his morning ride, still a quarter mile from home, a storm blew in from the southwest. The sky darkened and clouds billowed. The rain did not come, although the air felt thick and pregnant with it. The wind rose and howled like a woman in labor pains, but still the rain did not come.

Henry was seized with a sudden and terrible dread. What was it? Was Miss Smallwood in trouble, or . . . ? An image of his tower flashed in his mind like a premonition.

Although usually calm in any weather, his horse, Major, snorted and shied, perhaps sensing Henry's alarm. Henry urged Major into a gallop across the top of the headland, toward the tower they had rebuilt and upon which he had installed the bell only two days before.

Ahead of him, near the point, he saw Miss Smallwood, Lizzie, and Julian clustered around Rowan's easel, helping him pack up his supplies before the rain hit.

Henry rode past them to look over the edge. There, as he feared, was a ship, struggling to navigate the choppy seas to enter the haven.

His heart thumped. His pulse raced. This was it—the "next time" he had anticipated. There was no time to waste.

Emma Smallwood had run to the cliff's edge to see what had

drawn his attention. Seeing the ship tilting dangerously, she pressed a gloved hand to her mouth.

He called down to her, "Ring the bell. Hard!"

She nodded and whirled toward the tower. He turned Major's head and spurred him onward, galloping down the path toward the harbor.

Emma started toward the tower to do his bidding, but Lizzie caught her by the wrist, her face a sudden mask of hard lines and determination.

"Don't," she commanded.

"But . . . I . . . " Emma sputtered. "You heard what Henry said. He wants us to ring the bell."

Lizzie's eyes widened in apparent disbelief. "I didn't hear him say that. Not over this wind."

Emma tried to pull away, but Lizzie held her with a surprisingly tight grip.

"What are you doing? Let me go."

"I won't."

"Don't you understand—the ship is in trouble. Lives are at stake."

"What is that to us?"

Lizzie's cold voice, her casual disdain of life, struck Emma hard. Why had she thought she knew Lizzie Henshaw at all? Emma struggled against the girl's grasp. Though Lizzie was several years younger, she was strong. By comparison, Emma's daily routine of reading and teaching had done little to strengthen her arms.

Lizzie turned and shouted toward Rowan and Julian, several yards away. "She's trying to ring the bell. Come and help me."

Emma looked over her shoulder at them. Were they all in league together in . . . whatever this was?

Abandoning the easel, Julian came running, bounding across the grass. Rowan followed close behind. Emma knew that once they laid hold of her. She would never get loose. It was now or never.

She quit struggling for a moment, pretending to give up. She hung her head as though defeated. As she'd hoped, Lizzie's grip loosened fractionally. At this, Emma gave a great lift and downward lurch, as though bringing down an axe on a chicken's neck.

Lizzie cried out and reached for her again, but Emma reeled and slapped her hard across the face. The girl reared back and stumbled but kept to her feet, cradling her injured cheek with both hands.

Emma turned and bolted the few feet to the ladder and began climbing up as quickly as she could.

"You cow!" Lizzie yelled, shock and venom in her voice.

Emma didn't look down but felt Lizzie's hand raking at her cape hem. She jerked away, cleared the last rung of the ladder, and mounted the platform. She grasped the bell lever and pulled hard, over and over again until her ears rang and her head began to ache.

"I think you can stop, Miss Smallwood," Julian called up pleasantly. "The whole village has heard you by now."

"The whole county, I imagine," Rowan added wryly.

Would they trap her up there? Push the tower over with her atop it?

"You must forgive Lizzie," Julian said. "She was only concerned about our well-being. She knows whoever knocked down this tower before might come after us all looking for revenge, should they be deprived of a rich wreck." He sent a fond smile toward the irate young woman, still holding her face. "Isn't that right, Lizzie?"

Lizzie glared at him.

But Julian smiled in reply and said gently, "You were only trying to protect us, all of us. Is that not right, dear Lizzie?" he asked her pointedly.

From between clenched teeth, she ground out, "Yes, *dear* Julian."

He smiled up at Emma. "You see? Come down now and the two of you make up."

Lizzie seethed, "I will not '*make up.*' She hit me in the face. Did you not see?"

"I did." Julian looked up again at Emma with apparent admiration. "And I must say, I'm impressed. I did not think the tutor's daughter had it in her. She's not entirely the prim spinster I thought her."

Emma wasn't sure if that was meant as a compliment or an insult, but was too shaken to care.

"Just wait until Lady Weston hears of this!" Lizzie cried, lifting her chin.

At the moment, Lady Weston was the least of Emma's fears.

Rowan looked up at her earnestly. "Come down, Miss Small-wood," he urged. "You look very ill."

"I shall wait here, thank you," she said, forcing a cool, imperious tone. Never let them see fear, she recalled her aunt advising: of wild dogs or ill-mannered boys.

From the direction of the house, she glimpsed Phillip running toward them, Sir Giles and her father lumbering behind.

"Thank God," she whispered, realizing she had not thanked Him properly in far too long.

Knowing, or at least hoping, the three of them would not attempt to harm her in the presence of witnesses, Emma climbed gingerly down the ladder on trembling legs, too concerned about the ship, about Henry, to worry overly much about the impropriety of descending a ladder on a windy day above the heads of young men. They were not looking at her anyway; they were looking down at the struggling brig, talking in terse voices amongst themselves.

As much as she longed for the comforting presence of her friend Phillip and of her father and kindly Sir Giles, Emma made no move to join them.

Phillip approached ahead of the older men, and Lizzie ran to him, lacing her hands around his arm, face downcast, the picture of injured femininity.

The offended part of Emma wished to stay and defend herself, but she did not wait. Instead, she turned, pointed out to sea, and called over her shoulder, "A ship's in trouble. Henry's gone down to help!"

She expected Sir Giles, or at least Phillip, to follow her and lend aid as well.

But Phillip hung back, his head bent to hear what Lizzie was saying. No doubt vilifying Emma. Well, that could not be helped now. Vaguely hearing her father calling after her, Emma grabbed a handful of skirts and hurried down the path.

Slowing his horse at the bottom of the hill to round the sharp bend, Henry heard the bell above ring out at last, loud and strong. Thank God. He'd begun to wonder what had forestalled Emma, or if someone had disabled the bell.

Turning onto the sand road and galloping toward the beach, Henry saw the brig careening toward the far side of the harbor opposite the breakwater, her sails in tatters. He rode as fast as he could, reaching the beach as the ship struck rock beyond the harbor's mouth, turning broadside against the sea. Six frantic sailors lashed a yard line from the ship and from it jumped off into the water, desperate not to go down with the ship. The sailors floundered amidst the waves, struggling to keep their heads above the water.

Looking out at the crushing waves, Henry's heart failed him. Fear froze him to the saddle. The men would never swim in against that undertow. And he could not swim out to them. He doubted even the strongest, most experienced swimmer could manage the feat, and he had swum but little since boyhood.

He glanced down at the various fishing boats on shore. He could not row out over the bruising surf of the harbor's unprotected north side without capsizing. He glimpsed a rope in the bow of a boat, and an idea came to him. He dismounted, grabbed the rope, secured it around his waist, then leapt back onto his horse, his feet easily finding the stirrups by long habit.

*Gracious God, help me. Help those poor souls.* Taking the reins, he urged his horse forward. "Come on, boy. Let's go." Across the sands and into the water the obedient horse galloped. Icy water splashed up Henry's legs, then his waist, until he realized his horse was swimming. "Brave Major," he murmured.

Ahead, he saw the six men bobbing and gasping for air.

"Hold fast all together!" Henry called. Not sure they could hear him over the wind, he demonstrated by reaching up and clasping his own hands together.

The men made their way laboriously to one another and held on.

Henry tossed the end of the rope to the nearest man. He missed it and went under. Henry reeled it in as quickly as he could, then tossed it again. This time the man caught it. Suddenly a wave broke over Henry, stunning him with the force of the water, driving him back. He felt himself pulled from the saddle but gripped it with all the strength of his leg muscles and a hand to the leather straps. Robbed of breath, his lungs burned. Eyes closed, he felt dizzy and disoriented.

*God, help me!* he beseeched in silent cry. The wave passed, and Henry's head cleared the water. He sputtered for breath. He searched the sea around him, exulting to see the men still huddled together, the rope tied around the arm of the first.

"Come on, boy. Back to shore," Henry urged, signaling with his rein, knees, and voice.

The horse, heaving and snorting water from its nostrils, turned by degrees and, straining against the undertow and the weight of the waterlogged men, slowly pulled them all to shore.

The sailors, gasping and coughing, knelt in the surf, thanking God, Henry surmised, in a language foreign to his ears. Spanish, he thought. Or perhaps Portuguese.

But one man looked wildly about him. Then he reached up and grasped Henry's coattail. "Sir, my brothah!" he cried in accented English. "Hee's gone!"

Henry surveyed the small huddle of men—there were only five on shore. Disappointment slammed into him. *No . . .*

Searching the sea, the man pointed. "There!"

Henry looked and saw a head, then a desperate hand, before the man disappeared beneath the waves.

"Please, sir. I beg you," the man said. "Hee's my brothah."

For a moment their eyes caught and held. *Brother . . .* Henry's heart twisted. Dare he go out again? He hated to ask it of his horse, but as much as he loved and valued the animal, a man's life was more important.

*More important than my own?* he asked himself, then banished the thought. He had made himself a promise. A vow. He would not sit by and do nothing. Not again.

"Come on, boy. Let's go." He urged Major back into the surf. If the horse hesitated, it was only a momentary pause, yet Henry felt a tremor run through the massive muscles and knew the horse felt fear as he did.

Henry focused his gaze on the spot where the man had gone under. From the corner of his eye, a massive grey wall of water loomed into view. He took a gulp of air, stopped his breath, and ducked his head as the wave broke high over him. This time, Henry opened his eyes underwater and was amazed to see the sailor nearby, reaching up. The man managed to grab the stirrup nearest him. Henry reached down and seized the man's collar.

The wave passed. Henry's head broke the surface and he gasped a mouthful of air. He pulled the man with all his strength, but he was very heavy with his waterlogged clothing and likely water in his lungs as well. Henry wasn't even sure the poor man managed one breath before another wave broke over them. This wave knocked them over and rolled the horse upside down, so that Henry and the sailor were trapped beneath him.

*Lord, help us,* Henry prayed desperately.

His horse quickly righted, and Henry gasped for breath, yanking the sailor's head above water. Major turned toward shore and swam, then walked with Henry and the half-drowned sailor onto the beach.

By this time, a few others had arrived on the scene. Mr. Bray and the sailor's brother rolled the poor man on the ground until a good deal of salt water sprang from his mouth.

The sailor coughed and sputtered, and his brother fell to his knees, first praising God, then leaning down to kiss his brother on each cheek.

Wearily, Henry dismounted. His legs nearly buckled beneath him, and he leaned against his horse, wrapping an arm around his neck in gratitude, and for support.

Suddenly, Miss Smallwood appeared before him like a beautiful mirage. Her green eyes, bright with tears, looked huge in her pale face, her pink lips vibrant in contrast. Her hair had come loose in the wind and framed her face, fair strands flying loose and brushing her cheeks and mouth.

"You did it," she breathed. "My heart nearly stopped when I saw you go under. Now I know how you felt standing on shore all those years ago. I felt so helpless watching you. All I could do was pray."

He looked into her eyes. "Did you?"

She nodded. "How I prayed you would live."

And then she was in his arms, leaning into him, pressing herself against his sodden chest, her cheek against his shoulder. He knew he ought to keep her at arm's distance—she would get soaked, catch her death. Instead he wrapped his free hand around her waist—her very small waist—and drew her nearer.

For several beats of his heart they stood like that, still. Savoring her warmth, her nearness. His other hand still lay on Major's neck, in a strange triangle embrace. Man, woman, horse. Then sounds from around them broke into his awareness, and perhaps into hers as well, for she slowly righted herself, pulling away, her color high with embarrassment.

"I am just so glad you are all right," she murmured in excuse, head ducked.

For one second more he allowed his hand to remain at her waist, relishing the feel of the deep curve between ribs and hip. Then he realized that for him to feel that specific detail meant she wore no coat, only a thin cape over her frock.

"Emma, I'm afraid you're soaked through. Sorry about that."

"Sorry?" She gave a little laugh. "Don't be ridiculous. Not when you've spent most of the last thirty minutes underwater."

Had it only been that long? It had felt like hours. He let go of his horse and his legs wobbled again, but through sheer stubbornness he kept to his feet.

He said, "You had better go back and change into dry things."

"So should you."

"Yes. But first I shall see to this valiant fellow." He patted Major's neck once more.

Emma patted the horse as well, and for a moment their fingers touched.

"A valiant fellow, indeed," she echoed softly.

And when Henry glanced at her, his heart tightened to see her looking not at his horse as she said the words, but at him.

Sir Giles and her father appeared on the scene, fussing over Henry and asking questions of the constable, Mr. Bray. Sir Giles put his greatcoat around Henry's shoulders and her father, belatedly, did the same for her. Emma avoided their gazes, feeling self-conscious. But she was relieved to see nothing in Sir Giles's demeanor or her father's to suggest they had seen her embrace Henry.

Mr. Bray asked what he should do about the rescued men. Henry said they could be sheltered in one of the Ebbington cellars that lined the beach, and Sir Giles agreed, assuring the constable he would have food and blankets sent down. Mr. Bray thanked the Westons for their generosity and said he would oversee the arrangements.

While the men discussed all this, Emma glimpsed several villagers tentatively approach, taking stock of the situation—the rescued sailors, the constable, Sir Giles—and then turn away in resignation.

Derrick Teague lounged against the doorjamb of his whitewashed cottage, looking directly at her. The smirk on his rugged face told her he *had* seen the embarrassing embrace. When Henry turned to see what had caught her attention, Teague retreated inside.

Finally the donkey cart was summoned to deliver them all back up to the manor, Henry's weary horse tethered alongside.

*It is against the sometimes shadowy backdrop*
*of upper and middle class elegance that*
*the real drama of life in Cornwall——red*
*blooded, crude and vigorous——is enacted.*

—R. M. Barton, *Life in Cornwall*
*in the Early Nineteenth Century*

# Chapter 22

During the ride back, Emma remained silent. Within her, elation wrestled with dismay. She had embraced Henry Weston. She had struck Lizzie Henshaw. Both acts were completely unlike her normal reserve. What had come over her?

When they reached Ebbington Manor, Sir Giles urged Henry to take himself directly inside, but Henry refused, insisting he would see to his horse first. Sir Giles went with him into the stables, determined to send the groom to ride out for the physician, though Henry insisted he was fine.

Rowan and Julian hurried from the house and followed them, peppering both with questions about what had happened down at the harbor.

Emma entered the manor, damp and spent. She slogged through the hall, dreading the inevitable confrontations ahead. Her father followed behind, full of concern and questions.

"Please, Papa. Let us wait until we are upstairs alone and I have changed into dry things."

Reluctantly, he agreed.

Emma retreated into her bedchamber and rang for Morva. She wondered if word of her slapping Lizzie had already reached the servants, and if so, whether the housemaid would even come. While she waited, she removed her wet outer garments and pulled on dry stockings.

A few minutes later, Morva entered, looking behind herself before closing the door. She turned to Emma and said timidly, "Lady Weston says, thee art to show thyself in the drawing room in half an hour's time."

Emma nodded. She had anticipated just such a summons. She half expected Morva to leave without offering to help her change.

Instead the housemaid came forward, hands clasped, eyes bright and eager. "I shouldn't ask, but I must knaw. Did 'ee really strike Miss Henshaw?"

Emma sighed. "I am afraid so." And apparently Lizzie had lost no time in telling absolutely everyone.

Morva helped her change, and afterward Emma wrapped a shawl around her shoulders to ward off the lingering chill. Then she walked to her father's bedchamber.

She told him everything that had happened. Well, not quite everything. She did not mention embracing Henry Weston, and thankfully, he had apparently not seen her do so.

John Smallwood somberly shook his head. "Emma . . . I am shocked. You actually struck Miss Henshaw?"

"Yes. She would not let me go—I had no other choice."

"But to strike another person, Emma, regardless of the provocation . . . I . . . I don't know what to say. It isn't fitting for our station. For a lady. . . ."

"Then perhaps I am not a lady, because I would do the same again given the situation."

"But the ward of our hostess? A girl so much younger than yourself? Really, Emma. That was reckless. Imprudent."

She turned to face him. "Papa, do you not understand? Henry Weston commanded me to ring the bell. To sound the alarm, to rouse help for the crew of that floundering ship. And Lizzie held me by the arm to prevent me. What was I to do?"

"She must not have understood the situation. Or misunderstood your aim. You might have reasoned with her, instead of resorting to violence."

"Reason with her—for how long? Till one of the crew drowned? Half the crew?"

"Surely it would not have come to that."

Realizing further argument was futile, Emma held her tongue and drew her shoulders back. "I had better go down. Lady Weston has asked to see me."

"Apologize, my dear—for all our sakes."

Emma sighed. "I will do my best to make peace if it is within my power to do so."

She left her father and made her way down the stairs and into the drawing room. Lady Weston's domain. Her throne room where she sat as judge.

Around the room sat the jury—Julian, Rowan, Phillip, Lizzie, and Sir Giles. How Emma wished Henry were there as well.

When the footman had closed the door behind Emma, Lady Weston glared at her in righteous indignation. "You struck my ward? A girl of barely seventeen?"

"Yes. I am not proud of it. But she would not let me go and I felt I had no other recourse."

Lizzie said pitifully, "I thought Henry meant for *me* to ring the bell. And I was about to go up, but *she* held on to *me*. I think she wanted to do it herself, to impress Henry, since she's obviously in love with him."

Indignant, Emma snapped, "That's not true!"

One of Lady Weston's eyebrows rose high. "Which part?"

Instead of answering, Emma turned to Rowan. "You must have seen me struggling to free myself."

Rowan screwed up his face. "I saw the two of you struggling, but I cannot say with certainty who was trying to restrain whom."

Emma turned to Julian. "You remember. You told me Lizzie held me back because she feared the wreckers—or whoever knocked down the warning tower—might take revenge if we raised the alarm."

Julian blinked innocently. "Did I say that? I don't recall it."

Apprehension needled through Emma. There was nothing else she could say. It was their word against hers. And three to one in the bargain. If only Phillip had been there. But he hadn't run out until after she rang the bell.

Emma forced her chin to remain level. She had done nothing wrong—well, nothing so terribly wrong. She would not hang her head in shame like a convicted criminal. Though that was certainly the way Lady Weston and even Phillip seemed to be regarding her. A swift glance at her old friend stabbed her in the heart. He clearly believed Lizzie's tale of injustice. How painful to see the disillusionment and disappointment in his eyes.

Emma clasped her hands to stop their trembling and waited for Lady Weston to pronounce judgment. To send her and her poor father packing, most likely.

Sir Giles spoke up. "No doubt a big misunderstanding all around, my dears. The important thing is that lives were saved, thanks to Henry. I sent him up for a hot bath and have insisted Dr. Morgan pay a call to make certain he is all right. I shall speak to Henry about this matter later, but for now, he has had enough trouble for one day. We shall postpone any further discussion about this until tomorrow."

Emma thought Lady Weston would object, but she said nothing, merely flicked a hand in Emma's direction and turned her head as though she could not stand the sight of her.

Knowing herself dismissed, Emma turned and walked from the room, feeling several pairs of eyes on her back. It was nearly time for dinner, but she had no appetite. She went upstairs, reported the conversation to her anxious father, and retired to her room early. To think, to worry, and perhaps. . . . even to pray.

Later that night, Emma was already in bed, though still wide awake, when someone knocked softly on her door. Instantly, she tensed. Was it Lizzie, come to retaliate? Or, whoever drew that picture, ready to make good on his threat?

*Now, Emma,* she admonished herself. Whoever had sneaked into her room previously had not bothered to knock.

She climbed out of bed, drawing her wrapper around herself, and tiptoed to the door.

"Who's there?" she asked, detesting the tremor in her voice, her weakness. She pressed an ear against the door to listen.

"It's Henry." After a pause, he added, "Weston," as though she wouldn't know which Henry he was, or as if unsure where they stood in terms of formality. It seemed foolish to stand on formality now, when she had stood in his arms, wet and pressed against him, only hours before.

What did he want? Surely not to continue that embrace. . . . She swallowed at the thought.

She unlatched her door and inched it open. He was fully dressed, unlike her, and held a candle on a humble pewter holder.

"I am sorry to disturb you," he said. "Were you asleep?"

"Far from it."

"That's what I was counting on. I know it isn't done, but may I come in?" He held up his free hand, palm forward. "I only want to speak with you a moment."

Relief and foolish disappointment entwined in her stomach.

She supposed it was little worse than him being seen standing outside her door late at night. And truly, after the whole world had seemed to turn against her, she welcomed a chance to explain. Would he believe her, when the others had not? Why should she think that?

She nodded and opened the door. He slipped inside, and she shut it quietly behind him.

His glance skittered around her bedchamber before returning to her face. "Is your room always so dashed neat?"

"I am afraid so. Though you must forgive the unmade bed."

"I shall try," he quipped, but then his expression sobered. "It has been a difficult day for you, I imagine. I have heard Lizzie's version of events, but I should like to hear yours. I know you to be an honest woman, Emma Smallwood, for all your annoying perfection."

311

She pulled a face—regretful, self-conscious. "Hardly perfect."

His brows rose. "You did slap her, then?"

"I did."

"My goodness. I should have liked to see that."

She shook her head. "No, you wouldn't. It was not funny."

"You're right. I think humor is my way of coping with a stressful day."

She nodded, scanning his face feature by feature, as though cataloging them for one of her lists. "Are you all right? After . . . everything?"

"I think so, yes. And Dr. Morgan concurs."

"And the sailors?"

"Davies tells me they fare well enough—he and Jory carried down food and blankets several hours ago."

"And your horse?"

"Well rubbed down, in the warmest stall with the warmest blanket and an extra portion of oats."

"He deserves it."

"Yes, he does." He studied her face. "What happened after I left you on the point?"

She told him everything, ending with, "At the time, Julian said she did it because she feared retaliation from the wreckers. Whatever the case, I ought not to have struck her. Not in the face. And not so hard."

Henry grimaced and ran a hand through his wavy hair, still damp from his bath. "She had it coming."

She waited, expecting him to add, *"If what you say is true,"* or something like it. But he did not.

Her heart squeezed in relief. "I'm afraid no one else believed me, as you probably know by now. Even my own father is very disappointed in me. He is certain Lady Weston will insist on dismissing him on my account. And perhaps, considering everything, that would be for the best."

"Never say so. I shan't have you leave in undeserved disgrace. Besides . . . Adam would miss you."

"And I him."

For a moment their gazes caught and held. She wondered if he was thinking of their embrace on the beach, as she was.

He cleared his throat. "Well . . . I had better let you get back to bed. I shall speak to my father in the morning and clear up everything."

"Thank you." She wondered if they would believe him. After all, Henry was not on the best of terms with several members of his family. Perhaps he'd chosen to believe her only to spite Lady Weston.

She didn't care. Having one ally was such a relief, she could have kissed him then and there.

Perhaps it was well, then, that he had decided to take his leave.

In the morning, Henry rose early and met with his father in the library. Phillip joined them. Henry assured them that he had indeed asked Miss Smallwood to ring the bell and believed she had acted honorably, considering the precipitous situation. Time being of the essence, a slap may very well have been the most expedient method for removing herself from Lizzie's grasp.

Sir Giles looked bewildered. "But why would Lizzie seek to impede her?"

Henry hesitated. "Perhaps it was as Miss Smallwood said—Lizzie feared retribution from the wreckers."

"Julian denied saying that, by the way," Phillip added. "We have only Miss Smallwood's account of it."

"It's the most plausible explanation," Henry insisted. "We all knew retribution was likely, especially after the tower was knocked down. What possible motive could Miss Smallwood have to lie about it?" He glanced at Phillip, surprised he did not come to Miss Smallwood's defense. Henry began to doubt he'd correctly guessed the identity of Phillip's "lovely girl of humble circumstances."

Sir Giles countered, "What motive could Lizzie or your brothers have to lie?"

Henry had his theories about that, but he was not ready to voice them. He hoped he was wrong.

Phillip said, "Lizzie claims Miss Smallwood held on to *her*. She said she thought Miss Smallwood wanted to ring the bell herself to impress you, because . . . she's in love with you."

Shock ran through him. "Ridiculous! Level-headed Miss Smallwood would never resort to such a juvenile act. She is not some jealous schoolroom miss, whatever Lizzie Henshaw might say . . . or be. And certainly not when lives were at stake, no matter how she felt about me."

Phillip frowned. "There is no call to malign Lizzie." Then he asked, "How . . . *does* Emma feel about you?"

Henry fidgeted. "She barely tolerated me when I was in Longstaple. We get on better now, mostly because of our mutual interest in Adam. But don't worry—I don't flatter myself it's anything more than that."

Henry thought of the way Emma had looked at him, clung to him on the beach. He blinked away the image, as well as his irrational reaction. If Phillip *was* worried or jealous, he certainly didn't show it.

Sir Giles shook his head. "Be that as it may, there are now hard feelings between her and Lizzie—and Lady Weston, I fear. She was not happy I invited Mr. Smallwood here in the first place. And after this . . ."

"He has done nothing wrong, and neither has his daughter. Please do not allow her to dismiss them unjustly."

Sir Giles sighed. "Easy to say, my boy. Difficult to accomplish." He rose. "I shall see what I can do to smooth her feathers."

When he left them, Henry looked at his brother, who was gazing out the window lost in thought. He said, "I must say, Phillip. I am surprised by your lack of loyalty to the woman you supposedly love."

Phillip winced, but his focus remained distant. "I want to believe her, I do. But . . . I've never known Miss Smallwood to behave dishonorably."

Henry stared. Realization . . . confirmation . . . washed over him. Phillip had revealed the true object of his affections, misguided though they were. The relief Henry felt was tainted by the knowledge that Phillip's choice would likely lead not only to his own unhappiness but also to further discord between him and Lady Weston.

Henry left Phillip ruminating in the library. He crossed the hall and turned down the back passage, thinking to have a word with Mr. Davies before setting out to visit the rescued sailors himself.

He was none too pleased to see Derrick Teague leaving through the rear door beyond the steward's office. Henry recognized that greasy, dark red hair from behind. What possible business did that man have at Ebbington Manor? Had he met with Davies, or someone else?

Henry called after him. "Mr. Teague."

The man glanced over his shoulder but did not stop.

Henry caught up with him on the path outside and matched his stride. "What were you doing here?"

The man smirked. "Just paying a call."

"On Davies, or someone else?"

Teague's eyes glinted. "Be that thy business, lad?"

"If it involves Ebbington Manor or the Weston family, then yes, it is."

"Thee don't rule the roost, do thee, lad? So don't give thyself airs."

Anger rushed through Henry at the man's insolence. "If you will not tell me, I shall have to return to the house and ask around to learn whom you spoke with and why. I had better not discover you have been threatening anyone of my family."

The man looked more amused than alarmed, which disconcerted Henry.

Teague said, "Careful, lad. Thee may not like what 'ee find."

Henry fisted his hands, barely resisting the urge to strike the man. "Good day, Mr. Teague." He turned and stalked back into the house, and into their steward's office.

Davies looked up from his desk when Henry entered.

"What did Teague want with you?" Henry asked.

The steward's mouth formed a silent O for several seconds before he replied. "Oh, he comes by now and again."

"Why? What business has he with you? With any of us?"

"Aw, you know Teague."

"No, I don't. Enlighten me."

Davies shuffled the papers on his desk. "The man always has some scheme in mind, or something to sell. Most of it pure stuff and nonsense. I shouldn't worry about it if I were you."

"But I do worry, Davies. And your words do not reassure me. Name one thing we have bought from Derrick Teague."

"We've bought nothing."

Henry stared into the man's face. Davies might be telling the truth, but he was clearly uncomfortable. Something was not right.

"Good," Henry said. "I don't want us doing business with that man." He decided to leave it at that for now. He would talk with his father, and have another look at the estate books, before pushing Davies further.

But first he wanted to visit the rescued sailors and make certain they had everything they needed. Davies would wait. He hoped Teague would as well.

Guessing his intention, Davies said, "By the way, sir. Do take heed along the shore. I've never seen such high spring tides, and so late in the season. You saw how rough the water was yesterday. I think we're in for a powerful storm before long, and serious trouble with it."

Henry had never known the steward to be wrong in his reading of foul weather. "Thank you, Davies. I shall keep an eye on the sky, and the tide."

Henry thought of calling for his horse, but after what Major had been through the previous day, Henry decided the animal deserved a rest. He would walk instead.

As he strode across the headland, bristling with yellow gorse, Henry reviewed what he knew about Derrick Teague.

Mr. Teague had been in trouble with the law more than once for his wrecking activities, Henry had learned from Mr. Bray.

Mr. Bray often acted as salvage agent for companies who owned ships or their cargo. After a wreck, they authorized Bray to cellar as much of the cargo as could be salvaged and sold, sometimes at a reduced price, say, in the case of grain that had gotten wet, or casks that had cracked on the rocks.

A few years ago, a ship carrying a cargo of wheat had struck the chapel rock. Mr. Bray had collected the landed sacks of wheat and stored them in the stone-and-brick cellars built under the cliffs for that purpose. The ship was dashed to shatters soon after the wheat had been taken out of her. Thankfully, the crew had been saved.

People from throughout the parish had been offered the wet wheat at a low rate. Only three shillings per bag. Mr. Bray had assured everyone that, when the grain had been washed, dried, and new winnowed, it still made fine bread.

But Mr. Teague and a friend of his—a man with a very bad character—weren't satisfied to buy the wet wheat at a low rate like everybody else. They broke into the cellars and stole a cartload of sacks. But the thieves were found out.

Teague turned king's evidence against his friend, and the man was sent to Bodmin jail. For some reason Teague had been allowed to pay for the wheat he'd taken and let off without punishment. It was neither the first nor the last time the man had avoided consequences for his crimes.

Turning down the cliff path toward the harbor, Henry thought of all the losses along these shores and exhaled deeply. He thanked God again for enabling him to rescue the sailors this time. He was eager to see how they fared.

As Henry approached the Ebbington cellars where the men had been sheltered, he noticed all seemed quiet and peaceful. *Good.* He knocked on the cellar door, producing a scrambling of many feet and the mutterings of several men in a foreign language.

"Who ees eet?" a man asked, in obvious alarm.

Henry frowned. This was not the welcome he'd expected. "Henry Weston," he replied. "We . . . em . . . met yesterday when your ship went down."

The door opened a tentative inch. Eyes nearly black appeared, framed by hair as dark as his own. "Ah! Meestah Weston!" The golden-brown face broke into a smile, showing two gold teeth, and the door opened wide in welcome.

This man—the leader and, as Henry soon discovered, owner of the ill-fated ship—was the only one among them who spoke

English, albeit somewhat broken English. He explained that they had been harassed during the night by men wanting to take what few belongings they had managed to salvage from the wreck—three large woven sacks, two of oranges and another of lemons, as well as several casks of port, which the excise man would be sure to take an interest in.

"He say he keel us if we don't give heem"—he gestured toward one of the casks—"pipe . . . ?"

"Cask."

"Jes. He take two."

"Who was it?"

"I don't know hees name. Big man. How do you say *cabelo vermelho* . . ."

"Red hair?" Henry prompted.

The man nodded vigorously. "Jes."

Teague, Henry guessed. He did not relish another confrontation with the man but knew one was necessary. Henry had not risked his life to save these men only to have them killed by a greedy wrecker.

They spoke a little longer about the men's plans to return to Portugal as soon as a ship might be found. Bray, it appeared, had offered to assist them. Satisfied the men had all they needed for the time being, Henry stepped to the door to take his leave.

The men warmly thanked Henry again with embraces and even kisses to his cheeks, which Henry bore with a grimace and relief that no Englishman was there to witness their enthusiastic gratitude. The men insisted he take one of the sacks of oranges as a small token of their appreciation. Not wanting to offend their pride, he agreed and thanked them.

He wondered if Miss Smallwood liked oranges.

But first he went to call on Mr. Teague.

He knew the man lived in one of the cottages lining the harbor but did not know which one. He asked a lad in knee breeches, who pointed to the last cottage on the row, set apart from the others, white with a thatched roof.

Praying for wisdom, Henry knocked on the door.

Teague opened it with a lift of his brows. "Well, well."

"Mr. Teague."

"Weston." The man smelled of port, his teeth stained purple.

Henry began, "I understand you paid a call on the sailors recovering from shipwreck and near drowning."

"Oh? When was 'ee down to see that lot? Surprised 'ee'd soil yer fancy boots."

Henry ground his teeth and forced a calm tone. "I have just come from there. Those men are staying in our cellars as our personal guests. It was kind of you to pay a call. Very neighborly, I'm sure. But if you pay another, I shall be obliged to pay a call on our new excise man—who, I understand, is not as easily bribed as the last."

"Only taking my due, wasn't I? I didn't take it all."

Henry longed to call the man a thief, to remind Teague that not only had the crew survived but the owner of the cargo as well. But in Teague's bleary-eyed, belligerent state, Henry decided it would be unwise to provoke him further. He would never change the man's mind about right and wrong. And the threat of the excise man was likely the only warning Teague would take to heart.

Henry began the return trek to Ebbington Manor. The walk up the cliff path seemed more arduous than he ever remembered it. He supposed his strength had been sapped during yesterday's rescue, and his leg muscles had yet to recover. The sack over his shoulder did not help matters.

Finally reaching the house, Henry wanted nothing more than to go upstairs and fall back into bed. When Lady Weston hailed him from the drawing room as he passed, he stifled a groan.

"Hello, Henry. How is the hero of the hour?"

"Fine. I have just been down to see the sailors."

"You needn't have done so. Davies would have gone down for you. They are in good health, I trust, thanks to you."

"Yes, but no thanks to Mr. Teague."

Lady Weston's brows shot up. "Mr. Teague?"

"He stole from them during the night—and from us, come to think of it, as he forced his way into the Ebbington cellars."

She stared at him. Looked about to say something, but then noticed the sack slung over his shoulder. "You didn't confront him, I hope, or demand back whatever it was he took?" Her fingers fiddled with the lace at her throat.

"I did confront him. But he was already drunk on the port he'd stolen."

"Then what is in the sack, if I may ask?"

"Oranges—a gift from the sailors." Remembering his manners, he asked, "Would you like one?"

She wrinkled her nose. "No thank you. Too messy to peel. And I don't care for the white membrane."

"Very well."

Henry turned to go, but she called him back.

"Henry?"

He faced her once more and saw her hesitate.

She said, "Have a care with Mr. Teague. He is not a man to be trifled with, or threatened lightly."

Henry was not certain whether to be touched by her concern or suspicious of it. "My threat was not a light one, madam. It is very real, I assure you."

Leaving her, Henry went in search of Miss Smallwood.

He found her upstairs, sitting at her father's desk in the schoolroom.

"Miss Smallwood."

She looked up in surprise, and if he was not mistaken, pleasure.

"Mr. Weston. How fare the sailors?"

He tilted his head to one side, curious. "How did you know I'd gone to see them?"

"I didn't," she said. "I suppose I assumed."

He wondered if she realized she had just paid him a compliment.

"They are all but recovered, I'm happy to say. Though exhausted." He decided not to trouble her with the tale of the theft. He lifted the canvas sack from his shoulder and set it on the desk, extracting an orange from within.

"Do you like oranges?"

"Of course. Who does not?"

"Lady Weston, actually. She doesn't like the white membrane between peel and fruit."

"It does take time to remove. But I find many of life's pleasures are that way. A bit of effort adds to the enjoyment."

He smiled at that. "Here." He handed her several. "It's only right I should share them with you, since you did your part in ringing the bell."

She shook her head. "I shall accept two. One for my father and one for myself. Oh . . . May I take one to Adam? Unless you prefer to do so yourself."

That she thought of his brother prodded warmth in his chest.

He handed her another orange, holding on to it as she reached out to accept it. For a moment, they both held the fruit, their fingers touching around the orange—the fruit of his labors.

"Thank you," she said, with a slight wrinkle between her brows as she looked down at his hand, still holding the orange.

"Thank *you*," he echoed, stressing the final word.

Looking at her soft green eyes and the curious curve of her sweet mouth, he suddenly wished he might peel an orange then and there and feed Emma Smallwood section by section and kiss the juice from her lips. . . .

*Steady on, Weston,* he admonished himself, and turned to deliver the rest of the produce to the kitchen.

⁂

Emma took an orange to Adam, helped him peel it, and then enjoyed watching his delight in eating it. Afterward, she encouraged him to wash his sticky hands, then played a game of chess with him. She was impressed at his skill. Henry was evidently a good teacher.

Later, she took the other orange to her father and was relieved to find him in better spirits than she'd expected or hoped for. He told her that he'd had a good long talk with Sir Giles and was happy to report that the business with the tower had been cleared up, for the most part, and they faced no imminent threat of dismissal. Sir Giles had also told him about his eldest son, Adam, assuming Mr. Smallwood had likely heard rumors if not the whole story by that point. Her father confessed himself shocked to learn there was another Weston, though empathetic as to the reasons he had not been told before.

Offended on Adam's behalf, Emma bit back the retort burning on her lips, reminding herself that it had long been commonplace to conceal any imperfect members of one's family.

When their conversation tapered off, her father suggested they play a game of chess together. Emma had to confess that she'd given her set to Adam and had, in fact, just played a match with him.

"But he would play another, I am certain, Papa. Shall I take you to his room and introduce you?"

Her father hesitated. "Thank you, my dear. I should like to meet him, but . . . I am conscious of my hostess's preferences in this matter. I don't wish to offend."

She huffed. "Very well, Papa. But it is your loss."

He looked up, taken aback by her crisp tone. "Emma." Hurt shone in his round eyes.

She sighed, feeling guilty. "It is only that I know you would like him, Papa. Adam is the sweetest-natured young man I know. He is very talented and a good chess player already, though he has only recently learned the game."

"Is he indeed?" her father said, impressed, though he did not change his mind about meeting him.

She was disappointed in her father, she couldn't deny it, but nor would she say so aloud. Not when he was doing so much better.

She squelched the desire to stalk off in a fit of pique. Instead she steeled herself and suggested a game of backgammon.

He met her gaze. Apology and forgiveness were exchanged in wordless understanding born of long and deep familiarity.

"Backgammon?" he said, the ember of hurt in his eyes sparking into interest. "Now you are speaking my language."

She smiled and feigned enthusiasm, although she cared little for the game. Sometimes that's what you did for the people you loved.

That night, Henry awoke with a start.

Someone loomed over his bed, repeating, "Henry? Henry? Henry?"

Henry had been deep in a dream, and it took his mind a few seconds to realize Adam stood above him. Bright moonlight shone through the windows, illuminating his brother's pale face and wide eyes.

"What is it?" Henry sat up and swung his legs from the bed. "What's wrong?"

"Emma."

Henry's heart lurched. "Emma? What's happened? Is she all right?"

Adam shook his head gravely.

Henry leapt to his feet, grabbed his dressing gown, and stepped to the door. "Where is she?"

Adam ducked his head, sheepish, perhaps remembering that Henry had asked him not to go into other people's bedchambers, especially at night.

"In her room?" Henry prompted.

Adam nodded.

"Is she ill?"

Adam made no reply but followed along as Henry hurried down the corridor and up the stairs. Passing the landing, he grabbed the candle lamp left burning there without missing a stride.

His stomach twisted. *Lord, let her be all right.* He had so hoped all the strange suspicions reeling through his head were wrong. Overwrought. Surely no one would do her any harm. Not for ringing an alarm bell. Not in revenge for a single slap. . . . Surely not. But as revenge for the resulting loss of a rich wreck? A chill ran over him. *Please, God, no.*

Reaching her room, Henry saw that Adam had left the door ajar.

Unless someone had been in there since Adam came to wake him. Or was in there even now. . . .

Henry pushed open the door. All was still. Light from a full moon illuminated the room—Miss Smallwood's bed and the prone figure upon it, bedclothes bunched at her waist. Stepping nearer, the light from his candle lamp fell on her white nightdress. And the blood-red stain on her chest.

His heart hammered against his breastbone. For a moment he stood, paralyzed, staring at her pale face, so still. The large stain like a red blossom on her breast. Grief and anger punched him in the lungs so hard, he could barely draw breath.

In the next moment he dropped to his knees beside the bed and reached for her wrist. Closing his eyes to concentrate, he felt the soft *ta-tomb* of her heartbeat. *Thank you, God.*

He opened his eyes, just as she opened hers and focused on his face in a dreamy vagueness. Was she barely conscious? Weak from blood loss?

"Emma, who did this?" He reached for the neckline of her nightdress, determined to see how bad the wound was.

When his fingers touched the linen, her hand flew up and caught his wrist, eyes snapping wide and alert.

"What are you doing?" she demanded.

He pointed to her chest. "You're bleeding."

She looked down at herself and, seeing the large stain by candlelight, gasped and sat up, her own hand going to her chest. She pulled her loose neckline forward and looked down to her skin beneath.

She shook her head. "I'm fine. I'm not hurt."

"Thunder and turf!" Henry exploded. "What is going on here?"

Behind him, Adam whimpered.

She huffed. "Don't yell at me. You're not the one waking up to find a man looming over your bed."

"Actually, I was. Adam came to wake me." He gestured toward his brother cowering in the threshold, then turned back to Emma. "Sorry. But you gave me a devil of a shock."

Using his candle lamp, Henry lit the candles on Emma's side

table and washstand. That's when he saw the blood-red handprint on the wall.

"What on earth . . . ?" He gingerly touched a finger to the red substance and found it thick, viscous. . . . He lifted it near his nose and sniffed. No acrid smell of blood.

"Adam?" Emma said toward the door. "It's all right. I am not hurt. I am perfectly well."

Henry glanced over his shoulder and saw Adam straighten and take a tentative step forward.

Emma held out her hand toward him. "I'm fine. I'm not hurt. See? It's not my blood. Probably just paint. A trick, that's all."

"Trick?" Adam echoed in confusion.

"A joke. But not a very funny one."

Adam shook his head. "I don't like tricks."

*Nor do I,* Henry silently agreed.

***

In the morning, Henry asked Miss Smallwood to wait downstairs and directed Morva not to clean Miss Smallwood's room, nor move the stained nightdress from the bed. Then he bade Lady Weston, Sir Giles, Phillip, Julian, Rowan, and Lizzie to join him there.

Miss Smallwood had wanted to keep it quiet, to handle the incident her own way—by not reacting. But Henry could not stand by and do nothing. A line had been crossed, and he had had enough.

Apparently his stepmother agreed. She looked around the room at the red handprint and stained nightdress, listened to Henry's description of events, and threw her hands in the air.

"This is the outside of enough! Really, husband, I must put my foot down. I warned Henry what might happen if Adam was allowed to wander about the house at will. And look at this! Bloodstains in Miss Smallwood's room. A clear threat if ever I saw one. Really, I must insist we put more effort into making other arrangements for him elsewhere. Perhaps Mr. Davies might be given the assignment. He might very well succeed where Henry has failed. And until then, I must insist that Adam's bedchamber door be locked at night. For his own safety as well as ours. No harm was done this time, but who knows what his faulty mind and violent fits might occasion the next? Shall we all be murdered in our beds?"

Sir Giles's shoulders slumped. He appeared grieved indeed.

Henry hurried to defend his brother. "Adam did not do this. It is not the sort of thing he would conceive of. His mind works very literally, not in pretense. Besides, he was terrified when he came to wake me."

"And how did he know of it, if he didn't do it?"

Henry should have foreseen that question and avoided provoking it.

Lady Weston added, "What was he doing creeping about at that hour otherwise?"

Sir Giles asked soberly, "Did he see anyone else coming from her room?"

Henry fidgeted. "No. Not that he mentioned."

"Ah . . . so he was in her room. Again," Lady Weston said. "No doubt the same person who took Miss Smallwood's journal and returned it with that gruesome picture. Can you deny the connection? How else would he know about the apparent blood in Miss Smallwood's room?"

"Yes, Adam was in her room," Henry admitted. "But remember this was his room as a boy. Of course he feels the right to come in here. Why you insisted on putting him in the north wing, I'll never understand."

"Did he also feel it right to threaten her life, this usurper of his room as he sees it?"

Henry shook his head. "I don't believe that. And you wouldn't either if you had seen him cowering in Miss Smallwood's doorway. He thought it was all real."

"Perhaps he is a good actor."

"You allow he is that clever? That talented?"

She lifted one shoulder in a shrug. "It isn't talent to try to save one's own neck. It's instinct. An animal trying to flee a trap triggered by his own misstep."

Julian spoke up. "I don't know, Mamma. Look at the size of that handprint on the wall. It was made by a hand far larger than Adam's. Larger than even Rowan's hefty paw. In fact, I'd say the only one of us with hands that big is Henry himself."

"What are you talking about?" Henry scowled at his half brother. "I didn't do this."

"Are you certain? It sounds like something you would do. We have all heard about the pranks you pulled on the tutor's daughter when you boarded at the Smallwoods' school."

Henry looked at Phillip, but Phillip only shrugged. "You did pull a lot of nasty tricks on her."

Henry frowned, but before he could object, Julian continued, "How different is this than putting mice in her bed, or forged love letters under her door?"

"That was a long time ago," Henry said. He lamented ever telling his brothers tales of how he used to torment Miss Smallwood. He would pay for it now.

But better him than Adam.

"Upon my honor, I did not do this," he said. "I have not pulled a single prank on Miss Smallwood since she arrived." He looked around at the assembled faces. "But someone has."

Lady Weston narrowed her eyes at Henry. "Why do you look at us? Surely you don't accuse one of us?"

"Yes, madam. I most certainly do. Who among us has reason to want to frighten Miss Smallwood—perhaps as an act of revenge?"

Lady Weston glanced at Lizzie.

The girl blanched. "It wasn't me."

"Someone did," Henry insisted. "And I intend to find out who. And when I do, beware."

Henry stalked from the room. He had barely made it to his study and sat at his desk when his valet came in, hands behind his back, nose pinched in the air, and lips twisted in disgust.

Henry sighed, dreading more problems to deal with. "What is it, Merryn?"

"Really, sir. Far be it from me to complain, to bemoan my unfair lot in life. To serve a master who not only neglects his fine garments, but cruelly abuses them—and therefore me—in the bargain."

Merryn lifted something in two pincher fingertips, as though a foul rat by the tail.

Henry looked, frowning.

In his hand, his offended valet held one of Henry's own gloves by the cuff, its palm and fingers stained dark red. The color of dried paint . . . or blood.

The mystery of how the large "bloody" handprint had been made had been solved.

The only questions remained . . . Who had done it?

And why?

*Pleasant it is, when over a great sea the*
*winds trouble the waters, to gaze from*
*shore upon another's great tribulation.*

—Lucretius, Roman poet and philosopher

# Chapter 23

As Emma thought back to the events of the previous night, and Henry's report of how the morning's confrontation with his family had gone, she found herself concerned as much for Adam's fate as for her own safety. She feared what the misinformation being spread about him, and the resulting and increasing ill will against him, might mean for his future. Emma wished she could think of some grand plan, some *coup de grâce* to put an end to the campaign against Adam, but she could not. She had only one idea. One small plan to attempt to turn the tide in his favor. She didn't know if it would work, but she had to try.

She had no opportunity on Sunday, but on Monday Emma sat on an antique settee in the hall outside the music room, hoping her plan would succeed. It was the time of day Lady Weston usually left the drawing room and retired to her bedchamber to write letters and nap. Emma hoped she would not stray from that routine today.

Footsteps signaled someone's approach. Emma leaned back, her head near the door, pretending not to notice anyone or anything except the music. She held her breath as Lady Weston walked toward her, head tipped to one side, regarding her curiously.

"Pray, what are you doing, Miss Smallwood?"

Emma put a finger to her lips. "Shhh. I'm listening."

Lady Weston frowned at being shushed but cocked her head to the other side. "Ah. Julian has learnt a new piece. What talent that boy has."

"I agree."

"Why do you not go inside to hear better?"

Emma shook her head. "I don't want to disturb him. I think he's . . . struggling with a few notes. He's not quite himself today."

"Nonsense," Lady Weston insisted. "His playing is superb." She listened for several moments longer. "In fact, he has never played better."

Lady Weston took a step closer to the door and closed her eyes to savor. "That is truly beautiful. I wonder what piece that is. Do you know?"

"No."

"I shall have to ask him."

"I doubt he knows the name."

"Don't be foolish. Of course he knows. Unless . . . are you suggesting it is a piece of his own invention? That would astonish even his proud mamma."

"No, I am certain he has heard it somewhere before."

Lady Weston huffed. "Well, enough of this standing in the yard like the lower classes who can't afford a seat. Let's go in." She reached for the door latch.

Emma laid a gentle hand on her sleeve. "First . . . let's just peek in. Quietly. I'd hate to disturb such a talented musician mid-movement."

"Oh, very well," Lady Weston whispered. She gingerly inched open the door. Through the gap, she looked across the music room with an indulgent, expectant smile on her face.

Her smile fell away. She stared, dumbfounded, her mouth drooping.

Unable to resist, Emma rose on tiptoe and looked over Lady Weston's shoulder. There at the pianoforte sat Adam Weston, eyes closed, playing with a slight nodding of his head.

For several moments longer, Lady Weston stood stiff, listening, as if unable to believe what she was seeing, or hearing. Then she slowly, quietly closed the door. Emma slipped back into her seat.

"It is not Julian after all," Lady Weston murmured.

"Oh?" Emma said noncommittally.

Lady Weston looked at her sharply, but Emma offered no explanation. Nor did she mention she had seen Julian walking out to the stables with Mr. Teague half an hour ago, just before she had asked Adam to play.

"You tricked me, didn't you?" Lady Weston asked in soft wonder, her tone lacking the asperity Emma would have expected.

"Yes," Emma whispered, meeting the woman's gaze and willing her eyes to communicate all she felt. And her deep wish that Adam's family would come to appreciate him. To accept him.

Lady Weston hesitated, then wandered away, lost in thought.

After Adam finished playing, Emma walked with him back up to his room. A quick look at the chatelaine watch hooked to her bodice told her it was nearly time to go up to the schoolroom for the afternoon lessons. She thanked Adam again for playing for her and hurried upstairs. She had not seen her father since they had dismissed Julian and Rowan after the morning class.

When she entered the schoolroom, she found Rowan already seated at the table, bent over his sketchbook. But there was no sign of her father.

"Good afternoon, Rowan."

He looked up. "Hello, Miss Smallwood." He handed her a folded letter. "I was asked to give this to you. I gather your father won't be joining us."

"Oh?" This was news to Emma. He hadn't said anything to her. She unfolded the note and read.

*Emma my dear,*
*I have walked down to see the Chapel of the Rock, since you mentioned how impressed you were with the place when Mr.*

*Weston showed it to you. I should be back in time for afternoon lessons.*

*J. Smallwood*

Her father, gone down to the Chapel of the Rock . . . alone? What was he thinking? Had he even thought to check with Henry about the tides? Emma was certain she had mentioned the danger of the place, and the varying "safe" periods for venturing out to it.

A pinch of worry knotted her brow and stomach. *Steady, Emma,* she told herself. After all, her father was a highly intelligent man. A teacher, for goodness' sake. He would not simply walk out into the sea upon a finger of rock without taking precautions.

Yet her father, although no longer melancholy since coming to Ebbington Manor, was still somewhat out of his element there on the coast, being unaccustomed to the sea.

She glanced at the note once more. Noticed the somewhat shaky hand, the scrawled signature. Was he nervous about something? It wasn't his usual neat hand, though she recognized the customary J and S of his signature at his typical slant. Was it a bit odd of him to sign his name instead of *Papa*? Being almost always together, they had rarely if ever had occasion to send each other letters, but she found the closing cold. Was he still disappointed in her for striking Lizzie?

She decided to consult Henry's red notebook to check the tide tables herself. She hoped he would not mind. She excused herself from Rowan and went down to Henry's study. She believed Henry had ridden off somewhere for a meeting. Still, she knocked softly. When no one answered, she let herself in.

Her gaze swept his cluttered desk, where she had last seen him retrieve the book, but saw no sign of it. She hoped he had not taken it with him for some reason. She swiveled around the room, looking at his shelves and cabinets. A red spine on the bookcase caught her eye and she went to it, slipping out the volume. She sighed with relief, glad to find the book. Apparently he or an industrious maid had tidied up after she had last been there. Perhaps he'd decided her system of a place for everything and everything in its place had merit after all.

She opened the volume and found her way to the current week's table and that day's estimated tides. She compared the numbers to the time on her watch. Good. Still three hours before the next high tide. Plenty of time for her father to reach the chapel and return safely.

Emma replaced the book exactly where she'd found it and went back up to the schoolroom. Rowan was still bent over his sketchbook, though Emma could discern little progress. She walked to her father's desk to review the day's lesson plans and see if anything else needed doing. Now and again she glanced at her watch or looked out the window. She would see the point, the warning tower, and a patch of grey sky. But no sign of her father.

Grey sky. Not blue. Were they in for some weather? The tide tables, of course, were no guarantee against unexpected storms.

Julian came in and took his seat. "Mr. Smallwood not joining us today?" he asked.

"He should be here anytime now," Emma said, keeping a calm tone, reminding herself it was foolish to worry. "He went for one of his walks. Down to the Chapel of the Rock."

"Did he?" Rowan said. "I thought he was going—" He broke off suddenly and glared at Julian. "What? Why did you kick me?"

Julian turned to Emma. "I don't want to worry you, Miss Smallwood. We all know it's dangerous down there, but I am sure he'll be fine. He has been down there before, I trust? With you or Henry?"

She frowned. "Not that I know of. Not with me, in any case."

"I hope he knew to check the tides."

A blast of wind shook the schoolroom windows and whistled in through the cracks.

Rowan shook his head. "I don't like the sound of that."

"Davies said he smelled a storm brewing, and he is always right," Julian added.

"Did he?" Emma asked, anxiety prickling through her. "Did he happen to mention this to my father?"

Julian shrugged. "Not that I know of."

Emma stood abruptly, her chair legs screeching against the schoolroom floor.

"I had better go and check on him. You two, please read—" she consulted her father's notes—"the *Iliad*. From where we left off yesterday until . . . well, until I return."

Rowan groaned, but Emma did not relent. Her mind was filling with irrational images of her father being swept from the rocks as he walked back from the chapel.

She stopped in her room only long enough to pull on her half boots and pelisse. It took several precious minutes to lace the boots, but she knew she could make up the time by walking faster and more surefooted than she could in her flimsy low-heeled slippers.

When Emma descended the stairs, she noticed Lizzie in the hall, sitting in a straight-backed wooden chair near the front door. Hearing Emma's footfalls, she looked up from the *Lady's Magazine* she'd been flipping through. "Where are you off to?" Lizzie asked.

The two young women had formed an uneasy truce since the incident with the bell tower, but Emma guessed the warm camaraderie between them was gone forever.

"To find my father. Have you seen him?"

"I saw him leave on one of his walks, but that was some time ago now."

"Apparently he's gone down to the chapel."

"Really?" Lizzie's brows rose. "In this wind?"

Emma swallowed. "If anyone asks, please tell them where I've gone."

Lizzie nodded, and Emma turned to the door.

"Emma?"

Emma turned back. "Yes?"

Lizzie looked sheepish. "I am sorry. For everything."

Surprise washed over Emma—surprise and relief. "Thank you, Lizzie. I'm sorry too." She gave the girl a small smile and opened the front door.

"Emma?"

Emma turned back once more.

Lizzie hesitated. "Be careful."

Emma hurried through the garden, out its gate, and across the windy headland. She took long strides just shy of a running pace, her eyes sweeping the coast path for any sign of her father. Or of Henry returning from his meeting.

She saw no one.

She was halfway across the headland before she realized she had come outside with neither gloves nor bonnet for the first time in years. *Take hold of yourself,* she silently commanded. This was no time to lose her wits. Tendrils of hair pulled loose and blew across her face. She looked up. Yes, the sky was growing greyer by the second, and the wind was strengthening. Surely her father would notice and make haste home.

She reached the point and looked out, briefly scanning the ocean to the horizon. No sign of a struggling ship, nor of any vessel at all. She looked down at the rocky finger and the chapel at its tip, noticed how the waves hit the sides of the narrow peninsula but did not wash over it. Yet the sea was definitely turbulent today, and with the rising wind, the waves would only increase. She saw no one about. Was her father still inside? It was difficult to judge from that height if the door was indeed closed, or if that appearance was just a trick of shadow on the recessed doorway. Perhaps her father had already begun his return trip, but she could not see him on the steep path hugging the cliff's edge.

She turned and hurried down the path, recalling how she had done the same after ringing the bell, driven to make certain Henry was all right, to help him if she could. She felt a similar urgency, a similar dread now, but why should she? No ship lay breaking apart on the rocks. No lives were in peril.

At least she hoped not.

Emma steeled herself. The tide table estimated another two hours remained before the causeway was in danger of being submerged. And Henry had assured her the estimates were very accurate.

Still her heart beat hard and her stomach twisted as she made her way around the bend, hoping every second for a glimpse of her father coming up. Had he stopped to catch his breath? Gone into the village?

*Where are you, Papa?*

Henry slowed his horse at the crossroads. He had taken his usual shortcut to the main road. Left would take him into the village, straight ahead would take him into Stratton, and right would take him south to his meeting with Mr. Trengrouse about commissioning one of his lifeline-shooting devices for the Ebford Harbor.

Henry glanced at the signpost. He knew perfectly well what each carved wooden sign indicated, yet his gaze lingered, noticing how the uppermost signs trembled. The wind was rising. He was not usually put off by the prospect of a little wind and drizzle. He glanced up at the sky. Were they in for worse?

He became aware of a pinching in his gut, a nagging thought just out of recall, as if he were forgetting something. Something important.

"Whoa." He drew Major to a halt and for a moment sat at the crossroad, thinking. Listening.

*Turn back. Go home.*

Was it his own voice—his conscience—or God's still, small voice? He was not certain, but he had learned from repeated error not to ignore these quiet proddings, whether of conscience or of God. Mr. Trengrouse was expecting him, but Mr. Trengrouse could wait.

Henry turned Major's head and made his way back toward Ebbington Manor. As he rode, he felt the urgency building within him. Was he still worrying about Miss Smallwood after the incident with the fake blood, and the strange tussle at the bell tower? Was that it?

Ahead of him, he saw Mr. Smallwood walking, stick in hand, on one of his walks south. When Henry neared him, he hailed, "Hello, Mr. Smallwood. Everything all right at home?"

"Yes, my boy. As far as I know."

"Good. Well, don't go too far. Looks like we're in for some weather."

"Just to the Upton cemetery and back." He lifted a sketched map in his hand. "I don't mind the damp."

"Well then, enjoy your walk." Despite Mr. Smallwood's words, Henry felt unsettled and continued on toward Ebbington Manor. In the back of his mind he wondered why Mr. Smallwood would walk to the Upton cemetery, and especially at this time of day. Apparently his daughter was conducting the afternoon lessons in his stead.

Reaching the estate grounds, Henry rode to the stables. There the groom hurried out to take charge of his horse, appearing surprised and none too pleased to have him return so soon, causing him more work.

"Leave him saddled," Henry said. "I . . . forgot something . . . and will likely be on my way again in a few minutes."

The young man nodded, and Henry hurried into the house by the rear door.

Suddenly Rowan rounded the corner, nearly barreling into him. "Henry!" He gaped in alarm, then quickly recovered. "Thought you'd left for your meeting."

"I had. What are you doing down here? Why are you not in the schoolroom?"

Rowan stuck out his lower lip. "No one up there. We're having the afternoon off, apparently."

Henry studied his brother's expression, part chin-high defensiveness, part sheepish blush and furtive eyes.

"Where is Miss Smallwood?" he asked.

"Gone to look for her father."

"Oh? Why?" Henry thought of the grey skies and rising wind.

Rowan hesitated. "She thought he might have gone down to the chapel, but I don't think he would."

"To the chapel? Why would she think that?"

Rowan shrugged. "That's what she said."

"Dash it," Henry murmured and took the stairs by threes. He

didn't slow his pace until he'd reached his study. He looked on his desk for the tide book but didn't see it. *That's strange.* He always left it on the desk, for convenience sake, since he consulted it whenever he went down to the chapel and regularly made new estimates. Had she taken it? He certainly hoped she'd consulted it.

He looked this way and that until he spied it on the bookcase. *Emma* . . . he inwardly chided. A place for everything and everything in its place—whether he liked it or not. He snatched the book from the shelf and flipped it open to the current week. He frowned, and looked at the preceding days to see if he had somehow made a mistake. Then his finger traced that day's column once more and his heart seemed to skip a beat. The times marked for that day were incorrect. And not in his writing, though a close facsimile. He lifted the book and peered closer. Thunder and turf! Someone had scraped off the ink—taking a thin layer of paper with it—then written in new times. Wrong times.

God in heaven. The tide was on its way in. And with the wind rising and a storm brewing . . . it was far from safe to be venturing out to the Chapel of the Rock. In fact, it was dashed dangerous.

He hurried downstairs. Noticing the darkening sky through the hall windows, Henry detoured to the lamp room for a lantern.

He lit the glass-and-tin oil lamp, then ran outside and back to the stables for his horse. He took the reins from the groom, gripped the lantern handle, mounted, and urged Major into a gallop.

Why on earth would Emma think Mr. Smallwood had walked down to the chapel today of all days, when he had shown no inclination to do so before? When, in fact, he was walking south toward Upton.

Something was wrong about all this. Very wrong.

⁂

Emma stood on the beach, at the place where the sand ended and the rocky peninsula began. She surveyed its length—the waves crashing against it from the open sea, sending white spray nearly up to the path at its center.

"Papa, are you there? Papa!" she called toward the distant chapel, but quickly realized yelling was futile. The wind swallowed her words as she uttered them, gobbling them midair, like hungry gulls diving for tossed breadcrumbs.

She should have passed her father if he had gone back, but she had not. She would never rest, or forgive herself, if something happened to him when she might have prevented it. She had to go. She would move quickly, bid him come immediately if he was there, or satisfy herself if he was not. There and back. Every moment she stood there, the water would only get higher. . . .

She stepped out onto the first rock.

As she walked farther out into the sea, the wind strengthened, whipping her skirts and loosening her coil of hair. She held the billowing fabric against her legs so she could look down and see the path in front of her, to gauge the flattest rock, the next step with the surest footing. She consoled herself that at least she was not getting soaked. The wind brushed mist across her cheeks and through her stockings, but the waves still broke several yards away. She hurried on.

Nearing the chapel, she climbed the steep steps, missing Henry's guiding hand, his firm, confident presence. Ahead of her the door was closed, as it had appeared from above. She supposed her father might have shut it behind himself to keep out the worst of the wind as he surveyed the interior and perhaps prayed in relative peace.

She lifted the latch and pushed open the door. It took a moment for her eyes to adjust to the dim light seeping in through the high slit windows.

"Papa?" she called, her voice quavering, echoing against the sandstone walls. "Are you in here?"

Only the roar of the sea and the cry of distant gulls answered. Had he fallen asleep on one of the rotting pews? Her gaze swept the baptismal font, the slumping benches, the moldering altar. She walked to the chapel's far end, to the bricked-over wall that had once led to a larger nave, long lost to the waves.

Empty. No one was there. Then where was her father? Had he come here, but only briefly? Or had he decided against coming to the chapel and gone into the village instead for a bracing toddy or some such? Is that why she had missed him?

She heard something, a scraping sound of wood against stone and whirled. The door opened farther—someone was coming in. She tensed, hoping it was not a stranger—or worse, Mr. Teague. It took her a moment to recognize the figure standing backlit by the outside light, lantern in hand.

When she did, her heart rose in relief.

"Henry! That is . . . Mr. Weston."

But no answering smile or friendly salutation greeted her in return. "What are you doing in here, woman?" he snapped. "The tide is rising."

She didn't like his superior, criticizing tone, the implication that she was feather-brained. "I came looking for my father. Your little book said there was plenty of time. Are you telling me you were wrong?"

"I was not wrong. Someone tampered with the numbers."

Emma's stomach dropped, and her irritation with Henry fell away. "Who?"

He crossed the chapel in long strides and held out a hand to her. Not in supplication but in command. "We shall debate theories later. Let's go. My horse is tethered on the beach."

She tentatively reached out and gave him her hand. "Have you seen my father?"

He turned, tugging her along beside him. "Yes. He—"

The chapel door slammed shut, followed by the sound of a key scraping in the lock.

"Hey!" Henry called. "We are in here!"

He dropped her hand, set down the lamp, and ran to the door, trying the latch in vain. "Open the door!" He pounded on it like a vengeful blacksmith at his anvil. "Open the door, I say!"

She added her voice to his, hoping its higher octave would pierce the wood. "Hallo! We're in the chapel. Open the door."

They listened for a reply. Nothing. Nothing save the wind and the waves. Even the gulls had flown inland.

"Hallo?" she repeated plaintively. "Is anybody there?" She glanced at him and said, "Perhaps it has just blown shut."

Henry struggled with the latch once more. "And locked itself?" he said darkly. "Hardly."

"Who would lock the door?" she asked, face puckered. "I thought you had the key in your study."

"I did. But obviously someone took it." He put his shoulder to the door and butted it like an angry ram.

"Careful!" Emma urged. "You'll hurt yourself."

He hesitated, intense green eyes locking with hers. "Do you not understand, Miss Smallwood. If we do not get out of here, we may do worse than hurt ourselves. We may even die."

Fear flickered across Emma Smallwood's face, and Henry immediately regretted voicing his ominous thoughts aloud.

"Surely you exaggerate, Mr. Weston," she said coolly, clearly determined not to panic. "The tide was not so high when I crossed over and the wind is . . . Well, I have certainly seen worse wind since coming to Cornwall."

He made no reply, choosing not to reiterate his prediction of doom, or Davies's warnings of high tides and an approaching storm. Instead he began circling the chapel, looking out one narrow window, then another, trying to see someone to hail. To blame. Or to find some way of escape. But it was hopeless.

Even with Emma's enticingly small waist, she would never fit through one of those narrow slits.

He moved instead to the bricked-up doorway that had once led to the rest of the church. Perhaps it might be weaker than the thick sandstone walls that had stood the test of years and storms. If only he had some sort of tool. He looked down at the oil lamp he had brought for light. The sturdy metal base might be used to bang against the mortar and loosen the bricks. But it was unlikely to work, and he would surely lose the flame in the process and had no way to light another. If only he had thought to bring a knife . . . or a pistol. He reached up and set the lamp in the window facing the village, hoping someone would see it, and kept looking for a way out.

"Besides," Miss Smallwood added. "My father will soon guess where I've gone and sound the alarm."

"How do you know that?"

"Well, when he doesn't find me in the schoolroom, he will guess that I've gone looking for him."

"Why did you think he had come here?" Henry asked as his long fingers continued to probe the bricks, looking for cracks, a weakness in the wall.

"Because he left a note."

"Did he? Are you certain it was his writing?"

Doubt clouded her eyes and tightened her features. "Oh . . . I don't know. Something did strike me as odd about it."

"Miss Smallwood, I passed your father walking south when I rode back to the house."

She gaped at him. "If he didn't plan to come here, why would he . . . Why would anyone write a note saying he had?"

He looked at her grimly but did not voice his suspicions.

He saw a chill pass over her. She said weakly, "Well, Lizzie knows where I've gone. As do Julian and Rowan."

Pain lanced him. Would either of his half brothers lift a finger to help her?

She added hopefully, "And surely someone saw you coming in this direction?"

"Maybe. But I didn't think to tell anyone where I was going."

"That was not very wise."

He whirled. "I had other things on my mind," he snapped. "And may I say, your coming out here today was not wise either."

She swallowed, and the offended retort he saw building within her fizzled away, unspoken. Her shoulders slumped. "You are right. I came charging down here without thinking it through. Like something you would have done."

He huffed dryly and returned to his inspection. "Like something I did do." Why had he not thought to look for the key? To be on his guard?

"Look, let's not argue," she said. "Let's figure out a solution. We are both of us clever. I am certain we can think of something."

"You think all you like." He inhaled deeply. "I am going to pray."

*. . . behold, the four winds of the*
*heaven strove upon the great sea.*

—Daniel 7:2

# Chapter 24

When the first wave splashed through the westward window, Henry heard Emma gasp from across the chapel. It was soon followed by another whitecap, smacking the slit and sloshing onto the stone floor, wetting her half boots. Henry, who had been banging away at the bricks with a sharp rock he'd found, looked over at Emma, and for a moment both stilled, their eyes meeting in silent understanding. Then he resumed chipping with renewed zeal, and she ran to the door, tried once again to open it, and began yelling for help once more.

Henry's mind whirled with thoughts of what might happen to them if a powerful storm struck during record-breaking tides. On one hand, Henry was ready to accept his fate if need be. He had enough faith in eternal life that he was not terrified by the prospect of death. Then again, he would prefer to live another fifty years first, God willing.

But he was not ready to accept Emma Smallwood's death. Not at the hands of someone of his own family. And not while she had doubts about God. Her fate rested like a heavy burden across his shoulders—heavier than a waterlogged sailor, than six of them— weighing down his heart.

As he prayed, he worked. He believed God heard his prayers but did not think the Almighty wanted him to sit idly by, waiting for Him to do everything while Henry reclined at his ease. From the Old Testament Henry had gleaned that even when God promised to give His people the land, He still expected them to go to battle. To do the work. So he prayed and continued to chip away at the mortar.

But it was taking too long.

A quarter of an hour later, the water was up to their ankles, streaming through the westward and southern windows in a steady flow punctuated by bursts as waves crashed against the chapel, shaking the building to its ancient foundations.

They'd tried to batten the west window. But the waves pushed aside each obstacle they'd lodged there. Might the violent sea wash away the chapel as it had the rest of the church—and them with it? If the rising water level didn't drown them, that might.

From the other windows came patches of stormy grey daylight. It was unlikely anyone would see their lantern until darkness fell. Would the tower still be standing by then?

Across the chapel, Emma paced through the water, still searching for another way of escape or another tool with which to help him chip at the mortar. He noticed her shiver. Of course she was cold. What an idiot he was. Warm enough from his constant effort, he rose and splashed through the water toward her, removing his greatcoat as he went.

Guessing his intention, she shook her head, protesting, "I'll swim in it."

*You very well might,* he thought to himself but thought it wiser not to voice that dire prediction. "Then here," he said. "Hold this for me."

She accepted the outer coat, folding it in her arms to keep it above the water while he struggled out of his frock coat with some difficulty, both from the snug, precise cut and from the numbness of his hands.

"Forgive me," he murmured, standing in shirtsleeves and waistcoat.

She said, "I am not offended by your shirtsleeves, Mr. Weston. I hardly think propriety is our primary concern at present."

He held out his frock coat to her. "Wear this."

"But it's yours. You'll freeze."

"Nonsense." He draped it around her, allowing his hands to linger on her shoulders, to bestow what comfort he could. "I am a hardy Cornish lad, while you are a thin-skinned inland lass."

She looked up sharply, as though offended, then managed a wobbly grin.

Good. She realized he was teasing. How unfortunate that they were only now beginning to understand each other.

She handed him back his greatcoat and laced her arms through the sleeves of his frock coat. "Thank you, kind sir." She dipped an elegant curtsy.

He chuckled at her plucky courage, her attempt at humor at such a time. He bowed in his best formal address. Rising, hand to his heart, he said, "My honor and pleasure, Miss Smallwood."

For a moment they looked at each other and a warm cable of attraction held them. Then another wave burst in and doused them both. Icy water penetrated his fine linen shirtsleeves, wetting them through and sending shivers along his skin.

Emma gasped at the shock of cold, and the moment passed. He pulled on his greatcoat and while he worked the fastenings, he insisted she do the same.

Then he returned to his work. He took one more strike at the mortar, and finally a crack appeared. A thrill of success rose up in him only to be doused the next second. For through the crack, water rushed forth in a thin, high-pressure stream. It was too late. Even if he managed to chip away a hole, their way of escape was now completely underwater. The tide had come in, and the stormy waves had raised the water level even higher. In fact, he had just worsened their situation by opening another aperture, albeit a small one, for water to enter their shaky sanctuary.

No doubt noticing the cessation of his chipping efforts, Emma looked over, hope brightening her eyes. She looked from his face down to the shooting leak, and the hope faded. She bit her lip, probably fighting against tears, and his heart ached to see it.

*Lord, please help me save her!* How he longed to be her rescuer, her brave knight. To prove he was more than the mischievous trouble-maker she remembered and likely still thought him.

Outside the storm worsened. Wind and waves buffeted the stone walls. Water cascaded through the west and south windows with each new wave, and the water level inside the chapel rose to their knees.

Henry sloshed over to the stout, waist-high baptismal font. Its decorative cover was long gone, likely stolen years ago by some young vandal on a dare. Henry yanked a still-sturdy board from a sagging pew and laid it over the top, then gestured Emma over to him. "Come. Let's get you up on the font. You'll be drier there."

She looked at him earnestly. "Is there nothing else we can do?"

"Not that I can think of. Besides pray that someone sees the light and realizes we're out here."

"But even if they did, the causeway must be underwater by now."

"Perhaps not." He held out his hand to her. "Come."

She stared at his hand; then her eyes darted back to his face. He guessed why she hesitated. To accept his hand was to accept defeat—that there was nothing to do but wait to drown or be saved. He knew how much Emma Smallwood liked—longed—to be in control. To solve her own problems. She detested feeling helpless, to be at anyone's mercy. He didn't like being at anyone's mercy either, unless that "person" was God. And that's where they were, he realized. Helpless. And at God's mercy.

"Come," he repeated, remaining where he was, hesitant to walk toward her, to force his hand. He wanted her to come to him. To surrender.

Emma realized there was nothing she could do. For the first time in her life, she acknowledged the problem she faced was outside her control. She had likely been just as helpless at her mother's sickbed, but Emma had never accepted that inevitability. She had never ceased to consult medical books and herbal dictionaries, looking for a cure. She had kept the room spotless, overseen the

347

preparation of the most healthful invalid meals and beef teas. Plied the apothecary with endless questions, and sought a second opinion from a Plymouth physician when her father had not bothered. Not that any of it had availed in the end, but she had *tried*. Strived.

Now there was nothing she could do to affect the outcome—no second opinions to seek, no books to consult, no father to cajole, no Aunt Jane to call upon. There was nothing to do but pray. Was it hypocritical to turn to God now, when she had done her utmost to be independent, to make her way without Him until this point? She supposed it was. But was that not true of so many deathbed prayers? When one looked upon the prospect of one's mortality and eternity beyond?

She walked through the water, her steps made slow and arduous by heavy, sodden skirts. Her eyes remained fastened on his.

Another wave sprayed through the window, pelting Emma's face. Her eyes filled with tears, too many to be blinked away, and salt water both warm and cold ran down her cheeks. She saw answering tears fill his eyes. And somehow she knew the tears were not for himself but for her.

Reaching him, she placed her hand in his. "All right," she whispered. "I understand."

Together, they turned toward the font. Eyeing it, Henry gauged its height. "I shall have to lift you."

"I'm too heavy."

"Nonsense." He put his hands on her waist, its slimness somewhat disguised by the coat of his she wore. He lifted her, a bit of an effort with her waterlogged skirts but accomplished handily nonetheless.

For several moments, she sat atop the font, his hands still on her waist as he stood before her, her hands lingering on his forearms. Her face a few inches above his now that she sat perched on the font. He liked looking up at her.

Had he not always done so?

The water reached the top of his tall boots and ran down inside them. He gave an involuntary shiver.

"You must come up here too," she said. "You're freezing."

"There isn't room for two and I'm fine."

"I insist, Mr. Weston. I shall not sit here as though on some throne while you stand in frigid water. You'll catch your death."

Her lips parted in chagrin at her unfortunate choice of words. Then she began gathering her skirts around her. "Give me your hand," she commanded.

"Yes, madam. With pleasure."

Using his uplifted hand as a brace, she gingerly rose to her feet on the board, untangling her skirts as she did so.

"Careful," he warned.

She stood, and he was relieved she managed to not fall headlong from her perch. She said, "All right. Your turn."

He began to protest, "I don't think that is—"

She extended her hand to him. "Please."

He saw something in her eyes that shut off further objections. He considered various options for ascending the font without knocking her off. This was no time for a game of king of the castle.

His legs were long enough that he could raise one foot to the edge of the font. The water weighed down his other foot, but he thought if he got enough momentum, and levered himself up with his hands, he might make it.

She said, "Take my hand and I'll pull you up."

"I'm afraid I'll only succeed in pulling you down with me."

"I have a good stance. Let me help you." She grinned. "Just try to remain vertical so you don't butt me with your very large head."

He smirked up at her. "One wonders how I've found hats to fit me all these years."

"I imagine your hatter is exceptionally well paid."

He placed his hand in hers but warned, "If I start to fall, let go. Do you hear? I don't want to have to put my back out lifting you up again."

How ironic that they were teasing each other at such a time. Better than shouting or wailing, he supposed. Yes, much better.

Pushing with his standing leg and bracing arm and allowing Miss

Smallwood to help pull him up, Henry managed to heave himself up to his feet. He overshot the mark a bit and felt Miss Smallwood sway backward. He wrapped his arms around her, pulling her safely against him.

"Th-thank you," she murmured.

He did not let her go but kept his arms around her. What a sight they must make: two tall people standing pressed together atop a font. "Well, we made it," he said lightly, trying to dispel the tension of the unsaid things between them and the encroaching danger.

"Did we?" She looked down at the rising water, then up to the high ceiling. "One step closer to heaven . . ."

"You do know we can't ascend there on our own power . . . ?" he asked hopefully.

"I do know. I did not sleep through all those Sunday sermons in Longstaple, as you did."

A grin tugged at the corner of his mouth. "I am glad to hear it."

Emma's answering grin fell away as quickly as it formed. She whispered, "I'm sorry."

"For what?" Henry asked.

"I was not talking to you."

"Oh . . ." he breathed in awe.

She shook her head. "I should not have joked about heaven. For I am all too aware that I am not all I should be. Not worthy to face God on my own."

"None of us are," he whispered. "That is why our merciful God sent His beloved son to suffer and die—to cover our wrongdoing."

She nodded, though her eyes remained distant, anxious.

He inhaled a ragged breath. "I don't presume to know what you believe, Emma. But I do know that God loves you and forgives you. And if you acknowledge Him as the only one who can truly save you, save anyone, He will. Maybe not here and now in this world. But in the next. Forever."

She looked up at him, a smile slowly forming. "I think you've missed your calling, Henry Weston. Perhaps you ought to have gone into the church."

He grinned. "At the moment I'm wishing I had not gone into this *particular* church, but . . ."

She chuckled, even as tears filled her eyes once more. "I am mostly sad for my father. He was just beginning to recover from losing his wife. And now this."

He nodded. "I thought of that too."

"At least he'll have his sister," Emma said.

"Yes." Henry agreed. "Your aunt Jane is quite a remarkable woman. I've always liked her."

"And she you."

"The only Smallwood female to like me in those days, I'd wager. Then or since."

"That's not true," Emma said; then she ducked her head, self-conscious.

Henry looked at her cheeks, suddenly pink in her pale face, and felt unexpected pleasure warm his heart. Perhaps Emma did like him after all. Then he noticed the slightly bluish cast to her lips. Careful not to jostle her, he left one arm snug around her and gingerly loosed the other, moving his hand up along her arm to her face.

She watched, her expression uncertain, as he slowly lifted his hand toward her mouth.

"Your lips are blue," he whispered.

She pressed them together, the act restoring a bit of color. Not enough.

He touched his thumb to her lower lip. She jerked back in surprise, and again he tightened his hold to keep her from losing her balance. When she resisted no further, he slowly traced her lower lip, then moved to the upper, circling her mouth and wishing he might do so with his own. Leave it to a man to become amorous at a time like this, he thought wryly—but he made no move to stop himself. Returning to her lower lip, he dragged his finger across its fleshy firmness, feeling his chest tighten at the sight. Yes, he had to kiss her.

He leaned down, looking into her eyes, and seeing no resistance there, lowered his mouth.

"Emma...." he breathed and touched his lips to hers. Her cool lips were warmed and softened under his touch. He kissed her again, more fully, and felt her lips move against his, kissing him back. Satisfaction and pleasure filled him. Pleasure lanced with regret. Why had he waited so long?

He held her close, relishing how her tall, willowy body molded itself to his, supple and firm, yet soft in all the right places.

She snaked her arms up from between them, and wrapped them around his neck in a most un-bluestocking-like fashion that made him forget he'd ever been cold.

He deepened his kiss, her mouth melding to his. He wanted to make up for every lost second, every missed opportunity from the past or unlikely future. He wanted to savor her, breathe her in, and thank her creator for everything about her. From her elegant figure to her soft lips to her keen intelligence. Even her confounded love of order. If only they had more time.

He broke away to catch his breath, but his mouth was soon drawn back to her skin, kissing her temple, her forehead, one cheek, then the other.

"Mr. Weston," she breathed shakily. "I . . . I think—"

"I think you might call me Henry at this point, don't you?" he teased.

He glanced down at the water level. Was it his imagination, or had it remained the same as before they climbed atop the font? It certainly didn't seem to be rising as rapidly as it had been. Henry would take all the time he could get with the woman in his arms.

He caressed her cheek. "Do you think it funny that we are standing on a baptismal font to stay out of the water? Or is it just my odd sense of humor?"

Emma looked into Henry Weston's face with wonder. Her heart beat rapidly from their kiss and the rush of affection she felt—affection which he evidently returned. She had never felt about Phillip the way she did about the man holding her in his arms.

Suddenly the tower shook. Emma gripped Henry's shoulders

in alarm, and he tightened his hold around her waist. He began reciting the lines from an old hymn in his deep, masculine voice, stroking her cheek with his free hand as he did so.

> "Then let the wildest storms arise,
> Let tempests mingle earth and skies;
> No fatal shipwreck shall I fear,
> But all my treasures with me bear.
>
> If Thou, my Jesus, still be nigh,
> Cheerful I live, and joyful die;
> Secure, when mortal comforts flee,
> To find ten thousand worlds in Thee."

The words echoed within the stone walls, off the carved Greek gods of the four winds, and into Emma Smallwood's soul. She breathed, "That is beautiful."

He nodded. "It is. And I take no credit for it. Philip Doddridge wrote those words some sixty years ago."

"And still very fitting today." She swallowed. "Especially today."

Then Emma paused, belatedly realizing that she had indeed heard the words echo off the walls. Had the roar of wind and waves abated somewhat?

She looked toward the west window. "I'm sorry you never got to live the life you wanted. Or see the world. Have an adventure."

He chuckled low in his throat. "Oh, no? I'd say we were having quite the adventure, you and I. They always said to be careful what you wish for, but I wouldn't listen." He sighed theatrically.

She grinned, the act pushing a fat tear from each eye and down her cheeks. Traitorous tears! She was trying so hard to be brave. In control of her emotions.

"And what did you never get to do, Emma Smallwood?" he asked lightly, brushing the tears from her face.

"Nothing that really matters, in hindsight." She shrugged. "Though I would have liked to travel. And perhaps encourage Aunt Jane to live her life. Live enough for the both of us."

"No ordinary dreams? Of marriage, perhaps? A family?"

She ducked her head. "Perhaps." Tears filled her eyes once more.

He cupped her face in both of his hands and kissed her again.

From outside, Emma heard the sound of a voice. Or was it her hopeful imagination, transforming a sea gull cry into a human call?

"Did you hear that?" she whispered, breaking the kiss.

He angled his head, alert, frowning in concentration.

Fragments of words penetrated the chapel door. Followed by the clear peal of a bell. *Clang, clang, clang.*

The warning bell.

Henry and Emma looked at each other, eyes locking. Then Henry gripped her arms. "You stay here."

Henry jumped down into the thigh-high water. Clearly some of it had drained out through escape routes too small to do Henry and Emma any good. Even so, the cold water stole his breath.

Gritting his teeth, he slogged to the door, noting that the water level had risen nearly to its latch. Reaching it, he banged on the upper part of the door with his fist. "Open the door! We're trapped in here!"

He paused. Listened.

"Not so close to the breakwater!" Julian's voice. "What are you doing?"

"We have to reach the door." Rowan's lower voice.

"You're going to get us both killed."

"Give me the key."

"Let's go back." Julian's voice rose. "The waves are too high!"

"Not yet. Give me the key."

No answer. Henry held his breath.

"Dash it, Julian," Rowan growled. "Give me the key."

*Crack*—the sound of a blow. Fist upon flesh, followed by a thud.

What was happening? Finally there came the sound of metal scraping against metal. A key turning in the lock.

Henry raised his hand to the latch. What awaited beyond? A wall of water? Glancing over his shoulder to assure himself Emma still stood atop the font, Henry jerked the latch and felt it give. The door pushed inward by the force of the water, which rushed in up to his waist but no higher. Relief swamped him. *Thank you, Lord!*

Outside the door, where steps normally led down to the rocky path, now flowed choppy water, compliments of the storm and spring tides. Though the waves were still heavy, it seemed the storm had subsided. The sea covered the causeway so that the distinction between harbor and open sea was barely discernible. And there in the harbor, partially protected by the breakwater, rocked a small fishing boat. Rowan stood in the bow, legs spread wide. Behind him, on the floor of the boat, Julian struggled to his feet.

Rowan sat down at the oars and pulled hard.

Glancing past the boat to the shore, Henry saw Derrick Teague standing there arms akimbo, Major tossing his head, and Lizzie running headlong down the sand road toward the beach. Had she rung the bell?

Henry called, "Rowan, thank God you've come."

Rowan fought the waves to maneuver the small craft back to the door of the chapel.

From behind Henry came the sound of a splash, and he turned to see Emma wading toward him. Henry met her partway, taking her hand and leading her to the door.

Outside Rowan struggled against the waves to keep the boat close. Straining against the oars, he said, "Julian, throw Henry the rope."

"Julian . . . !" Derrick Teague called from shore, warning in his voice.

"Throw me the rope," Henry commanded, stretching out his hand.

Julian looked from Henry, back to Teague on shore. He appeared torn, his loyalties divided. He looked instead at his twin. "You hit me!" he shouted, rubbing his jaw.

"It's less than you deserve," Rowan snapped. "Now throw the rope!"

Instead, Julian launched himself at Rowan headfirst, knocking his larger brother against the prow.

"Stop it, Julian!"

The boat quickly moved away from the chapel.

Julian snarled, "Nobody hits me, jackanapes."

Rowan cocked his fist back and punched him again.

Julian reeled and lost his balance. He toppled backward off the boat, splashing into the churning water.

On shore, Lizzie screamed, hands pressed to her cheeks.

Rowan paled but sat at the oars once more and rowed hard back to the chapel.

Julian's head appeared above the surface, sputtering and cursing.

Keeping an eye on Julian, Henry said to Rowan, "Miss Smallwood first."

Struggling to keep his balance as the vessel lurched in the waves, Rowan stood and tossed Henry the mooring line himself, his face tense. "Come on," he called. "This is only a lull in the storm. The worst is yet to come, according to Davies. Let's get out of here."

Henry hurried to comply. Holding the rope and bracing his leg against the doorjamb, Henry extended his other hand to Emma. "In the boat, Emma."

"But, what about Julian?"

"First, you get in."

Emma took his hand and extended her other to Rowan, awkwardly half climbing, half falling into the boat.

"I'll kill you for that, Rowan," Julian yelled, though he was clearly struggling to keep his head above water.

Henry climbed in behind Emma. The boat rocked violently, even though the water in the south side of the harbor was somewhat less violent than the open sea beyond. Henry took the oars, trying to keep the boat from facing broadside in the waves.

"Throw the rope to Julian," Henry ordered between gritted teeth.

Rowan shook his head, face white. "He might capsize us. Intentionally."

"We have to save him," Emma cried.

Rowan looked at Henry for a decision.

Henry nodded and yelled to Julian, "Hang on. We'll tow you to shore."

Lips tight, Rowan threw the rope to Julian. Julian grasped it and pulled his head higher out of the water.

Julian's weight added more burden, but Henry rowed with all his might, muscles straining, lungs burning.

The boat nearly capsized more than once, then finally scraped its belly against sand.

"Praise God," Henry sighed.

"Amen," Emma echoed.

Probably drawn by the bell, villagers appeared along the harbor, Mr. Bray among them.

Derrick Teague strode into the surf, grasped the struggling Julian by the arm, and hauled him up onto the shore. Scowling, he tossed Julian onto his back as so much flotsam. "Botched that, didn't 'ee, lad."

Julian coughed and rolled to his side, waterlogged and hacking but safe.

Henry helped Emma from the boat, then paused where he was, resting his hands on his knees, panting in exhaustion. He glanced over at Teague, saw the man glare at him and fist his weathered hands. Henry doubted he had the strength to fight the man at present.

Teague took a step toward him, but Mr. Bray gripped his shoulder.

Teague jerked free and wheeled on the old constable. "What?"

Bray said gently, "I was only going to thank you for helping the lad. Why not go home now while you're ahead?" The constable said it kindly, yet there was a tenor of steel beneath his words. The men's eyes locked.

Teague looked away first. "That's right. I was helpin' the lad. Remember that." He turned and stalked away.

Lizzie ran to Henry, splashing through the surf, heedless of her gown. "Oh, Henry! I saw the light in the window and your horse on the beach. That's when I rang the bell. I was so worried, knowing you were trapped inside." She threw her arms around him.

Henry knew the girl looked upon him as an older brother and resisted the urge to put her away from him. Instead he awkwardly patted her shoulder. "Well, thankfully Rowan managed to reach us in the boat."

Henry glowered over her head at Julian and shouted, "What the devil were you thinking, Julian? You have a lot of explaining to do." Seeing the crowd gathering, Henry added more quietly, "But we shall wait and have it out in the privacy of our own home. Understood?"

His brothers nodded, but Lizzie continued, almost desperately, "I never thought it would come to this. Never!"

Mr. Smallwood jogged onto the scene, face flushed, breathing hard. Had he run all the way from the house? His anxious eyes riveted on his daughter. "Emma!"

Good, Henry thought. Her father was there. She would be safe while he dealt with the chaos that was his family.

Soon after, two carriages rattled onto the beach. The Westons' landau, driven by their coachman, followed by the two-wheeled cart, driven by the groom.

Sir Giles hopped down from the landau, looking more spry than Henry had seen him in years. Henry guessed he had heard the bell and ordered the carriages. Now, surveying the sodden lot of them—and the assembled, gawking crowd—the baronet took charge. Ignoring their protests and urging haste, he herded his sons toward the family carriage.

Henry allowed his father to lead him into the landau, his half brothers arguing and Julian's eyes flashing dangerously—though one eye was sure to be black-and-blue before long.

He tried to catch Emma's attention across the way, but she was deep in earnest conversation with her father. Henry would have to talk to her later. Assuming she would ever want to speak to him—to any Weston—after this.

Emma was relieved to see her father alive and well, when she had feared him in danger but a few hours before. He held her tightly, and she embraced him in return.

"Thanks be to God, Emma. Are you all right?"

"Yes, Papa." She noted his flushed face and labored breathing with concern. "Are you?"

"Now that I know you're safe, I am." He panted to catch his breath. "I was partway to Upton before I suspected I'd been tricked. I hurried back and when I found that forged letter in the schoolroom and no one else, I feared the worst. I alerted Sir Giles and ran down while he called for the carriages."

He held her a little away from him, anxiously studying her. "What happened?"

Emma glanced at the curious onlookers and hovering groom. "I shall tell you later. All right? When we're alone."

He followed her gaze, and the groom quickly ducked, feigning interest in the harness. "Very well."

Emma looked across the way. Henry was being led into his family's landau, fussed over by Sir Giles. Henry glanced in her direction and their eyes met across the distance. She saw his lips move but could not make out his words over the shouting of his brothers and the roar of the wind, increasing once more. She shrugged and shook her head, meaning *I can't hear you.* Who knew how he interpreted the gesture. He lifted a hand, in salute or in farewell, his face downcast in regret.

Seeing Henry join his family in the fine landau, leaving her and her father to ride alone in the cart, felt like a splash of cold water in her face, waking her from a vivid dream to stark, grey reality.

Realization seeped into Emma like water oozing through a hundred cracks in the wall of her being. *He would never be allowed to marry you.* Surveying the dozen yards between them, she knew what separated them was far more than physical distance. Henry Weston was the son of a baronet, and his likely heir. He would be Sir Henry after his father's death, and she would still be plain Miss Smallwood, tutor's daughter. No birth of distinction, no connections, no wealth. The line of demarcation between them was clearer than any actual line drawn in the sand.

Henry's damp coat hung on her, as heavy as chain mail. Her

knees trembled under its weight. Emma thought of all that had passed between them in the chapel. The way he had looked at her, held her, kissed her. The words he had said. But that had been when he'd thought they would not live to see another day.

Fingers of misgiving kneaded her spine. Had it all been runaway emotion?

She wondered what he was feeling now. Embarrassment? Regret? Might he feel he had inadvertently committed himself to her when he had hoped, perhaps even planned, to marry Miss Penberthy or some other wealthy young lady like her? The last thing Emma wanted was for Henry to feel trapped, obligated to her out of duty alone. She wanted his genuine, unreserved love or nothing at all. Seeing him now, seated with his family, Emma thought the latter the most likely eventuality.

Across the harbor, waves battered the chapel with renewed fury. Emma shivered, wind cutting through her wet clothes like a knife. Noticing, her father removed his coat and draped it around her.

As he helped her into the waiting cart, a terrible rending shuddered through her. A violent cracking, as though a frozen pond had been struck by a mighty fist.

She turned and saw the beleaguered chapel lean and then keel over, crashing into the water with a great splash. The hungry waves licked it, consumed it—and in a matter of moments, buried it beneath the water. Gone forever.

Around the harbor people stared, stunned. Emma looked at Henry in the landau and saw his gaped mouth. His grief.

*Poor Henry,* Emma thought. He'd loved that place. How disappointed he must be.

She inhaled deeply. At least he was alive.

*And so am I,* she reminded herself. And that was enough. It was time to be thankful.

And to start living.

*The lofty pine is oftenest shaken by the winds;*
*High towers fall with a heavier crash; And*
*the lightning strikes the highest mountain.*

—Horace

# Chapter 25

Mindful of Henry's admonition to wait to discuss the matter in private—and aware of the coachman's curious looks and listening ears—the Westons were a somber, silent party on the ride up the cliff.

They reached the manor, shivering and spent. Lady Weston and Phillip were there to meet them, all concern. Sir Giles, ignoring the questions and protestations tumbling one over the other, shepherded his sons inside and called for hot baths for all.

"Very well, Father," Henry allowed. "But afterward, we need to talk. All of us."

The Smallwoods arrived in the cart, and before they went their separate ways, a meeting with all involved was set to commence in two hours' time.

As she stepped past him on her way inside, Emma solemnly handed back his coat, folded away and all but ruined, like his hopes.

At the appointed time, they all assembled in the drawing room, some begrudgingly, some eager to learn what had taken place, and why. Henry was somewhat surprised to see both his half brothers enter the room of their own volition. True, Henry *had* instructed the footman, Jory, to keep an eye on Julian, just in case. But apparently he came under no duress. Was he so convinced of his own innocence—or his ability to prove himself so?

Lady Weston sat in her customary chair; Sir Giles stood behind her. Emma Smallwood and her father shared one settee, while Lizzie and Phillip shared the other. Rowan and Julian each took armchairs of their own. Henry stood by the fire, hand on the mantel. The only Weston absent was Adam. But Henry was only too happy to spare him what would no doubt prove a trying confrontation.

Without accusing anyone, Henry began by giving a summary of the day's events: The forged note Miss Smallwood received. Mr. Smallwood walking in the opposite direction to the Upton cemetery. Henry following Miss Smallwood to the chapel and both being locked in—and would have been swept away when the chapel fell, had Rowan not reached them in time.

When he finished his summary, he turned to Julian. "Why did you do it?"

"Do what?" Julian asked, eyes wide in faux innocence, one of them shadowed by a burgeoning bruise.

"You know very well what. Lock us in the chapel."

Julian crossed his arms. "I didn't do that. Rowan did."

Rowan frowned. "That's a lie, Julian."

Julian turned his head and pinned Lizzie with a look. "Tell them, Lizzie. Tell them who did it."

Lizzie wrung her hands. She bit her lip, glancing from Henry to Phillip and then nervously back at Julian. She whispered, "You did."

Julian's face contorted. "You unfaithful—"

Foul words seemed about to follow, but Henry quickly silenced him with a stinging grip to his shoulder.

Changing tack, Julian shrugged. "*If* I did, it was only meant to be a joke."

"A joke?" Henry exclaimed. "To lure Miss Smallwood down there just as the tide and a storm were coming in?"

"Well, I couldn't know *when* she would go, could I? Or how bad the storm would be."

"Are you going to tell me you did not change the times in my tide book, that you did not write that note, mimicking Mr. Smallwood's handwriting, telling Emma he was going to the chapel when you knew very well he was not?"

"I didn't give her the note." Julian jerked his chin toward his brother. "Rowan did."

Rowan threw up his hands. "Well, how was I to know it wasn't real? Lizzie told me Mr. Smallwood had given it to her on his way out. She asked me to deliver it since I was going up to the schoolroom anyway. I had no idea what the letter was about. I didn't suspect forgery—not until Miss Smallwood told us her father had written to say he'd gone to the Chapel of the Rock."

"But *you* sent her father to Upton on a wild goose chase," Julian insisted.

Rowan nodded. "I admit I lied when I told him I'd seen several graves with the name Smallwood in the Upton cemetery, and gave him a map with a few wrong turns to lengthen his trip. But that is all I did." He glanced at the tutor. "Sorry, Mr. Smallwood." He looked back at his brother with a frown. "I thought the plan was to buy ourselves an afternoon without lessons. I had no idea you tampered with the tide table. Or took the chapel key. Had I known everything you planned to do, I would never have gone along with even that much."

"Do you expect anyone to believe that?" Julian scoffed, with a covert glance at his mother. "You admit to getting the old man out of the way. And failed to tell Henry about the forged letter. And yet you expect everyone to believe you had no part in the rest? Ha."

"I believe him," Lizzie said quietly.

Julian glared at her. "Turning against me now—is that it?" His lip curled. "I had thought to spare you in this little mock trial of Henry's, but if that's how you're going to behave, then forget it. Let's tell everyone how you knowingly gave Rowan a forged note to deliver, for I knew he would suspect it if it came from my own hand." He glanced at the others. "It was not my first forgery, you see." His eyes glinted with a strange pride.

"But I never thought you would take it so far," Lizzie said. "That you planned to trap her there until . . . until it was too late."

Lady Weston, Henry noticed, had sat rigid and uncharacteristically silent throughout the testimony. Now she suggested hopefully, "But, Julian . . . surely you meant to go back out and unlock the door. But the water rose too high before you could do so. Is that not right?"

Henry heard the restrained desperation in her voice, but Julian made no reply.

Lizzie turned plaintive eyes toward Henry. "We had no idea you might go out there too. Or I never would have gone along with it."

He looked at her, incredulous. "It was acceptable to lock Miss Smallwood in the chapel, but not me?"

Lizzie ducked her head. "I don't say it was right. But she is nobody to us."

Henry noticed Emma flinch at the words. Angry indignation mounted on Mr. Smallwood's face, and in his claw-like grip on the arm of the settee, where he sat beside Emma. She apparently noticed as well, for she laid a restraining hand on his.

Lizzie continued, "When I realized Julian still intended to go through with it, I rang the warning bell, hoping to stop him and bring help."

"Why did you do it, Julian?" Mr. Smallwood asked, expression thunderous. "What has my daughter ever done to you?"

Julian huffed. "Interfere—that's what. Sticking her nose into private family affairs. Eavesdropping. Pointing out incriminating notices in the newspaper, forcing Mamma to suspend . . . certain activities. Causing Phillip to come home midterm and . . . confuse a particular young lady. . . ."

"That's not true," Phillip protested.

But Julian went on, undeterred, "Turning Henry's head, when he is meant to marry Miss Penberthy or someone like her. Ringing Henry's dashed bell. Mr. Teague does not appreciate that tower one bit. It was he who suggested that a warning to Miss Smallwood would serve as a warning to Henry as well."

"Mr. Teague?" Sir Giles's face puckered. "What has that reprobate to do with her? With any of us?"

"Far more than you know, Papa. Or would want to know, I'd wager." Julian turned to his mother. "Would you not agree, Mamma?"

Lady Weston stared back at him, face pale. Slowly she shook her head. "Julian . . . you cannot think I wanted this. I . . . I never thought you capable of such . . . deviousness."

One brow arched high, he challenged, "Are you not impressed?"

"Impressed?" Again she shook her head. "I am shocked. Disappointed. Afraid for you. When did you become so coldhearted? So . . . unscrupulous?"

"Oh, don't be modest, Mamma," Julian said with a wicked grin. "We all know you deserve the credit, coming from a long line of West Country smugglers, as you do. Wouldn't Grandfather Heale be proud?"

Her mouth fell ajar. "Ungrateful, spiteful boy. My papa devoted his life to overcoming my grandfather's reputation, to bring our family up in society. And he succeeded. Now, that is enough. I will hear no more of this."

"What is the matter, Mamma?" Julian asked archly. "Afraid Papa will learn of your dealings with your friend, Mr. Teague?"

Lady Weston's eyes sparked with anger. "He is not my friend, Julian. As you well know. We are business partners at best."

"Business partners?" Sir Giles repeated, incredulous. "What sort of business would you have to conduct with a man like Teague, who everybody knows to be an infamous wrecker?"

Julian said, "Oh, he may have been a mere wrecker in his younger days, but he is far more now. Much more sophisticated."

"Teague—sophisticated? Bah."

"He no longer merely helps himself to cargo but instead has become a dealer, finding profitable markets for things that would bring only a fraction of their worth here in our poverty-stricken parish. But in Bristol or Bath or even London . . . ? My, what people are willing to pay."

"But I still don't see what that has to do with us."

"Why, Papa, I am surprised you don't know. Mamma is Mr. Teague's patroness. She lends her name whenever he finds something particularly valuable among the cargo or taken from some half-drowned shipowner or his lady—say jewels, or a fine watch, or precious metals of some kind. A man like Teague trying to sell these things would, of course, raise suspicion of theft, given his unfortunate reputation. But when he produces a letter on the stationery of Lady Violet Weston, explaining that unfortunate circumstances have forced her to seek a buyer for a few of her family heirlooms, and would said buyer promise the utmost discretion to avoid embarrassing her husband, Sir Giles, Baronet? Well, that opens doors and purses which might otherwise remain closed to Derrick Teague."

Sir Giles stared at his wife, shock slackening his facial muscles, making him look older than his fifty-odd years.

"Is this true, madam?" he asked. "Can it be? Do I know my own wife so little?"

Lady Weston lifted her chin. "If it is true, it is your fault as much as mine. If you were not so ineffectual as head of this family, I might not have been driven to it. Where do you think the "family money" I've poured into the Weston coffers has come from all this time?"

He grasped for an answer, sputtering, "Your . . . dowry or . . . marriage settlement. I don't know."

"Both depleted long ago, thanks to your mismanagement. I had to think of my boys, didn't I? As younger sons, they would have nothing to secure their futures, if not for the money I've brought into this house. You ought to be thanking me instead of castigating me."

Sir Giles slowly shook his head. "No, madam, I cannot thank you for being in league with a known criminal. For dragging my family's good name to the level of a Teague."

Julian smirked. "It's ironic, isn't it, Mamma? You, the *fine* lady, so desperate to climb the social ladder, to secure prestigious marriages for your sons. All to further distance yourself from your grandfather's crimes. And what do you do? Jump into the very gutter you claim to despise."

Shame suffused Violet Weston's otherwise pale face. She clasped her hands and said stiffly, "A mother does what she must for her children."

She turned to her husband with a feigned casual air. "I would think twice before considering legal action against either Teague or me. For if I am ruined, you are ruined with me. No one would believe a woman raised such sums without her husband's participation and *superior* knowledge."

It was likely true. And Henry could not stand the thought of his innocent if naive father being punished—further damaging the Weston family reputation—for something he had no part in beyond, perhaps, willful ignorance or neglect.

Emma's mind reeled with all the new information. She felt terrible for Sir Giles, for Henry, for them all.

Henry faced his stepmother. "And I would think twice, Lady Weston, before threatening Sir Giles. Consider, my lady—your precious Julian nearly succeeded in killing Miss Smallwood and me today. If anyone ought to be considering legal action, it's—"

"Not intentionally," Lady Weston interjected.

"Oh? The tampered tide book and forged letter contradict you."

"No one will believe you. I will simply tell them you've always held a grudge against my natural-born sons."

Rowan stood, eyes blazing. "Then *I* shall give evidence against Julian," he said. "I'm tired of protecting him, of covering for his escalating wrongdoing. First the trouble at school, then the pranks on Miss Smallwood—the letters, the drawing, the blood—and now this."

Dismay widened Lady Weston's eyes. She pleaded, "But, Rowan, he's your brother."

"So is Henry, but Julian nearly killed him today. Along with Miss Smallwood, who has been nothing but kind to us since she arrived. I have been on Julian's side—the wrong side—long enough."

"Me too," Lizzie echoed.

"Oh, shut up, Lizzie," Lady Weston snapped. "Or shall I tell everyone why you are really here, in my house, as my ward?"

Lizzie paled and immediately pressed her lips tight.

"What do you mean, Mother?" Phillip asked. "She is your cousin's daughter."

"My cousin? Ha. I might be very distantly related to her jade of a mother, but Mr. Teague is no cousin of mine. But he has become my keeper. Once we had . . . worked together for a time, he realized he held leverage over me. With his newfound wealth, he wooed Lizzie's mother. But she left him after only a few months, leaving the girl behind. He pressured me into taking Lizzie in, to give her every advantage—and keep her happy—or he would expose me. I only said she was a relative to explain her presence here."

Lizzie hung her head in shame.

"So what if she is Mr. Teague's stepdaughter?" Julian exclaimed. "I knew it and I still love her. And I won't have you being cruel to her, Mamma. We are promised to each other, and when we're older, we plan to wed."

Lady Weston's brows rose. Incredulous, she blurted, "Love her? Love Lizzie Henshaw? Marry her? I won't hear of it."

Emma digested this revelation as well. *Julian* was the younger brother Lizzie had once promised herself to—not Phillip, as she'd first thought. Emma supposed Julian was less than two years younger than Lizzie, but he had always seemed even younger—until today. Emma supposed that what at fifteen and seventeen seemed a gulf, at thirty and two-and-thirty would be a trifle hardly worth mentioning.

Lizzie sniffed. "Well, that's fine with me, Lady Weston. For I don't love Julian anyway. Another Weston has won my heart."

Lady Weston turned brilliant, angry eyes on the girl. "Your heart? I don't think you have one, you little fortune hunter. Do you think I would allow any Weston to marry you—the daughter of nobody, stepdaughter of a thief? How dare you even think such a thing? The Westons will marry young ladies of good birth and breeding."

"That's for him to say. Not you," Lizzie insisted, looking away and feigning an interest in the candle chandelier.

Lizzie's former words echoed once more through Emma's mind: *"I fear I have fallen hopelessly in love with . . . an older Mr. Weston."* And when Emma had asked if this older brother returned her affections, Lizzie had said, *"I think so. Oh, I dearly hope so."*

So Lizzie loved Phillip. Not Henry. But the realization brought little comfort. Emma had been foolish to ever believe it of Henry. A man like Henry Weston would no more marry Lizzie Henshaw than he would marry her, Emma Smallwood.

The seconds ticked by, but Phillip did not declare his love for Lizzie. Had the girl misread his feelings? Or was Phillip reticent to speak up in the presence of Lady Weston, or even Emma herself, whom he had allowed the others—if not Emma herself—to believe he'd been interested in romantically?

*This is becoming very awkward,* Emma thought. *They cannot want us present to hear all this.*

She tugged on her father's sleeve. Their eyes met in silent message.

John Smallwood rose, stood erect, and spoke with impressive firmness. "You must excuse us. These are private family matters, and we prefer not to be involved. And considering what Emma has suffered today, I think it best if we prepare to depart without delay." He offered Emma a hand and helped her to her feet.

Sir Giles began to sputter in protest, but her father lifted his hand.

"No, Sir Giles. I will not stay and have my daughter subjected to further danger or insult." John Smallwood's once meek, subservient tone was notably absent. "If either of us is needed to present evidence or written testimony, I trust you will let us know."

Sir Giles bit a worried lip and then cleared his throat. "May I ask for your mercy, my friend, in allowing me to handle this in my own way, without bringing in the law? Rest assured, Julian will face consequences. But I don't wish the reputation of my other sons to suffer for his wrongdoing."

Mr. Smallwood considered this. He looked at Emma, and she nodded.

"Very well," her father said. "You may count on us for discretion. In the meantime, if we might trouble you for a carriage to take us into the village first thing in the morning? That is, assuming you can assure my daughter's safety one last night. Or shall we leave before nightfall?"

Emma was in agreement about not bringing charges against Julian Weston, but she doubted she would sleep well until they had put many miles between them.

"Of course, of course," Sir Giles said, regretful and considerate at once. "I shall personally guarantee Julian gives no one any further trouble. In fact I shall post guard outside his room to make certain there is no more nighttime mischief. Then tomorrow I will decide what is best to be done with him."

Julian sneered. "Oh, really, Father, I hardly think that's necessary." He looked to Lady Weston. "Mamma, tell him."

But Lady Weston only shook her head, refusing to meet Julian's eyes. Her momentary outburst had faded, leaving only shaken disillusionment in its place. She looked ten years older. A wilted flower, its head suddenly too heavy for its fragile stem.

Emma felt the same way. Legs weak, she wrapped her hands around her father's arm for support and walked with him from the room.

She noticed with both relief and sinking sadness that not one other soul objected to their departure.

It was surprising, really, how quickly their weeks at Ebbington Manor could be packed away into trunks and valises. Morva came in to help Emma with her frocks and undergarments, while Emma stowed her books and gold-rimmed teacup. Henry's valet, Merryn, had been sent up to assist her father, because the footman who usually did so had been assigned to stand watch outside of Julian's room.

The schoolroom took the most time—extricating their own texts, maps, and papers from those belonging to the Westons.

After an uneventful night, Emma rose early, relief and dread mixing in her stomach, making her queasy. She thought, *This is the morning we leave Ebbington Manor forever.*

Morva arrived and helped her dress. Then Emma excused herself, leaving Morva to finish packing and close up the trunk.

Emma walked down the corridor, passing a cot still set up across Julian's door, though the footman had already risen. She turned into the north wing, feeling none of the trepidation she had once felt, only sadness and loss at the thought of never seeing Adam again. Probably not Henry either.

She knocked softly.

"Enter."

Her heart lurched. Not Adam's soft voice—Henry's.

So early? She hadn't anticipated that. Emma doubted she had the courage to face him at the moment. She turned away, thinking to spare them both the awkward encounter, the stiff, polite farewells.

Behind her, the door opened—more swiftly than she'd expected.

"Emma . . . um, Miss Smallwood."

She winced, then forced a neutral expression as she turned back.

Henry stood in the threshold, looking expectant yet guarded. Did he fear she'd come to extract some commitment from him? Cause a scene?

She blurted, "I've come to say good-bye to Adam. But if you are talking, I—"

"Come in. He'll want to see you. I have been easing him into the idea, so hopefully he won't become upset."

How ironic that the one person who would be truly sorry to see her go was the one Weston she hadn't even known existed when she arrived.

She dipped her head and passed by Henry into the room, unable to meet his eyes.

Inside, Adam sat at the small table near the windows, idly playing with a tin soldier. He did not rise or even straighten as her boot heels tapped across the floorboards, but she did notice him glance at her from the corner of his eye.

She sat in the chair opposite and recognized the boxed chess set on the table. "Hello, Adam," she said gently.

His eyes flitted up and away. "Hello, Emma."

She projected brightness into her tone. "I am going home today."

"Henry told me. I want you to stay."

She noticed that though he fidgeted with a tin soldier, he grasped something else in his other hand. Tight.

"We put your chess men in a box," Adam said. "Henry says I should thank you for letting me play with them." He took a long breath at the end of his speech.

Emma's stomach knotted. "You are very welcome, Adam." She asked softly, "What are you holding?"

Adam looked down at his left hand for several moments. Then he gradually unfurled his clenched fingers. Within lay the white queen.

Adam took a long look at the piece, then slowly extended his hand toward her.

From somewhere behind her, Henry said quietly, "He doesn't want to let her go."

His words reverberated through Emma's heart. Was he speaking of more than a chess piece? Was he speaking for Adam alone?

Emma swallowed. "You keep it, Adam. It's yours now. I gave the set to you. I didn't come to collect it. I only came to say good-bye."

Adam nodded, apparently relieved.

Emma rose and forced a smile. "Will you shake hands with me before I go?" She held out her hand, wondering if the gesture would repel him.

For a moment Adam stared at her trembling hand. Then he released the soldier and reached out, grasping her hand in a tight squeeze, then immediately releasing it.

He may as well have squeezed her heart.

"Thank you, Adam," she whispered, feeling tears sting her eyes. She blinked rapidly, not wishing to cry in his presence—or Henry's. "Good-bye."

He did not echo that phrase, but gave a jerky little nod instead.

She turned to the door, swiping at the corner of one disobedi-
ent eye.

Henry followed her out into the corridor, softly closing the door
behind him.

"Miss Smallwood," he began. "I—"

*No, no, no,* she thought. She did not want to hear his apologies
or explanations.

She hurried to interrupt him. "There is no need to say anything,
Mr. Weston."

She could not quite look into his face but focused instead on his
hurriedly tied neckcloth, and told herself to breathe.

He said, "I can understand why you might feel that way. After
yesterday, I would understand if you never wanted to see any of us
Westons again. But I hope you will forgive me one day."

"Forgive you?" *For which part,* she wondered. For the words he'd
spoken, never guessing he'd live to be held accountable to them? Or
for the kisses they'd shared, never guessing they might obligate him
to a woman he had no intention of marrying? She said only, "Were
you somehow responsible for yesterday's misadventure, after all?"

"Not directly, no. But I keenly regret not realizing what Julian
was capable of. And I regret ever mentioning the boyhood pranks
I pulled on you at Longstaple. I should not have done those things
in the first place. And I cannot help but think my example had a
part in leading the boys astray."

"You are not responsible for your brothers' actions."

"Still, I wish I might have prevented it somehow."

She nodded. "Well, we are both safe now. That is all that matters."

"Is it? Is that truly all that matters to you? It isn't all that matters
to me."

"Please, Mr. Weston. Think no more about it. I don't wish you
to say anything or do anything out of misplaced feelings of obliga-
tion or duty."

"But, Emma . . . Miss Smallwood . . . yesterday . . . the words we
spoke. The things we—"

She cut him off. "That was yesterday. When we thought we would not live to see another day. It is understandable that our emotions should run away with us. You need not worry. I shall not hold you accountable for anything you said. And I hope you won't hold me to anything I may have said either." She chuckled nervously.

"It grieves me to hear you say so, Miss Smallwood."

"Oh?" She swallowed. "Which part?"

He hesitated. "I meant everything I said." He winced as though in pain, eyes and mouth pressed tight. "Though it is true that now . . . certain family obligations must be seen to. And I may not be at liberty to pursue . . . any of those . . . subjects upon which we touched in the chapel. However—"

The words *we touched in the chapel* . . . echoed through Emma's mind, and she felt longing rise in her. She mentally shook herself and took a deep breath. "Mr. Weston, as I said, do not make yourself uneasy on my account. There is no need."

He opened his mouth, then closed it again, thinking the better of what he'd been about to say. Finally he said, "There is one subject I hope you will own, one choice of the heart you will not cast aside in the light of day, or in light of Weston wrongdoings. Do not cast God aside, Emma. Not now that you've begun praying again."

*You misunderstand me,* Emma wanted to say. *I cast aside no one. Nothing. I would happily cling to every word spoken, every prayer uttered, every embrace shared. If I could. If you loved me. If you were not duty-bound to marry another.* If Lady Weston objected to any of Sir Giles's sons marrying her ward, what would she say about Henry marrying a mere tutor's daughter?

He squeezed her hand. "Tell me that was not runaway emotion as well?"

Emma's throat convulsed, threatening tears. Not trusting her voice to convey all she felt, she shook her head and whispered only, "It was not."

Soon their things were packed in the boot of the Westons' traveling coach, which Sir Giles insisted carry them all the way home.

He would not hear of them traveling post or by stage, not after Miss Smallwood's ordeal. He himself inspected the groom's work, checking to make sure their trunks were securely tied down and that the hamper of food for the journey had been placed inside. He bid the coachman and groom take the utmost care of their passengers.

Then Sir Giles turned and shook her father's hand. "I am sorry, but Lady Weston is . . . indisposed and unable to see you off personally. She sends her regards."

Rowan stepped forward and apologized again for his part in the previous day's ordeal.

Her father said, "You erred, my boy, but in the end you saved my precious daughter. So the rest is forgiven and forgotten."

"Thank you, sir." Rowan shook Mr. Smallwood's hand and thanked him for everything. "I regret you are not able to stay with us longer," he said earnestly. "You are a good teacher."

Her father beamed with pleasure at his pupil's praise.

Lizzie stood to the side, hands clasped, her former flippant attitude gone.

She tentatively approached Emma. "I am sorry, Miss Smallwood. Truly I am. I had no idea Julian planned to take things so far. I am very glad you are all right."

She appeared sincerely penitent, and Emma wanted to believe her. She hated to think she had been so wrong about the girl. She wanted Lizzie to be a good woman, especially if she might yet marry into the Weston family one day, despite Lady Weston's objections.

"Thank you," Emma managed. "Um, where is Julian? Not still confined to his room, I trust?"

Lizzie shook her head. "Worse. Sequestered with his sorely disillusioned mamma."

"Well, good-bye, Lizzie," Emma said, feeling her throat tighten. She turned toward the carriage.

Phillip appeared before her, his face somber and sheepish. "I am sorry, Emma. I still can't believe all that happened."

She nodded. "Nor I."

"I regret my own behavior as well. I realize I may have led you to believe—"

"No, you did not," Emma interrupted, aware of Lizzie standing a few yards off, watching Phillip's every move.

Phillip persisted. "But I did not stand by you as a friend ought."

"It is all right. I understand." Feeling tears prick her eyes, Emma quickly changed the subject. "What will you do now?"

"I leave for Oxford this afternoon. To try to make things right."

She managed a small smile. "I am very glad to hear it."

Phillip gave Emma a hand up into the coach, then went to bid farewell to her father.

From the carriage window, Emma saw Henry step outside and shake her father's hand. He did not approach the carriage. But once her father was settled and the traveling coach lurched into motion, Henry met her gaze through the carriage window. He raised his hand in silent salute and somber farewell.

# Chapter 26

v

Several times during the carriage journey home, Emma felt her father's concerned gaze on her profile. She knew he worried about her, that he was anxious for her to speak, to prove she remained her stalwart, steady self. For once she hadn't the energy to oblige him.

Eyes fixed on the window, barely seeing the passing countryside, Emma murmured, "It's sad, isn't it?"

He replied, "It is sad, yes."

When she said no more, he expounded, "But we have seen the like before, my dear—time and time again, have we not? Permissive parents who spoil their children, who live selfish and immoral lives and are then, against all logic, shocked and remorseful when their children follow their example."

She nodded vaguely. She had not been thinking of Julian Weston, but was relieved her father had misunderstood. She did not completely agree with her father but kept silent, not bothering to point out that a similar upbringing had produced four very different Westons—not to mention Adam.

She thought once more about her earlier notions of the four brothers and four winds. She had pegged Phillip as the mild and friendly west wind, and she supposed she had been right, although his loyalty had wavered. She now knew that Rowan, despite first impressions to the contrary, meant well but occasionally blew overzealously, like the south wind. And the east wind, with his violent and disorderly personality who enjoyed creating storms? Julian. She had erred most in judging Henry, who was not as cold and fierce as the north wind she had once believed him. And she had not even known about the fifth Weston brother when she'd crafted her futile theory.

In the end the myth didn't matter. What mattered in reality was a person's character, what he did with the life and abilities God had given him, and his daily choice to act honorably despite the selfish tendencies and weaknesses shared by all humans.

What about her? What would she do now, with the life God had given her?

They arrived in Longstaple that evening, after six or seven hours on the road, stopping to change horses at various coaching inns along the way or to stretch their limbs and take refreshment from the hamper provided by Mrs. Prowse.

Her father directed the coachman to take them to Jane Smallwood's home, as their own house was still let. They could not, after all, go charging in and ask the tenants to quit the place that very day, without proper notice.

Emma hoped Aunt Jane would not mind their unannounced arrival, for there had been no time to send word.

Aunt Jane greeted them in surprise, and tentative pleasure mingled with concern. Were they all right? In good health? Had something gone wrong to force them to return ahead of schedule?

Emma said they would tell her all by and by, but for now could she possibly allow them to stay with her for a time?

Of course they were welcome, Aunt Jane insisted. Emma might sleep with her, and her brother might have the room recently vacated by the pupil Jane had escorted home to help her ailing mother.

Grateful to have a familiar place to stay with one so dear, Emma heaved a sigh of relief and instructed the coachman and groom to set their trunks in the corner of the entry hall for later removal. She thanked the men, offered them a gratuity—which they politely refused—and suggested a good inn that would put them up for the night before they undertook the return journey.

After they had gone, Jane Smallwood ushered her brother and niece into the snug parlor. "Come, my dears. You must have tea. And Jenny and I will put together a little something for you to eat."

"Don't go to any trouble, Aunt Jane," Emma said. "We have eaten well enough on the journey, though tea sounds heavenly."

A few minutes later, Jenny brought in the tea tray with a plate of shortbread and her aunt's old, chipped tea set.

Emma glanced from it to the fine rose-and-white china in the corner cabinet. Seeing it pinched her heart. She rose abruptly, held up a wait-a-minute finger, and went to her valise. From it she withdrew her gold-rimmed teacup and saucer, removed its tissue wrapping, carried it to the table, and set it down with dramatic flair.

"Now I shall take tea." Emma eyed the tray. "And a piece of shortbread with it."

Her father's mouth dropped open in alarm. "My dear, have I forgotten your birthday?"

Emma chuckled, "No, Papa."

Her father looked at her, bemused, and Aunt Jane's eyebrows rose nearly to her hairline. When Emma offered no explanation, her father cleared his throat and asked his sister for the village news. Then they drank tea and spoke of inconsequential details of the journey—the conditions of the roads, the inns, the comfort of the coach. But all the while Jane Smallwood's large green eyes searched her niece's face in unspoken concern.

Too weary to bother with the trunks, Emma borrowed one of her aunt's freshly laundered nightdresses. Aunt Jane helped her out of her traveling clothes and unfastened her long stays. Jane hung up her gown while Emma slipped the nightdress over her head and climbed into her aunt's bed.

Emma glanced at the bedside table and saw the familiar letter propped there, next to the book about steam engines. "You still have Mr. Farley's letter, I see. Gathering dust like your tea set."

"And your teacup. Until now," her aunt replied glibly.

*And our hearts,* Emma added to herself.

Aunt Jane kissed Emma's forehead and promised to be up soon, after she made sure her pupils were settled in for the night.

Lying there alone, Emma picked up the letter. She had not read it in quite some time, but she still remembered the gist of it—Mr. Farley's admiration of Jane's loveliness and intelligence, and his desire to deepen their acquaintance.

The image of Henry Weston's face, looking at Emma with warm admiration, appeared in her mind. She tried, in vain, to blink it away.

Aunt Jane came in a few minutes later, interrupting Emma's reverie. She undressed and sat on the edge of the bed so Emma could unlace her stays. She then pulled on her own nightdress and slid under the bedclothes, the bed ropes rocking with her movement.

Emma asked, "You never answered him?"

Jane glanced at the letter in Emma's hand. "No. I never did."

"Why not?"

Jane paused, running her hands over the nappy quilt. "I don't know. At the time, I was not ready to think about such things. I had a school to run. And girls' seminaries are usually run by unmarried women."

"Not always."

Jane sighed. "I don't know, Emma. I just . . . never wrote back, and neither did he. And time went by and with it the opportunity."

"He obviously admired you a great deal."

Her aunt turned to face her. "Yes. Though who knows if his admiration would have lasted."

"Of course it would have. You are the best of women."

Jane patted Emma's hand and winked at her. "You are only a tiny bit partial, I know." Jane gently took the letter from her. "Sometimes I don't even read it—I simply look at it. A reminder that I once had an admirer, though briefly. And now and again when days go badly, or finances are tight, or my dear brother and niece leave for a season . . . then, yes, I allow myself to think of what might have been."

"What might yet be."

"Oh. That ship has sailed, Emma." Her aunt returned the letter to its place, raised herself to blow out the candle, and settled back down again. "By now, Mr. Farley has no doubt found a more suitable, amenable woman to fill the role of Mrs. Farley."

"You don't know that, do you?"

"No. But I imagine it is so. I tell myself it is to shield my foolish heart from disappointment should I ever hear confirmation of that fact."

"Why not write and ask?"

"And have my letter read by Mrs. Farley? Or put Mr. Farley in an awkward position, having to explain a letter from another woman? I think not."

Jane was silent for a moment, then asked gently, "Are you going to tell me what happened in Cornwall?"

And so Emma told her aunt in briefest terms about the pranks at Julian's hand and the ordeal in the chapel.

Her aunt reacted with the expected shock and many questions, which Emma answered as best she could. Finally Jane's questions ended, satisfied at least for now. Emma felt spent. Wearier than ever.

She had not told her aunt what had passed between her and Henry. She was not ready to reveal the words and embraces the two of them had shared. They were her secret, her letter from an admirer to save for cold spinster-evenings, to warm her like faint embers from the past.

Her aunt said nothing for several long minutes, and Emma thought she had fallen asleep. Then Jane rolled over to her side, facing away from Emma.

"I was always fond of Henry Weston," she murmured on a yawn. "More so than Phillip, in all truth."

Had her aunt somehow guessed her feelings for Henry? She certainly knew her well enough to do so. Emma said only, "Were you?"

"Mm-hm."

Emma had heard it before, but she liked hearing it again. For Emma was fond of Henry Weston as well—futile though it was.

In the morning, Emma dressed with the help of Jane's maid.

"Where is my aunt this morning?" Emma asked casually while Jenny fastened the back of her frock.

"Already busy belowstairs, miss."

*Belowstairs?* Emma's curiosity was piqued. "Doing what?"

The girl grinned. "You had better go and see for yourself."

Emma went downstairs, passed through the parlor, then followed the back stairs down to the kitchen. She found her aunt in the small scullery, up to her elbows in soap and water. On the worktable were stacked rose-and-white china plates, cups, and saucers.

Emma laughed. "What in the world has got in to you?"

"I could ask you the same thing." Jane winked. "Now are you going to help me or not?"

Emma rolled up her sleeves and dove in.

That afternoon, Emma went through the books she had asked her aunt to store when she and her father had left for Ebbington Manor. Among them she found a volume of military battles to send to Adam.

During her search, she culled a hefty stack of books she did not need anymore. These she dusted, boxed up, and asked her father to carry over to the vicarage to see if the clergyman might have use for them—or if he knew of any poor children who hadn't any books. Her father was certain Mr. Lewis would put them to good use.

Content, Emma turned to find Aunt Jane staring at her, hand on her hip and eyes narrowed in speculation. "Who are you, miss, and where is my book-hoarding niece who went away to Cornwall?"

Emma grinned and swatted her playfully with the dustcloth.

But her aunt wasn't playing. Eyes earnest, Jane asked, "You are so changed, Emma. Is it because you thought you were going to die?"

Emma thought. "That was part of it, yes. But there was more to it than that."

"Oh?"

"Two things made me realize how much I really wanted to *live* and not waste any more time. One of those was realizing how uncertain life is. I truly thought I was going to die that day in the chapel, but we might just as easily have died on the carriage journey home. Only God knows the number of our days. . . ."

"And the other thing?" her aunt prompted.

Emma nodded thoughtfully. "A long, long look out a narrow west window."

A few days later, Emma and her father paid a call on their tenant—the vicar's sister who had let the Smallwoods' house while her husband was away at sea. Over tea, in their own sitting room, Mrs. Welborn introduced them to her sister, Miss Lewis, who was staying there now as well. Emma noticed that her father was quieter than usual, and guessed he felt it awkward to discuss business matters in the presence of a guest. But eventually John Smallwood cleared his throat and politely broached the subject of reclaiming their home early.

Mrs. Welborn frowned and said she would find it very difficult to vacate at present, because she was near her term, and her sister had traveled no small distance to help with the birth and the other children.

Apparently seeking to soften her sister's refusal, Miss Lewis added warmly, "But we are terribly sorry to inconvenience you."

Emma personally thought it would be rude to break the lease if the tenants were unwilling, especially given the circumstances, but feared her father would not agree. Seated across from Mrs. Welborn and Miss Lewis, Emma waited nervously for her father's rebuttal. When he didn't speak, Emma glanced over and found him looking at Miss Lewis, the vicar's charming unmarried sister. He smiled and gallantly said that the ladies might have the house for as long as they needed.

Emma nearly spilled her tea.

For Emma's part, she was happy enough to remain with her aunt and even began assisting her with the lessons as they had always dreamt of doing someday—should her father ever be able to part with her. Emma liked teaching and found girls easier to deal with than boys in the classroom. Even so, she missed having males around. At least, one male in particular.

Her father, however, was uncomfortable in a house full of females. And, not wishing to impede his sister's capacity for paying pupils, he approached the widower vicar about lodging in his spare room. The Reverend Mr. Lewis, perhaps feeling guilty because his sisters had taken over the Smallwood house, was only too happy to oblige.

While Emma helped her father settle into his temporary home, Mr. Lewis told them that during their absence he had been approached by a member of the local gentry. The wealthy man had long wished to sponsor a charity boys' school in Longstaple, and he had asked the vicar if he might consider undertaking the project and heading up the school's board of governors. Mr. Lewis had hesitated to accept the time-consuming project. But now that Mr. Smallwood had returned and was free of other responsibilities, Mr. Lewis asked if he might consider working with him in planning and building the school, and then serving as its headmaster.

Yes, her father decided, surprising Emma yet again. He would like that very much indeed.

One evening, a week after their return, Emma and her aunt sat in the parlor together after the pupils had gone to bed. Jane was rereading one of the travel diaries they'd both enjoyed, and Emma held a geography book. But in reality she was doing more thinking than reading. Finally Emma rose, unfurled the book's fold-out map, and spread it over her aunt's lap.

Jane looked from the map to Emma's face, eyes wide in question.

Emma knelt beside the chair. "Come, Aunt Jane. Let us go on an adventure of our own. Why should we merely sit at home and read of other people's travels? We could do it, you and I. I have a little money put away from my mother. And you have the summer vacation."

Jane opened her mouth, thought the better of what she'd been about to say, and pressed her lips together. Then she looked at Emma, eyes twinkling. "Well, it would not hurt to research the possibilities, I suppose. In fact it could be quite fun. We might list our favorite places from travel diaries and begin a tentative itinerary."

"Are you saying you'll go?" Emma asked eagerly.

Her aunt shook her head, holding up a warning finger. "I am saying I shall think about it."

Emma was only too eager to begin a list.

*It is better to learn late than never.*

—Publilius Syrus, first-century writer

# Chapter 27

Emma and Jane spent several cozy evenings over tea, maps, and dreams.

Venice topped their list of longed-for destinations. But very quickly, they realized that both the cost and time to travel all the way to Italy were far beyond their expectations. The sea voyage alone would take two and a half to three weeks each way, depending on weather and the winds.

They investigated the possibility of sailing to France and then attempting the overland route but learned that would take even longer, and it would be quite dangerous and expensive to cross the Alps.

Two of Jane's pupils were taking the entire summer off because they had brothers at Oxford who would be home for most of July, August, and September. But the others planned to return home for only one or two months. Jane could ask someone to take her place. But it would be difficult to find a willing and capable woman to do so. If Jane *did* go, the journey itself would take six weeks or more, giving them at most four weeks in Italy. That would leave only a fortnight for Jane to prepare for the new term when they returned. That was *if* all went well and they experienced no significant delays.

The cost of a two-and-half-month journey . . . ? Well beyond their combined means.

Eventually, Jane removed the spectacles she'd been wearing to review estimated expenses, rubbed her eyes, and sighed. "Perhaps, Emma, we ought to start with something closer to home. There are many places here in England we haven't seen. There is nothing to say we cannot have an adventure in our own country."

As much as she hated to admit defeat, Emma knew her aunt was right. She swallowed her disappointment and said brightly, "Perhaps a tour of the north. It would take only a fraction of the time and a fraction of the cost. Derbyshire is reputed to be absolutely beautiful."

Her aunt smiled at her, approving of her courage in the face of disappointment, perhaps even more so than her choice of alternate destinations.

Henry found himself sitting in his bedchamber, once more looking through the mementoes in his cigar box. The chess piece was gone, of course, now in Adam's possession. As was the perfume bottle, which he'd returned to Adam after showing it to Phillip. Instead, Henry turned his attention to the fragment of letter he had from his mother: *"Be brave, my dear boy. And remember."*

He had been meaning to once again ask his father to see the remainder of that letter. His father had put him off the last time he'd asked, but that had been years ago. Perhaps now that Henry was an adult, Sir Giles would not mind allowing him to see whatever it was his mother had written before she died.

Henry went downstairs and found his father where he usually was at that time of day—in the library reading the newspapers and answering correspondence. He and his father had spent a great deal of time together in the library during the weeks since the Smallwoods' departure. There had been much to see to—deciding what to do about Julian, severing all ties to Derrick Teague, and confronting Davies for his role in the business.

When all was revealed, Henry decided their steward's main fault was his blind loyalty to Violet Weston, whom he had known since her girlhood, when he'd served as her family's butler. Realizing the Westons' financial problems several years ago, Davies had suggested Lady Weston agree to Teague's proposal—that she lend her name to the man's merchandise for a share of the profits. Davies had acted as go-between. But the steward had quickly come to rue the day he had suggested the arrangement, because what began as a stopgap measure soon became a trap, an ongoing yoke, with increasing pressure from Teague to continue.

After hearing the steward's account of things, which Lady Weston confirmed, Henry and his father decided not to sack Mr. Davies, but rather to put him in charge of arranging to pay back what they could to ship owners they'd wronged.

Meanwhile, Sir Giles made arrangements for Julian, spent a great deal more time with Rowan, and wrote to Phillip to make certain he finished the term well before returning home for the summer. Henry was pleased to see his father rise to the occasion and reclaim the reins of the family. This had left Henry at liberty to pursue his plans for a stone tower on the point.

Now entering the library, Henry asked, "Do you still have Mother's letter? The one this was torn from?"

Sir Giles took the scrap Henry held forth and squinted at it through his reading spectacles. Then he sighed, unlocked a lower desk drawer, and from it withdrew a box not so unlike Henry's cigar box. He rummaged through the papers inside until he came to one with a ragged edge, read a few lines to confirm its contents, and then looked up at Henry.

"I hope you won't be angry with me. It mentions Adam, and since your mother and I had decided not to speak of him and to keep his whereabouts quiet, I thought it best not to give you the whole letter. Please remember that I was in mourning at the time, and perhaps not thinking clearly."

*The whole letter?* Henry wondered. He asked, "Was the rest addressed to you?"

Sir Giles shook his head and handed him the letter.

Henry sank into a nearby chair, the breath going out of him when he saw the salutation in that dear hand.

*My dear Henry,*

*Have you any idea how much I love you? When I look at your young face, so handsome and intelligent, my heart squeezes with love for you. It saddens me to see your eyes losing their spark of carefree innocence with the passing of each day. Yet I hope you don't lose your childhood when you lose me. For I shall always be with you. Just a memory away.*

*Please look after your little brother even after you are grown. There is no one with whom you will share more common bonds. Phillip is very young, and I know he will not remember me. Selfishly, that thought brings tears to my eyes.*

*I hope you, being older, shall remember me, Henry. But don't feel guilty when my memory fades. That's how life is. The present crowds out the past, and for the most part that is how it should be. I don't want you to hang on to the past, to grieve overmuch (though perhaps a little would be nice).*

*I imagine your father will remarry in time, though hopefully not too soon. And when he does, I want you to know it is all right to love your new mamma. I want you to. Don't resent her out of loyalty to me. We all want to love and be loved. We all want affectionate arms around us from time to time. Well, most of us.*

*I don't know what to say about your brother Adam. He is different. He doesn't like affection the same way you and I do. Yet I love him. How could I not? I pray we have made a good decision regarding his upbringing, as well as yours and Phillip's. God forgive me if not. Mr. and Mrs. Hobbes will take good care of him, I know.*

*Oh, the hopes I have for you, my son. I don't care if you are renowned, build some great invention, or sway the nation with powerful oratory. I want you to possess what is really important. What brings true and lasting joy, not the fleeting happiness dependent on circumstances and so easily taken away. Cling to your childlike faith in God and the way of redemption He provided through His Son. For I want you with me in heaven someday, Henry. Though not for many, many years!*

*And when you reach manhood, I hope you will choose a wife with a loving, loyal heart. Not a vain woman who is merely beautiful on the outside—for that will fade with time and, in my case, illness, as I know from the evidence of my looking glass. Your father says I am still beautiful to him. And that is enough for me.*

*Make your life count, Henry David Weston. For when you reach the end of your days, you will not look back and wish you'd garnered more money, or power, or fame. You will look back and wish that you had been a better parent, spouse, friend, and Christian. And you will wish for just a little more time with those you love. This I know full well.*

Henry's eyes burned. His chest squeezed with both sadness and joy. How he missed her, missed having her in his life all these years. Yet what an inestimable gift to receive this letter—especially now.

"Thank you, Father," he said hoarsely.

Sir Giles regarded him warily over his spectacles. "You are not angry with me?"

Henry shook his head. "I am grateful."

The next day, Henry stood at one of the front hall windows, watching his father lead Julian out to the carriage. Sir Giles was taking him to meet the ship where Julian would serve a former navy captain—an old friend of his—who had purchased his own merchantman with prize money from the war. Julian would be gone for at least two years. They all hoped the captain, who had gained the obedience and respect of hundreds of men in his time, as well as the rigors and harsh discipline of shipboard life, would instill responsibility and a sense of right and wrong in Julian.

Privately though, Henry feared only God could accomplish such a transformation now. He wondered if facing legal action for his wrongdoing might have been good for Julian. But as his brother, he was relieved Sir Giles had decided to give him this second chance. At the very least, sending him to sea would keep Julian from getting into more trouble in England.

Lady Weston stood a few feet away from Henry, at the next window. He glanced over and saw the tears glimmering in the woman's eyes, though as soon as she realized he watched her, she averted her face and blinked away the evidence. The act reminded Henry of Emma Smallwood. Always determined to appear strong and in control.

Henry said gently, "I know this is very difficult. It is for all of us, but especially for you. I know how close you and Julian are."

He saw her throat convulse. Her mouth tighten. Her fingers twist and retwist the handkerchief in her hand. He realized she waited for him to say something else. To say, *"But you had it coming."* Or *"But what did you expect?"* Something cutting or critical.

It smote his conscience.

When he said no more, she managed a weak nod.

Words from his mother's letter returned to him. *"I imagine your father will remarry in time. . . . And when he does, I want you to know it's all right to love your new mamma. I want you to. Don't resent her out of loyalty to me. We all want to love and be loved. . . ."*

Henry swallowed the lump of reluctance—the fear of rejection—and said quietly, "I am sorry . . . Mamma."

The twisting handkerchief stilled. He held his breath, and apparently, so did she. Would she sneer at his use of the term after so many years of refusing to do so? He deserved no less.

She glanced over at him almost timidly, perhaps fearing a smirk of irony awaited her. He met her gaze evenly, earnestly.

Tears, the ones she had fought so hard not to show him, filled her wide eyes and flowed down her powdered cheeks.

Again the slight nod. Then a whisper so soft he barely heard.

"Thank you, my boy."

Three weeks after their return to Longstaple, a letter arrived, addressed to both her father and herself. Emma recognized the handwriting as belonging to Rowan Weston. At least, she hoped it was Rowan's writing and not another of Julian's forgeries. She carried the letter to the vicarage to allow her father first opportunity to read it.

He did so, then handed it back to her, saying, "I suppose it is well he plans to study art under a master, for if he wished to come to the Smallwood Academy at last, he would find lodging with Mrs. Welborn and her brood a rude welcome indeed."

Emma agreed and read the letter.

*Dear Mr. and Miss Smallwood,*

*I hope this letter finds you both well and happy. Once more I apologize for the misdeeds that befell you during your stay at Ebbington Manor. And for my foolhardy part in that final disaster, I can never apologize enough and pray you will forgive me.*

*I wanted you to know that I am leaving Ebbington to study under a master artist. Had Henry not convinced Father to offer me this opportunity, my desire would have been to come and study with you there in Longstaple, though it is presumptuous, I know, to think you would have welcomed me.*

*Julian has been sent to sea to serve a former navy captain—an old friend of Father's. We all hope the discipline of ship life will improve his character. I shall miss my brother, I cannot deny it. Yet at the same time I feel free, as though a heavy yoke has been removed from around my neck, one I barely realized was there but now feel the relief of its absence. Mamma says I stand two inches taller than I did only weeks ago. She no doubt exaggerates, as mothers do.*

*Lizzie is gone as well. Mamma and Henry escorted her to Falmouth to rejoin her mother. And though Mamma would never admit it, I think she had grown fond of Lizzie and will miss her, regardless of her connection to Mr. Teague.*

*Mamma looks forward to happier news for the Weston family soon. She still hopes for a wedding in the near future with Miss Penberthy as bride. But after recent scandals, I fear she hopes in vain.*

*The rocky peninsula looks so bare, so naked without the chapel perched there, and Henry and I are not alone in lamenting its loss. A local man, a magistrate, has bought two of my paintings, which depict the Chapel of the Rock as it stood for so many years. "A way to preserve local history," he said.*

*I say, much-needed funds to finance my art studies.*

*I still can hardly believe the chapel fell in that storm, only minutes after you, Miss Smallwood, and Henry were freed from its confines. For all my mistakes, I am happy I was able to come to your aid, in the end.*

*I wish you both long and happy lives,*

*Sincerely,*
*Rowan Weston*

Emma was happy for Rowan's good fortune and held no ill will toward him. Nor did she feel any vindication in learning of Julian's fate. Life at sea could be very hard, from what she had read. And brutally dangerous. She felt sorry for him. And sorrier yet for his parents.

Emma could not help but wonder if Lady Weston still hoped that Henry—or Phillip—would marry Miss Penberthy, especially now that Lizzie had left Ebford. Emma could more easily imagine either of them married to Tressa Penberthy than Lizzie Henshaw. She wondered if Phillip had resolved to give up Lizzie, or if he pined for her. And what of Lizzie herself?

Emma would have liked to have known more about how they all fared—Phillip, Sir Giles, Adam, and yes, Henry. Still, it was good of Rowan to send a note. Though he was not the Weston she most wished to hear from.

*A remarkably temperate, sober, steady man,*
*in a certain town in Cornwall, who is in*
*every way qualified to render the marriage*
*state desirable. Any agreeable lady, who*
*feels desirous of meeting with a sociable,*
*tender and kind companion, will find*
*this advertisement worthy of notice.*

—The *West Briton*, 1828

# Chapter 28

On a fine July day, Emma went out for a walk, a new habit she had taken up since her return from Cornwall. She stopped at the vicarage to pay a call on her father and was surprised to find the vicar's younger sister, Miss Lewis, there as well, taking a short respite from her sister's children to visit her brother. And perhaps, Emma wondered, to visit John Smallwood as well? Emma found she rather liked the idea. At least, she liked seeing the happy twinkle in her father's eyes—something absent for far too long.

Returning to her aunt's house a short while later, Emma stepped into the former butler's pantry, which served as Jane's office. There, she found her aunt reading the post. She started at seeing Emma and abruptly hid the letters behind her back.

Curiosity and suspicion flared through Emma. Had her aunt received news of Henry's engagement—is that why she didn't wish Emma to see it?

"How guilty you look, Aunt. I can only guess what the contents of such a letter must be if you feel you have to conceal it from me. You likely wish to shield me from some unhappy news. . . ."

"No, my dear. You are quite mistaken."

"Am I?"

Impulsively, Jane thrust forth a letter. Emma glanced at it and saw it was addressed to *Miss Jane Smallwood*. Emma could not immediately identify the hand, yet it seemed vaguely familiar. With a questioning look at her aunt, who nodded acquiescence, Emma unfolded the letter. It began with *Dear Miss Smallwood,* and was signed *Mr. Delbert Farley*.

Emma read only the opening line before realizing the letter was indeed none of her business.

*"My dear Miss Smallwood. How pleased I was to receive your letter after all this time . . ."*

Emma's gaze flew to her aunt's face. Her blushing, becoming face. Stunned, Emma asked, "You wrote to him?"

"I did. My niece would give me no rest until I did so. Neither would my conscience." Her dimple appeared. "Or my heart."

The two women smiled at each other—smiles born of shared secrets and dreams yet unrealized.

Emma reached out to squeeze her aunt's hand. Only then did she realize Jane's other hand remained behind her back. . . .

Her aunt's eyes sparkled but she shook her head. "You have pried enough from me for one day, Emma Smallwood."

Emma continued planning their Derbyshire itinerary, including the celebrated beauties of Matlock, Chatsworth, Dovedale, and the Peak. But a few days later, Emma realized even their more modest tour was unlikely to occur.

Delbert Farley came to call.

Emma met him soon after he arrived, as he and Jane were about to depart for a stroll together around Longstaple. He was a dapper gentleman in his midforties with a charming smile and intelligent brown eyes—eyes which lit up every time he looked at Jane.

That evening, Emma made the rounds and checked on the pupils in her aunt's stead. Passing the stairwell, she overheard Mr. Farley taking his leave below.

"May I call on you again, Miss Smallwood?" he asked.

"I would like that," her aunt said without hesitation. "And please, call me Jane."

Mr. Farley returned the following week. He and Jane spent the afternoon together, and then Emma and her father were invited to join the two for dinner that evening. As they ate, Mr. Farley told them about his life in Bodmin as well as the engineering advancements he hoped to implement in his china clayworkings there. He, in turn, asked her father insightful questions about the proposed charity school and discussed books with Emma. How could Emma fail to like him?

It was clear from Jane's smiles and manners that she liked him a great deal as well. And though Emma prided herself on not making snap judgments, she thoroughly approved. A kinder, more gentlemanlike, better suited companion for her aunt, Emma could not imagine.

After dinner, Jane and Emma withdrew from the dining room to allow the two men to get better acquainted.

Jane led Emma into the office and whispered, "Emma, I want you to be the first to know. Mr. Farley has asked me to marry him."

"Oh, Aunt Jane!" Emma took her hands. "I am so glad. Have you accepted him?"

"Yes. But, I am afraid this means our tour of Derbyshire will have to—"

"Of course we shall have to forgo our little tour," Emma rushed to say. "You and Mr. Farley will want a wedding trip instead, I imagine."

"Only a short one. He can't leave his business for long."

"I understand. I am so happy for you."

Her aunt's large eyes grew anxious. "Are you terribly disappointed?"

"No!" Emma protested. "I would not choose a trip over your happiness for the world."

"If you are certain . . ."

"Of course I am." Emma squeezed her aunt's hands. She was happy for her. Truly. Though at the same time, she felt dangerously close to tears.

A few days later, Emma went out for a walk at her regular time. As usual, she stopped by the vicarage to see her father. She was pleased to see how well he was faring, happily occupied with both his fledgling interest in Miss Lewis and his plans for the charity school.

Emma was contemplating similar plans of her own. Jane had offered her the opportunity to take over the girls' school when she married Mr. Farley and moved to Bodmin. But only if she really wished it. She urged her niece not to hurry into a decision but to give herself time to see if that was what she really wanted. The thought of a useful and secure future ought to have made Emma happy. And she was happy.

Mostly.

On her way back to her aunt's house, Emma walked past the coaching inn. She paused in front of the destination boards, which listed the various places one might go from there and the schedule of departure times. *Penzance, Exeter, Bristol, Bath . . .*

Emma sighed. Would she ever go anywhere?

"Miss Smallwood!" a voice hailed her from several yards away.

Startled, Emma turned, stared at the approaching figure, and felt her mouth fall ajar. She blinked, yet the apparition remained. Came closer.

Henry Weston—handsome in green coat, buff trousers, and boots—strode across the lane.

He seemed about to approach her directly but then paused several feet away. The appealing smell of bay rum came with him.

He bowed formally. "Miss Smallwood. A pleasure to see you again."

"Mr. Weston." She curtsied. "I . . . am surprised to see you here."

"Evidently. You look quite shocked. I hope you are not sorry to see me."

"No. Not at all. What brings you here?"

He looked directly into her eyes. "I came to see you."

Emma's heart thumped against her breastbone, but she told herself not to raise her hopes. She reminded herself of what he had said to her before she left: " *. . . certain family obligations must be seen to. And I may not be at liberty to pursue any of those subjects upon which we touched in the chapel. . . .* "

What if he had come to tell her he was engaged to Miss Penberthy? Was she supposed to congratulate him and wish him happy? Her stomach knotted. She would need to govern her expression and emotions with all her former restraint if she were to accomplish the feat.

She looked up at him from under her lashes, half in expectation, half in illogical fear of what he might say. He stood there, staring down at her.

Nervously, she blurted, "Your family . . . are in good health, I trust?"

"Yes." He hesitated. "That is, I don't actually know about Julian. He has been sent away to sea as consequence for his actions. And we have yet to hear word of him."

"Rowan wrote and explained Julian's situation," Emma said. "How is Lady Weston taking it?"

"It has been very hard on her, as you can imagine. However, I will say her disillusionment with her favorite has improved her relationships with everyone else: my father, Rowan, Adam. Even myself. So at least some good has come from Julian's disgrace."

Henry waited until a noisy farm wagon had passed, then added, "And as far as Lady Weston herself, she says she is relieved to be free of Teague's demands at last. Apparently she had wanted to extricate herself from his dealings for some time but was unable to do so while he held the secret over her."

"No more threats from Mr. Teague?"

He shook his head. "Not yet, anyway. He's been too busy trying to avoid the new excise man."

She asked, "How is Adam?"

"Very well, thank you. Mrs. Prowse dotes on him. And Father often plays chess with him of an evening."

Emma's heart lifted. "Does he? That's wonderful!"

Henry added, "Adam always wins."

They shared a smile at this.

"Lady Weston has even taken to listening to Adam play the pianoforte. I think it soothes her loneliness for Julian."

Emma nodded, imagining the scene.

Henry inhaled deeply. "All this has been quite a call to arms for my father. He has taken up his role as head of the family with renewed vigor, I'm happy to say. He's determined to take my brothers in hand while there is still time. And to release me from my responsibilities on the estate, at least for now."

"I am happy for you, Hen—Mr. Weston." She managed a tremulous smile.

He pulled his gaze from hers to the destination boards, and crossed his arms. "And you, Miss Smallwood, what are your plans for the future? Going somewhere?"

"No. That is, my aunt and I had planned to travel. But she has recently become engaged to be married, so . . ." Her words trailed away on a shrug.

Henry glanced at her. "That's too bad. About the trip, I mean. Not the marriage. Your aunt told me about your travel plans in one of her letters."

Emma stared up at him. "Letters?"

"We've exchanged several, yes."

Incredulous, she asked, "You and . . . my Aunt Jane?"

"Yes. You know I've always been fond of her."

"And she you . . ." Emma murmured, but felt her brow furrow. She stood for a moment, lost in thought, then realized he was looking at her expectantly. "Oh! Pray pardon my manners, Mr.

Weston. You must come to Aunt Jane's house. She will be so happy to see you."

"Actually, I have just come from your Aunt Jane. She told me you'd gone for a walk and suggested where I might find you."

"Did she? Oh." Emma felt even more flustered now. "Well, you must come and take tea with us."

"With pleasure." He bowed, then gestured for her to lead the way.

As they walked she asked, "And how is Phillip?"

"He finished out the Trinity term well and is now home for the summer."

"I am glad to hear it."

"So were we. Relieved and proud."

Tentatively she asked, "And Lizzie? Rowan mentioned something about Falmouth in his letter."

"Yes, Lady Weston and I escorted her there to rejoin her mother. She did not want to live with Teague." Henry shook his head. "I cannot say her mother seemed pleased to see her again, unfortunately."

"I am sorry to hear it." And Emma found she truly was sorry for the girl.

Henry continued, "With Phillip home for the summer, Lady Weston was only too happy to deliver Lizzie to Falmouth. She hopes to end the unfortunate connection, as she saw it. She still believes Phillip might yet marry Miss Penberthy, but on that score, we shall have to wait and see."

"Is Phillip terribly disappointed?" Emma asked.

Henry pursed his lips in thought. "You know, I don't think he is. Lizzie's somewhat sordid connections coming to light, not to mention her part in Julian's schemes, seems to have dampened his interest."

"And Lizzie's?"

He shrugged. "Perhaps I am cynical, but I think she was relieved to depart with no harsh consequences and an impressive wardrobe in the bargain."

Emma chuckled ruefully at his observation, knowing it was probably true, at least in part. Had Lizzie really loved Phillip, or had she only seen him as an entrée to a better life? Emma guessed her feelings had been a bit of both.

At Aunt Jane's door, the maid, Jenny, let them in, sizing up the returning gentleman caller none too subtly. Untying her bonnet, Emma asked Jenny to let her aunt know she and Mr. Weston had returned and requested tea for three. Noticing a few curious pupils milling about, Emma led the way into her aunt's private office.

In the confines of the narrow room, Emma was taken once again by Henry Weston's height, broad shoulders, and sheer masculinity. How intense his golden green eyes were as he looked at her. How she had missed him. Her fingers itched to trace the lines of his face, the grooves on either side of his mouth, his lower lip. . . .

She looked away first. An awkward silence followed.

To her relief, Jenny brought in the tea things a few minutes later, the tray laid with Emma's own gold-rimmed teacup and two of her aunt's. "Thank you, Jenny. That will be all."

After Jenny left them, Emma asked, "Will you take tea?"

"No thank you."

She was surprised but relieved he'd declined. She wasn't certain she could have poured with trembling hands.

"Will you be seated?" she offered, gesturing to the guest chair.

"No thank you," he repeated. "I prefer to stand."

Her teacup caught his eye, and Henry leaned down and picked it up from its saucer. He angled the cup to see the fine hand-painted image of Venice on its side. "I remember this cup. And I remember you threatening us within an inch of our lives if we dared touch it. And heaven help us if we broke it."

"That was a long time ago, Mr. Weston," she said quietly.

Eager to change the subject, she thought of what Henry had said about Sir Giles releasing him from estate responsibilities. She asked, "And what will you do with your newfound freedom? Follow the west winds? Embark on your long-overdue grand tour?"

He chuckled softly, but the laughter did not reach his eyes. "I do hope to travel," he said. "But not alone."

She swallowed. "Oh?"

Henry pulled something from his coat pocket and unfolded it. "Here is my itinerary." He held the piece of paper toward her. "What do you think of it?"

Emma accepted the single sheet and glanced at the list of Italian destinations—cities, churches, ruins, *palazzos,* and *pensiones*—preparing to offer some polite comment. Instead she stared. She turned to her aunt's desk, opened her notebook, and compared it to their own Italian itinerary—the one they'd had to discard. Except for the handwriting, the lists were identical. She glanced up at him, lips parted in astonishment.

He stepped nearer. "I had hoped to travel with my wife, but she is, as yet, unavailable."

Her neck heated. "Oh . . . why?"

Henry dipped his chin and raised his brows. "Because she has yet to agree to marry me."

He took her hands in his.

Emma looked down at their joined hands in disbelief. She breathed, "I don't understand."

He lifted one of her hands to his lips, pressing a warm kiss there, his breath tickling her skin. "I asked your aunt for a copy and she obliged. I hope you don't mind."

How could she mind when she could barely breathe?

"But . . . she never said a word to me."

"It was our little secret."

He brought her other hand to his mouth and kissed it in turn.

Emma's heart hammered. "But . . . Lady Weston would never approve."

He looked into her eyes and said, "I love you, Emma Small-wood. And I would marry you whether Lady Weston approves or not. But I think she'll come around. Her pride in Weston superiority has suffered a fatal blow. After everything that happened, I realize you may be reluctant to take the name Weston, but I hope you shall."

Emma studied his strong, earnest face, and searched his eyes for sincerity.

He gripped her hands tighter. "Will you marry me, Emma Smallwood? Will you be my wife and make me the happiest of men?"

Emma needed to understand. "But . . . you let me leave. You didn't say anything. I thought . . ."

"*I* thought you would want nothing more to do with any of us, and with good reason considering your treatment at my family's hands." He took a breath and continued. "But even knowing you might very well refuse, still I had to try. I wrote to your aunt to test the waters. And she wrote back, hinting that all was not, perhaps, lost between us. Which, of course, lent me courage. But I would have come even had she not written back. Courage or no."

Emma shook her head in disbelief. "Henry Weston lacking courage for anything? Inconceivable."

"You obviously have no idea of the power you hold over me."

"Power?" She shook her head. "What power?"

"The power to make me happy or miserable for the rest of my life."

Emma felt a grin tickle the corners of her mouth. "I think I should take great pleasure in doing both." Her grin bloomed, and she leaned into him.

He wrapped his arms around her. "I certainly hope for more happiness than misery."

She raised her arms and cupped his face in her hands. "I shall make every endeavor to make it so, my love. In fact, I shall add it to my list."

He chuckled, a chuckle that deepened into a murmur of pleasure as she stood on tiptoe, bringing her mouth near his.

He whispered, "Does your list include kissing me, Emma Smallwood?"

"Yes," she murmured. "Items one through four." She pressed her lips to his and felt a thrill of pleasure run through her. She pulled back slightly, looked into his eyes, and the intensity she saw there thrilled her even more. She kissed him again, angling her head to form her mouth more firmly to his.

He pulled her close, kissing her back with passion that stole her breath and left her knees as firm as pudding. Fortunately, he was holding her so tight she did not fall.

He broke their kiss at last, only to begin placing kisses on her temple, cheek, and chin. "Is that a yes, Emma?"

"You know it is."

Tightening his hold around her waist, he lifted her off her feet and whirled her around the narrow office, accidentally knocking a glass vase and her china cup from the tea tray.

In a flash, Henry released her and lunged for the gold-rimmed cup, catching it just as the vase hit the floor and shattered.

Emma stood stunned, hands pressed to her mouth.

"That was close," Henry said, rising with the rescued cup. He blew out a relieved breath. "That would have ended my chances, I imagine."

She looked down at the broken, insignificant vase, imagining her cherished cup in fragments of green and gold. But instead of the grief she expected, she felt an unexpected bubble of mirth rising up in her. Of freedom. She chuckled. "I would have married you anyway, clumsy fellow, even had you broken it."

He lifted the cup to his eye level and inspected it once more. "You know, this poor cup needs a partner. When we go to Venice on our wedding trip, I shall buy you a matched set."

She smiled. "I'd rather have the other wedding gift you once promised me."

His dark brows rose. "Oh?"

"You once vowed that if I ever married, you would perform the dance of the swords at my wedding breakfast."

A slow grin stole over his handsome face. "I was hoping you forgot." He set down the cup and stepped closer. "Do you also recall what I promised to wear while dancing it?"

The brazen man didn't so much as blush, but Emma felt her cheeks heat at the thought.

His eyes twinkled as he drew her close once more. "Though perhaps we ought to save that particular performance for our wedding night."

Emma's cheeks burned all the more.

The door creaked open, and her aunt popped her head in, expression uncertain. "I heard something crash. Is everything all right?" Jane looked from the broken vase to Henry, his arm around Emma, to Emma's smile. Surprise and delight brightened her aunt's face.

For a moment they all stood there, the smiles of aunt and niece widening as they looked at each other. Scores of unspoken words passed between them, enough words to fill a book.

"Better than all right, from the looks of things," Jane said, dimple blazing, and slowly closed the door, leaving them alone once more.

Emma leaned up and kissed Henry again.

She was certainly glad she'd had the pleasure of drinking from that cup. But she would not have chosen it over the man in her arms for all the world.

# Author's Note

Thank you for reading *The Tutor's Daughter*. I hope you enjoyed it. Now for a few historical notes.

For anyone tempted to think poorly of parents who would send away a child like Adam Weston, I wanted to mention my inspiration for this character's situation. One of Jane Austen's older brothers was cared for, along with a mentally disabled uncle, by a family who lived in a nearby village. I had read a little about this before, but a recent visit to the Jane Austen Centre in Bath, England, brought this little-known fact back to the forefront of my mind. The museum guide told us that young George Austen was sent to live with a foster family due to some mental or physical impairment, though the extent of his disability is not known with certainty. (Some suggest he had epilepsy and may have been deaf and unable to speak as well.) There is no record of George visiting his family after he was sent away and none of Jane's existing letters mentions him. However, the Austens did pay for his upkeep, and Jane's father wrote of him, "We have this comfort, he cannot be a bad or a wicked child." Some authors have criticized the Austen family, and others have defended them, reminding us that, given the era, the Austens behaved humanely and responsibly toward George, who lived peacefully and comfortably for seventy-two years, far longer than Jane herself. I tend to agree.

Also note that the Mr. (Henry) Trengrouse mentioned in the book was a real person from Helston, Cornwall. After witnessing the drowning deaths of over one hundred men during a shipwreck, he devoted his life and fortune to the invention of lifesaving equipment, such as his rocket line apparatus.

Another real person mentioned in the book was John Bray.

As is often the case, truth can be stranger—and more difficult to believe—than fiction. With that in mind, if you had difficulty believing that a man on horseback could rescue shipwreck victims, I am happy to tell you that I based that scene on the firsthand account of John Bray, who actually performed such a rescue as recorded in his *An Account of Wrecks, 1750–1830 on the North Coast of Cornwall.* For the descriptions of shipwrecks, wreckers, and law regarding them, I relied very heavily on this slim volume, not printed until after Mr. Bray's death.

John Bray lived his entire long life around the area of Bude, Cornwall, the inspiration for the fictional coastal village depicted in this novel. My husband and I had the pleasure of visiting Bude during our second trip to England—a serendipitous, unplanned stop in our whirlwind tour of Devon and Cornwall. From our hotel on the north side of the harbor or "haven," I spied a large red-stone manor high on the cliff opposite and instantly thought, "I want to set a book there."

When we asked a local woman, she told us the place was called "Efford." Further research revealed that the house was Efford Down House, and built by the same family who once owned Ebbingford Manor, an even older manor house nearby. I based fictional Ebbington Manor on a combination of these two historic houses.

My husband and I enjoyed walking up the cliff and along the scenic coast path to take in the wild, windswept views. Atop this headland stands an octagonal tower which inspired my Chapel of the Rock. It is actually a former coastguard lookout, known as Compass Point, built in 1840. From this vantage, we could also view the rocky breakwater extending across the harbor below. (According to Ecclesiastical record, there *had* once been a chapel out there, where a monk kept a fire constantly burning to warn of the rocks beyond. But that chapel washed away centuries ago.)

There is something thought-provoking and reverent about the stone octagon high on the headland. Something soul-stirring about looking out its narrow slit windows toward the endless sea beyond. If you ever have the opportunity to travel to Cornwall, I hope you will visit the lookout. In the meantime, I invite you to visit my Web site (www.julieklassen.com) to see a few photos of this beautiful place.

Before I close, I would like to thank my husband, who bravely drove on the "wrong" side of narrow roads lined with stone walls so I could see the southwest of England. Thanks, honey.

Fond appreciation goes to Cari Weber and Raela Schoenherr for their brainstorming input and insightful reviews. To Connie Mattison, special education teacher, for reviewing the Adam sections. And to Mark Sackett for suggesting flower varieties for a Cornwall garden. I would also like to thank my pastor, Ken Lewis, my agent, Wendy Lawton, my editor, Karen Schurrer, and as always, my readers. I appreciate you all.

# Discussion Questions

1. How would you compare education by private tutor with other forms of education you may have experienced (home-schooling, classical academy, boarding school, public school, etc.)? Would you have enjoyed being taught by a tutor? Would it have been an effective way for you to learn? Why or why not?

2. Do you have anything in common with the main character, Emma Smallwood? (i.e., Do you like to make lists? Have a place for everything and put everything in its place? Like to be in control and are reticent to ask for help?) How would you say Emma changes during the course of the novel?

3. Emma admits that, since her mother's death, she rarely prays because she has come to believe that God no longer answers her prayers. Have you ever struggled with your relationship with God after a loss or when it seems as though your prayers go unanswered? What would you say to someone struggling in this way?

4. What role does Emma's teacup from Venice play in the novel? Why is it significant?

5. Have you, like Aunt Jane, ever refused or postponed a romantic

relationship for career (or other) reasons? Have you ever re-sisted other change in a similar way? How can we discern the best choice to make when we come to such points in our lives?

6. Imagine if you, like Emma, had grown up with a houseful of young men coming and going. How do you think this might have affected your upbringing and perspective, your relationships with both men and women in later life?

7. How would you diagnose Adam's "disorder," or would you? Were you surprised to learn people like Adam were often raised elsewhere during this time period (including one of Jane Austen's brothers)? Is it understandable that different people will care for a loved one in different ways even in this day and age? What are your feelings about that?

8. Were you surprised by anything you learned about Cornwall, shipwrecks, "wreckers," or the lack of lifesaving equipment in the early 1800s? What did you find most interesting?

9. Did you have a favorite character in this story? Why did you like him or her? What thoughts did his or her situation prompt about your life?

10. How would you characterize the book's theme or message? What spoke to you most in the story?

**Julie Klassen** loves all things Jane—*Jane Eyre* and Jane Austen. A graduate of the University of Illinois, Julie worked in publishing for sixteen years and now writes full time. Three of her books, *The Silent Governess* (2010), *The Girl in the Gatehouse* (2011), and *The Maid of Fairbourne Hall* (2012) have won the Christy Award for Historical Romance. Julie and her husband have two sons and live in a suburb of St. Paul, Minnesota.

For more information, visit www.julieklassen.com.

# More Regency Romance From Julie Klassen

**To learn more about Julie and her books, visit julieklassen.com.**

To escape marrying a dishonorable man, a lady disguises herself as a housemaid. When she finds herself entangled in intrigues both above and belowstairs, will love or danger find her first?

*The Maid of Fairbourne Hall*

Olivia Keene is fleeing her own secret. She never intended to overhear his. Now that she has, she is left with no choice but to accept a post at Brightwell Court. But when an attraction develops between her and Lord Bradley, their hidden pasts could threaten all their hopes for the future...

*The Silent Governess*

An ambitious captain, a beguiling outcast, and a mysterious gatehouse... Will he risk his plans—and his heart—for a woman shadowed by scandal?

*The Girl in the Gatehouse*

## ✸BETHANYHOUSE

Stay up-to-date on your favorite books and authors with our *free* e-newsletters. Sign up today at bethanyhouse.com.

f  Find us on Facebook.

Free, exclusive resources for your book group! bethanyhouse.com/AnOpenBook

anopenbook

# More Regency Romance From Julie Klassen

To learn more about Julie and her books, visit julieklassen.com.

Charlotte Lamb, a fallen vicar's daughter, flees to London's Milkweed Manor and is mortified when a former suitor—a physician her father rejected—is in charge of her care. Yet he harbors some secrets of his own...

*Lady of Milkweed Manor*

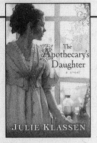

When her father falls ill, Lilly Haswell must take over the family apothecary shop, despite the law that forbids women from practicing the science. When suspicious eyes uncover the truth, have her actions condemned the family legacy and stolen her chance at love?

*The Apothecary's Daughter*